THE BAKER'S GHOST

THE BAKER'S GHOST

A MYSTERY BAKED TO PERFECTION

Gerard Fioravanti

THE BAKER'S GHOST
Copyright © 2023 by Gerard Fioravanti
Published by Groovy Corporation Publishing NY

This book is a work of fiction. Names, characters, places, and incidents either are the products of the author's imagination or are used fictitiously. Any resemblance to actual events or locales, or persons, living or dead, is entirely coincidental.

Printed in the United States of America

Library of Congress Control Number: TX9-333-148

First Printing, August 2023

979-8-218-25825-2 Trade Paperback
979-8-218-25826-9 E-book

Book design by Glen M. Edelstein, Hudson Valley Book Design

Edited by Caroline Tolley and in part by Art Lizza
Copy Edited by Amy Knupp and Heather Rivera
Illustrations by Domenic Rizzotti IG@Domenic.Design

For Steve

CHAPTER 1

IT WAS A DEAD space, literally. Well, at least I thought it was.

The floor-to-ceiling windows at the front of the store draped in craft paper from top to bottom, hardly letting any light pass through. The air was dank and moldy, immediately triggering my asthma. I called out a soft "Hello?"

Steve, my partner, scanned the walls for a light switch.

I looked down at the well-worn tiled floor, trying to scuff out what I thought was dirt. Turned out to be cracks. "The leasing agent said three o'clock. It is now five past three. I'll bet she's looking for parking." The sour smell in the air made me think of rotting dough, and the space looked abandoned. Made me wonder if the previous pizzeria owner just up and left? Hmm? Not sure.

"Probably."

Excuse me, my man, may I interrupt at this point? I must put my two cents in now before he goes any further. You see, I'm so eager to move this story along that I must fill you in on some info. I know it's a dead space because I made it so. There's more to it than you think, and you have no idea what I've been through.

Dude, I'm so tired of people traipsing around here, thinking they can be successful business owners in this town. I believe I should have the final word if they want to occupy this space. Just look at the last owner, or should I say look down at the last owner, six feet under somewhere. I haven't seen the dirt bag yet, but when I do, I will have a few unkind words for him. He treated the children horribly. All they wanted to do was help, but instead he chased them away like they were a pack of stray kittens looking for a home. We live here in this crib too, and I'm not going through that again, no way. He got what was coming to him and then some.

Anyway, back to the story and these guys. Oh, wait, you'll have to excuse me; I didn't tell you who they are. I'm so stoked to be able to tell parts of this story, that I forgot to introduce our main characters. Gerard is an extraordinarily talented baker. His partner, Steve, is an interior designer at heart but spent many successful years in the publishing industry instead. They are trying to decide if this location on Main Street in Harrington, New York is a good spot to open a patisserie.

I think I dig these guys. I'll think about it more when they finish their tour, considering that I do love pastries, and who doesn't? I can really go for a delectable cream puff, or a chocolate éclair filled with custard. I can almost taste the powdered sugar all over my upper lip, and the sweet chocolate glaze sticking to my fingers. Oh, to be alive again would be fantastic but my life, well, let's just say it was cut short. Wait, I'm getting ahead of myself, and I don't want to give too much away in one chapter, but our guys just entered the empty storefront. Well, maybe I should say they entered my home, den, or whatever you want to call it. I've been here so long that I should call it home, or should I say, I've been stuck here for years, and I feel much older than I am, too. Catch my drift?

I could sigh all day about it, but I won't. I know, I know, I'm getting this all off my chest in a single breath, but there is so much to tell you.

Anyway, they stepped farther into the store, letting the glass door close, the For Rent sign swinging back and forth behind them. I always liked how that sign swung back and forth, especially when I scared the bejesus out of the potential new renters. They can't even say the word ghost. All they say is ga-gos-gos and run like hell out the front door, letting that little sign swing just as fast as they can run. I must say, I do have some fun around here with these pranks. I dig it; can you dig it?

But there is something different about these two guys. They have a good aura about them; maybe they're a good fit for this space after all, not like Franco the previous owner; he was so harsh.

From the first day I met the children in the hallway, Franco was as miserable as hell, yelling at the top of his lungs for them to go away. They ran behind me in fear asking for help, startling me, wondering what was going on. The oldest stood up to my waist while the youngest hugged my leg, crying. I saw Franco standing under the doorframe, gazing upon us as we huddled in silence. Not a word was spoken as he stared in the distance, trying to seek us out as if we were invisible, maybe we were, I'm not sure, and he slammed the door shut with such force. What a putz this guy was.

This went on for years. I stayed out of it as Mr. Clayton, the building proprietor, instructed me to. He could see and hear me at times, and he tried to console me as I was upset about being, well, being dead!

I was the new kid here amongst the spirits and had to make my keep. He watched over the children like a grandfather would and let them use the artwork supplies. I tried to help Franco with pizza making but he swatted me away like an annoying fly. Oh, he could sense that someone or something was there. But for some reason he couldn't see me although he was able to see the children at times. His wife and staff thought he was crazy and laughed at him when he yelled at the children to go away. He definitely needed to take a chill pill.

They just wanted to help, but he lost his mind one day when the children knocked over his bottle of vodka onto the marble tabletop and ruined his dough. It was an accident, but he screamed quite a few obscenities, and chased them as best he could, limping his way to the back of the kitchen. He had an old bullet wound from shooting himself in the leg a year ago.

I was so angry and took too much energy from the lights above that I surprised myself, blowing out one of the fluorescent bulbs overhead. He screamed, having no idea I was waiting for him when he rounded the corner to the hallway. I slammed him into the wall with all my might like one of those wrestlers on Saturday night television. I was even more surprised at my strength than anything else. I had no clue I could physically do that to a living human. I was proud of protecting the children and kind of felt like a big brother.

Franco, on the other hand, bugged out and became disoriented, shaking his head and grimacing as he cradled his left arm. I guess I hurt him, angering him a bit more as he looked around. "Who did that?" he sputtered. "Who's here? Show yourself, so I can kill you with my bare hands!"

I grabbed the children and raced into the hallway, stopping short of the single overhead light. I didn't move, nor did the children next to me. We stood in silence as we saw this young girl in white race toward us from the darkened depths, draining the energy from the single swaying lightbulb overhead, creating a blinding white light to a shattering mess. Glass flew everywhere as she passed through us, draining all our energy, too. Dude, we collapsed into a heap, watching with wide eyes. I never thought what she did was even possible. What a nightmare; I had so much to learn.

She showed herself to Franco as a ghostly angel at first, floating above him. I could see his lips quivering. But then she contorted her face, pulling in all different directions. I hugged the children tighter for I feared her myself as I was bugging out. We listened to Franco scream as she turned into a ghoulish monster with two heads, and back again, turning from white to gray to black with the face of a skull, holding a sword inches away from his chin. Franco never stopped screaming, from one terrorizing apparition to the next. This guy was tripping, and his eyes showed his fear more than his screams as he clutched his chest and began breathing heavily. I believe she did some damage to his ticker. He closed his eyes in horror as his wife came running and screaming to his side. The young girl in white smiled at us and sped away like a shooting star.

That was Franco's last day at the pizzeria.

Now the children are happy and ready to make cookies, well, we shall see. I don't want to rush things, since I must break these guys in first with a few paranormal pranks. I don't want to scare them like the girl in white does. But I'm feeling a bit peevish now. I always liked that word, peevish. My grandmother used to say it all the time before taking a nap. Well, this took a lot out of me, and I need to recharge. I'll let my man Gerard tell his story, but I'll be back for I am the baker's ghost.

Just then, the door flew open behind us, and we turned around at the same time, as if a bus were coming through.

"Hi, guys. Sorry I am late. Parking is so bad out there today." A woman with a short, energetic frame rushed forward to greet us, extending a handshake to Steve as if she were in a hurry. "I'm Sawyer Lambert. You must be Gerard. So nice to meet you." She whipped her brunette hair over her shoulder.

"Hi, Sawyer. I'm Steve. He's Gerard." Steve smiled his signature charming smile. "Everyone thinks I'm the baker because my upper body is bigger than his."

"Oh, I'm sorry." She spun toward me, hair now whipping the other way. "It's nice to meet you both."

She is going to get whiplash one day. I smiled back. "Nice to meet you. We spoke over the phone."

"Yes, we did." Her eyes twinkled in amusement. "You didn't tell me how handsome you both are."

Steve was quick to say, "It's the lighting. When you are in your forties, everything looks good in dimmer light."

"I'll remember that when I catch up to you." Sawyer grabbed my arm and smiled a flirty smile. "Are you guys' business partners?"

"Yes, and life partners, too."

"What a power couple you two make." Sawyer pumped her grip on my arm.

"Thank you," we replied in unison.

"How did you guys get in? Do you have a key already?"

"Key? No, the door was open."

"Really? Thought it was locked." Sawyer released her grip and walked farther into the empty shop, indicating the walls and ceilings of the gloomy space. "Oh, well, as you can see or sort of see, it's fifteen hundred square feet. Front access here, and there's an alleyway in the back for deliveries and garbage takeout."

Steve asked, "Do the lights work?" He was still looking around for a wall switch.

"Ah, no. The power is off, unfortunately, but I can roll up the paper on the window to let some more light in."

"That would be great."

Sawyer went right for it, rolling up one of the paper curtains to let enough light in to see the layout of the space, exposing a view of Main Street, with plenty of traffic flow.

I want this space, I thought. I visualized the sign above the front window—Fiorello Patisserie—for all passersby to see. I gave my attention back to Sawyer.

"As you can see, this is the front of the store, with about eight hundred square feet of space being used. Everything you see here comes with it. The space is as-is."

I looked at the red laminated table, wooden chairs, and the full straw dispenser. "Straws, too?" I chuckled.

Steve rolled his eyes.

"Straws, too." Sawyer smiled wide. "From what I understand, you want to put a pastry shop in here?"

"Yes."

"The town needs a good one, so I hope you're good." Sawyer leaned over, raising her hand to her mouth as if to tell me a secret. "There are a lot of critics in this town."

"Madam, he is an excellent chef." Steve stared at her. "One of the best, if not the best on Long Island. He has won awards and makes the best darn carrot cake."

Sawyer backed away with widened eyes. "Okay, then. Would you like to see the rest of the space?"

"Yes, please." Steve winked at me.

We walked around the front of the space, taking photos, and picturing the café we had dreamed of in our minds. We talked about rent and taxes and any other town fee that might come along.

I crunched the numbers in my head and felt comfortable with the total, adding a few hundred dollars just to play it safe.

As I opened the door to the kitchen, I at once averted my face. "Dear God, what is that smell?"

"Pee yew! I'm sorry, guys, I had no idea it smelled so bad in here."

There was a closet on the right. Steve grabbed a hanger to keep the door pried open to let some air in. "It's not so bad. All this place needs are a bottle of bleach and some good old elbow grease."

"Yeah, and maybe a cart to get rid of the dead bodies." I rolled my eyes.

"Oh, stop. There are no dead bodies in here." Sawyer shuffled in. "At least I don't think so," she mumbled and bit her bottom lip.

I smiled to reassure her that I was only joking as I took in the open work area. A center worktable, a marble table against the left wall, bins stored under another worktable just on our left. "Looks perfect." But something was troubling me. Why did the place look like the previous owner just went up and left? It did not make sense to me. The bins were full of flour and sugar. There was definitely food rotting somewhere, as I knew that smell. A chef's knife lay on the marble table next to a spill of flour as if recently placed.

Sawyer pulled out a flashlight from her purse. "A Realtor is always ready." She shined the light around the room.

CRACK! The sound came from behind us, followed by a long squeak. We turned around to see the kitchen door slam. *BAM!*

We all jumped. Sawyer let out a small scream.

"That was scary." I looked over at Steve, whose face had gone sheet white. "You, okay?"

"Yeah, I'm okay. It was a cheap hanger. We're good."

The smell of rotting food grew stronger as we walked closer to the built-in refrigerator and freezer.

"Is there a dead body in there? Is that why the space is for rent?" Steve looked over to me as I shrugged my shoulders.

"No, no dead bodies, maybe some old dough rotting away. Easy cleanup as far as I can see, and there are no rotting zombies." Sawyer kept that smile going, but I saw a smidgen of doubt.

We walked past the ovens, and three compartment sinks to the back of the kitchen. I did not want to open the refrigerator. The smell around it was so sour. We passed the dry pantry with a few scattered cans of tomato paste and oils. A pile of flour and dirt was pushed into a corner.

Sawyer stepped ahead to open the rear door to the hallway. It was a heavy metal fire and security door. She pushed the release bar with all her might and shoved the door open. The cracking noise was scary on its own.

It was a hallway. Not an outdoor alley. Lit up with a single bulb hanging down from the fourteen-foot black-painted ceiling. The bulb moved as if someone had tapped it with a slight touch or as if caught on a gentle breeze. The dark gray hallway walls led past the neighboring art supply store and then curved around to the right, emptying out into an open alley behind the Italian restaurant on the corner and the neighboring bar.

"This is the hallway/alleyway. It exits to Wall Street, the adjacent street where the trash is picked up." Sawyer had her flashlight ready, as if she were looking around an attic for an antique of some kind. All I could think of was a creepy-looking doll sitting on an old sewing box with half its hair and one eye missing.

Sawyer waved us on, "Follow me."

"Uh, no, thank you. You cannot even see the exit door. I will stay here with the rotting body. That is one scary hallway. I won't be going down there."

"What's got you so scared?" Steve questioned me. "Come on, Sawyer, I'll finish the tour." Steve looked to me, "Chicken." Then jokingly, he added, "I think I saw a chopped-off hand in the pile of debris on the floor."

I looked behind me so fast as Sawyer laughed. Steve laughed, too, as I grabbed my right wrist. "Just go and hurry back." I stood there with the flashlight in one hand as I held the door open with the other.

I could imagine the kitchen full of workers making the best desserts ever. I could hear jazz music playing as the cappuccino machine swirled its steam.

My thoughts stopped short.

I felt something approaching me from somewhere between the cans of crushed tomatoes and the pallet of flour bags behind me. It was suddenly freezing cold as the hairs on the back of my neck stood up like a literal cold wave from the right of me. Invisible, it brushed against me with cold pressure, as if I had walked by an open freezer door, causing me to hold my breath from the icy breeze. I had never felt anything like this before. It continued past me, radiating coldness without stopping as it entered the hallway. Sensing something but not knowing what it was, I followed whatever it was with my eyes, holding the door tightly in my grip. I could not see it, but something was there. It left me to approach Steve and Sawyer as they came into view from around the corner, chatting away.

"What the hell was that?" I whispered.

I noticed they did not seem to feel a thing, nor did they comment on how cold it was in the hallway.

"So, what do you think?" Steve nodded his head to convince me.

"Uh, yeah, I… I like it." I did not want to say anything about what I'd just experienced.

"You don't sound convincing."

Sawyer stood by his side with a gleeful smile. "I can make a deal with the property owner. He's desperate to rent it out."

"Okay," I flatly said it, trying to let the feeling of unease pass. My palms were already sweaty and cold; maybe it was nerves kicking in. I wanted this space and thought it would be perfect. "Yes. Where do we sign?" I looked past them one more time, peering down the hallway, and thought, *I am never going down there. Ever.*

CHAPTER 2

A FEW MONTHS OF renovation later, we arrived at the patisserie to celebrate the hanging of our sign, Fiorello Patisserie. Steve had been working closely with the contractor on designing the front of the café, while I worked on the kitchen. I was concerned over how old the equipment was because periodic maintenance could get awfully expensive. The double-stacked convection ovens seemed to be working fine, holding at the right temperatures. The walk-in refrigerator and freezer were purring away, or should I say chilling away now that new compressors had been installed on the roof.

The café resembled a fine Parisian bistro. The floor tiles were a busy connecting pattern of creams, burgundy, and chocolate. Bistro chairs and tables filled the room as the rose-gold ceiling warmed the atmosphere with its glow of copper.

We popped some champagne as the sunset-orange lightbox sign with burgundy lowercase script was hung. Looking up at our name in lights made us feel like the patisserie was finally complete.

"Cheers, and here's to us." I clinked my paper cup against Steve's.

"Yes, to us and to Fiorello Patisserie. May every croissant rise, may every cake taste delicious, and may every customer fall in love with it."

"Hey, I like that. Have you been working on that?"

"No, I just made it up."

"Ha. Witty as ever."

"Ah, you know me, always on my toes." Steve grinned from ear to ear, clinking my cup again as Ralph, the contractor, turned the sign on.

We had combined our surnames, to create the name Fiorello. When translated from Italian, it meant *little flower*. We left New York City, where Steve worked as a publisher for a travel magazine and I as a pastry chef. We moved to Harrington, Long Island, a few years ago with our West Highland terrier, Figaro, to have a little more green in our world. Unfortunately, Figaro passed away a few months ago, and I felt the time had come to devote all our energy to opening our own business. I missed Figs like crazy.

Our contractor, Ralph, took us on a tour of the completed work. The kitchen sparkled, my reflection practically shining in the stainless-steel finishes. The guys had done a tremendous job of cleaning every nook and cranny. No more mold and no more rotting zombies anywhere.

We added some rolling racks, shelving, and a granite top for the center table and replaced the ceiling tiles, adding energy-saving overhead fluorescent lights.

Ralph led us to the white marble-top lowboy table and pointed to the lights overhead. "I noticed a problem with these lights. They seem to blink occasionally. Not sure where the problem is coming from, though, but we did notice that when they flicker, we sometimes hear a banging sound coming from the back of the kitchen." He let out a huge sigh. I thought my sighs were bad, but this guy even beat me. "The sound seems to be coming from inside the walls somewhere."

We stood in silence and listened. I was concerned. "Is there an electrical problem?"

Steve spoke freely. "If there's a problem, fix it."

"We've tried several times. I replaced all the wiring, the fluorescent end caps, and bulbs. I have no idea what the banging is all about, but it scared the crap out of Tom, my electrician. He got a bad vibe back there and said he won't work in that hallway by himself anymore."

I gasped as my eyes widened, and I thought of the bad vibes I had had a few months ago when I stood by the hallway door. "Er… What type of bad vibes? Like someone-watching-him bad vibes? Because I know how he feels."

"Yeah, exactly, and definitely not a happy feeling. That's one creepy hallway."

Okay, wait a minute, I'm about to bug out here. Here's my two cents about the hallway. I happen to like it back there; it's not creepy but it is cold, dark and quiet. I can have some down time, and recharge without being disturbed. As far as Tom goes, if he would do his job instead of wasting time and money sending messages to his mistress maybe I wouldn't be so aggressive. He's a bad seed. I sensed it from when he first started working here. He deserves to be freaked out and spooked.

"Oh, stop it. That's nonsense." Steve threw a dismissive hand in the air as he walked around the center worktable. I looked at the shiny green granite top as I listened to him. "Bad vibes, voodoo, scary things. It is probably a water pipe banging back and forth when someone runs the water or flushes the toilet. It happens in my home when the washing machine pumps water in. I am not worried about it. What other problems are there?"

"Ah. Okay. Well, I can ask the plumber again about the water lines, but I know all the work we did is solid around here." Ralph blew out a lot of air as he sighed again. I could see Steve's authority threw him off a bit. "Nothing else wrong that I know of. Oh, wait, yes, the floor."

Steve and I both looked down at the floor. I even took a step back, thinking maybe I was stepping on something.

"This part of the floor, from where I stand to that wall, and to the back kitchen wall, is the original floor. Now, from here to the kitchen door is all new tiling. The old tiles were cracked and busted."

"Sweet. I noticed they were worn out. Thank you for replacing them. It looks great." I followed the line he was talking about. It was an area from the end of my lowboy refrigerator to the doors. The lowboy itself, dough sheeter, and walk-in boxes were all on the old tiles.

"All right." Steve looked around. "So, we're good to go? Ready to make some pastries?" He smiled at me.

"I was born ready, with a whisk in my hand."

Ralph laughed. "Yes, you're ready to go, everything works. If you have any problems or concerns, please, call me. I'll come right over."

We all shook hands. Steve handed him a check for the balance due. I let out a gulp that I am sure even the rotting zombies heard. I have a ton of money riding on this venture, and it had better pay off.

We escorted Ralph to the front door and locked it behind him.

"This is great, the patisserie came out so nice. I love the molding and the white marble countertops." I ran my hand along the counter.

Steve followed me and went behind the counter. "He did an excellent job. Do you want a cappuccino?"

"*Oui*, no sugar, cocoa on top, please."

Bang! Bang! Bang!

I jumped at the sound coming from the front door behind me. I quickly turned around to find a blonde woman knocking and waving. She held a paper in one hand, her sweet smile contagious. Even before I met her, I knew I would like her.

As I reached for the doorknob, I could see it jiggling from left to right, but the woman was not turning it from the outside, she had her hands by her side. I hesitated for a moment and went ahead to unlock the door, her smile grew wider and brighter. "Hi, may I help you?" I asked.

"Hello." She extended her hand. "I'm Annie Banks. I was wondering if you are hiring. I'd like to apply for a pastry chef position."

"Why, yes. I am looking for another assistant. I am Gerard, the pastry chef. Would you like to come in?"

"I would love to, thank you." Annie stepped in as I held the door for her. "Oh, it's so nice in here. So, Parisian. Who's your decorator?"

"I am," Steve chimed in from behind the counter. "I'm Steve, and you are?"

"Hi, Steve, it's so nice to meet you." Annie extended her hand. "I'm Annie Banks, your first employee."

Annie Banks? How? She's my homegirl but she moved away from

here years ago. I haven't seen her since high school. Damn, she is as beautiful as ever, my first crush, and my last. What is she doing here? I can't believe this… hey sunshine, remember me? She wants to work here?

"Really? Well, thank you for letting us know. Although we hired a few already, but I'll double-check the order in which they were hired when I have a moment."

Annie laughed and handed me her resume.

I smiled, too, and looked at her qualifications. "Would you like a cappuccino, Annie?"

"I'd love one, thank you." She made herself right at home, taking a seat at one of the bistro tables and slipping her coat off her shoulders. "Nice café, guys. I like this place. I get a good vibe in here."

"Thank you." I sat across from her as Steve brought over her cappuccino and sat next to me.

"Well, this is a spur-of-the-moment interview." Steve looked at her resume.

"Yes. I want the job. I need the job, and I am sure you will be happy with my performance and my skills. As you can see from my resume, I have been in the business for the past five years and have worked in several pastry shops. I moved back to Harrington four months ago, just waiting to come in and apply for the job. So, regardless of what you are thinking now, I know I'll be working here."

Steve and I just stared at her with smiles on our faces. *Who is this charming woman?* I thought. "Okay then. I guess this interview is over."

Now it was Annie's turn to stare. She thought otherwise and went for it. "So? When do I start?"

Steve nudged me and we both kept our poker faces on.

Annie took a sip of her cappuccino. "This is so good." She smiled a nervous smile.

I smiled back, "You seem to have enough confidence in yourself. I hope you have enough confidence in your work and in letting me show you what I want you to execute on a daily basis. I'm fair, honest, and I know what

I want in my product as well as in the pastry chef who works for me."

"Does that mean I have the job?"

I held my hand up and continued. "This is my kitchen and my house. I have hired a few chefs already who come well trained. I know because we have worked together before. As confident as you are, I want you to be open and learn the way I bake and how they bake. I don't want to see you making products your way unless you discuss it with me first."

Annie listened and took another sip.

Steve chimed in, "Can you show up on time at five in the morning?"

"Yes. Yes. And yes! Can I see the kitchen?"

I smiled. "Yes." I liked her and I had a good feeling about Annie. I think she would work well with my other chefs, Hana, Kate, Jada, Laurent, and Antonio. She was just the person I had been looking for to round out my new team.

I could see the excitement on her face as we all got up from the table and headed for the kitchen. Steve held the door open as I escorted her in.

"This is perfect." She looked around with delight at all the equipment, her eyes focusing immediately on the wall in front of my marble table. There, in perfect size order, were all the knives and utensils on the magnetic strip. "So clean and organized."

"Yes, that's me, Mr. Organized."

"When do we start baking?"

"Are you working now?"

"No, I'm ready to come on board."

"How does Tuesday sound?" I wanted to see how willing she really was.

"I need to find a sitter. Um…" She looked around and darted her eyes back and forth to think of an answer. "I'll be here. I will figure it out. What time, five?"

"Five in the morning, okay?"

"Yes, I will leave him with my mother. It will all work out."

"How old is your son?" I looked over to Steve as he asked the question.

"He just turned six. Sweetest thing on two feet." Annie pulled up a photo on her phone to show us. "This is Danny."

"Oh, sweet. He's a cute kid."

"Thank you. His father, on the other hand, is a sack of dog poop. Excuse my French."

"Well, this is a French patisserie," Steve chimed in as he looked at the photos.

We all laughed, breaking the tension.

"I've been divorced for seven months now."

"Congratulations." It was all I could think of to say.

"Thank you, it's been a rough road. I'll tell you about it one day, but I'm originally from Harrington. I just moved back here to be closer to my family."

"Yeah, sure, I understand. I'm sure we'll have plenty of side-by-side chats."

The fluorescent light above the marble table blinked. It was barely noticeable, a quick half a second at the most.

So, Annie has a son, that's crazy. I need the whole skinny on this. Who's the father, is what I'd like to know because Banks is her maiden name. I guess the jerk she married was so bad that she had to change her name back.

"So that's what Ralph was talking about. Huh." Steve and I looked up at the light.

Annie looked up, too. "Is there something wrong?"

"Ah, no, not that we know of. Our contractor told us that this overhead light flickers once in a while. I now know what he means."

"Gerard don't focus on it. It is barely noticeable. We'll call another electrician as soon as we start making some money around here, okay?"

"Yeah, sure, no worries." I gave my attention back to Annie. "So, this is the end of the tour. Do you want to work here? I'd like to offer you the position."

"Yes! I thought you'd never ask." Annie smiled from ear to ear again. It was a sweet and sincere smile.

I extended my hand for a handshake. "See you on Tuesday?"

Annie accepted and shook my hand. "Yes, and every day after that."

"Great, I'm looking forward to working with you, too." I escorted Annie to the door. "Thank you for barging in. I think we'll work well together."

I locked the door again and stared at the knob, feeling good about this new development. "What did you think, Steve?"

"I think she's fine. I like her. She has a spark, and she will do well with the rest of the staff. Definitely an asset to the business. Do you agree?"

"Absolutely," I replied. *I am going to keep my eye on that one and this doorknob.*

And so, will I. Well, well, well, this is a sweet change of events. Dude, I haven't had a heartfelt feeling like this in years. Annie, my first high school crush. She liked me; I know she did. Oh, my heart just skipped a beat. I almost feel alive again. We had a thing for each other, but it never materialized. That jerk JT got in the way. He was always in the way. Why we let him do the things he did I will never understand. We went along with it. The stealing from the High Street Shop-mart, the constant lying, cheating on tests, smoking, and drinking between classes. What was I thinking? What were we all thinking?

And here I am. I wonder if she will be able to sense me around her.

CHAPTER 3

TUESDAY CAME QUICKLY AS my staff, and I began to fill up the walk-in refrigerator and freezer with storable items. Cookie dough, genoise sponge cakes, rainbows, truffles, macaroons, curds, pastry creams, and croissants, of course. We were getting all the mise en place together and getting along fine. I was aiming to open to the public by Saturday, June third.

Laurent and I made puff pastry, pâte brisée, pâte sucrée, and three recipes of perfect croissant dough. Hana, Kate, Antonio, and Annie produced cookies, cakes, muffin batters, and scones. Rock music streamed in the kitchen while Steve played opera up front in the café.

We hired a few high school students for the afternoon shifts to help customers, clean up, and to take the trash out through the hallway. I did enough, and that was one chore I would not be doing, especially through that creepy place. I am not sure what I felt that day back there by the hallway, but I did not need to be reminded of it either.

Steve came through the kitchen door with a pizza so we could break for lunch. He was as eager as I to turn the custom-made sign around in the window to Open. Open was written on one side and Closed on the other side in three different languages—English, Italian, and French. "Okay, lunch, people." Steve set the pizza down. "So? How is everyone doing? Almost ready to open?" He looked at me, knowing no one else would know the answer to the question.

"We should be ready by Friday with a vast selection of pastries, cakes, and cookies. I'll have the high schoolers scoop cookies this afternoon."

"Who's coming in later for training?"

"Rick, Vincent, Lucas, Robert, Jase, Julie, and Nora." I reached over to my table to pick up the schedule. "Tomorrow afternoon we have Tony, Alex, Raquel, Deanna, Jon, and Constantine."

"That's a lot of people to train," Steve sighed.

"You got this, Steve," Kate blurted out on a giggle as she picked up a slice.

"You know how patient I can be."

We all laughed. Steve had the patience of a hand grenade in midair.

Hana got Steve's attention. "Steve, we should be done by three today, just in time for the afternoon staff to come in."

"Okay, good. I will be up front decorating if you all need me. I bought some fleur-de-lis sconces at an antique store and two art deco mirrors to hang up."

"Oh, that sounds lovely," Hana replied.

"He's always shopping at garage sales or antique stores," I snapped back.

"That's right! That's how I do!" Steve bellowed as he pushed through the swinging door. I smiled and followed him with my eyes as he left. As the door swung back and forth like a pendulum in a grandfather clock, I saw a black shadow outline of a person, like a cutout figure in the door's reflection as it swung back to the same spot. My smile disappeared when the door stopped moving, it looked just like that, a laminated burl-wood swinging door.

Annie saw me staring and found her cue to ask me, "Are you okay?"

"Uh, yes. I'm fine." I tried to regain my focus. "I thought I saw something weird, but I'm okay."

Annie nudged up next to me. "So, tell me, how long have you been baking and how did you start?"

"Ah, what?" I had zoned out.

"Were you a child baker or did you pick it up along the way?"

"Oh, I'm sorry." Shaking off the disturbing image on the door, I continued, "I was a child baker. I used to help my mom, and my grandmother who lived downstairs from us."

"Really? I did, too. I baked with my mom." Annie paused. "Are you from Harrington? Where's your family from?"

"No. I grew up in the Bronx. My mom's name is Ann, too, although it is really Annina. She grew up on a farm in the Bronx, whereas my dad's family lived in an apartment building."

"Farms in the Bronx? Are you first-generation or second?"

"Second." I brought over a stool.

"My first baking experience occurred when I was about six years old. I had just started kindergarten shortly after my grandmother, my father's mother, came to live with us in the basement apartment along with her daughter, my Aunt Angie.

On my grandfather, Giacinto's fortieth birthday, my grandmother surprised him with a waffle iron as a present. I am not sure why a waffle iron, but nevertheless, many years later, I would have the distinct honor of inheriting that waffle iron. One reason I was so proud of that was because Grandma Anna had the initials *GF* engraved in the center to honor her loving husband. The *GF* gets imprinted into a wafer cookie one makes in the waffle iron.

They would make GF cookies with the waffle iron as a Christmas tradition. I would race downstairs as the smell of these sweet, buttery cookies came wafting up to our apartment. My older siblings never got quite as excited as I did, and soon Grandma let me help her mix and roll the dough into two-inch-long logs. Then Aunt Angie would take the logs one by one and place them in the hot iron and squeeze it down over the gas burner on the stove. I was not allowed to flip the iron over by myself, but Angie would do it with me, making me think I had done it alone. "Yay," she would exclaim as the other side of the cookie was cooked. She knew exactly when to flip it and exactly when to remove the cookie so that it was perfect on both sides, a golden color, and light brown edges.

I don't think she ever burned a single one. She would remove each cookie ever so gently with a butter knife and place them on the cooling rack. Grandma would smile as she smacked my hand as I tried to reach for one, eliciting light, slightly wicked laughter from Angie, who would say sympathetically, "Oh, Ma, let him have one." Words I was always excited to hear.

"No, not yet." was usually my grandma's response. She was nice—but tough. Then she would smile at me and say, instructively, "Okay, now, Gerard, watch," as she sprinkled powdered sugar over the edges. "See? Don't get any powder in the middle on the GF, okay?"

My grandfather's initials were in the center. I always thought it was made for me because I had the same initials. It was like magic watching the powdered sugar fall ever so gently over the cookies, so artfully around the perimeter but never in the center. Finally, Grandma would pick out a still-warm cookie and hand it to me with a smile wider than my own. And her expression blossomed with satisfaction as she watched my happy face light up and my eager hand reach for the cookie.

It was sweet and I was as happy as a kid could be.

There was no other name for the cookie, nor could I ever imagine calling them anything else, even to this day we call them GFs after my grandfather. I never met him, but boy, oh, boy, I thought he was one lucky guy to have a cookie named after him.

And I never met my mother's parents either, Antoinette or Raphael, they passed away before I was born. They had owned a farm in the Bronx on Metcalf and Story Avenues—if you can imagine a farm in the middle of one of New York City's five boroughs. They worked the farm along with their children, my mom being the oldest of five. It's curious, but although my mother's name, officially, was Annina, growing up, we always called her Ann or Annie. I wouldn't actually learn of her real first name until one day, decades later, when she needed help getting a copy of her birth certificate from city hall, and I happened to look at the correct spelling on the document.

My mother told me, Grandma Antoinette was always in the kitchen cooking breakfast, lunch, and dinner—and little things in between. There was enough food to feed the family as well as the neighboring farm workers who knew they could stop by the farm to get a delicious meal, where most of the food came directly from the farm.

"So, I think I have a little bit of both ancestors' genes and personality in me, especially my grandfather Raphael. He worked on the farm with his hands. My dad was a carpenter and my mom cooked and baked. I guess I am my parents' son."

"That's so cool. What a nice story. Better than my broke-ass family with a drunk for a father." Annie smirked as she threw her paper pizza plate away.

I could see the looks on the chefs' faces, from happy about my story to an *I do not want to know about it* look.

"But my mother did make a chocolate ricotta cheese pie, which was really good. I'll make it for you one day." Annie forced a smile.

"Sure Annie, that sounds delicious." I smiled back.

"Hey, G. Where is the waffle iron now?" Antonio took the final bite of his pizza.

"It's right over here in the corner behind the swinging door," I pointed.

"Oh, so that's what that is." Kate was clearing off the center table and giggling. "I had no clue as to what kind of pastry tool that was. It's so big and heavy."

Jada picked it up off the table and flipped it back and forth. "Wow, your grandmother must've had some major arms swinging this thing around. It's so heavy."

Jada handed it to me. "Yep, this is it. I haven't used it in a while, but I'm sure I will again." I opened it up to show everyone the initials and hung it back up on the hook for good luck and to remember my family.

I eyed the burl-wood laminated door as I passed, looking for the shadow image of a person or even to see my own reflection, but to no avail.

By the way, just to give you the lowdown on this, that wasn't me he saw in the reflection on the swinging door. This place, or should I now call it a patisserie, has more than one haunting it. Sometimes it's like Grand Central Station back here. But I let them pass through, just as long as they don't overstay their welcome, and get on my nerves.

Some of these chefs have their own deceased family members whose spirits pass through, and that shadow figure he saw is unfamiliar.

I'm not bugging out about it, but I don't like it either. It could be shadow man is back and that's not good, for anyone. I'll have to keep an eye on that. But the children will stay, they were here before me, and they make me laugh and feel young again.

Sounds like Gerard came from an awesome family. Sort of reminds me of me when I was young or should I say younger, rallying to my mother's side to make chocolate chip cookies. Gosh, I miss her. I remember Annie's father was a mean son of a bitch. Always yelling at his wife and Annie. If I remember correctly, she ran away twice. Once to my basement. My mother set up the old sofa so she could sleep there, and she went to school after her creep of a father went to work. This went on for a month during my sophomore year. Yes, she had a tough life at times.

That was when I fell for her, and I was crushed when she put me in the friend zone. I thought we might turn into something special. Geez, I've known her since fifth grade, and I never made a move on her, and never wanted her to think I was weird, so I guess you can say I kept her in the friend zone, too. Things could've been a lot different.

Pictured: Raphael Orsini, family cousin Frank DiNunzio, Francis Orsini, Maria Orsini, Antoinette Orsini, Philomena Orsini, and my mom Annina Orsini.

GF Cookies.

4 Tbs	Unsalted butter, soft at room temperature
6	Extra-large eggs at room temperature
¾ cup +1 Tbs	Granulated sugar
4 cups	All-purpose flour, sifted.
2 tsp	Baking powder
2 Tbs	Anisette liquor
1 Tbs	Vanilla extract
1 Tbs	Milk
	Confectionary sugar for dusting

In a large mixing bowl or in a stand-up mixer, cream the butter and sugar. Beat in the eggs one at a time. Add the vanilla and the anisette. Beat mixture again. Sift the flour with the baking powder. Add half of the flour mixture slowly to the batter with the mixer on the first slow speed until incorporated. Add the milk and follow with the remaining flour. Stop and scrape the bottom of the bowl to incorporate all the dough. Remove the bowl from the mixer and finish kneading the dough by hand on a lightly floured surface to form a smooth dough but do not overwork the dough.

The dough can be used right away. Be sure to preheat the waffle iron first. Prepare the pizzelle maker according to the manufacturer's instructions.

Roll the dough into a log and cut pieces about a half-inch wide and one inch long. Cook according to the directions on your pizzelle maker. They will be lightly golden when cooked, but still soft—remove quickly with a fork or tongs to a cooling rack. As the next cookie is baking, the first cookie will cool and become crisp. Dust the edges with powdered sugar.

The cookies may be stored in an airtight container for up to one week (if they last that long!).

Yields approximately three dozen.

Enjoy!

CHAPTER 4

OPENING DAY!

Most bakery chefs start their workdays at the bleary-eyed hour of five in the morning. I was no different.

I arrived at the patisserie with nervous jitters, like the first day at a new job, wondering if the citizens of Harrington would like my pastries. I unlocked the door and stepped inside locking it behind me. Looking around the empty café, I imagined soft French café music playing in the background while customers drooled over which cake to purchase. I smiled only to myself.

I reached for the kitchen door and entered, flipping the lights on. "Good morning kitchen!" There was a comfortable silence about the place, save for the familiar whirring hum of the compressors working to cool the large walk-in refrigerator and freezer. I hung up my hoodie and emptied the contents of my leather messenger bag Steve bought me on our last trip to Paris.

First things first, I thought to myself. Turn on the ovens and the proofer (which was an electric steam box that helped the croissants, morning pastries, and brioche rise quicker). Turn on my laptop so we could have some music while we worked. For some reason, we did not receive a radio signal here. Maybe the building was made of lead, I do not know. And most importantly put on a pot of our morning brew coffee, a select blend of dark roasted Columbian and Italian espresso. The aroma alone will wake you up.

Next, I opened the door to the walk-in fridge. Dozens of croissants, prepped the night before, lay in neat rows on several trays slid into a free-standing rolling rack inside the walk-in fridge. They must first be slowly defrosted with a refrigerated proof overnight. It was opening day and I expected half the town to visit the pastry shop to see what it was all about.

I was guiding the rack out of the refrigerator when I first heard a sharp, chilling sound, almost a screech. I stopped dead in my tracks, my feet straddling the doorway saddle of the walk-in.

I did not dare move. I think I held my breath in fear and doubt, listening, straining to hear amid the dead silence. It registered right away as a voice, sweet and light, yet terrifying. I was terrified! My heart was beating in my throat. It was definitely a woman's voice, calling my name in a piercing shriek, as if to get my urgent attention.

"*Gerrraarrrrdd!*"

I stood frozen in the doorway, the cool condensation from the fridge cascaded down and out like an eerie ground fog across the floor. My eyes scanned as much of the kitchen as I could see, fearful that someone else was with me. No such luck—or should I say, no such easy explanation—I was alone, standing somewhat ridiculously half in, half out of the walk-in refrigerator, too scared to move, my hands gripping the gleaming cold bars of the stainless-steel rolling rack. I think the hairs on the back of my neck stood up.

But I did not panic; there had to be a logical explanation. I looked down at the wheels of the rack, and I smiled like every movie detective who had just solved a great mystery.

Yes. That must be it. It was the wheels that had squeaked. Except that when I resumed pulling the rack out of the walk-in, they did not squeak at all, they rolled smoothly.

I was baffled, but there was baking to be done and I tried to put my thoughts aside. I pulled the rack completely out and closed the refrigerator door. It shut smoothly, without the slightest squeak. I turned to the rolling rack and made my way over to the proofer, where I began to load the trays of croissants.

Coffee.

That is what I needed. Maybe it was just me.

My man, my man, this guy is jittery. We wanted to wish him well, and here he is freaking out over a simple hip-hip, hooray greeting. He has no clue as to how much energy the young lady utilized just to say his name. Although, I do feel he knows we're here.

Rest up, kid. Don't be upset because you think you scared him, and don't storm out of here like you did the last time, young lady. This is your pad, too.

You've been here longer than me and have claimed the land but you're in and out of here like a flint half the time and all you do is stare at me. You could at least tell me your name.

I rushed through the swinging door to the area behind the counter, where I tried to pour myself a cup with my trembling hands. "What the hell was that? It sounded like a woman calling my name." I gave in to the fear, I was talking to myself as I reached below for the half-and-half.

Taking a sip of coffee, I closed my eyes for a brief second to let the stress slip away. "Ahhh," I exhaled. I was still a little tight from what had just happened. I eyed the kitchen door, knowing I had to go back in there and get moving.

I took another sip, determined as I went into the kitchen to load up the now fully heated oven. I stopped in front of my laptop and opened my music playlist tapping the shuffle button.

"Here we go, first song to be played in the kitchen on opening day is?" I needed a distraction and music always set the mood. I recognized the opening chords right away from the song Bittersweet. "Alright, nice memorable random song, like bittersweet chocolate." I tried to put the nervous feelings away and reached for a tray of almond croissants, I looked around as if I were being watched. Working quickly with the oven door open, I had positioned the rolling rack close enough to grab the trays immediately one after the other and load them directly into the oven. I was starting to settle my mind and get back into the flow of my routine, singing the chorus to the song but as I grabbed the last tray with the blueberry ginger muffins on it, I saw something that freaked me out.

It whipped past me in a flash in my peripheral vision.

A bright white light that either zipped past me or seemed to pass right through me like an X-ray, so quickly I could not tell which. Then it turned abruptly, zigzagging around the center table and out the kitchen door in an instant. I am sure that my mouth dropped open, and my eyes bulged out.

"What the hell was that?"

I felt frozen in place and yet shook uncontrollably at the same instant. I tried to absorb what I had seen—or thought I had seen: It had a flowing white tail trailing behind it like a woman's beautiful gown, and it had blown past me like a chilly gust of wind out of nowhere and hurriedly raced out the door.

Wait, wait, wait. Don't freak out and don't go. Oh geez, she showed herself again. First with Franco, and now this guy. I'm not even able to do that. How did she do that? Why? Is it because she's much older than me, and more powerful? I'm going after her this time. Wait up sunshine!

That is when I knew it had to be a ghost or spirit of some kind, though why and where it came from, I had no idea. As I stood there mesmerized, listening to my pounding heart, all I could think was: *Who needs coffee after that? Something even stronger might be in order.*

Right at that moment, the front door clicked open, and Chef Kate walked in. I think she was about to say, "Good morning," but the shocked and confused expression on my face must have alarmed her.

"What's wrong?" she asked instead, deep concern in her voice.

I tried to regain my composure.

"Kate, did you see anything strange when you came in here?" I asked. "Anything?" I thought for the sake of my sanity, *please give me something.* The truth was that I could not believe I actually saw what I knew I had just seen. It could not be real. I needed her to confirm this. Kate pursed her lips and shook her head.

"No, nothing unusual. Why? Was I supposed to see something?"

"No, no, I guess not," I answered, trying to hide my consternation. "I made a pot of morning brew," I deflected, hoping Kate would not notice that my hands were still shaking.

"Great," she replied, and walked toward the front counter to pour herself a cup.

Maybe it was me and the lack of sleep combined with opening-day jitters. But I refused to believe that. I was always on my game when I was at work, even in the wee hours before dawn. Somehow this time I was turned around and tricked. I had that palpable, heart-pounding feeling, as if someone—or some phenomenal presence—had been in the kitchen with me, had played a joke on me and managed to escape just before I caught them. At the same time, I felt played by my own senses.

I had never experienced anything like this. I thought about the reflection I had seen in the swinging door the other day and the cold pressure sensation I felt by the back hallway when Steve and I first saw the space. I really did not have time to think about this, but could there be a ghost here in our about-to-open café?

Blueberry Ginger Muffin

1 lb	Soft unsalted butter (preferably at room temperature)
2 Tbs +1 tsp	Ground ginger powder
1 lb.	Granulated sugar
4	Extra-large eggs at room temperature
1 pound + 4 oz	All-purpose flour sifted.
1 Tbs + 2 tsp	Baking powder
1 tsp	Salt
4 oz	Whole milk
18 oz	Fresh Blueberries

Note:

For conventional ovens preheat oven to 400 degrees and lower to 350 degrees after 5 minutes

For convection ovens, preheat oven to 350 degrees and lower to 325 degrees after 5 minutes.

In a five-quart stand-up mixer with a paddle attachment, cream the soft butter until it is a soft pomade texture.

Mix the sugar and ginger together and add to the butter. Mix for three minutes, set the mixer on a slow speed, and add the eggs one at a time until incorporated. Stop and scrape the bottom of the mixing bowl to make sure the butter and sugar mix are not stuck to the bowl. Turn the mixer back on and mix for three minutes or until homogenous.

Alternate adding the dry ingredients together and the milk in two or three turns of alternating.

At this point, the blueberries can be folded by hand with a rubber spatula. You do not want to turn the batter blue by using the force of the mixer.

Scoop twelve muffins into paper baking cups in a muffin pan and bake for twenty minutes. Turn the muffin tray around and bake for approximately another fifteen minutes, depending on the oven type or if a convection fan is used.

Use a thin paring knife to check if muffins are done by inserting it through the top center. Knife should come out clean.

Yields eighteen muffins.

CHAPTER 5

"**I THINK I SAW** a ghost this morning." There I said it. I blurted it out while everyone munched on lunch wraps from the deli around the corner. Hana stared at me with her wrap still in her mouth, deciding whether to bite and chew or scream and run. I could even see some ranch dressing dripping from the corner of her mouth.

Laurent laughed. "A ghost?"

Annie looked around the room. "Why would you think you saw a ghost?" The chefs were waiting for an answer. I took a deep breath and told them what had transpired earlier that morning.

Jada took a step back from where she was standing not to be in line of the ghost trail.

"Oh, please." Laurent finished his drink. "Maybe it was the headlights of a car passing by, reflecting off the window?"

"Ohhhh! Now I know why you asked me if I saw something this morning." Not knowing what else to say, Kate looked me in the eye from across the kitchen as if she wanted to communicate with me mentally.

I averted my stare. I was still a little shaken up. This was opening day, and all I could think about between finishing a cake and how many croissants were left was what I had heard and seen this morning.

Steve pushed open the swinging kitchen door with a carrot cake in his hand and immediately noticed the kitchen was as quiet as a mouse. "What's going on? Did someone die?"

"Uh, maybe?" Antonio whispered, loud enough for us to hear between Steve's rapid-fire questions.

Laurent, Kate, and Annie laughed.

"Why are you all so quiet?" Steve shot me a look.

I said nothing as I looked up from my salad.

"I need a happy birthday sign, please. This is the first birthday cake going out, so make it memorable."

"I'll do it," Hana ran to the rack in the back of the kitchen to get a fondant plaque and a cornet of chocolate.

"Everything is fine." I was not about to tell Steve about this morning, not yet anyway. I was sure he would make fun of me somehow. I quickly asked him, "How's it going up front with the new staff?"

"So far so good. They are doing what they are supposed to be doing, and the customers are behaving. That is all I can ask for. Did your chefs save some wraps for the front staff?"

"Yes, there are a few leftovers." Kate was consolidating the sandwiches onto one plate for Robert, Rick, Julie, Nora, and Alex.

"Okay, good. I'll wash some of those pots and bowls by the sink while they have lunch."

Rick was the first to come into the kitchen. "Hey, Annie, there's some guy out here who wants to say hello."

Annie was startled. "For me? Who would ask for me? I'm sorry, I'm not expecting anybody." Anxiously taking her apron off, she apologized one more time before heading out front.

"No need to apologize, it's fine," I tried to assure her. "We all have a visitor now and then."

She saw him as soon as she opened the kitchen door. Folding her arms across her chest in self-protection mode, she looked the guy in the eye. "What do you want?" Annie sounded annoyed and spoke loudly enough for every customer to hear.

"Well, that's a nice way to greet your ex-husband."

"It's ex-husband for a reason. What do you want?"

"I wanted to say hello and wish you well. Geez."

"Since when, Brenden? You never supported anything I set out to do and keep your voice down."

"Me? You're the one who's shouting."

"Whatever."

A customer tried to walk around them to get a look at the cookies on display. She smiled at Annie then smirked at Brenden.

"Excuse me, I'm sorry I'm in your way." Annie stepped aside.

"No problem," the customer answered. "Thank you and I think you're handling this problem quite well." She smiled and rolled her eyes toward Brenden.

Brenden sighed as Annie smiled. "Thank you."

"How's Danny?"

"He's fine. My mom is watching him. It would be nice if you spent some time with him, or is it too soon to take him to the bars to pick up girls while your wife is at work? Oh, I'm sorry, ex-wife."

"Okay, we're still living in the past, I see."

"Yes, only when it comes to what you did to me. Why are you here? I do not have time for your bull-crap. I have to get back to work."

Brenden bit his upper lip. "JT was released from prison today. I picked him up, drove him back to Harrington, and I thought I'd pass by to say hello since I was in town."

"JT? They let him out?"

"He served his time, and they reduced his sentence for good behavior."

"Is that him outside leaning on the car?" Annie could see the guy named JT in a white button-down shirt, smoking a cigarette. "He looks different, guess prison aged him some."

"Yeah, that's him. You want to come out and say hi?"

"No, thanks."

"He always liked you, you know. Old high-school-sweetheart type of thing that you were."

"Were? Come on, Brenden, it was never like that, and you know it. JT went away for manslaughter." Annie focused back on the ex. "I have to go back to work."

"He always claimed he was innocent."

"Uh-huh. Please do not come back here, and do not come back here with him. He gives me the creeps. I like this job and I want to keep it. Don't ruin this for me like you did everything else."

"Ah, come on, don't be like that."

"Bye." Annie headed back to the kitchen, leaving Brenden alone.

"All right, nice seeing you, too." Brenden shook his head.

Annie opened the kitchen door just in time to hear Steve scream.

I leave for five minutes, lose the girl in white amidst the spirits, and all hell breaks loose. What is happening out there? Jeepers creepers, Brenden married Annie? When did that happen, and what is he doing here? Oh, I've got to see this. I'm pushing through, get out of my way you people.

"Owww!" Clunk-Clunk-Clunk. "Where the hell did that come from?" He watched a white bucket roll away. "Damn thing hit me in the head."

We all turned our attention to Steve, who stood by the sink, rubbing his head. "Am I bleeding?"

"No, it looks fine, no blood."

"How did that bucket fall off the top shelf?" Steve asked me.

We both looked up in unison at the top shelf, which was clearly about two and a half feet higher than the top of my head. The chefs shrugged their shoulders too.

Laurent suggested, "Maybe it was half off, half on the shelf and the vibration from the spray hose caused it to fall."

Steve concluded, "Maybe or maybe someone pushed it off."

Just then, there was a banging noise in the wall. Boom! Thud! Knock. Call it what you will, but I heard it, and Kate heard it, too. She looked at me as I widened my eyes and shrugged my shoulders, having no idea where the noise came from. It sounded like it came from behind the wall by the kitchen door.

It was just an empty bucket. Lighten up.

Why is this jerk out of jail, and why is he here? This is insane, a nightmare. Twenty years have passed, and I'm still stuck here. I can only travel so far before I must come back and recharge. Why doesn't somebody let me out of this prison, and set me free? Huh? Why am I still here? Could Annie, JT and Brenden be the reason? I am so angry right now; can't you people hear me banging? This is a warning people; I am bugging out, damn it. They are troublemakers. Now, get them out of here, and don't ever let them come back.

"All right, back to work. I am okay and you are all crowding me. You know I'm claustrophobic." Steve shooed us away.

Robert pushed through the swinging door and called me. "Hey, G." That was my new nickname around here—G. "What's up?"

"There's a woman out here named Sawyer and she wants to say hello."

"Oh, the Realtor. I will be right out. Hey Steve, Sawyer is here. Do you want to come out and say hello?"

"No, my head hurts, but ask her if there are any ghosts around here."

There was a moment of silence as everyone lifted their head up from what they were doing to look at Steve. Then they all turned around and looked at me. If not for the oven and the walk-in hum, you could have heard a pin drop.

"And why do you say that?"

"Don't know, maybe it's my sixth sense because my other five senses are pointing in that direction."

"Well, after what I saw this morning and now this, I think something is up, too."

I didn't say another word but walked out the kitchen door to say hello to Sawyer as Steve yelled out, "What did you see this morning? Casper?"

"Yep!"

Jada stopped piping a whipped cream border on a strawberry and cream cake and slowly raised her head. "Oh, my God. Don't even think that."

Robert was oblivious to what was happening and scanned the kitchen with a mouthful of a turkey wrap and said, "What's going on? Why is it so quiet in here?" Nothing comes between a seventeen-year-old high school student and food.

CHAPTER 6

"Hi, Sawyer." I extended a handshake.

Sawyer avoided the hand and went for a hug. "How are you? The café looks great and busy, too. I love the way the whole place came out. It looks so Parisian. *Très bon!* Absolutely amazing."

"Thank you or should I say, *merci, madame.*" I noticed a woman standing next to her. She stood patiently, waiting with her hands folded in front, her purse strapped over her shoulder, and a smile from ear to ear, waiting to be introduced. I acknowledged the waiting friend with a nod.

I also noticed two guys standing outside, leaning on a car with their arms folded, looking at the sign above. I thought one of them had just been in the patisserie speaking with Annie. *Wonder what they wanted?*

Sawyer distracted me. "Here, I brought you and Steve a little something." She handed me a bottle of champagne. "Where is Steve? Is he here?"

"Why, thank you. This is so nice of you. Yes, he is. He's in the kitchen. He, uh—" I was cut off.

"Let me introduce you to my friend. This is Mary Cartelli, food writer for the *Long Island Post*. I told her all about you and the opening of the patisserie."

"Nice to meet you, Mary." We shook hands and I looked around for Steve. I wanted him to be here.

"Nice to meet you, too. Your patisserie is fantastic. I loved your croissant, it is delicious, flaky, texture is delicate with evenly spaced air pockets, and the lightness about it is perfect. *Très bon.* I don't think I've ever had one like this, except for that time I was in Paris."

"Merci beaucoup Madam. I would like to offer you both a café, but I guess you've been here for a while?"

"Yes, we sat in the corner trying a few of your delicious pastries. I must say I haven't had anything I didn't like, and your carrot cake is simply the best I've ever had." Mary giggled as she patted her belly. "I'll be writing my review of Fiorello Patisserie for next Wednesday's issue. Is that okay?"

"Why, yes, that's fine and quite nice of you. Thank you. I hope it's favorable."

"All I can say is you better start making more croissants and carrot cake."

Sawyer butted in to say, "Harrington has needed an upscale place like this for a long time. So happy you guys filled the void."

"Thank you. I would like to offer you something." I turned to Sawyer. I had a question, and it was on the tip of my tongue.

"No, we're fine, and besides, a food critic likes to be incognito. Otherwise, it seems like a biased opinion." Mary winked at me.

"Yeah, I catch your drift. No problem."

Sawyer grabbed my arm. "We must get going. Tell Steve we said hello, congratulations, best wishes, and all that jazz."

"I will, I will. Thank you again, especially for the bubbly. I will share it with my staff." I had a feeling my question was going to have to wait.

"Oh, one more thing." Mary grabbed my other arm as they both kept me in place as if I were leaving the party. Little did they know I might have a full day ahead of me. The number of customers coming in and purchasing baked goods was overwhelming. I watched for five minutes, and everyone who walked in bought something.

Mary continued, "Have you heard of the Prestigious Honoré Awards?"

"Yes, I have. It's for Long Island restaurants."

"Well, this year they created a few new categories for pastry since the patron saint of pastry chefs is Saint Honoré. There is the best dessert category, best pastry chef, and best pastry shop. Excuse me, patisserie." Mary giggled again as both of her hands were now on my arm. "You should enter."

"I don't know, I… I just opened my shop." I thought fast of how I hated being competitive. So much jealousy among the competitors, always throwing dirty looks to someone. The question I had started to ask slipped to the back of my tongue.

Sawyer was listening attentively. "I will nominate you."

"You will?" Sounded like I was about to be roped in. I guess I had to say yes to make them let go of me.

"That would be perfect," Mary exclaimed. "The event is in a few weeks at the end of the month. I'll send you the details, and from what I can see and from what I think, you will sweep the awards in all three categories." Mary winked at me and finally let go of my arm.

"Why thank you, thank you both. I'm beside myself right now trying to take this all in."

"You'll do fine. And make that carrot cake." She looked up at me and closed her eyes with a wide smile. Sort of like the smile you give the sun after a few days of rain. I could almost hear her sigh.

"Maybe I will. Email me the details and I'll get back to you."

I turned back to Sawyer and that question I had pushed through. It no longer sat on my tongue. "Is this place haunted?"

You want the lowdown now because you better believe it is my man. I'm standing right here at the front window; can't you see me? For twenty years I've been stuck between the earth and these walls. Some of the others have been here much longer than me. I'm young compared to most but now determined to keep that bastard away from here.

Look at them. Leaning on the car all smug, smoking and laughing like the old days. What a putz, I can't understand why Brenden is still rubbing elbows with him. He used to be my best friend, for God's sake.

Looks like I'll be on my guard. I have a bad feeling, something's going down.

Sawyer looked up to me with a stunned expression. Puzzled by what I said, she lowered her chin as if to speak, but nothing came out.

I spoke softly as I didn't want to sound the general alarm in front of brand-new customers. "Ah, let me put it another way. Did someone die here? Is that why the space was available, and the place seemed to be left behind in a rush?"

Mary touched my arm again to lean in on the conversation.

Sawyer finally closed her mouth and connected with her thoughts. "Noooo!" She laughed as if I had just said the funniest thing she had ever heard. "Don't be silly, Gerard. No one died here."

My heart instantly slowed down a few beats from hearing that one sentence alone. *No one died here, thank God.* I breathed a sigh of relief as Sawyer continued.

"The previous owner had health issues. He tried to sell the pizzeria but passed away from congestive heart failure at the hospital. Why do you think it is haunted? Look at this place. It's beautiful. Nothing scary at all around here."

"Just the hallway."

"I'll agree the hallway is a bit dodgy. Maybe ask the landlord, Mr. Clayton, from the art studio next door, to clean it up for you." Sawyer tried to pass it off.

"Maybe I will. I'm sorry, I had to ask." I looked up at the front door and noticed a line had formed outside. "Oh, my goodness."

"Wow, you better get to work and make more croissants. Looks like the word is out." Mary patted my arm. "Nice to meet you. Don't forget the review is next week and the awards at the end of the month. Best wishes to you and Fiorello. *Au revoir,* Gerard."

"*Au revoir,* madams." As they left, I caught a glimpse of the two guys outside getting into the car they had been leaning on and driving away.

I kept my smile on my face as I looked around the café. "Welcome to Fiorello," I spoke loudly enough to no one in particular. The first thought that came to mind was the fact that no one had died here in the patisserie. The second thought was more important. There was a line forming from the counter out the front door. It was going to be a great opening day.

CHAPTER 7

I may be exhausted, but I can still tag along for the ride and see what they are up to. Being a ghost comes with flaws. We aren't on the go twenty-four-seven. I need to rest just like you do and recharge myself. I'll sit in the backseat and listen; these idiots won't even know I'm there.

BRENDEN PULLED OUT OF the parking space, turned the radio on, and drove down Main Street.

JT turned it off.

"What did you do that for?"

"Just tell me one more time why Annie didn't want to come out to say hello."

"Dude, why are you getting bent all over this?"

"I'm not. It's just that I've been in jail for twenty-four years. I finally get out and she thinks I'm creepy?"

"JT, why does this bother you? Annie broke up with you in senior year of high school, moved away and dated a few other guys, came back, and married me, of all people years later. We had a kid six years after that, and she divorced me because I…I had an affair." Brenden stopped for a red light. "She has nothing to say, nor does she want anything to do with you or me for that matter."

"Okay, fine, I get it." JT sighed, looking out his window at a young mother pushing a baby stroller while window-shopping. "Maybe I'm rushing it, but I just thought I could reconnect with the past, and the first person I wanted to say hello to won't and thinks I'm a creep."

"Dude, from what I remember, you didn't have much of a relationship with her anyway. Let's not forget you went to prison for manslaughter."

"She dumped me; complaining I was too rough with her. It's so hard to please a woman." JT shook his head with a laugh.

"Ah, you forced her to have sex with you under the bleachers at homecoming."

"Yeah, that was fun." JT slapped his knee and chuckled. "I know she was your wife and all, man, but I miss all those years. She was so sweet, like a candied apple." JT closed his eyes as he reminisced.

Brenden cringed, trying to get the image of JT and Annie out of his head. He wasn't there that day, but he was always afraid of JT and of what he was capable of. "It's okay. We didn't hook up until a few years later." Brenden had to reconfirm his life with Annie again and again, always thinking and feeling JT was angry with him for taking his girl.

"Yeah, the girl was up for grabs when I went away. I get it."

"That was after high school."

"Annie was all I had. I never got over that. That was my only relationship with a woman before I went away."

"And you never got over it?"

JT thought it over before answering. He replied simply, almost in a hypnotic state and without any emotion, "No."

Brenden closed his eyes and bit his tongue. *Why can't people just move on?*

"Go. The light's green."

Brenden stepped on the gas and looked over at his sulking friend. "Now that you're out of jail, can I ask you a question, friend to friend?" Brenden checked the traffic in the rearview mirror and then glanced at JT.

"What?" JT replied as if annoyed.

Brenden turned off Main onto Carly Street, pulling over in front of JT's mother's home. The faded and chipped, green-painted home had seen too many days in the sun. All the blinds were drawn. The chain-link gate was opened halfway with a worn and crooked Beware of Dog sign, hanging by one metal link, inviting anyone to walk in.

"Since it's just you and me here"—Brenden looked JT right in the eye—"did you kill him?"

JT unbuckled his seat belt with a chuckle. "You're kidding me, right?" Brenden held his stare.

"I told you I didn't kill him. Everybody was on him, and I got screwed."

"I believe you, maybe it was your friends, Johnny and Kenny, they were with you, but everyone else in this town thinks differently."

"Yeah, sure. You were there too. Somebody stabbed him."

Brenden's heart jumped a beat. Rehashing and opening old wounds were not how he wanted to spend his day. "Yes, I was but not really. I left before it went down."

JT flung his prison backpack over his shoulder, staring at his childhood home with a bit of sadness, and mumbled, "Looks like I never left." Slamming the car door closed, he leaned in the open window, getting Brenden's attention. "What do you think? Did I?"

Brenden did not say a word. He locked eyes, hoping to find the truth somewhere in his friend's hollow stare.

JT smiled and began to snicker. The snickering turned into an explosion of laughter as he sauntered up the walkway.

Brenden looked straight ahead, with his knuckles white on the steering wheel. He shoved the car into drive and took off just like he had twenty-four years ago.

Dude, you did do it, you stabbed me to death you crazy bastard, and you Brenden, are a chicken ass. You could have saved me, but you let this happen, too, and for what? For what?

What did you gain from this? Annie? You even screwed up that relationship. You both make me sick. Your day will come, and I'll be on this side waiting for you. Waiting to pounce on you unexpectedly, like you did to me. You didn't have to kill me, you psycho, I did nothing wrong.

I've had it, I'm going back.

CHAPTER 8

STEVE'S MYSTERIOUS MISADVENTURES CONTINUED in the days that followed. It seemed just about every time he helped by washing mixing bowls and utensils at the sink, a bucket fell off the top shelf, just missing him—when it did not actually plunk him right on the head. He continued to insist it was only happening to him, but it was happening frequently and to a lot of different people. Okay, not every time, but we were cautious around the sink, looking up a lot. We brought in a level to check the shelves and even tried to force a bucket off by yanking and rocking the shelves. I have to say it took a lot of effort to make even one bucket move.

The odd events had become noticeable to the point of distraction. We joked nervously about the banging in the wall and the buckets dropping, but we weren't terrified enough to run out of the café, yet.

Curses really flew from Steve's mouth. "W-T-F?" he shouted. "Every time I'm at this damn sink these buckets fall. What the hell is that all about?" Then, practically stammering, he looked at each of us, "Are you guys playing some sort of joke on me?"

Then Steve revealed what we were all thinking: "I think there's a ghost here," he fumed. "I really do. And for some reason, he has it out for me."

Hana and Kate tried to cover their smirking faces with their hands, while the chefs tried to go back to work, suppressing any more laughter. And even if the falling bucket phenomenon had happened before, that was the first time that Steve, shall we say, *raised the specter* that there actually might be a ghost in our patisserie.

Steve shouted a warning to the so-called ghost. "When I die, I'm coming back here to kick some ass. So, you better run because I'm going to find you and mess you up."

"He's already dead," Kate kidded him. "You can't do any more damage."

But Steve was having none of this. "Oh, yeah. You wait." He marched up to the front of the store and was clearly convinced by now that something out of the ordinary was happening.

Oh, please, take a chill pill, I'm half your age, and more agile. Besides, that was an accident this time. I like you, Steve, you're the man. I wouldn't intentionally hurt you. You're quite genuine, straight to the point, and funny as hell. You don't take any bull-crap from people, and I must take my frustrations out on something. Just happens that empty plastic buckets are easy to push around.

I turned my attention back to my task of making Mexican wedding cookies, the crunchy, buttery pecan cookie that melts in your mouth. It had lots of butter but no eggs. When I baked these, I scooped them onto a sheet of parchment paper, positioning them six across by eight down, giving them plenty of room to spread.

Out of nowhere, an individual sheet of parchment paper came flying out of the box and sailed off, as if in the sway of a light breeze, eventually landing on the floor. But there was no light breeze, no wind at all, and there was no one near the box that had been stationary on top of the rolling rack next to the small metal table.

We looked at each other bug-eyed, standing stock-still, with that look on our faces that said, *it was not me* or *did you do that?* or *do not look at me!* There were usually five of us in the kitchen, and we were nowhere near the box of parchment paper.

Nor were the sheets hanging half out of the box. Had that been the case, I might have reasoned that it was the work of gravity pulling them out, perhaps an air current we did not feel. But they were tightly in the box, and it did take at least a little effort to pull one out. I looked around the room in hopes of an answer but did not get one.

I picked it up off the floor and tossed it in the garbage. Hana looked at me over her glasses with raised eyebrows. She saw the look on my face, and we all glanced at each other. Hana pursed her lips and swallowed hard.

By the look on their faces, I guess that didn't go over well, girls. Listen up children maybe they don't need our help just yet. Let's wait till they're really busy, and then all the children can pitch in. I think I would've made a great father; these children keep me busy, it's like running a daycare sometimes and that's no lie.

It's nice to see Annie, my sweet girl. My heart goes out to her, we could've been something good, something special. I think she would've been an incredible wife and mother to the right man, like me.

Three o'clock rolled around quickly around here. We had only been open a few days, and my chefs seemed to have found their groove when it came to getting the work done and getting out on time. They worked well together, helping each other out like any experienced team would.

After the opening weekend mayhem, I was in cookie production mode. We didn't make the typical bakery spritz cookie dipped in chocolate with sprinkles. In fact, you would not find a sprinkle anywhere in our kitchen. We had twenty distinct types of cookies, ranging from chocolate chip, oatmeal, biscotti, and linzers to tuilles and meringues. Something for everyone, but without sprinkles.

Kate rested her arm on my shoulder and pointed to the clock. "Hey, Rard, it's almost quitting time, but I'll stay a little longer to help you get some of these cookies done."

"Sounds good, thank you. Maybe you can prep out cranberry orange biscotti? I'm almost done with the Mexican wedding cookies."

"Okay."

"All right, we are out, see you tomorrow." Hana was packing up her bag as Annie and Antonio were heading out the kitchen door only to let Tony, Julie, Nora, and Jase in at three o'clock.

"What is this, the changing of the guard?" Hana laughed as she waved goodbye.

They all laughed as Tony started marching in place. There was always a comedian in the group. I knew because I liked to make jokes as well.

Oh, I'm going to have fun with this kid. He thinks he's too cool for his own good. He reminds me of me a little bit.

Tony had finished washing a load of mixing bowls and pots at the sink and started to put the dry utensils away. He proceeded to hang up some whisks on the S hooks, which were inserted into the bottom of metal wire shelves on the wall over and next to my table.

I started making some oatmeal raisin cookies. The recipe went back to my childhood, passed down to me by my mother when I graduated from culinary school. She did not remember where it originated, but when a cookie was this good, who cared?

"Excuse me," Tony reached past me to hang up one of the whisks.

"Yeah sure."

Abruptly, the S hook popped out of the metal shelving rails. Up and out right before he could hang the whisk on it and fell onto the metal tabletop right next to me, bouncing around, making a loud clanking noise. It startled the daylight out of the both of us.

"Whoa! What the hell?" Tony exclaimed. "Did you see that?"

"No," I spoke somewhat sarcastically, "I was watching the knife, so I don't cut off my fingers." But when I glanced over, an ashen-faced Tony had a blank, shell-shocked look all while clutching two whisks in his hands.

"The hook just popped out. I mean, the hook had to move up and out to fall like that, right?" He stood there waiting for an answer. I did not have one.

"I didn't do it, if that's what you are asking," I testified. I liked to play tricks, but this was not one of mine.

"Yo, G, I didn't do it either, but how did that happen? What do we have—ghosts in here or something?" Tony was trying hard to smile, because by this point, he really thought I was messing with him. Or maybe he hoped I was messing with him because he did not really want to believe in his own ghost theory at sixteen years old.

From the corner of my eye, I noticed Kate staring back and forth between Tony and me. I was sort of speechless. I didn't want to scare the kid, nor did I want to lie to him.

"I have no idea." I shook my head. "But if you must know, I think we do have a ghost in here." I let out a heavy sigh.

"Say what?"

"I mean, something is going on around here, so maybe they or it is playing with you."

Geez man, I'm trying to help. Can't a guy have some fun and play a practical joke without everyone bugging out? I'm a nice guy, I promise. I miss the human connection, and it gives me something to do. I learned some tricks in the kitchen by watching Franco.

I took a deep breath and returned my attention to making the cookies like it was another day in the shop. I had work to do, and besides, there simply was no other explanation I could think of.

"Are there are ghosts here? Who are they? Yo, I don't like being played." Tony eyeballed the room suspiciously, from me to Kate, from floor to walls, and eventually toward the ceiling, as if the answer were hanging up there somewhere.

Well, in a way, it was.

Kate laughed at Tony's animation. "Maybe there are."

"Tony, listen, the other day buckets fell from the top shelf over the sink and hit Steve on the head. Parchment paper flew out of the box. I heard voices and saw a white ghostly image."

Tony's eyes bugged out. "And you're all still working here? No one quit yet?"

"Yes, and no one quit yet. We just opened. I'm not about to run away."

"Damn!"

The S hook mishap got Tony nearly a half dozen times over the course of a couple of days.

Each time, he bellowed, "What the hell is going on here? This place is haunted. Every time I go to put these whisks away, the hooks pop off. Someone is messing with me. C'mon, show yourself, tough guy." With a shake of his head, Tony walked back to the sink.

I would show myself tough guy, but I don't know how to do it just yet. Besides, why do you people want to fight me? Keep that attitude up, and I will get my friends together and give you a fight, although we'll have the advantage. We can see you.

Kate tapped me on the shoulder. "Here's the biscotti dough. Do you want me to put it in the walk-in box, or are you going to bake it now?"

I looked at the clock. Almost three thirty. "Leave it here. I'll roll it into logs now and bake it tomorrow."

My table faced the wall, so there was not much to look at as I rolled out the biscotti dough. I sometimes gazed to the front of the store or out the windows, but on this occasion, I admit I was staring mindlessly at the utensils hanging on the magnetic board.

Suddenly, one of the offset spatulas just started flapping back and forth for no reason, twanging against the magnetic board each time it knocked against it. I thought to myself: *What the heck, maybe I bumped it by rocking the table.* But I had to dispel that theory. The solid marble-top table and the spatulas were at least seven inches above the table line.

It kept rocking back and forth as if someone had just pushed on its handle to make it swing or someone was trying to pull it off the magnetic bar and was having a tough time with it. No such luck. I was the only one near enough to have done that. And I hadn't laid a finger on it. I tapped Kate on the shoulder. In the tight quarters of the kitchen, we worked back-to-back. She turned around and saw the swinging spatula. Her jaw dropped as I pointed out what was happening.

Hey, you, leave that alone. This is my crib; you two guys don't belong here.

Well, we used to belong here, isn't that right, Richard?

Yes, it is Giuseppe. This used to be our hangout before you came along, kid. So, don't get yourself in an uproar.

Used to is the key phrase, now out you go. I said go!

Oh, he's a tough guy too.

Don't rush us kid. We'll be back from time to time, just so you know.

I hate some of these spirits passing through. Everyone wants to join in the act.

Come on Giuseppe, let's blow this joint. See ya later kid. Next time we might not be so nice.

By the way you dorks, I'm not a kid!

"Oh, God!" Although I kind of got the sense that she was thinking: *See no evil, hear no evil, speak no evil!*

There was a whole row of utensils on the wall, but just one spatula decided to swing and twang against the metal magnet. I reached out to grab it, and Kate yelled out, "No, don't touch it."

"Why?"

"It's scary, that's why. Maybe if you touch it, more things will happen."

I pulled my hand back and kept working. "But how do we stop what's happening?"

"I don't know. Who can we call? Did you ask the landlord next door if he has witnessed anything like this?"

"Not yet. I haven't had the clear mindset yet to say, 'Excuse me, Mr. Clayton, but are there ghosts here?'"

Kate laughed her nervous laugh. "Yeah, I know what you mean. It sounds silly."

"You should get going. Your husband's going to think we're having an affair."

Kate laughed. "Oh, my God, that's too funny. Have a good night, guys."

"Nite." I felt something bump into me as I turned around and ignored it.

Sorry, G, I didn't mean to barge through, but something is wrong. I can sense it, Annie is in trouble. I should've followed her like I always do, but this kid and those guys sidetracked me. I gotta skitty out of here.

Mexican Wedding Cookies

Note:

For best results, cookie dough can be made a day or two before and stored in the refrigerator or at least four hours ahead of time.

Preheat conventional oven to 350 degrees or convection oven to 325 degrees.

½ pound	Unsalted butter soft or at room-temperature
1 cup	Powder sugar/confectioner's sugar, sifted.
½ tsp	Vanilla extract
½ cup	Roasted pecan flour*
	Small pinch Salt
1 ¾ cups	All-purpose flour sifted.
	Cookie trays lined with parchment paper.
2 cups	powder sugar/confectioner's sugar, sifted, for tossing and coating the cookies.

In a stand-up four-quart mixer, use the paddle attachment. Cream the butter first to a smooth, creamy consistency free of any lumps. Add the sifted powder sugar and mix until it is smooth and creamy again. Add the roasted pecan flour and salt and vanilla extract. Mix again, stopping to scrape the sides of the bowl. At the first slow speed, begin adding the flour slowly in three batches. Scrape down the sides and bottom of the mixing bowl. Mix again on a slow speed for two more minutes.

Remove from the mixer. Roll small balls or use a scooper, tablespoon size, and place on the sheet tray, leaving room between each cookie, approximately two inches, allowing them to spread freely.

Place the tray in the preheated oven for five minutes. Turn the tray around and bake for approximately five minutes until the cookies are lightly golden brown around the edges. Could take a few minutes longer, depending on the oven. Over-baking can produce a harder cookie.

Remove the tray from the oven and place them on a cooling rack.

Set up a bowl with the remaining two cups of powder sugar and your cookie storage bin next to it.

When the cookies are cooled, toss a few at a time in the powder sugar until they are completely covered. Gently remove them and place in your storage bin without eating them all first. Store in a cool location for up to one week if they last that long.

Yields approximately three dozen.

** Roasted Pecan Flour—Preheat conventional oven to 350 degrees or convection oven to 325 degrees. Measure one cup of pecan halves and spread them out on a parchment-paper-lined sheet tray/cookie tray. Place in the oven for ten minutes. Turn the tray around and roast them for about another ten minutes. Check the pecans to see if they are roasted by breaking one or two in half. Also, your kitchen will take on the nut aroma, letting you know they are roasted. Do not let them get dark in color or they will become bitter. Place the cool nuts in a food processor and grind them to a fine grind.*

CHAPTER 9

HANA, JADA, ANNIE, AND Antonio had left together that same day at three o'clock, about forty-five minutes before Kate.

"Good night, ladies, I will see you tomorrow." Antonio waved as he walked to the corner of Wall Street.

"Wait up, Antonio, I'll walk with you." Jada hurried to catch up.

"Where did you park, Hana?" Annie was looking for her cigarettes in her purse.

"I'm up the street at the broken meter." Hana smiled as if to say, *Ha, I am beating the system.*

"Well, good for you. I parked in the lot across from the post office."

"Oh, yeah, I thought of that until I saw the broken meter. You know someone is going to park there. Why not me?"

"It looks like the town caught up with you." Annie pointed up the street.

"Whaaaat? Oh, no. I hope I didn't get a ticket."

Town maintenance workers were replacing the broken parking meter. "Damn it! I guess I'll be walking with you in the morning."

"I guess so. Have a nice night, Hana."

"You, too, Annie."

"Can never find my lighter when I need it."

"Do you need a light?" The voice came from behind her. Annie looked up from the depths of her purse. *Geez,* she thought to herself. *Can't I look for my own lighter without getting hit on?* Afraid to turn around, Annie kept walking.

"Hey, Annie, why the rush? Do you want a light?" The man behind her increased his pace to catch up to her.

This time Annie realized it had to be someone she knew. Who else would call her by name? It was not Brenden. "Do I know that voice?"

With her hand in her bag and a cigarette dangling from her smiling lips, she turned around. She did a double take as fear and horror took over and the cigarette fell from her lips. Stalling for time, Annie kept her hand in her bag. She had given up on finding the lighter. Without taking her eyes off the man, she felt around for and wrapped her hand around the can of pepper spray.

"Oops, you dropped your cigarette. Let me be a gentleman and pick that up for you."

Annie quickly looked around for somebody else she might know as she watched Hana's car pull out of the parking spot. "Damn it," she whispered as the man in front of her began to stand up straight. The red baseball cap JT wore had a brownish stain on top. Focusing on the nuances rather than the situation, she took a deep breath as the brim passed inches from her face. Everything moved in slow motion, giving her time to see the details of his wrinkled shirt with what looked like lint from the dryer hanging on his sleeve.

Contact, face-to-face, eye to eye—there was darkness there, hollowness, loneliness, shattered beyond repair. *What happened to him?* Thoughts spun. She had to get out of this encounter.

Without a man in her life to make her feel protected, Annie had to face her own fears. Even with pepper "Jack" spray in her grip, she still felt vulnerable. She mustn't show her fear. She flipped off the cap of Jack and put her index finger on the trigger. She had named the pepper spray Jack, her protector, the one who would do the damage so she could get to safety. Standing on the corner of Main Street, USA, she did not think she needed it, not yet.

Not saying a word, Annie and JT stood in silence. Instead of handing her cigarette back to her, he flipped it around and proceeded to put the cigarette between his lips. Was he smiling or was it that devilish grin she had never forgotten? After lighting the cigarette with one swipe of the lighter, smiling as he inhaled and exhaled smoke into the air, he removed the cigarette from his lips and offered it back to Annie.

She stared at it as if it were a snake on a stick. In high school, she would have kissed JT first and let him put the cigarette between her lips. Looking from the cigarette to him and back again, she mustered up, "No, thank you."

"Okay then." He put the cigarette in his own mouth and inhaled again. "What's the matter, Annie? You're not happy to see me?"

Finding her courage, Annie stood her ground. "Hello, JT."

"See? That was easy and pleasant." JT took another drag off the cigarette. "Nice day today, not too hot."

Enough of this chitchat. Annie thought, *I need to go home to my son.* "What do you want, JT?"

"Pffff! Why would I want something? Can't I just say hello?"

"Why are you following me?"

"Well, that's a false accusation. I was merely window-shopping on this beautiful afternoon and happened to see you drop a cigarette. I was just offering help to a damsel in distress." JT smiled, revealing his yellow teeth, most of them or just the ones that made it through prison without being shattered by all the fights that took place.

"Thank you. I… I must be going."

"Aw, why so soon? We have a lot to catch up on, you know. I've been away for a long time; you married my best friend and had a kid." JT stopped. He took another drag and exhaled, shaking his finger in Annie's face. "That's right. You had a kid. Your second kid if I'm not mistaken."

Annie's eyes bulged out. *Who the hell told him?* Her mind started to race in every direction.

JT saw the look on her face. Bam! Waste no time, the damage was done. "Oh, I'm sorry, the cat got your tongue? I'm not supposed to know. The father of your unborn child is not supposed to know you went and had an abortion?"

Annie felt anger rise faster than the prick in front of her picking up her dropped cigarette. She took a step back, thinking maybe she could make a run for it. The car was only around the block. "It was a miscarriage. Who told you that? Brenden?"

"Never mind who told me. Let's just say it was a little bird, you little whore." JT smiled that devilish grin that was beginning to look more psychotic by the minute.

"Whore? Who the hell are you calling a whore?"

The maintenance workers replacing the broken meter heard Annie loud and clear from two parking spots away and stopped what they were doing.

"Why, you, my dear. From what I remember, you wore the title well."

Annie was burning up with a fiery rage. *I don't need this in my life, not now, not ever.*

JT saw her face contort, providing him with some humor.

"Oh, it looks like someone just sucked on a lemon." JT laughed.

"You… you are a murdering psycho!" Scared but not going down without a fight, Annie thought, *I will spray Jack in his eyes and run like hell.*

"Ha! I think you said that wrong. I didn't murder anyone, you did."

The shouting match caught the attention of some passing window shoppers. A young mother almost dragged her daughter out of earshot.

"You forced yourself on me at homecoming, under the bleachers, you bastard, while your horny-ass friends watched! They watched me cry and begged you to stop. No one helped me. No one heard my cries over the marching band as I struggled to get away from you. Why would I want your kid?" Reliving this horror brought tears to her eyes.

"I didn't rape you if that's what you're insinuating." JT's conversational tone made it seem as if the assault had never happened. He nonchalantly continued, "We were dating, having fun, like high school sweethearts." JT smiled through his rotting cigarette-stained teeth. "You liked it rough, from what I remember. Oh, maybe that is why you and Brenden divorced. He turned into a whipped mama's boy. I think you need someone like me, and if you think playing rough is inevitable, then sit back and enjoy it honey." Laughing, JT threw the cigarette on the ground and smashed it out with his well-worn boot.

"You bastard!" Annie had enough and pulled Jack out of her purse, letting him have it, pressing down on the pump trigger.

Her aim was dead on. It was too late for him to stop her. The damage was done.

JT shrieked, "My eyes! My eyes!"

They were instantly burning as if they were on fire and turning redder than the devils. JT tried to stick one hand out to block the spray and cover his eyes with his other hand. "You bitch!"

"Stay away from me, JT. Don't ever come near me again or I will kill you!" Annie took off faster than ever as some onlookers started to gather. One of the maintenance workers dropped his tools to rush over.

"Damn bitch!" JT stumbled backward into a tree that lined Main Street and rubbed his eyes, which only made the burn worse. *All those years in prison and first week out and this damn bitch does me wrong.*

An elderly woman walked over, clearly not privy to what had happened, and spoke. "Do you need help, sir?"

"No, ma'am, I'll be fine."

JT turned away from the crowd and the approaching maintenance workers and dabbed his eyes with his red bandana. "I'll be fine. It was just a lover's quarrel." Thinking Annie might have called the police, he wasted no time walking away, mumbling to himself, "Yes, I'll be fine, but she won't. This ain't over."

Damn, it looks like I'm too late. Where's Annie? Hope he didn't hurt her, but it looks like she might have hurt him. Or somebody did. Maybe she ran to her car.

Fumbling for her car keys as her tears fell, Annie kept looking over her shoulder, making sure JT hadn't followed her. Relieved to be in her car with the doors locked, she let out a good cry, and all she could relive in her mind was that October night, 1981, at high school homecoming.

Crying now and crying then, all she focused on was Eddie's face. JT was drunk and relentless in his attack on her, his boys vigilant on the lookout. Eddie, her neighboring childhood friend, the good boy who mowed her lawn and walked with her to school, quiet and shy for the most part and whom she believed had a constant crush on her. A romantic relationship never developed, but best friends was all she wanted, and Eddie stepped aside when JT entered the picture.

Oh Annie, I never thought you could love me; you were distant at times when I wanted to move forward. I gave you space, and you went for him. I knew he was no good for you, I should've warned you. He was dark and twisted and still is. I want to hold you in my arms and tell you it will be okay. Please don't cry. You're safe now, he's gone. I can hear your thoughts, Annie. Can you hear mine?

"Get off me! Dear God, help me!" Annie had tried to punch JT in the face.

"You know you want me, baby. Stop your bitching, you bitch!" JT had laughed at Annie.

"JT, that's enough. Get off her!" Eddie approached JT with a toughness he didn't normally display. "This isn't funny anymore." Eddie grabbed JT's shoulder to pull him off. "I said let her go! You're hurting her!"

"Here Mister tough guy, take this!" JT swung out with his right fist and hit Eddie in the side of his face. Like a rag doll, Eddie collapsed to the ground, out cold.

Annie cried out as the other boys looked on.

"Let's get out of here, guys." Johnny egged on the other boys to leave. "Let's go, JT."

Annie lay helpless, bruised, and shaking as the band played. No one to help her or to hear her cries as she looked to the one boy who had tried to save her, Eddie, extending her arm to reach him…

Tap-tap-tap.

Annie screamed as Kate tapped on her car window. "Annie? Are you okay?"

CHAPTER 10

"ARE YOU OKAY, ANNIE?"

"Yes, I'll be fine. Still a little shaken up, but I'll be okay."

"All right, if you need to take the day off, leave early or something, please just tell me so." Annie gave me a nod as Hana gave her a hug. In fact, we all hugged her. Fiorello family style. I swear you could hear a pin drop as Annie told her story; it was so intense.

I've been a boss for a few years and always find it hard to separate myself from all the staff drama. Everyone has drama and sometimes you must step back from it in hopes it does not affect the job. So far so good as I pushed open the kitchen door. I could feel my shoulders tightening and my stress level creeping up. Maybe I should schedule a massage. I poured myself a cup of morning brew and thought, *Now I must deal with my employee, afraid to come and go from work, always looking over her shoulder for this JT guy. Bad enough we just opened a patisserie, hired new people, and trained staff. There is a review coming out, a pastry competition that I got roped into, and oh, let us not forget we think the bakery is haunted. Cheers!* I lifted my shaking hand and took a sip. Ah, the simple pleasures of a good cup of coffee in the morning.

As the chefs settled into their job duties, I went up front into the café to read my emails, especially the one from Mary Cartelli about the pastry competition.

Dear Gerard,

It was so nice to meet you the other day at your patisserie. Your pastries are amazing. You can find my full review in the Long Island Post. I'm sure you will find it most favorable. :)

Attached are the details for the Prestigious Honoré Awards.

Good luck, best wishes, and I'll see you at the award ceremony in a few weeks.

All the best,

Mary

I let out a big sigh and thought, *here we go.* Finishing my coffee, opening the attachment, I read the rules and fine print. Besides the best dessert, best pastry chef, and best pastry shop categories, they had added one more—best childhood dessert and cookie.

Huh. My name had been *added* in all four categories. Well, looks like I have work to do. The event was in three weeks on a Monday at a local venue. All bakers and pastry chefs had to be ready at seven a.m., which would not be a problem for me.

I could make those GF cookies along with… That was as far as that thought went. I froze. A cold breeze touched me, as if someone blew on the back of my neck. But it was not an outdoor breeze, nor could it have come from an air-conditioner vent. I shot out of my chair with an alarm.

You need to watch out for her. Dude, you can sense me, I know it. I just wish you could hear me. Annie is in danger as long as that dirt bag JT is alive. He is relentless and has been out to harm her even more since yesterday. He doesn't care who gets hurt along the way. Be it you or one of your chefs, you're all sitting ducks in my opinion. Open your minds people, and listen to me…

The feeling was uncanny, unmistakably moving from left to right, almost sluggish, as if someone were passing behind me so close that they had to actually touch me. The hairs on my neck stood up. I felt like I was in a movie, as if in a dream sequence in which the environment around me was surreal. There was nothing there. It was the same feeling and sensation I had felt when we first saw the space and I held the door open for Steve and Sawyer. I could not see anything, but I sensed something was there. I followed it with my eyes as it passed, watched the kitchen door swing ever so gently. It was one more scary moment, except that more than just seeing something weird happen, this time I felt something weird, too. I paused to let this chill pass me. *Who was that? What was that?* I gulped nothing but dry air. I did not even want to blink as part of me wanted to see whatever it was.

I stood in the morning darkness in the café part of the patisserie, by myself with my cell phone in hand, looking at an email. I heard my staff and the music playing in the background. I waited for someone else to scream, cry, or exclaim, "What the hell was that?" But there was only silence.

I picked up my coffee with a shaky hand and walked back into the noisy kitchen.

Kate looked at me right away. "What's the matter?"

"You okay, Rard?" Hana noticed the look on my face as well.

"Yeah, I'm okay, I guess." I tried to explain it to them, but nobody else had felt the presence except me. Again. Lucky me.

I confess I hadn't felt that scared in a long time, probably not since I was a kid. This haunting, or whatever it was, was getting more real day after day. I had teased Steve for claiming the ghosts were targeting only him, yet now for some reason, I'd been singled out. No wonder the previous owner had up and left this place intact. *I'll have to pay a visit to Mr. Clayton next door and see if he can fill me in on what is happening around here.*

"You're giving me the chills." Kate rubbed her arm as she proceeded to the oven, shaking it off.

Just then, Laurent walked in with a copy of the *Long Island Post.* "Look, here it is."

"Morning, Laurent." I always liked to say good morning to everyone before getting involved in any conversation. My momma taught me some manners.

"Morning, boss. Are you okay? You look a little pale." Laurent opened the paper to find our review.

"I'm okay."

"He thinks he saw the ghost this morning," Kate chimed in, putting a hot tray of croissants on the rolling rack. She held her oven-mitted hands in the air, shaking them as if to scare me.

"You'll have to work a lot harder now to scare me apparently."

Everyone laughed.

Annie nudged in between Laurent and I to read the review.

*"Exceptional. Best croissants west of Paris
and east of New York!"*

That is all I read and of course I stared at the five stars. So proud of my staff, my partner, Steve, and myself for making this dream come true of bringing Fiorello Patisserie to life. Job well done. I congratulated the chefs for their consistent demanding work, their expertise, and love of pastry.

Some of the other highlights in the review were the service by Steve and his staff, the décor, the crisp and fresh pastries, the flourless chocolate cake, the cookie assortment, and the carrot cake being the best, hands down.

Antonio's grin went from ear to ear. We all patted him on the shoulder for making the best carrot cake ever. Even though it was my recipe, props went to Antonio for his consistent bake and making the cream cheese frosting perfectly smooth, creamy, and not overly sweet.

I felt blessed, with nothing but gratitude for my staff and the work they did to make it happen.

"I have one more bit of news."

"What's that?" Kate raced for the oven as the timer was going off.

I reread, out loud this time, the email for the Prestigious Honoré Awards. "We've been nominated in all four categories, best dessert, best pastry chef, best pastry shop, and best childhood dessert and cookie."

"That's amazing and we just opened." Jada put the paper down after rereading the review.

"So, what are we going to make?" Annie chimed in.

"Definitely the carrot cake for the best dessert category."

"Good idea. They'll all have seen the review and want to try it." Hana pointed at Antonio. "Your carrot cake is going to be famous."

Antonio raised his hands in the air. "Oh, my goodness, I better make more."

We all laughed.

"Then, for best childhood dessert and cookie, I was thinking of making the GF cookie along with some gavajunes."

"What the heck is a guavajune?" Kate stood with one hand on her hip, as she egg-washed the loaves of brioche to be baked.

"Not guava but gava, gavajune like the month of June."

"That's an odd name. What is it?"

"It's a fried flaky dough filled with chocolate, jam, and chickpeas."

"You're going to deep fry this doughnut?"

"It's not a doughnut, it's a sweet brisée dough. No frying. I'll bake it.

"Chickpeas?" Jada scrunched up her face and stuck her tongue out as if to say, *that sounds gross.*

"Yes, sautéed chickpeas in butter. See, as a kid, growing up, we did not buy cookies for the holidays; we made them ourselves, and on the weekends when we would visit family and friends, we brought over a tray of home-baked goods. All my aunts had their own variations of the same recipe. Some were filled with prunes or figs, others flavored with rum, wine, or vermouth. My mother created a filling made with chickpeas, nuts, chocolate, honey, and jam. Who would've thought this would make such a really great pastry?"

I had everyone's attention. "As if there weren't enough other desserts to go around at Christmas. Still, I don't think these flaky fried pastries ever lasted until New Year's. Well, in my house they didn't."

"Sounds interesting, especially with the booze." Kate laughed on her way to the oven.

"Oh, God," I lightened up from the memory, "I still remember this from when I was a kid. My mom would try to get us up early..."

"Gerard, time to get up. Come on, let's go and get out of bed. We have to make the gavajunes." Mom stood over my bed. "Come on, Michael, you, too." Michael and I shared a bedroom. He's three years older than me.

"Aw, come on, Mom, five more minutes. Please?" my brother and I lamented, almost in unison.

We're on Holiday break from school, and all we wanted to do was sleep till next year, or even until my tenth birthday, which was in January.

"Five more minutes. That's it." Mom ordered, leaving the door wide open

to show she wasn't kidding. It was eight thirty in the morning. Who baked so early? Little did I know, years later, I'd be halfway through my day at this point.

I crawled out of bed. I could smell the sweet aromas wafting from the kitchen. Walking down the hall, rubbing the sleep from my eyes, I saw my mom mixing her pasta dough by hand on the wooden birch board made by my dad. My dad was an excellent carpenter. He renovated the kitchen in the home I grew up in, he made all the kitchen cabinets, and he made me a bedroom dresser for my first apartment when I moved out. He was always making something.

"Oh, good, you're up." Mom smiled and giggled a bit. "Look at your hair," she chuckled. I had crazy pillow hair as a kid. It was so thick it stood up on its own. I made a stick-out-your-tongue face to make my mom laugh. She always did.

These days she makes fun of my balding head. Some things never change.

"Get the wooden spoon from the drawer and stir the chickpeas on the stove."

They were on a low simmer. I could smell the sugar and butter mixture in the sauté pan about ten feet away. But of much more immediate interest was the rich chocolate melting slowly in a double boiler on the stove's backburner, right behind the chickpeas I'd been instructed to stir. My stomach growled. Simmering chickpeas were both my obstacle and my opportunity—if I was quick. Still in my pajamas, I shuffled over to the drawer with all the utensils, opened it up, and took out the wooden spoon. Then I walked over to the stove. The logistics were good because Mom's back was to the stove. I kept eyeing the chocolate. I gave a quick glance over my shoulder to make sure she was not looking. She was kneading her dough and humming to a big band tune playing on the radio.

I stood on my tippy-toes and raised the spoon nonchalantly over the chickpeas but then proceeded past them and over to the melted chocolate. I glanced back one more time before making my move.

I got this, I thought to myself. Oh, yeah, just a spoonful of chocolate for breakfast would be oh so great.

I dipped the big spoon deep into the chocolate and raised it ever so slowly. It was melted and dripping thickly off the spoon, as if in slow motion. It was pure as silk. I could almost taste it. I looked from the spoon to the chickpeas. They can wait, I decided. And as I carefully retrieved the spoon over the pot of chickpeas, being careful not to spill a drop, I shot one more cautionary glance *toward Mom. She was still humming and kneading her dough.*

I opened my watering mouth in anticipation of the best, most decadent breakfast ever. I could smell the caramel in the chocolate. Soon it was right under my nose.

"Hey, Mom!" Michael shouted. "Look at what Gerard's doing!" He was standing at the entrance to the kitchen, pointing at me accusingly.

Busted!

Oh, I was so close.

But his abrupt shout startled me. The spoon shook up and down in my hand, splattering chocolate everywhere. Up my nose, on my pajamas, on the stove, on the floor—I am sure some of it even hit the ceiling. Although I did manage to get some of it in my mouth before Mom swiveled around so fast and amazingly caught the spoon in midair by the chocolaty end.

"Gerard!" she scolded, "I told you to stir the chickpeas!" But then she started to laugh. "Look at your face. Go wash up and get ready to help me." Apparently, I was constantly a source of amusement for my mom!

"Yeah, go wash up," Michael consorted, reinforcing Mom—at my expense.

Mildly shamed and covered with chocolate, I headed for the bathroom as Mom went back to kneading her dough. But I turned back to catch Mike licking a finger he had just slyly dunked into the pot of melted chocolate, grinning at me so diabolically. He stuck his tongue out at me. I just sighed. Boy, he was fast.

"Oh, my God, little Rardy covered in chocolate." Hana led with her bolstering laugh. "That is so funny."

That was slammin' and funny as hell. I like this guy. He is definitely the man around here.

"It was. Good times back then."

"Well, I would love to try one of those gava java things." Kate laughed. She was the adventurous one with a gazillion taste buds waiting for something new.

"Okay, I'll make a batch in my spare time."

"That means never. You work fourteen-hour days already."

"I know, I have had no life since I opened this pastry shop. I actually used to bike ride, go to the gym, watch a movie, but I'll figure it out." I walked over to my worktable and gazed up at the monitor for the front of the store.

Although the day started off quietly enough, and at five a.m., all was well, now at five forty-five a.m., it was still a bit dark out, so early in the morning. I noticed a stream of light coming from the ceiling in the front café of the patisserie. It was like someone held a spotlight above the camera and shined it down to the floor. It swayed from left to right ever so slowly, sometimes pausing and staying completely still.

"What is that?"

Kate looked over my shoulder. "I don't know."

"That is weird." Laurent was trying to roll out some sucré dough, and I was getting in his way.

I walked out front while Hana watched the security monitor. My thought was to try to get caught in this shining beam of light. No such luck. But it just kept moving in a slow sway, back and forth across the customer area. I went back into the kitchen and decided to record the video of this latest weird phenomenon to show Steve later. Maybe he might have an idea of what it was, but I doubted it.

I helped Hana finish scooping out the carrot zucchini muffins and stopped the video recorder after about five minutes.

Steve came in at six thirty with a small bouquet of sage. "Good morning."

"Morning, Steve." We all spoke in unison, but before I could utter a word about the review or the random beam of light, Steve continued.

"Here, I picked up this sage from the market. It's supposed to keep ghosts and evil spirits away."

My man Steve, what are you doing? No, you don't. Are you kidding me? Do you want to see me go from zero to sixty in a nanosecond? I'm calling you out on this. The next time you're at the sink, you better be wearing a helmet.

We all stared at the sage as if it really had magic powers.

"Really?" Annie seemed unconvinced.

"Yes, really. For whatever reason, ghosts do not like the smell of it, so they stay away. Didn't you ever see a scary movie where they burn sage to keep the evil spirits out?"

Yes, for evil spirits, but we are not evil. This is my home you're trying to push me out of. And to think I like you, Steve. This is totally unnecessary. The children are going to be so upset, they hate that smell. They are going to freak out on you.

"Are you saying we are living in a scary movie, Steve?" Kate took out the final tray of chocolate croissants from the oven.

"Ha-ha. Yes! The boogieman is hiding in the closet, Frankenstein is in the freezer, and the Mummy is in the HVAC room."

We all laughed.

"Life is scary enough. Apparently around here, too."

"Ain't that the truth." Annie rolled her eyes.

I had a feeling she was thinking about yesterday's encounter.

"Don't worry. You'll be okay." Antonio rubbed her shoulder as if to say he would protect her.

"Somebody get the stepladder, please." Steve saw a spot and hung the sage in the kitchen on the latch for the outdoor sign timer box. It's in the back of the kitchen, right past the restroom, high enough so no could pull it down. "There, that should work."

We looked at each other and at the hanging sage. We shrugged our shoulders, not knowing what to say.

I thought to myself, *I can roll with the punches well in life, but what the heck are we getting into now? Ghosts, spirits, paranormal activity, and we are still here?* I was surprised no one had run away yet. Do I have an option? I don't think I do. I was in this for the long haul.

I had invested so much money, time, and a career to have my own business, I needed to do what it took to make the shop successful in every way, shape, and form. I sighed loud enough for everyone to hear me. *My plate is almost full. There is enough on it and enough to do. What's next, a silver platter of more gray hair or, in this case, will my hair turn white from seeing a ghost?*

CHAPTER 11

WE PLAYED THE VIDEO clip back from when I was up front reading my emails, and sure enough, at the two-minute, thirty-five-second mark, a foggy cloud of light came through the front door. A huge white mass but with speed and a direction set. Quick and fast, it made turns to come in the kitchen door behind the counter.

So, they can see me? No way, do I really look like that? A blob? I'm much better looking, always was and always will be. Even with these chest wounds.

"Whoa, you see that?" I pointed to the screen.

"Oh. My. God," Hana chimed in.

"What is that?" Kate was having her coffee.

We all took a deep breath and replayed the clip repeatedly.

Steve grimaced, "Looks like a dust ball. Maybe it's an electric tumbleweed."

Kate burst out laughing and almost spit her coffee out.

On slow motion, you could see it make a turn as it came through the front door, through the display cases, and into the kitchen.

Hana spoke with a quiver, "But what is that?" She looked around the kitchen as if thinking it might reappear behind her.

"I don't know. Is it a ghost? Is it an orb? You can almost look right through it like it's a cloud or something," I was amazed. "Wait, that's me behind the counter. That is the same time I felt something pass by me. Oh, geez!"

I was fascinated with this video. I finally had visible proof that something was going on. Or so I hoped. But what was it, just another unknown occurrence happening around here?

"Come on, let's go. We must put all the croissants and breakfast pastries out. It's almost seven already." Steve rushed us along. "We can look at it later."

He was right. The time had flown by. I decided I'd play with this video again later. "Hey, Steve, did you see the review this morning?" I reached for the newspaper.

"Yes, I read it online." Steve smiled from ear to ear. "Congratulations everybody. I expected nothing less. Now let's get to work you shitbirds, and let's show this town what this patisserie is all about."

We all laughed, and Laurent let out a roaring "Yeeaaah!"

I went back to focus on the monitor and swinging beam of light. I took a duster from the maintenance cabinet and went to the front of the store. Reaching up, I dusted the camera lens.

Hana shouted from the kitchen, "Oh, you got it. That beam of light is gone."

"Wow, it was just a spider web after all, but that doesn't explain the electric dust ball or mass or orb or alien that came through this morning."

"No, it doesn't." Kate narrowed her eyes to me. "What the hell, Gerard?"

"Don't ask me, Kate, I haven't a clue." Well, at least they believed me now that something had passed me that morning.

The front door chime went off and Steve greeted the first customer. Only no one was there. He made his way back into the kitchen when it went off again. He turned in his tracks and headed back out front. "I'm sorry, I thought no one was..." and then his voice trailed off.

He stood at the counter, looking at the front door. The chime went off again.

Hey Steve, can you see me on the camera display? I'm standing right here by the door like a dork.

"Gerard," he called from the front counter. "Something is wrong with the front door. The chime is going off and no one is here."

"What, why?" I shouted from the kitchen and gazed up at the monitor, thinking I could maybe see something happening.

"It's going off and no one is coming in, that's why!" he shouted. "How am I to help these people if they keep playing ring and run? The nerve."

We all laughed. We did find it quite odd.

Steve looked at me accusingly, like I should know why the door chime was going off for no reason.

"Don't look at me!" I bellowed.

"Is there a short in the system or something?"

"I have no clue and I'm too busy to try to figure it out right at this minute."

"Well, I don't like pranks. You're right, we're getting too busy for this!" Steve thundered, as Kate looked my way, smirking.

I just shrugged my shoulders and thought, *I hope today goes smoothly.*

The chime went off again, making my heart skip a beat. I could not show my staff that I was scared or nervous, because if they were, and I was, then we had a problem. I looked at the monitor again only to be relieved that the morning staff was marching in.

Yeah, sure, plow right through me. You have no idea what that does to me.

"It's about time you kids got here," Steve shouted out, as he made a fresh pot of morning brew. "Let's go. It's going to be a busy day."

"What's going on? I need an espresso. Anybody else want a café?" Robert went straight to the espresso maker.

No, thank you was the general opinion.

Steve confronted Robert. "You're seventeen years old, off from school, and you need an espresso to get moving? Why so lazy? When I was your age, I was out and about, heading for the beach. Then I would sleep all day."

Robert laughed at Steve as he made an espresso.

I started to tell Robert about some of the things that were happening. He just laughed it off and tried to make a joke out of it.

No one in the kitchen was laughing. Jon, on the other hand, thought it was sick to have ghosts. Lucas thought we were weird, "Oh, great, now some ghost is going to drag me down that creepy hallway when I take out the garbage?"

We laughed at the thought of it, but I kept a solid face. As the captain of this crew, I should try to keep it together.

Robert set the cup under the spout and pressed the short espresso button. He stepped toward me to finish a point he was making about how, when you died, your spirit went straight to heaven, or maybe the other place, but that was it, he insisted. Life was over and spirits did not hang around to annoy the living on this earth.

"But ghosts do." I was arguing life after death with a seventeen-year-old. I wasn't even sure myself, but I did believe in ghosts, spirits, heaven, and hell, and some kind of life after death. There had to be something more after we died.

"Ghosts? We have ghosts here?" Raquel looked like a deer caught in headlights. She looked from me to Laurent to Kate and Annie.

"No, I don't know what's going on. All I know is that the review came out today and that we are going to be busy, so please ignore what was said and set up the front. Thank you."

"Come on, Raquel, I'll help you." Robert went to retrieve his espresso, but he could never explain who moved the cup while the espresso machine was still dripping espresso. Because when he went to retrieve it, the cup was a good inch from the spout, and all the espresso had dribbled all over the counter. Yet somehow, a tad of espresso was in the cup, and the drips down the side of the cup proved that it had been moved while the espresso was still dripping.

Suddenly Robert looked as if he had just seen a ghost. "Okay," he allowed. "Maybe there is something going on here. I've made dozens of espressos and cappuccinos this week and this never happened to me before."

"See?" I cautioned. "They're listening to us, and they want you to believe." I started to laugh a bit. "That was pretty weird, don't you think?"

"I think you're putting me on," he replied, and with that, Robert laughed it off, shaking his head, "It was probably just a vibration."

"Ha-ha, now who's making things up?" I just smiled.

"Gerard, leave the kid alone and leave the ghost alone. I'll take care of them. You and your staff take care of what you do best and make pastries."

Robert didn't believe in ghosts, or so he said. But he also knew me well, and he ought to know that I would not play around with him. He is the son of one of our friends, youngest in a family of four siblings just like me. He has a great personality with a yearning to learn about everything life has to offer. Except ghosts.

Leave the kid alone? Why would I do that? At least now I put a smidgen of ghostly truth in his head, and yes, young lady, there are ghosts here. We do exist, people.

That smell of sage is starting to get to me. I may have to go now but you won't get away with it. It doesn't always work like you think it does, that's the fact jack.

CHAPTER 12

HANGING THE BUNDLE OF sage seemed like a promising idea until I came in the next morning at four forty-five a.m. to find it lying on the floor.

I gasped when I turned the lights on in the kitchen. "What the hell is that?"

I changed my shoes at the closet, pondering what might have happened and how the sage might have gotten there.

I walked to the rear of the kitchen and looked up at the timer box and down at the sage. It hadn't been thrown or tossed; it was right below it. The string was still tied securely, and the loop was still together. So, what caused it to fall off? Now we had a new mystery. At first, I thought, again, that someone was playing a joke. But I realized that I'd been the last one out of the kitchen the previous night, and the first to arrive in the morning (such is the life of a business owner, always working).

"Oh, my God!" *The ghost did this? Who did this? Is this their way of telling me to throw the sage away?* My heart was skipping beats, I looked around me in all directions. I even walked ever so slowly to the back hallway door. I stopped and took a deep breath and exhaled, knowing if I turned the corner and found the back door unlocked that I'd freak out. I walked a few more steps to see the door in full view. I focused on the deadbolt. It was locked. Relieved, but I panicked. I pushed the door. It was still locked. I took another deep breath, sighed, and walked back over to the sage on the floor again.

My hand shook as I bent over to pick it up. I got the step stool and looked closer at the latch. The sage had to be pushed up and over to come off the latch. Just like the S hooks that popped off when Tony was putting the whisks away.

I started to feel vulnerable, alone, on top of the ladder, with my heart now in my throat with a bouquet of sage in my hand that a ghost or whatever wants me to throw away. I placed the bundle of sage on top of the timer box and immediately got down off the ladder. *Now let's see what happens.*

I walked back to my worktable, peering over my shoulder to make sure the bouquet was not following me or jumping off the box. I sighed and watched the monitor for a minute to see if any electric balls of dust or orbs were passing through. Nothing, but I was startled as I saw Hana open the front door. *Damn, this ghost stuff is making me jumpy. It is starting to get on me.*

"Morning!"

"Morning, Hana."

She saw a frightened look on my face. I could not hide it. "What happened now?"

"Nothing. I'm waiting for something to happen and looking for that dust ball to come through again."

"Oh, just another day at the café?"

"Uh-huh."

"Well, maybe the sage worked and is keeping the ghosts away."

"Ha!"

"Oh, don't say that. That's a scary ha."

The front door opened, and we both looked at the monitor to see the rest of the chefs coming in.

"Good morning." I placed my hands gently on Hana's shoulders and turned her around to face the back of the kitchen. The chefs had that *what are you doing* look as they stood in silence, "Do you see the sage hanging?"

"What? Oh, no, it's gone?"

"Where's the sage?" Kate stood next to Hana.

"I found it on the floor this morning."

"Oh, my God!" Kate backed away. "No way."

"Yes way. I got so scared when I came in and saw it on the floor. I thought it was a dead mouse at first, but as I got closer, I realized it was the sage." My heart dropped and I shook internally. "I picked it up and placed it on top of the box."

"Oh, yeah, I can see part of it." Hana pointed to the box.

"Maybe the ghost is trying to tell you something." Annie passed by us to get an apron.

Maybe? Maybe is right baby girl. None of us like it or the smell of it but it won't keep us away. Uh- uh, no freaking way and don't go starting trouble like Franco the pizza guy did.

"Or maybe they're telling you they don't like the sage and they want you to get rid of it." Kate went to the walk-in refrigerator to get the morning breakfast going.

"I don't know, but let's see what happens."

"Café anyone?" Annie went to brew a pot.

Just then, the lights over my worktable blinked.

"Oh, my God, did you see that?" Kate put the muffin tray down and ran behind Hana and me.

Electricity perks me up like coffee does for you. We are made of electrical matter and there's no better way to recharge myself than with some fluorescent bulbs. Please, don't tell me you never saw a light bulb blink before. It was probably your grandmother.

"I saw it, but I don't believe in ghosts that much." Laurent set up the workspace to make tart shells for the day. "There has to be something wrong with the lights."

"There is nothing wrong with the lights. We had them checked out. I think we have a ghost. I really do."

"Great. Just what I need is to work in a haunted bakery." Jada followed Annie to get a cup of coffee.

"How is this even possible? Maybe if we ignore the idea, it'll go away." Laurent was ready and rolling out sucrée dough on the dough sheeter.

I nodded along with him, thinking maybe he was right. I set up my laptop and streamed good classic rock and roll music, and we all worked in silence for a while.

"I like this music in the morning." Annie nodded at the music selection.

I nodded back. "How's life this morning?"

"Good."

"You don't sound convincing."

"I'm okay, especially when I'm here or at home. It's the in-between time that gets me nervy."

"Have you seen JT out there lurking in the shadows?"

"No, not at all. He is persistent, from what I remember, and he always got what he wanted."

Yes, he is. I don't think we've seen the last of that freak.

"Did you notify the police?"

"Yes, but they can't do anything if no crime was committed."

"Well, just make sure you come and go from here with someone until this blows over."

"Don't worry, I will."

Little did we know about the person across the street, standing in a dark doorway, watching us from the time I arrived, to the time the chefs arrived. If I had turned around when I entered the patisserie, I might have seen the glow of his cigarette.

CHAPTER 13

LATER THAT MORNING, I received a phone call from a customer, Kerriann, asking for a favor.

Kerriann was an author and had just finished drafting a novel. The story revolved around a female pastry chef, and she wanted to know if she could use our shop to shoot the advertising trailer for the book. She explained that she would bring her own cameraman to get a shot of a female pastry chef filling up a cannoli. She had been at the café opening day and knew right then that she had to film her segment here at Fiorello. Raquel was the only female working that afternoon, and she agreed to help Kerriann out.

Kerriann came by around three in the afternoon with her cameraman, who went right to work to set up the scene. It would only be about three seconds long. Raquel finished her shift, put some gloves on, and got to work filling up the cannoli. She was a star! Well, for three seconds at least.

"Where are all your chefs?"

"They went home about fifteen minutes ago."

"Oh. I was looking forward to meeting the talented team."

"Yes, they're quite talented. Maybe next time."

Kerriann and I started to chat, and she mentioned that she was also the author of a book called *The Ghosts of Long Island*.

"What a coincidence, I think we have some ghosts right here." I became quite engaged.

"Really? Why do you think that?" she asked.

I told her about the buckets falling and the banging.

"Wow! Buckets? Seriously? Sounds like you may have some spirit activity here. What else has happened?"

I proceeded to tell her about the falling S hooks, the flying parchment paper, the screechy woman's voice, and the cold breath on the back of my neck by the rolling rack.

Her smile disappeared. She knew I was serious. It turned out Kerriann was a ghost hunter, and she had heard all these things before. Some were true and some not so true.

Then I told her about the sage falling from the latch that morning. Her cameraman's mouth dropped open. "Oh, boy, are we done here?" he questioned in a slightly fearful voice.

You should be afraid, very afraid. If you fear us, we will unleash the gates of hell and swallow you up whole. I love being dramatic, too. I played a ghost, in a Christmas play, junior year in high school. Now it's real.

Kerriann ignored him, glancing up at the sage on top of the timer box. She looked as if she were contemplating the situation. She wasn't smiling.

"It was hanging here," I pointed, "and when I came in this morning, it was on the floor. I'm telling you, my heart dropped when I saw it." I might have gotten a little melodramatic in telling her this story.

Regardless, she listened intently.

I continued. "How did the bouquet fall off? I was the last one to leave last night. No open windows, no breezes from door closings or openings. And besides, the door is forty feet away. The security camera in the kitchen didn't pick it up because it's out of view back there." I let it all out.

"Sounds like you definitely have a ghost or spirit," she paused. "Do you know anything about the land or what was here before?"

"Not much," I replied. "Maybe we're on an old Indian burial ground."

"Who knows?" She laughed. "This town is so old, who knows what's underneath it. Keep an eye on things, and if you have more occurrences, call me and I'll come over. I'll bring my investigation partner, Joe, he is a medium, maybe we can help you out."

"Wait a second. What is the difference between a ghost and spirit, and why would either be here anyway?"

I'd tell you if you would open your mind and listen, but _nooo_, you're too nerved out to listen to me. She can't hear me either, she is too busy with other thoughts.

What's the use? This is turning into a long, drawn-out project. I kid you not.

"Ghosts are place-centered, meaning that, for whatever reason, they haven't crossed over to the other side. A spirit, on the other hand, could be our family, relatives, and friends, those who have passed on. They are where they are supposed to be. For me, I believe in heaven, so those we love are there, but they can come and go and oftentimes make their presence known. It's quite consoling knowing they never really leave us. Life continues and they help us on our journey. Sometimes you just must look for the signs. In either case, ghosts, or spirits, they can't harm you and you shouldn't be afraid."

HA! I'm angry to begin with, and I'll hurt you, if need be, so don't get me started, lady. You have no idea what it's like on this side.

"That's easy for you to say."

Kerriann laughed and continued. "It's just a matter of accepting them sometimes. Whatever you do, don't watch what's on television or in the movies. They make everything into horror, and it is just not like that. The work Joe and I do is positive. We concentrate on spiritual communication with the other side."

I folded my arms across my chest and took a deep breath. _I bought and now own a haunted pastry shop filled with ghosts, spirits, and paranormal_ *activities. No wonder the previous pizzeria owner had a heart attack and died. He was scared to death.*

Yes, he was, and I don't wish that on you. I think we can get along.

"How, uh, how do I get rid of them?"

"It's not always a question of how to get rid of them, but more of how to deal with and accept them. Try to ignore them, tell them to go away, that this is your place of business, and they should go elsewhere."

"You must be joking."

That's right, she must be joking, because we aren't going anywhere. This is my space and my home. You're the intruder, maybe you should buy some dessert and go.

"Quite the opposite. Playing with ghosts and spirits is a serious thing. Treat them like you would people. That's essentially who they are. If you respect them, they should respect you. Talk to them, tell them that you know they're here, but you need to work, and you don't need distractions."

I thought about this for a moment. I felt a bit overwhelmed, and all the muscles in my neck felt tighter than the folds in my croissants. "Okay, I'll give it a try, see what happens, and we'll see what Joe thinks when he comes by."

After a couple of takes, Kerriann and her cameraman finished filming and bought the extra cannoli that were filled. Raquel had made her acting debut and was all smiles, even though all that anyone would ever see of her in the finished video were her hands filling a cannoli. Show business could be brutal. Still, I guess you could say that Raquel had had her "close-up"!

Kerriann bought a flourless chocolate cake for her son, who was celebrating his birthday the next day. As she was leaving, Kerriann quipped, "Boy, if you died and had to have a heaven to go to, wouldn't you want to live here forever?" Then she breathed in deeply the aroma of the shop, as if trying to take it with her for as long as possible. "Mmmmm. There is such a great smell in this shop."

"Thank you, I hope it's the pastries you smell and not the dead ghosts or spirits."

"That's hilarious. 'I think I smell a ghost!' I have to use that on my next investigation. Call me later and we'll set something up with Joe."

I closed the door behind me, leaning on it as I stared at the timer box, catching a glimpse of some sage leaves barely over the edge. *Is this ghost trying to get my attention?*

Lucas walked through the swinging doors with a cake order in his hand. "What's up, G? What're you looking at?"

"Not sure anymore. I feel like I'm about to get on a roller coaster and it's not going to stop."

"Damnnn, you better hold on tight." Lucas stuck his fists out in front of him as if he were on a roller coaster holding on to the bar that secures you in, going up, twisting, and turning, going down the first steep hill all the while holding on to the order form, which was crumpled on one side.

I laughed so hard and so loud; all my wonders were swept away as I enjoyed the moment with tears of laughter in my eyes.

Laugh all you want, big guy. I'm not leaving; I don't think I can. You're going to have to learn to live with me. I guess I really am a ghost, and I'm here for a reason. Maybe some unfinished business with my baby girl Annie or that freak JT. The young girl in white must be a spirit, and I have no idea what the children are. By the way, that sage up there is a joke. We're here to stay so hold on tight.

CHAPTER 14

I'm sitting in the backseat of JT's car listening to his gibberish. You know the feeling you get when you think something is going to happen, and then it does. You scream, I knew this was going to happen. Well, I had that feeling and followed the chefs to their cars. But, more importantly I ran ahead of them and scouted out the parking lot.

My intuition was right, I spotted JT sitting in his car by the post office as if he was on a stakeout. He kept looking at his watch then toward the chef's cars, mumbling to himself and repeated again. So, I sat in the backseat and observed. I wish I could strangle him right now.

"Maybe is always the question, not the answer. It's that dumb answer for people who can't make a decision. It's yes or no, plain, and simple. Do you want to go out to dinner? Maybe. Do you want to go to the movies? Maybe. Do you want to hang out tonight? Maybe. Do you want me to beat him up? Maybe. Do you want me to take advantage of you again like I did in high school? Maybe."

Never mind his thoughts which clearly show he's a pathetic mess and tripping on God only knows what. Maybe if she had stayed with him, none of this would have happened. Then perhaps, I'd still be alive. I can't even imagine how Annie could be with him. Instead, I'm now watching this insane man laugh a bit wildly like a murderous clown at his own joke, banging on the steering wheel because he thinks it's so funny. Prison life definitely drove him over the edge.

"Do you want me to kill him now or wait till he has the chance to scream out no, please? Maybe."

He grabbed his pack of cigarettes and tapped them several times on the steering wheel. You had to pack them in there nice and tight for a good smoke. I remember doing that, too. Slowly he peeled the cellophane off with the thin strip that kept them fresh. I'm clearly in his head right now. He has no idea who he's conversing with.

"It's dried-up tobacco leaves. How fresh is that? Do you want me to go pick some fresh leaves for you? Maybe."

I believe he can hear me or at least my thoughts, hopefully I can keep this demented soul's mind occupied, so he leaves Annie and the chefs alone.

He huffed out a short laugh as he flicked the cellophane out the car window, still the litter bug, too. From this parking space on Gerard Street, he saw them coming around the corner. Of course, he had parked under a tree near the post office where he could then scope out the entire lot. I'm getting a little nervous here in the back seat. I think I'm about to lose my mind.

I feel like a spy on a stakeout. Oh, let me use my binoculars and get a better look.

He rolled his fingers up and put his hands over his eyes so he could pretend he was gazing through real ones, but there's no need to see everything. I gazed from him to Annie and the chefs and back again. He knew who he wanted to see. I watched them enter the municipal lot, the three chefs walking side by side. I kept looking from the chefs to JT, back and forth. I think I've a better chance of protecting her from here rather than being by her side. Maybe I can distract him, he is so childish.

"Oh, look how cute."

He was staring at Annie, on the end, puffing away on a cigarette walking with her head down. JT started humming an old nursery rhyme reciting it out loud. I kicked the back of his seat, but he didn't budge.

"Pat-a-cake, pat-a-cake, baker's man, bake me a cake as fast as you can. Pat it, roll it, mark it with a B and put it in the oven for baby and me."

When he tapped the open pack of cigarettes against his left wrist, five of his cigarettes came out together. He pushed four of them back in the pack one by one, leaving the middle standing alone. Dude, what in God's name are you doing?

He held the pack up looking at the single cigarette, he used it to block the two other chefs from view. I looked over his shoulder and could see Annie was in his sights. All I kept thinking about was, does this guy have a gun?

"Yeah, yeah, there she is, all nice and pretty. One cigarette soldier standing tall is all I need to salute you."

He brought the pack up to his mouth and bit down on the only cigarette standing. He tossed the pack of cigarettes into the console and reached for his lighter. With a flick of his thumb, he lit up, followed by a deep inhale to satisfy his nicotine addiction. I could smell the tobacco burning, not as unpleasant as the sage but close. He slowly exhaled and mumbled.

"Put a B on it for bitch, not Brenden."

He laughed and snorted as smoke blew through his nose.

"Well, Brenden is a bitch anyway."

He laughed again at his own joke, an audience of one or two I see, depending on who showed up at the right time. This dude is tripping. I wonder what other spirits haunt this sad soul of a man. He watched as the chefs gathered by their cars, chatting away. I need to distract him now. This isn't going to go down in a bad way, not on my watch.

"Oh, come on. Would you people get in your cars and go home already? I need to follow her and see where she is living these days so I can stalk the hell out of her before I go in for the kill."

Yeah, that's not going to happen you freak. He took a final drag and flicked the cigarette butt out the window, watching as it rolled into traffic, headed for the double yellow line. When a car came speeding up and crushed it, he hollered, "Woo-hoo, yeah, baby, *bam*. Smacked on, nailed it." He laughed his unhinged laugh while pushing his long locks off his face. I think I helped distract this dirt bag. I gazed over the parking lot and watched the chefs get into their own cars and drive away.

"Yeah! That's what I call another soldier snuffed out. Wait a minute, where'd they go? Are you kidding me?"

I was grinning from ear to ear and let out a short laugh. All I can say is thank you for stupid people. All three chefs were gone, cars and all. Panic set in his crazy head as he searched the lot across the way.

"Damn it! Where is she? How could they leave so fast?"

I laughed some more as he flopped back down into the seat of his mom's old boat of a car. Banging the steering wheel with both hands, he let out a scream loud enough to attract attention. With no one to talk to, he looked into the rearview mirror and spoke. I panicked for a moment that he could see me and stared right back into those killer eyes.

"JT, I told you to stay focused, but no, you had to play with cigarette soldiers trying to cross the street."

Staring straight into his own eyes and snarling his lip, he let the voices gather in his head. I spoke a little condescendingly, but I let him have it and I believe he heard me loud and clear. "You're an idiot. You can never do anything right. Thank God for that."

JT let his thoughts get the best of him.

"That was stupid of me! How could I let her get away?"

Let's see if I can mess with his head a bit more. "Momma is going to spank you when you get home. Did you change your socks this morning? Monkey see, monkey do, monkey is looking at you. He slowly rocked back and forth, humming to himself. I think I sent him a bit further over the edge.

"Pat-a-cake, pat-a-cake, baker's man, bake me a cake as fast as you can. Oh, I like that. Pat-a-cake, pat-a-cake, baker's man, bake me a cake without a hand! Chop, chop."

Uh oh, I think he is up to no good. That devilish grin appeared as his mind was conjuring his next move. I could feel his energy rising into a raging storm, and I'm being pushed out. I tried my hardest to smack him on the side of the head, but he didn't budge. He just continued to roar with his tormenting laugh. I'm not strong enough for this, I'm done for the day and need to recharge. I think I've had enough of him today too.

CHAPTER 15

I TOLD MY CHEFS about Kerriann's visit and how she wanted to bring a spiritual medium here to see if he could connect with the ghostly spirit that might or might not have taken up residence in Fiorello.

Kate shot me a quick glance as she rotated the croissants in the oven. "Oh, lordy lord, is this really going down?"

"Can we be here to watch?" Hana chimed in.

"Yes, and yes," I replied.

"This is ridiculous. She thinks there's a ghost here?" Jada sounded a bit nervous.

"I guess so. I'm not totally on board with this, but we'll see,"

"I'm not into this!" Jada's hand shook as she picked up her morning brew.

Kate laughed at Jada's expense. "Look at your hand. There's coffee shaking out all over the place."

Just then, we heard it—*boom, thud, bang, knock*—whatever you want to call it, coming from the inside of the walls in the back of the kitchen.

We all stopped what we were doing.

"What the hell was that?" Hana jumped.

"It heard us." Annie backed away, moving to stand next to Antonio and Laurent.

"Kate, you're the closest. Go check it out." My heartbeat picked up a few beats. I'm sure the chefs felt the same way.

"Ah, no, thank you, I'm quite okay where I am." Kate slammed the convection oven closed and came running to me, leaving Hana alone on the opposite side of the table. "Okay, Hana, you're closer now. You check it out."

Hana looked up and found us all on the opposite side of the center table. "No way." She dropped her paring knife and came running over to us.

We all laughed as she hugged Kate and me.

It doesn't take much to scare you all, but I need your attention. Listen up, JT is up to no good, he's planning something.

Kate asked, "Didn't Kerriann suggest telling it to go away?"

"Uh-huh." They all eyed me for an answer.

"Well?" Kate extended her arm out as if to let me lead the way.

"Why me?"

"Because you are the man in charge, boss man. It's your shop and Kerriann told you what to do."

"I hate this. I hate confrontations. I've never done anything like this before, and with a ghost, are you kidding me?" I let out a loud sigh. "Only if you come with me!"

"I'll be right behind you."

We walked past the ovens, the timer counting down from 1:11, 1:10, and so on. Slowly we crept along, past the walk-in refrigerator and sinks. My heart raced as Kate grabbed my shoulder, stopping us before the bathroom and the freezer.

"What do we say?" I whispered into Kate's ear.

"Tell them to go away."

"You do it."

"No!"

I took a deep breath, then, in a firm and loud voice, I spoke, "I don't know who you are or what you are, but please go away from here. This is my bakery, and we don't need any disturbances." My voice cracked like when I was twelve.

"A little nervous there?"

"What do you think?"

Knock! A one-time knock. Not a bang but a knock on the wall right next to us. We both screamed.

Boo! Dang, you people are so easy to scare. In fact, you scare yourselves more than I seem to scare you. But this is real, things are happening, and you need to be on your guard.

Beep, beep, beep, the oven timer went off as we jumped.

Kate pulled me back to where everyone else was. "Damn it, Gerard, that scared the crap out of me."

"Me, too. I think I wet myself." I made everyone laugh just as the timer beeped. I took the croissants out, appreciating the beauty of them, baked to perfection. Pulling myself back together, I spoke up again. "Hey, ghost person, leave us alone. We have work to do."

"Yeah!" Hana chimed in.

You people are bugging. This is hysterical. Wait, you, young lady in white, where did you come from? Why are you here?

Maybe I can help you get their attention. I know what's going on, I've been watching from time to time.

You want to help me? I, I don't even know your name.

Just stay back, I'll see what I can do. I was buried here a long time ago.

Here? In this kitchen? Oh, is that why you come here?

I'll explain one day.

One day? I've been here for over twenty years!

I closed the ovens and reset the timer. "Okay, we're good. Let's get going. We have things to do. Who wants more coffee?" I had to change the subject.

Everyone replied with a yes as I went to make a fresh pot of morning brew. *What just happened? How is this possible? Why? Is there a poltergeist, and who is getting dragged through Hell's portal first?*

"Yo, G." Antonio came up behind me, causing me to jump.

"Oh, ha, sorry, G. I didn't mean to scare you."

I laughed. "That's okay. What's up?"

"Can you help me with the scones?"

"Sure." I grabbed my cup of coffee and put on a fresh carafe for the chefs.

Antonio had to make a couple of batches of cinnamon raisin scones. We set the large mixing bowl on my marble table, where we turned the dough onto the floured surface.

We were scooping the scone dough out of the mixing bowl when I felt a completely different sensation from the cold breeze on my neck, I had felt a few days earlier. Directly under my right foot. It was a double tap, *knock-knock*. Like someone was tapping the bottom of my foot from somewhere beneath the floor.

"Antonio, did you feel that?" I whispered over so not to add more attention to this morning's activities.

"Feel what?"

"The ground under your feet? A bang. Like someone knocking?"

Antonio looked at me oddly. "No, I didn't feel anything." He was only two feet away from me.

Maybe I am losing it.

I glanced down at the floor, and it looked like the floor. I didn't want to freak them out again. It's the same floor, nothing odd, not so much as a loose tile anywhere.

I'm sorry, I tried.

Wait, don't leave me. I need help. Unbelievable. She took off faster than a jack rabbit.

Antonio smoothed out the scone batter on a tray. I wrapped it in plastic wrap, opened the lowboy refrigerator door, and took a step to the right so that Antonio could put that tray in. I knew I'd felt something there, and I watched as he stepped onto the exact same spot. Maybe he would feel the tapping floor now. But nothing happened.

He put the tray in without a remark and we cleaned the table.

After an hour, Laurent and I rolled out some tart shells and took the scones out for Antonio and cut them with a round cookie cutter. I traded spaces with Laurent, waiting for him to feel what I had felt. No such luck.

For the rest of that day, every few minutes, I just stared at the floor.

The rest of the morning was normal.

Steve walked into the kitchen and asked Hana to write a Happy Birthday sign for a black-and-white mousse cake. "This customer out there wanted a smiley-face cake. I said to her, 'Madam, we are a fine European-style French patisserie, and we don't make smiley-face cakes. That, my dear, you can buy at the supermarket across the street.' She whined, 'I used to have it when I was a child.' I graciously replied, 'Madam, you are no longer a child, and the only smile we want to see is yours after you've tried our black-and-white chocolate mousse cake.'"

"You did not," Kate laughed.

"I did so."

"What did she say?" I chimed in.

"Nothing, absolutely nothing. I was about to reach over the counter to close her jaw shut because she stood there gaping at me."

We all laughed.

"Then she gave in, 'I'll take the black-and-white mousse cake with a happy birthday sign please.' I replied, 'Very well, madam, nice choice. Then I complimented her on her beautiful necklace, and she smiled. I made her a cappuccino and we chatted for about ten minutes. She's a lovely lady."

"You are too much, Steve," Hana mixed up Bavarian whipped cream.

Annie went to the back of the kitchen to get the dried fondant plaque for the happy birthday sign.

It became apparent that neither Steve nor I were the only ones seeing or hearing strange things. I headed for the walk-in box with the tray of scones; I heard Hana and Kate squeal with excitement as the door began to close behind me. "Ahhhhh!" they yelled loudly.

I turned back quickly and pushed the door open, poking my head out around the side. I looked over at them in the work area. They were both staring back, their eyes bugged out like…well, like they had just seen a ghost! I could see Steve just beyond them. He was looking at me the same way.

"What did I do now?" I let Annie pass me with the plaque without a clue as to what had just happened.

"The rolling rack," Hana stammered. "It moved all by itself. Right after you went into the fridge."

Kate nodded her head vigorously.

"Oh, come on," I disagreed.

"No, no, no. It moved about a foot—from there to there." Hana pointed to the spot. She was shaking, the whisk up in the air as the whipped cream mixture dribbled down her arm. "I saw it move!"

I laughed. "Yeah, yeah, yeah."

Kate agreed with Hana. Steve was also nodding his head like a bobble-head doll. "I saw it, too," he testified. "I thought maybe you pulled it with you or something."

They all swore they saw it move. I walked back to my table. There was nothing I could say. I hadn't seen it.

Hana went to wash up. She stretched out her arms so that she could stand as far away from the sink as possible—and its overhead racks filled with plastic-bucket missiles.

Kate wrote the happy birthday sign and Steve just smirked at all of us. "Better call those ghostbuster people."

Like I said, the children love to help, and are all over the kitchen. It's like they go bananas around here sometimes just from the sweet smell of sugar.

CHAPTER 16

THE QUICK DRIVE FROM my home to the parking lot and then on to the shop at the ungodly hour of five in the morning did not bother me, and for whatever reason, I never felt afraid to open the patisserie alone. I locked the door behind me and could swear I saw someone smoking a cigarette across the street in the doorway of the town bar. Obviously, the bar was closed, but the entranceway was set back about two feet from the sidewalk, making it a perfect place to have a smoke or to dodge a few raindrops. I still felt like someone was watching me.

I walked through the café, ignoring the smoker. It was a hard habit to break. Sixteen years later, I still wanted a cigarette, but I never gave in, not even a drag.

Routine. Lights on, ovens on, unlock the walk-in boxes, set up the laptop, turn the coffee on, pull the breakfast rolling rack out of the walk-in refrigerator, fill the sinks up with water, and load up the proofer.

I streamed music from the internet and always started my day with some rock and roll music. I worked at a New York city radio station when I was younger as part of the morning show. I was hired as a laugher, yes, laugher, where I would laugh at the morning jokes and do coffee runs for the DJ's. If you know me well enough, you know my laugh is quite hearty and could fill a room. I still listen to the same station.

With the music playing loudly enough that you would have to say *what?* if you were having a conversation with someone, and coffee in hand, I loaded the proofer.

Tray by tray, I put them in until I grabbed the cheese Danish tray, and I heard someone say, "Put it here." Clearly in my right ear amidst the loud music. Not a muffled voice blended into the background, but a crisp, stern "Put it here."

I froze with the tray in my hand and raised my eyebrows, looking up as if a teacher wanted my attention away from my doodling.

As I darted my eyes around the kitchen, knowing perfectly well someone had spoken, it clicked that this was the same voice that had called my name two weeks prior when I took the rolling rack out of the walk-in refrigerator.

"Ah, who said that?" I asked, my voice short of cracking.

I love rock and roll music in the morning too G. Wait, a second. I could see the girl in white was bothering him. What is she doing?

Nothing, nobody responded, just the music playing as loudly as it had been before. I turned to the monitor ever so slowly, fearing the person smoking the cigarette across the street was now in the café playing a trick on me. Just me. I sighed heavily. "I don't like this." I lowered the music to a normal level as I finished loading the proofer. Alone with the voice in my head. Or was it?

Beep-beep-beep. The front door chime went off. The monitor for the front of the store showed there was no one. My heart pounded as goose bumps rose on my arms. I stared into the darkness of the café. It was not completely dark; the overhead lights were dim enough as if a night-light were on.

A bolt of light crossed the café. "What the hell is that?" My eyes bugged out. It looked like one of those stick lights that my Aunt Angie bought my brother and me while at the circus when I was eight. Swinging it around left a trail of light in the darkness of the circus tent. It passed from the left wall, across the café, into the glass display cases, and into the espresso machine.

My heart was now in my throat as I caught the kitchen door in my peripheral vision swinging ever so gently. "Oh, my God!" I swallowed hard. Music blared and the phenomenon that I was experiencing scared me to the point of wanting to see this happen again. What was it? I'd never seen anything like this before and not in any horror movie either.

Dear God. How did she do that? Wow, I am blown away, I can't even leave here without getting winded and she is all over the place. I've got to see what this young lady is up to.

Stock-still, I watched the kitchen door stop swinging, and I felt a sense of calm pass over me… almost telling me not to be afraid. Something was here with me. I could feel it, I could sense it, like having a spider's sense. I turned down the radio volume again in hopes of hearing something other than the water running in the sinks. "Oh, crap, the sinks." I raced over to the sinks, watching as the water fell from the middle compartment into the first compartment. I laughed nervously as I shut the water off.

Beep-beep-beep. The front door chime went off again. "Now what?" I leaned backward to see the kitchen door open, relieved to see Hana and Kate coming in to work.

"Morning, Rard!" Hana smiled as Kate waved.

I took a deep breath and sighed. "Morning." I dried my hands on my apron as I walked over.

"Where's Annie? You left her outside?"

"No. She sent me a text that she wasn't feeling that good and wanted to come in later." Kate rolled her eyes.

"Oh?"

"You know, female issues."

"Enough said. The coffee should be ready. I could really use a cup."

"Tired?"

"Not exactly." I told Hana and Kate what had happened over a cup of morning brew.

"And you're okay with this?" Kate folded arms across her chest.

"Yeah, how can you be so calm?" Hana asked, grabbing a couple of aprons for the others when they arrived later.

"I don't know. Something is here. Ghostly, spiritually, or paranormally, and it wants us to know it's here."

"Yeah, well, I hope it's one of the first two. I don't need to be dragged across the kitchen floor." Hana threw her arms in the air and shuffled across the floor, making a joke out of it.

"Well, I'm not scared." I tried to be a little convincing, if I was scared, then this ship would go down.

"Good for you." Kate patted my arm as if she were speaking to a nine-year-old who had just finished a jigsaw puzzle. "I like to be scared, but that's when I'm home cuddled up watching a scary movie on television. I don't need to be living a horror movie." Kate laughed but it was more of a nervous laugh.

Hana spoke up, pushing her black-rimmed glasses up. "Well, I don't like it either, but maybe we need to have this place smoked with sage and not just hang it. You know, like they do in those scary ghost movies."

"I don't know, but I feel like whatever or whoever it is, they're doing this for a reason." I took a sip of morning brew.

"Or this bakery is sitting right in the portal," Kate gazed around the kitchen.

"What portal?"

"I've seen enough scary movies to know that there's a portal or gateway to the other side and we're the portal."

"That's messed up. Now I'm really getting scared." Hana looked at me wide-eyed.

"Ha!" I said it just like that. "Portal? Where? Through the oven doors? Or how about here by the walk-in box wall?" I approached the wall with my right hand extended as if to send it through.

Kate stood there with her hands on her hips, looking at me as if I were the crazy one. Well, just a tad, aren't we all? I also love to have fun. As I hit the wall, I started to crumple my finger and arm as if they were going through, then slammed my body into the wall.

Oh, brother, you'd be tripping if you actually passed through. Laugh all you want but you have no idea what it's like to live here on a daily basis. No freaking idea.

Kate and Hana busted out laughing.

"If you went through, I would pee my pants and run out the door." Kate laughed.

"Me, too," Hana exclaimed. "Not coming back here again."

I laughed out so hard I almost cried.

Boom!

"Did you hear that?" Hana jumped.

We had all jumped.

"Make it go away, Gerard." Kate ran behind me, almost pushing me forward.

"Make what go away, or should I say who?" I was getting tired of this.

"What do we do?" Kate threw her hands up in the air.

"I don't know, ignore it?"

"How can we ignore it? This is happening to us. Like it or not, we are working in a haunted bakery fun house!" Hana shouted.

Kate looked at me. "Looks like you own a haunted pastry shop."

"Boo!" I shouted, making them both squeal in laughter. "All seriousness, we can't let this affect us or get the best of us."

"Easier said than done." Kate took over the baking and put the trays of almond croissants in the oven. "Something is happening around here, Gerard. Maybe we should call a priest."

"We have a ghost here, not a possessed croissant."

Hana brought out the muffin batters, trying not to let it all bother her. We all fell silent and scooped the muffins for the day while chitchatting about our personal lives.

The bottom oven door opened.

"Uh, the oven?" Kate gestured to it with the muffin scooper in her hand.

We stared at it, then at each other, afraid to move. Hana slowly walked over to it without a sound and gently pushed it closed, giving it a tug to make sure it was closed. It was and it needed a good pull to open it.

"Maybe it wasn't closed all the way?"

"No, I closed it, just like I always do." Kate looked at me accusingly.

"What are you looking at me for?"

"For assurance?"

"I believe you; I just didn't touch the oven, you did." I raised my eyebrows and gave her a wide-eyed look, making her smile.

"We need to put this honey wheat banana on the production list. We're almost out." Kate shook her head.

"Gotcha." I tried to feel normal about all the ghostly weirdness. I kept thinking about voices, portals, haunted houses, and my sanity. *This is not normal, nor do I want it to be the new normal.*

Hana came back to the table to help us finish scooping the muffins when the oven door opened again.

Kate screamed out, "What in the world?"

Hana jumped back. "How is this possible?"

I had had enough. I found the courage to face the situation. "Hey!" I yelled, making Kate and Hana jump again.

Come on, children, now you got him mad. I know you want to help but they are not used to us being able to help them bake. They need more time to adjust to us and that damn young girl in white.

"Oh, my God, Gerard's scary voice. I don't know what's worse, this paranormal crap or your scary voice when you're mad!" Kate looked at me with some fear in her eyes.

I continued speaking to the whatever. "Leave us alone. Go away, ghost, get out of here, whoever you are, and go to the light!"

And here we go, blah, blah, blah. I can't go even if I wanted to.

Silence.

"You think it heard you?"

I had a feeling it did.

Beep-beep-beep!

The front door opened, making us jump, with Jada and Annie walking in. I held on to the table and hung my head low.

"I could use a drink."

CHAPTER 17

LATER THAT AFTERNOON, AFTER the chefs left for the day, all the baking was done, and the high school students came to work, I found myself making notes of what had happened around the patisserie. It added up to too many unexplained occurrences. I'd come to terms with knowing that something was definitely happening beyond my control. Not sure why, what, or how it started, but it is freaking everyone out, including me. My guess was the previous owner got the crap scared out of him so much that he gave up. *Oh, God, I hope that does not happen to us.*

Your guess is right. Don't antagonize us and we won't antagonize you.

Steve pushed through the swing doors, interrupting my thoughts, but I took advantage of what was on my mind. "Hey, Steve, I think we should speak with Mr. Clayton next door about these ghostly paranormal happenings and see if he has seen any himself."

"What? Why? The guy is in his mid-eighties with one foot in the grave. Have you seen him lately?"

"No."

"He looks like he hasn't slept in a year, quite pale and disheveled. I wouldn't be surprised if he's the ghost."

I chuckled. "Really? He looked fine a few months ago when we signed the lease."

"Maybe he's ill. I'm not sure." Steve glanced at the clock. "He closes in fifteen minutes, but maybe we can go by tomorrow and ask him about Casper. I have to run some errands. Will you be, okay?" Steve took off his apron and hung it on a hook in the closet by the door.

I chuckled at his Casper comment, too. "Yeah, sure. Alex and Rick are cleaning up and Vincent and Deanna are tending to customers. No worries. I'll see you later."

"Okay, just make sure the kids put the garbage out after four. I don't want the town giving us a summons for putting it out earlier and clogging up the sidewalk."

"No problem. I'll see you later." I pulled a stool over and set my laptop up on the marble table. I thought it would be a suitable time to look over the rules and regulations for the pastry competition. I had to submit recipes for the two desserts and give a demo for one of them.

I sat back for a second, thinking how I'd be able to do the demo, and stared aimlessly at the knives and tools on the magnetic bar. Just a few days ago, one of those offset spatulas had twanged. If I stared long enough, would one be able to move it on its own? Not that I wanted it to. It was just a thought.

I logged in and filled out all the necessary information. The two recipes were easy enough to write up. The GF cookie used a straightforward creaming method followed by flour. The gavajune was a bit more involved, with a few extra steps to prepare before finishing the dessert. I had to make them in the morning at the event, so they were fresh. Maybe I would ask Hana to help me on that Monday. Why were they holding this competition on a Monday? But then I thought about it, and it made sense because most restaurants and pastry shops were usually closed that day.

I thought about the waffle iron and envisioned myself slinging GF cookies at the event. I could really put on a good show, make assorted flavors: chocolate, lemon, anisette, and maybe a savory with rosemary and sea salt.

"Hey, G! It is almost four. Can Rick and I put the trash out?" Alex snuck up, laying his hand on my shoulder.

"Geez, Alex, you startled me."

"Sorry, G." Alex proceeded to give me a high five.

"You want a high five for startling me?"

"Uh, yeah?"

"It seems like you want a high five for everything you do around here. I think not."

"Er, okay, no one has ever left me hanging for a high five."

"Welcome to the world, kid. It's not so high five-ish all the time."

"Are you really going to leave me hanging?"

"Yes." I turned around quickly with a smile. The kid made me laugh and had not let me down around there yet. "Alex, put your hand down or put some paper towels in it and go clean the windows, or better yet, go put the garbage out with Rick, okay?"

"I'm not doing anything until I get a high five."

"You're serious, aren't you?"

"Yes."

"Your poor mother. Do you do this at home, too?"

"Absolutely."

As he stood there with his palm facing me, ready to be sworn in as the high-five judge that he was, I shook my head and gave him a high five.

"Yes! Way to go, G!"

I turned back to my laptop with a laugh. "Get out of here, you crazy high fiver."

I like this kid too, sixteen, full of himself with a good sense of humor. I'm down with most of these kids. Come on Alex, I'll help you and Rick with the garbage.

Laughing to the back of the kitchen, Alex caught up with Rick. "Yo, Rick, G just gave me a high five."

I heard Rick reply, "That's nice. I'm about to carry garbage bags down this hallway and you're going around high fiving the boss."

I laughed even more. There was something about these kids that brought me right back to an earlier age. I knew one thing for sure, they kept me on my toes.

Getting back to my idea, I thought about baking off the gavajunes in the morning and bringing the waffle iron for the GF cookie demo. I jotted down my notes and what had to be done the day before and the morning of.

"Hey, G?" The swinging door opened, and Deanna came into the kitchen.

"Yes, what's up?" I gave her my attention.

"There's a woman out here who wants to talk to you about a pudding pie? I told her I don't see it on the menu, and I don't think we will make it. So, she threw her hand on her hip and demanded, 'Let me speak to the chef!'" Deanna imitated the lady's cobralike snake moves.

I shook my head like a cobra snake, "Well, Deanna, let's go see what she's talking about."

Deanna laughed at me.

I quickly finished up and logged out of the registration website. Standing up, I pushed the stool aside and heard a thud coming from the back of the kitchen. All I heard was Alex and Rick in the hallway joking around. Had to be the two of them.

Stopping at the hand sink, I reached for a paper towel, and I heard Alex and Rick talking.

Oh, oh, trouble approaching. Dude, I can feel it. How can this be? No way this is happening. Sorry, boys, get out of my way.

"Don't push me, Rick."

"I didn't push you. How could I push you when I'm over here?"

"Well, someone did."

I walked past my worktable only to stop when I heard my laptop close behind me. Fffthump!

I looked over my shoulder and gasped. "Oh, no, no, please let it be a gust of wind." I went ahead to the swinging door and took a deep breath.

More like a hurricane brewing. Move.

Deanna nodded toward the lady in question.

"Hello, may I help you?" There she was, in all her glitz and glory. I didn't know what to look at first. She was so busy, noisy, loud, and that was only about her appearance. The leopard-print flowing blouse was the main attraction, although her dyed black, or should I say her extra dyed black hair, was a big bouffant right out of the nineteen eighties. Her jungle-red lipstick was freshly adorned with a glossy finish. Her eyeglasses were so big that they took over half her face, with black trim and rhinestones. Bling, baby, it was all about the bling. The diamond pendant earrings seemed normal compared to the rest of her outfit with twenty gold and silver bracelets and her nails out to here with a shiny ivory finish, like a light cup of coffee with way too much milk.

"Yes, you're the baker?"

I glanced around the café before answering her. Vincent was clearing off the coffee bar, and she stood right in front of the counter, blocking anyone else's access if needed. She was lucky that I had attention to give her. I could give her some fashion advice, but I kind of enjoyed the craziness in front of me.

"Yes, I'm Gerard, baker, and owner, and you are?"

"Silvia. Nice to meet you."

"Nice to meet you, too. What can I do for you?"

"I asked the lovely young woman if I can order a chocolate pudding pie and she told me. you don't make that."

"That's correct, we don't."

"Why not?" Silvia blasted.

I blinked, unprepared for the rage in her voice. "We don't make that. It's something we just don't do."

"If I order it, would you make it?"

"No, I'm sorry. We make—"

Silvia cut me right off and almost shouted as she waved her index finger in the air back and forth as if I were a five-year-old who just drew on the dining room wall with crayons. "That's bad business."

"Silvia, we make a variety of different items. Chocolate pudding is not one of them." She wanted a stare down, but I was not about to play. "That's not bad business. What is bad business, is for me to make this chocolate pudding pie from scratch and try it at least three times to get it right or close to being right and charge you what? Twenty dollars? The twenty dollars does not even cover the cost, let alone the labor. You should go to the supermarket, buy the graham cracker pie shell, instant chocolate pudding mix, and a can of whipped cream, put it all together, and you are done. This is something you make with your grandson or granddaughter."

"I don't want to make it. That's why I'm here."

"I'm sure your company would love the fact that you made it."

"You see these nails?" She spread them out over her black leather bag. "These nails are like this because I don't cook anymore. I don't have to. I'm retired."

"They're lovely and I'm sure we may have something else to please your palate. Deanna, would you please show Silvia the flourless chocolate cake?"

"Yes, I would love to. It's right over here in the display case."

"Nice to meet you, Silvia."

"Nice to meet you, too, Gerard."

My pleasantries ended abruptly as I caught the swinging door moving in my peripheral vision. I quickly looked to my left in hopes that one of the boys was about to come through. The coldness passed right in front of me. The slight pressure of air pressing on my skin made me step back, and I could see Silvia felt it, too.

Pacing back and forth never solved anything but at least it gives me time to think. Get out of the way, lady, you are something else, I must agree. Hey Gerard, would someone please lock the damn door?

"Oh, I feel a draft coming through. I got a chill. Where's the cake?"

She had felt it. Someone else had felt what I had felt. How is that possible? Where did it go? I watched a man try to enter the front door. I say, try to enter because he seemed unable to open the door. He tried a few times to pull the door open, but it looked like it was slamming shut with every pull.

"Hey, Vin, what's going on with the front door?"

"I don't know. I'll check it out."

Vincent opened the door for the man trying to get in. He opened it with the ease of a two-finger push.

Damn it, what do I do now? He's in, like a vampire invited into a blessed home. You people can't do this to me. You cannot invite the murderer in. Dude, what in the name of God are you thinking?

"That was weird." I muttered to myself as I watched the man enter. "Sorry about that, um, maybe the door needs some oil."

"Oh, maybe it does." The man laughed as he pushed his long straggly hair off his face.

I tried to understand why he was laughing. I didn't think it was that funny.

Vincent came around the counter, "What can I get you?"

Don't serve him, get him out of here. There must be something I can do. Where's everyone when I need their help? No, they only show up to antagonize me. Help, can anyone hear me? Looks like I'm on my own. I have to concentrate.

"Oh, I don't know, something like a cheesecake will do."

"Right over here we have the Italian cheesecake made with fresh ricotta or we have the American cream cheesecake with fruit on top."

I could smell his cigarette breath five feet away.

"The American cheesecake is right up my alley." He raised his right hand to salute. "Proud to be an American. Ouch, what the heck?" His salute was almost a punch as he hit himself in the eye.

Got him.

"Excuse me, are you okay?" I thought this guy was slightly off, but I was willing to give him the benefit of the doubt.

He nodded and rubbed his eye. "May I have an expresso to stay?"

"It's espresso, with an s not an x," Silvia chimed in. "And don't smoke so much. You smell like a pack of cigarettes."

Silvia picked up her goods and marched out.

The man mumbled something and stuck his tongue out at her as she was leaving.

I rolled my eyes and whispered, "Hey Vin, keep your eye on this one."

"You got it, G. Anything else, sir?"

"Sir? You called me sir. I do not feel like a sir. Never did." He looked at Vincent with slight aggravation in his voice. "How much do I owe you, young man?"

"Uh, uh, that would be nine seventy-five, please. I was just being respectful."

What are you bothering the kid for, chill out, you asinine idiot.

"Of course." He took his wallet out of his pocket and watched it fly out of his hands to the floor. "How did that happen? Pardon me, that was careless."

He picked it up without saying a word, pushing his hair back again, and took the cash out of his wallet. "Here you go."

I watched the whole transaction, knowing the guy might be a little off or left of center. "Thank you, enjoy your pastry."

"Thank you. If you ever need help in the kitchen, I can be at your service, I have exceptionally good knife skills."

"Oh, well thank you, I currently have a full staff." I smiled and nodded. "Are you a pastry chef?"

Smart answer, Gerard, but don't converse with him. Keep your distance, this guy is trouble. I've been trying to tell you this. He might try something stupid.

"Heavens no, no, no. You could say I'm a butcher." He smiled a devilish grin and continued, "I like to carve with the tip of the knife and leave a beautiful scar."

I didn't know what to say after that. Who says things like that to people? I had a bad feeling. "A scar? On a side of beef?"

"Just on the skin." He spoke nonchalantly. "You know, something to be remembered by." He winked at me.

What the hell was this guy saying? Was he messing with me? Was he crazy? Was he trying to threaten me? I pushed his order across the counter. "Thank you for coming by. Have an enjoyable day."

"You have nice big hands. I'm sure it would be a shame to lose one in a knife accident." He kept his head down while looking at us. All I could see were the bottom whites of his deep brown eyes.

Gerard, my man, you're messing with a killer. Get him out of here, call the police, do something. He'll kill you and everyone else in here. Geez, can't you hear me?

I pulled my hand back as quickly as I could.

He noticed and smiled with a snort of a soft laugh. "Have a nice day, gentlemen."

The guy gave me the creeps. So, I stepped back and put my right forearm across Vincent's chest and slowly pushed him back to the rear counter with me.

Deanna was wiping down the cases and missed half of this encounter. "What's going on?"

I followed suit as we watched the long-haired guy take his café and dessert. He turned to the coffee bar and seemed to have stumbled, but it really looked like someone patted him on the upper back unexpectedly, causing him to fall forward a bit. Our eyes locked and I could see a bit of craziness in there, something that was not right. He looked at me with a *hey, what did you hit me on the back for* look. But he could clearly tell that it hadn't been me.

Why can't I push him like I did Franco and slam him into a wall? Geez, how much energy do I need?

"Damn, that guy is creepy," Vincent whispered as he cleaned the cappuccino maker.

Deanna passed by me. "Hey, G, that guy is making me nervous. Can I go in the kitchen for a while until he leaves?"

"Yeah, sure, I think I know how you feel."

We watched him for as long as we could without being so obvious, then went back into the kitchen.

"Hey, G, the Wi-Fi went down."

"What?"

"The security monitor went dark, and the music stopped."

"Hey, Vin, go in the back and reset the modem."

"Yeah sure."

"Uh-oh." The lights blinked over my worktable, the oven shut off, and my lowboy refrigerator turned off with the compressor chugging out, sounding like a car running out of gas. "Damn it, now what? A brownout?"

*　　*　　*　　*

Get out of here, you dirt bag.

JT looked around the café. "Who said that?"

Someone had spoken to him, but no one was looking at him directly or standing in front of him, like the gangster in prison, because he was sitting in his seat at the checkered table.

His mouth now full of cheesecake, he savored the creaminess and sweetness on his tongue. *Boy, our little cheffy girl can bake.* He dabbed at the corners of his mouth with a napkin. Momma always said, *enjoy what you're eating, but don't let the world see what you're eating.* Momma was always right.

I said, get out of here, now!

Whose voice *is that?* he thought, cutting another piece of cheesecake off the plate with his fork. He looked around the café. A young couple chatted over gelato, playing cutesy with each other, two women gossiped over a carrot cake, and a young hipster was on his phone.

Argh. This is making me so mad. I'm about to bug out on you JT, now you're in for it.

He raised his fork, circling it around as if conducting an orchestra at Carnegie Hall. He hummed to himself, enjoying the delectable cheesecake, when suddenly the fork in his right hand began to move on its own. As it moved side to side across his face, JT followed it with his eyes, like one of those games you play trying to figure out its next move.

"What's happening?" JT muttered to himself.

He felt pressure on his right wrist as he tried to resist the uncontrollable movement as his left hand felt glued to the table. He watched the fork like a pendulum swing.

Then up, up, up, up over his head, his right arm was out of his control as he watched the plastic fork go up above his head, but what went up must come down.

JT gasped. "What in the world?"

It came down, forcefully. As if someone pushed his right hand, the plastic fork, which he thought was going right into the cheesecake, entered instead into the meaty part of his left hand between the thumb and index finger.

"Ahhhhhhhhh!" Screaming out, JT stared at the fork stuck in his hand. Blood sprayed out, immediately flowing around his thumb.

You're a raw bloody mess. Now get out of here you putz.

JT was in too much pain to even listen to the voice in his head.

"Oh, my God!" the young woman with her boyfriend screamed, pointing across the café.

The hipster shouted out, "What the hell, dude!" as his phone flew from his hands. The two women looked on in horror, one of them clutching her chest, as he took the fork out of his hand. Screaming in pain, JT put a few napkins on the impaled hand to try and stop the bleeding. "It's okay, I'm okay. It's just a little blood." He wrapped his hand up as best he could, cringing from the pain. "I've seen worse. I… I'm a butcher."

Leave, you murdering demented asshole.

He stood up. *Whoever said that did this to me.* "Who, who said that?"

I walked right up to his ear. I said that you prick.

JT twitched to the right as if a fly buzzed in hie ear. "I want to know who said that!" He surveyed the other diners. They all fell silent. It was not them. They stared at him, wondering who let the weird man in the café. His eyes darted left to right, as he held his bleeding hand and panicked.

One more push, in your face, my old friend.

As he backed away from the table, his chair fell over with a *thwack*, and the remaining napkins on the table blew up toward his face, flying wildly in the air.

Hearing all the commotion from the front of the café, Vincent and I raced out of the kitchen. "What's going on? What happened?" Some customers had stood up, backing away in fear of the strange man.

The strange guy shot me one final evil stare before bolting out the front door.

What a nightmare, it's about time he left. That was exhausting to say the least. I can't believe I did that all by myself. I'm getting stronger, I can feel it. I hope he stays away for everyone's sake because I don't think I could do that again. He's looking for Annie, I know it. I must tell her or tell one of these chefs, but how? They are so closed minded. I need to think this out, seems like Gerard is my best bet. He can sense me; he just needs to open his mind a bit. Otherwise, I'll be scrawling words out on the walls with a chef's knife and that can take days. The energy to do that alone is massive.

I may tripping, but I think I need the young girl in white. I need her help.

American Cheesecake

Prepare 4 to 24 hours prior.

Preheat conventional oven to 350 degrees or convection oven to 325 degrees. Best made on low fan

Eight-inch springform pan or French cake ring.

1 1/2 lbs.	Cream cheese at room temperature
2 tsp	Vanilla extract
4	Extra-large egg whites at room temperature
1	cupGranulated sugar

Graham Cracker Crumb:

1 1/2 cups	Graham cracker crumbs
6 Tbs	Unsalted butter, melted.
1/4 cup	Granulated sugar

Sour Cream Topping

2 cups	Sour cream
3 Tbs	Granulated sugar

Note: Best made the day before.

For the graham cracker crumb mix:

Combine the graham cracker crumbs and sugar in a mixing bowl. Stir in the melted butter and mix well until the mixture is evenly coated.

Press the crumb mixture evenly onto the bottom of the springform pan or French cake ring. Place in the oven for five minutes. Remove from the oven to let cool before filling it up with the cheesecake batter.

For the cheesecake:

Separate the eggs keeping the egg whites in a clean bowl, saving the yolks for another use.

In a stand-up mixer with a whisk attachment, whip the egg whites to a medium peak. Slowly add the sugar and continue whipping to a stiff peak. Remove from the bowl and set aside.

Using a paddle attachment, beat the cream cheese with the vanilla to a creamy light texture. Slowly fold the stiff egg whites into the cream cheese. Finish folding by hand.

Pour the mixture into the prepared cake pan and bake for twenty-five minutes, until set with a solid jiggle in the center, most of the cake should be set.

Prepare the sour cream topping:

In a mixing bowl, mix the sour cream and sugar together.

After the cheesecake has baked for twenty-five minutes, gently spread the sour cream mix over the top and place back in the oven for another five minutes.

Remove from the oven and let cool to room temperature, then place in the refrigerator for at least six hours or overnight to cool completely.

To unmold the cheesecake, slide a thin paring knife or thin spatula carefully between the cake ring and the cheesecake and carefully remove the ring. Serve with fresh fruit.

CHAPTER 18

I WENT IN EARLY the next morning to get a head start on all the baking. I needed the ovens to bake cookies later for the weekend orders. Each of our twenty-two cookies stand alone in flavor, texture, and sweetness. Maybe I'll try some GF cookies and decipher my mother's gavajune recipe.

Before opening the door, I looked around to see if the smoker was across the street. I could not see anyone; it was too dark to even see a figure lurking in shadows. I locked the door behind me just in case and out of habit.

Time was of the essence in the morning. It was critical to have the mise en place in order because I only had a two-hour window to cook all the breakfast items. I could get up earlier, but I did need some sleep. Kate was extremely helpful in the morning; she took the reins to bake, so I could focus on something else.

As usual, I brought out the muffin batters so the chefs could scoop them into the tins as soon as they arrived. The lights flashed over my marble table, and I ignored them, but when the oven timer went off behind me, I jumped at least a foot.

BAAAH, BAAAH, BAAAH.

I turned it off and stared at both ovens, top and bottom. I never set the timers right away in the morning. I only turned them on when there were too many items baking at contrasting times in the oven, and there was nothing in them to set them for. I backed away.

"Okay, we good now?" I looked up at the lights and moved on, giving the monitor a peek, hoping someone would come in soon. I was starting to get the heebie-jeebies.

I need your attention, uh, hello, Mr. Baker. You need to listen to me. Come on, you can do it. Stop being a scaredy-cat and open your mind. You know we're here. Ghosts are real and, well, you know I'm here. Listen, see if this works. Hey, Gerraarrdd.

Setting the muffin trays on the table, I heard my name called. I froze in place, listening, listening for whatever was to follow. I counted to ten, one hand on the muffin bucket. Slowly, I turned around to look at the monitor, listening for I don't know what, but all I could hear were the convection ovens warming up behind me. I stared at the monitor and the darkness of the front of the café, waiting for something to appear in the café shadows.

Figures appeared at the front door. It was Hana and Kate. I sighed and hung my head as I heard the front door unlock.

Great, just when you think you're getting through, these two-walk in.

"Good morning, boss."

"Good morning. How are my two favorite bakers?"

"Aw, that is so sweet. What do you say to the other bakers?"

"The same."

"Ha. Thanks for making me feel so special."

"You're welcome, Hana. I always aim to please." I gave her a wink. "Where's Jada and Annie?"

"Annie is running late again, and Jada is wherever."

"Are they okay?" I handed Hana a scooper for the muffin batters.

"I'm sure they are fine," Kate interjected as she loaded the proofer with the raw croissants, chocolate croissants, brioche, savory croissants, and Danish.

"Uh, someone called my name before. The lights flashed over my table and the oven buzzer went off."

"Holy crap. All at the same time?" Hana stopped scooping, peering at me over her big black rimmed glasses.

"One after the other. Lights first, then the oven timer, and then my name. It was a man's voice this time. It was deep and it scared the crap out of me."

Kate started to put the almond croissants in the oven. "It's like I feel scared, but I feel excited about it at the same time. It's not like horror scary but it still freaks me out."

I laughed. "You mean you're scared but not scared enough to run away from here?"

Hana laughed. "That's messed up. Don't wish for more scary things to happen and it seems like most of it happens in the morning."

That's right, because I'm well rested from you people bouncing around this kitchen like it's an airport terminal. Like the time my mother and I went to see her sister in San Francisco, they changed the terminal gate at least four times with everyone running around like a chicken without a head.

"Seems like it, until yesterday afternoon." I smirked.

"What? Why? What do you mean?" Kate struck her baker pose with oven mitts on and on her hips.

"Well, this guy came in, real weirdo at first and…" The front door opened again letting Jada, Annie, Laurent, and Antonio in.

"Oh, great, keep me in suspense." Kate threw her arms up in the air.

"You're so impatient. I thought I was bad. Geez!"

Kate jumped in, "Okay, grab an apron and shut up. Gerard wants to tell us what happened yesterday afternoon."

"What happened, boss?" Laurent shook my hand. I always found it polite to shake everyone's hand in the morning and to wish them well, and when they left for the day with a thank you.

I told the story about what happened that morning followed by what happened yesterday afternoon.

"So, was this guy crazy or what?" Kate put the muffin tray on the rack and, with the oven mitts still on, popped her hands on her hips again.

"I don't know." I started scooping some chocolate chip cookies on the small metal table to stay out of the way. "He definitely fit the role."

"What did he look like?" Annie looked a bit unsettled. "I hope it wasn't JT."

I could feel Annie trembling and tried to console her by putting arm around her with some positive energy. She knew what he was going to say.

"Um, he was about six feet tall, a little taller than me. Stringy black hair, deep brown eyes, with a fair complexion."

"Oh, man, that sounds like him." Annie folded her arms across her chest.

"His hair was parted in the middle, and he smelt like cigarettes."

"Yup. That's him."

We all stopped what we were doing and stared at Annie as she started to tremble and cry. I'd seen this in movies, but she raised her apron up to her face and sobbed. "Why won't he leave me alone?"

"Hey, Rard, play back the video from last night." Hana raised a good point.

"I would if I could, but it's not there. From the time you see me go to wash my hands to the time after he left, the Wi-Fi went down. In fact, the lights flashed over my table and the oven shut off, too. It was like a brownout."

"Are you kidding? What the heck?" Jada questioned us, with a comforting arm around Annie.

"Seriously, it's not there. I tried to show Steve last night."

"This is nuts. What do we do? Call the police?"

"Can't. No crime was committed. JT did not threaten me per se, and I don't have any proof. He did say he was a butcher, liked to carve scars on meat and how it would be unfortunate for me to lose a hand. I freaked out. I pulled these sausage fingers back so fast."

Kate was the only one to laugh at my humor.

"This isn't going to stop, is it? He's going to keep stalking me." Annie wiped away her tears. "I'm so sorry. I feel like I'm the cause of all this."

"Don't feel that way. It is not your fault. The guy is crazy." Privately, I thought he was mentally unstable.

"Why is he following you, Annie? What happened? Why did he go to jail? You haven't told us the whole story." Kate was not going to let her off the hook now. "As far as we're concerned, this jerk is now stepping on our turf."

Uh, this is my turf foxy mama, don't ever forget it. You people need to be always on guard around here. Annie is not safe with JT on the loose. Damn Brenden had to bring him here. Always the puppet to that piece of trash. I should've kicked him between the legs when I had my chance the other day.

The light flickered again over my worktable. No one looked up, not even Laurent working right under it as he rolled out some sucré dough for the fruit tarts. I thought, maybe there is a connection here between what seems to be a blinking light, Annie, and this JT guy. Something was happening beyond my control, and I wanted to know what it was.

CHAPTER 19

"IT WAS MY SENIOR year in high school, September 1981, and things started out okay, even when JT asked me out. My two besties Nettie and Marie, and I, were walking through the halls to English class when JT and his gang surrounded us. We all started giggling, pushing them away, saying, 'Come on, we have to get to class,' but JT stood in front of me, not letting me pass."

I remember this like it was yesterday.

BAAAAH, BAAAAH, BAAAAH.
"Damn oven timer scares me every time. Can't we make it a nice wind chime sound?" Kate ran to the oven to turn the croissants around. "Keep talking, just speak louder."

"So, he asked me out for pizza after school to Little Z's and I met him there."

"What did you wear?" Jada asked.

"What did I wear?" Annie laughed. "I don't know. Probably something black. I was into the punk dance scene at the time and JT was still into the seventy's music and its fashion."

"The seventies had a fashion?" I chimed in. "We wore a lot of T-shirts, faded jeans, and sneakers back then."

That's what I wore too. I think Gerard is about the same age as Annie and me. Funny, I haven't changed physically but I have matured. Well, I think I have.

"Yep, that was what he wore." Annie smiled at me. "So, when I arrived, I saw JT and his friends, Johnny, Eddie, Christopher, Kenny, and Brenden, were all sitting in a booth being loud and annoying, acting like a bunch of clowns. I was ready to walk back out and leave when JT saw me and waved me over. He told his friends something and they all shut up and moved to a table on the other side of the pizzeria."

"Is that how you met Brenden?" Hana asked as she filled up a quiche—tomato with fresh basil and asiago cheese, to be exact.

"No, well, we knew each other in high school, but we really didn't connect until after college." Annie took a sip of coffee and continued.

As they got up, Eddie was the only one to say hello to me. I smiled, 'Hello, Eddie,' and he smiled back as he joined the others. He was so nice. I could never figure out what the hell he was doing with JT and his boys. It didn't make sense. He was always nice to me, smart, well mannered. He was the boy next door. I think he liked me and wanted to ask me out, but never got the chance.

You think? I adored you; you never once gave me the time-of-day baby girl. Now you tell me this. Gosh, all these years and now the truth comes out. You're breaking my heart. I'm dead, you're miserable, you have a son from that putz and now that other dirt bag wants you dead. And all of this could've been avoided if I asked you out?

He died around the block, across from the big supermarket, which was a bowling alley at the time."

"That's awful," Kate exclaimed emotionally.

Yes, it's true. I'm still here, too. Hello?

"He died while he was in high school?" Jada asked as she helped Antonio set up the cake rings for carrot cake.

"No, well, it was after graduation, maybe a few months later."

"Poor kid, too young to die. He was just starting out at that age. How did he die?" I asked, as Laurent, and I rolled out some more sucré dough.

"It was so sad. I moved to New Jersey to live with my grandparents after the whole homecoming thing when I found out I was pregnant, I had an abortion, finished out high school, and then went straight off to college. I never heard the full story, but from what I understood, JT, his friends, and the Mafia had something to do with it. JT was found guilty of Eddie's murder and went to jail. He always claimed he was innocent and had been framed by the Mafia."

Of course, he did. All he does is lie.

"You have got to be kidding me."

The chefs all had a comment as Annie dropped this bomb.

Laurent looked me in the eye, "Watch your back, boss. This JT guy sounds like a killer."

He is. You are all in his sights and he'll probably stop at nothing until he gets what he wants, and that is Annie.

I was speechless. This guy had been in my patisserie. Anxiety and fear crept in with my palpitating heart as I relived the conversation, I had with the wacko guy from yesterday afternoon.

"Why did you go out with this JT guy anyway?" Kate sounded annoyed.

"He was cute. He had that bad-boy image I liked." Annie winked at Kate and continued. "Eddie worked in the restaurant around the corner, you know, the small, skinny building next to the alley. The Mafia ran card and number games on the second floor, and I heard something about money and drugs were involved. I'm not sure, and Brenden never wanted to talk about it, so I never pushed him for more info. All Brenden would say was he believed JT, that the Mafia took Eddie out."

"Why would the Mafia want to kill an eighteen-year-old boy?"

"Like I said, I never heard the whole story, let alone the truth." Annie took another sip of coffee.

Hana looked at me. "Did you just say something?"

"No, you heard it too. I heard some inaudible chatter in my right ear."

"Yeah, I couldn't make it out, thought it was you." We both shrugged our shoulders.

"And JT was blamed?" Hana asked.

"Yep."

"Sounds like there's more to this story than what's been said. Maybe there was a cover-up?"

Hana shot me a look.

"Wow, that is so crazy! What happened when you had pizza with JT that day?" Kate was dying to know.

"Well, I sat across from him, and he was nice at first, not annoying like he was when the gang of them were all together. We spoke about what type of music we liked and then he slyly leaned over the table, 'I always thought you were hot, and I always wanted to ask you out, but never had the courage to do so.'

"Then he yelled out at the boys, 'Hey, Eddie, get us two slices of pizza and two sodas.' JT shouted it out across the room as he waved a five in his hand. JT stood up, gave Eddie the money, and then slid in the booth right next to me. I had nowhere to go, I was trapped between him and the wall. He was literally pressed right up against me."

Annie paused and she looked near to crying again. I had no idea where this story was going, but by the look on her face it was not going to end well.

"Eddie did what he was told and brought the food over. I smiled thanking him. I did hang out with Eddie a few times outside of school until JT found out, and I don't think JT liked that, because he said something like, 'I asked you to get us pizza, not to hit on my girl.'

We went to class together and lived next door to each other. Nothing ever happened between us other than chit chat, but no one believed that, especially JT.

I remember Eddie putting his head down and walking away with his long hair falling forward. JT wasted no time in taking a sip of his soda with one hand and putting his other hand on my bare knee. I was caught off guard."

Kate rotated the almond croissants around in the oven. "Not good."

"You're right, it wasn't good. JT went right into gear, put one arm around me, and started to kiss my neck and move his hand up my thigh. He was so aggressive, so quick. I… I froze and became quite angry, 'Stop it!' grabbing his hand under the table. He pulled me tighter and pushed my hand away. I remember him whispering, 'Come on, baby' right in my ear. I tried to pull his hand off my thigh again, and he smacked it away. He tried to play me, 'Relax, baby, we're just having fun,' smiling that devilish grin. I couldn't even look at him, but I do remember saying, 'I'm not that type of girl. Now get your hands off me.' He laughed at me. So, I made him stop by hitting him right where it counts.

"I must've hit him ten times and banged my hand against the table that many times as well. That got everyone's attention in the pizzeria. JT cursed at me, and I was able to push him off me as he was grabbing his crotch in pain. I pushed him out of the booth, right to the floor. I grabbed my soda, threw it in his face, and ran for the door."

"Bastard." Hana narrowed her eyes with distaste.

"I turned back when I got outside and saw all his friends rush over to him, but Eddie. He was looking at me through the big window, and we locked eyes for like a nanosecond, and he smiled at me, like he wanted to laugh."

"This guy sounds completely wacked, Annie." Hana put the muffin tray in the oven, and we all fell silent.

"Yep. High school drama, but it didn't stop there. He harassed me in school for the next few weeks. He even cornered me by my locker one day and growled, 'You know, that wasn't a nice thing you did to me at the pizzeria. Being your boyfriend and all, I thought we were more than that.'"

"He actually thought you were a couple?" Jada asked.

"I know, right? I told JT to stay away from me, but he just laughed disregarding me with something like, 'I'll never leave you alone till the day I die,' and walked away. It was rough and then came homecoming."

"Oh, you poor thing," Kate was quite emotional.

"I remember walking in with Nettie and Marie when JT popped out of nowhere, pleading to talk. I told my girls that I'd meet them in a few minutes."

Annie's tears had started to fall. Jada put her arm around her and gave her an encouraging squeeze.

"I still remember how he grabbed me by my arm, 'Come on, we need to talk.' We walked right past teachers and staff. It was like we were invisible to them. He pulled me under the bleachers. I was quite annoyed, 'What do you want, JT?' He looked around and suddenly his boys came out of nowhere. Next thing I knew I was on the ground amid empty potato chip bags, soda cups, and napkins." Annie stopped for a moment and folded her arms across her chest.

"No need to continue, Annie." I could see how distraught she was. We all could.

We all gave her a hug, one by one. I do not think there was a dry eye among us.

Yeah, not a good time at all. For either of us.

CHAPTER 20

STEVE AND THE MORNING staff arrived at seven on the dot. Setup was easy when you had three people doing it together.

Steve poured himself a cup of coffee, "What's with the chefs this morning? They all look like they just came back from a funeral."

"Just another day full of drama. Sun's up, drama is up," I replied.

"What happened now?"

"Remember the crazy guy from yesterday?"

"Yeah."

"Well, we just found out he's the guy who raped Annie when she was in high school. Then he went to jail for murder, and now he's out of jail stalking her."

Steve took a sip of his coffee. "Wow, that's a lot to digest first thing in the morning."

"I know, plus there was more ghost mischief this morning."

"We can't live and work in fear. Bad enough we believe this place is haunted. If he comes in here again, we call the police, and Annie better start carrying some mace in her bag."

"She does and she already used it on him."

"Did she file a police report?"

"I think she already looked into it, but no crime was committed. In fact, she assaulted him with the mace."

"Okay, way too much for me to get into. Hey, Annie."

Annie came up front from the kitchen, trying a smile that just was not working. "Hey, Steve, what's up?"

"Gerard just filled me in on what happened, and I want you to know we have your back. You are safe here. We all know what he looks like, and if he ever comes here again, we will call the police."

"Thank you, guys. Sorry about all this."

"No need to be sorry. He'll be the sorry one if I ever meet up with him."

We got a small smile from Annie, and she hugged us before heading back into the kitchen just as the front door chime sounded.

Beep-beep-beep.

Now, if only I knew morse code then I'd be able to speak to you, but given the way this is going, I doubt if you do, too. For God's sake people, now you know, Annie is in trouble. I could sigh all day and still nothing would be solved. I'll have to keep trying and figure something else out.

Steve and I turned to find an empty doorway.

When Annie was out of sight, I whispered to Steve, "I think this whole ghost thing has to do with Annie somehow."

"Where the hell did you get that idea from?"

"I don't know, it's just a hunch. Maybe a connection somehow. I'm not sure."

"Not sure?" Steve rolled his eyes. "The poor woman is crying her eyes out, and now you want to scare the crap out of her by saying she's the ghost whisperer?"

I'd hate to pop your bubble but she's not, you are. Or can be.

"No, I didn't say that, but I think something is definitely up."

"Yeah, but things happen even when she's not here. No way is she involved."

Steve put a lid on his coffee. "If this place is haunted, then there has to be a reason behind it. I really don't think a new hire like Annie brought ghosts with her."

The front door chime sounded, announcing the first customer of the day. Steve and I scooted out of the way to let Raquel take over.

"Come on, Gerard, do you want to go see Ernie next door?"

"It's kind of early."

"He's there. I saw his car pull up just before I came in. He has art classes at seven thirty. We can bring him some croissants and see what he knows."

"Yeah, okay. Maybe he can shed some light on this ghost stuff."

Good idea. Now hopefully Mr. Clayton can hear me. He doesn't always connect with me, but he does connect with the children and of course, they're not around. Nope, nowhere to be found. People come and go from this place but not me. I'm stuck here for life. Mr. Clayton says it's because I'm unsettled with unfinished work. How unfinished is it? My life was cut short. I was murdered, I'm dead, let me go. There's always something else to sigh about. Could this all be my unfinished work, saving Annie?

We left the shop and knocked on the neighboring door of the *Artist's Palette*. I stared at the open/closed sign hanging on the front door. It was a palette with twelve dots of assorted colors representing the numbers on a clock, with two thin paintbrushes for the hands of a clock. It was clearly set for seven thirty.

Mr. Clayton saw us and limped with his eighty-five-year-old bad hip to open the door but not before trying to smooth out the few gray hairs left on his pillow-haired head.

"Good morning, boys. What brings you here? Come in, come in."

"Good morning, Mr. Clayton. We brought you some croissants." Steve handed him the box Raquel had put together.

"Oh, my, thank you. Please, call me Ernie."

"You're welcome, Ernie. We know you have a class starting soon, and we just wanted to ask you a few questions. If you don't mind." I slipped my sweaty palms in my pockets.

"Is business all right next door?"

"Yes, yes, everything is fine."

Steve wandered around the studio, looking at all the paintings hanging on the walls. Quite a few were hung lower, at waist level, and Steve bent over to view them. "Why are these paintings hung so low?"

Ernie turned slowly and walked over next to Steve. "Oh, these were painted by the children."

"This one looks like a smudge and this one looks just like a dot," Steve pointed out.

Mr. Clayton laughed his almost silent laugh. "This is what they left for me. So, I have to show them I approve of their work and hang them up for all the students who take the class to see that art is in the eye of the beholder. What one person sees as art; another may see as a masterpiece."

"Well said, Ernie. Perfect advice for the young ones." I bent down to see the paintings and noticed the only color of choice was red.

"You mean the children."

"Yes, I am sorry, the children. That's what I meant."

Ernie folded his arms across his chest. "They like to be called children, not kids or young ones or even half pints. It's children." Ernie gave me a stern look.

Now you did it, you angered him. Now he won't open up to me or anybody else. Great, just freaking great. Might as well sit here and chill.

"Okay then, I apologize. Children it is." I raised an eyebrow when Ernie turned away and caught Steve's attention.

Steve threw his hands in the air and gave me that *I do not know* look.

"So, how may I help you boys?" He continued setting up, placing blank paper and small palettes with multiple colors of paint on each desk.

"We were wondering if you think the building is haunted." Steve said it ever so nonchalantly.

"Haunted?" Ernie shuffled from desk to desk without ever looking up, mumbling under his breath.

"Well, yes." I spoke up eagerly. "Have you heard banging noises coming from the walls or voices calling your name? Seen anything move on its own? And can you tell us what happened to the pizza guy who was here before?"

Steve rolled his eyes and shot me a that look, *you said way too much for this guy to answer*. I just shook it off.

"He died of a massive heart attack. I think he brought it on himself, to tell you the truth. He was always calling me and complaining about the children, saying they were terrorizing him. I was beside myself; how could these lovely children bother you? They are oh so nice. Sometimes I could hear him screaming through the walls, yelling, 'Get out!'" Ernie paused and shook his head.

Steve and I listened intently, but I felt a bit confused as we waited for him to continue.

Ernie scratched the top of his head. "Let's see, um, from what I remember he died in the hospital. His wife called me and said she wanted nothing to do with the place and wanted out of the lease. I was so happy when you guys came around to rent it." Ernie laid down the tiny paintbrushes. "I'd love to sit down and chat with you boys, but class starts in another minute."

"Yes, sure, sorry to delay you."

"Maybe we can speak again when I come back from vacation."

"Sure, that sounds great. Where are you going?"

"I leave tomorrow morning. I am going up to Ogunquit, Maine, to spend a month with my sister. I haven't had a chance to take any time off since my wife passed, and now that school is over for the summer, I thought it would be a good time to go."

With all due respect, yes, your wife was a lovely lady, Mr. Clayton. But seriously you're going away now? My only medium source and you're leaving. How am I going to warn Annie about JT? Even in the afterlife nothing is easy.

"Well, thank you for your time, Ernie. Enjoy your vacation." We all shook hands, and then Ernie opened the door to let the students in for their class. They looked so young, maybe seven or eight years old at most.

"Good morning, Mr. Clayton," was sung by the youngsters entering.

"Good morning, students." Ernie waved goodbye as we let the door close and walked back next door.

"Well, at least the pizza guy didn't die here."

"Yeah, but Ernie never said if the place is haunted or not." I opened the door for Steve. "And what's with the children?"

"That was creepy, to say the least, and did you notice he called the kids entering students, not children?"

"Yes, I did. Then who are the children?"

"Don't know."

CHAPTER 21

I CALLED KERRIANN LATER in the morning and told her about the recent goings-on in the kitchen. She was excited and thrilled to hear that we had caught an orb on film. But she was a little skeptical because she had never actually seen an apparition, or an orb as she called it in motion. She said to save the clip and watch out for more.

"More?" I questioned her.

"Yes, there might be more orb activity." Kerriann laughed.

Great. Now we have orbs flying around!

She said that she would be meeting Joe for lunch and the two of them would stop by.

I couldn't get that video, or what was going on with Annie, for that matter, out of my head.

We had just finished up for the day when Kerriann and Joe arrived. I don't know what I'd been expecting, maybe a wizard, but it was not an average guy, maybe a few years older than me, wearing khakis and a polo shirt looking for ghosts. Jada, Annie, Laurent, and Antonio had to leave, and as Annie stated earlier, "I've had enough drama for one day."

This is my chance, finally I can talk with someone. Hey, Joe, can you hear me? If you can, I know you can. I'm right here, look around.

I was about to show them the video clip when Joe interrupted, "Nice pastry shop. Do you make pignolia cookies?"

"Yes, we do," I answered. "They are—" But at once Joe cut me off.

He raised his index finger, as if signaling for our attention. "I'm sorry, but did someone die in here?"

Yeah dude, me, but well not here specifically but…

"What?" I tilted my head to the right. "I don't think so. Maybe…"

He cut me off again. "I think someone was murdered here. Excuse me," he abruptly started walking to the back of the bakery.

Now we're talking. Finally, someone I can talk to. Now listen up, Joe. I have a lot to say. First things first, my name is Eddie.

"Whoa! What was that all about?" Kate exclaimed.

"Seriously," Hana added, horrified.

I was speechless. I had sensed it from the beginning. *Someone died here.*

Kerriann leaned over, "He picks up on things sometimes."

"Sometimes?" I laughed. "I think picking up on a murder is a bit more, but the landlord and Realtor both said the previous owner didn't die here."

"Hmm, maybe someone else did."

I closed my eyes, sighed, and reopened them to find Kate and Hana looking at me. It all sounded profoundly serious. Had someone been murdered in this spot before I took the space over? And I now knew it was not the previous owner. So, who? Suddenly the light above my head flickered. I looked up and felt the fear creeping in.

I turned to Kerriann, "This overhead light flickers at times. Don't know why but I feel its ghost related and it's only this one. All the other lights don't do that, only this—"

Joe came back, interrupting us. "There seems to be the spirit of a Black man who died back there. Stabbed maybe… he is gurgling something. I couldn't quite understand him."

Hey, I'm here in the back. I didn't say I'm black, you must be kidding me. You don't understand me? Oh, my God, this is useless and who are all these other people here? Hey, you, get out of here. This is my medium time, not yours, you're clouding up my message. Please, this is important, let me speak to him.

"Saying something like he is black. Maybe he is African American or in the back. Couldn't follow what he was trying to say."

"What are you talking about?" Hana sounded confused.

Kate gasped, raising her hand to her mouth, and keeping it there.

I was eager for an answer, "Who is he? Do we know him?"

"Don't know," Joe replied. "He's just hanging out back there. Can't understand him too well. Wow, there are a lot of dead people trying to get through."

Concentrate, Joe, I'm right here next to you. Don't pay attention to the others, they're just passing through.

Lucas and Rick stopped what they were doing and came over to listen.

Rick raised his hand as if he were in a classroom, "Did you just say there's a dead guy back there?"

Lucas, on the other hand, threw his hands on his hips and then pointed to Rick. "You're taking the garbage down that hallway. I'm not about to be dragged into a portal by a dead guy."

We all laughed at Lucas.

Now, it's a damn comedy. Come on, kid, keep it up and I'll drag you both down the hallway. This is so frustrating.

Kerriann consoled him, "No one's going to drag you. They only do that in movies."

And then Joe smiled as if he had solved a murder from one of those whodunnit shows.

"Um, you're telling me some guy died back there and you're just smiling about it?" There was an uncomfortable silence.

"I got the chills," Kate rubbed her arms.

Joe smiled a bit wider. "So, what's going on here? You saw an orb or something?"

I paused, still waiting for Joe to explain as I pointed to the monitor. "Who's the dead guy in the back?"

It's me, Eddie. What do I have to do to get your attention? Tap dance?

"I don't know. I couldn't understand him. It could be just some random soul picking up on my medium ability, looking to communicate."

"Oh, that's all." I waved it off like what he said made sense to me. Behind Joe, Kate and Hana gave me a wide-eye look.

I played the video clip. I told them about the beam of light. "Now look towards the door. You will see a ball of light come racing in."

Yes, that's me and the children. We live here. I'm standing right behind you, exhausted, and willing to communicate and tell you everything, if you would only be willing to listen.

I stepped back to watch Joe and Kerriann's reactions.

Kerriann let out a big gasp and Joe stood quietly and calmly told me. "Play it again."

So, I did, and I told him to look at the floor to see the other particles of light.

Joe's eyebrows shifted. "Wow. Will you look at that?"

I realized that this was as exciting as Joe got, but the truth was, his eyes were glued to the monitor.

Kerriann tried to get his attention, "Joe, I've never seen an orb in motion. That is an orb, right? Joe?"

Joe stared at the screen, "That's a nice-size orb. It's pretty big, I haven't really seen one that big before. See, it's a mass of energy. Usually, they are transparent and rounder, like those small ones, but this one is huge." He pointed at the screen.

"So, there is more than one?" I questioned the findings only to realize I already knew the answer.

"Yeah," Joe gestured to the back of the kitchen. "And you have a spirit back there, too."

What? You don't like the way I look. No one said I must dress the part of a ghost by wearing a sheet over my head and yes, I'm a nice spirit most of the time.

I raised my hands. "Great, we have a haunted bakery. It's official! Orbs, spirits, and one of the biggest masses of energy either one of you two has ever seen. And you've been doing this for how long?"

Kerriann and Joe giggled.

I didn't find it funny or entertaining at all. Hana and Kate didn't say a word, they stared at me with bulging, incredulous eyes and the blank expression of shell-shock victims.

I felt a powerful adrenaline rush. "Wow! Like, these things really do exist," Amazed with fear in the forefront and the knowing—or should I say the believing—coming second.

"Uh-huh." Kerriann nodded. "I may have written a book, and I've done investigations before, but I've never seen anything like this."

"Great."

"But they won't hurt you."

"Why not? Could they? How do you know they will not? I mean, they do things around here with buckets, spatulas, paper flying, my name has been called a few times, and there's some dead guy hanging out back there. Next thing you know, they'll chop us up with knives and throw us in the oven."

Kerriann laughed. "Come on now, that won't happen."

Wanna bet, lady? We are more powerful than you think we are.

But I was serious, at least a little bit. "The oven door has been opening by itself lately and the timers keep breaking. Who knows?"

Steve pushed through the swinging door. "Can I get some help out here, please?"

Lucas and Rick went out front to help. Joe and Kerriann assured us whoever was haunting us wanted to say hello and to be recognized.

"Well, it's a crazy way to say hello," Hana quipped.

"The more you welcome them and recognize they are here, the more likely they will stay here, and that could bring on trouble," Kerriann warned.

I showed them the next clip from the night before, when I'd left the camera running in the kitchen.

"Oh, my gosh, look at that," Kerriann was clearly intrigued. "There are orbs all over the place."

The clip captured me turning off the lights and leaving the kitchen for the night, the camera being still in night-vision mode. There was no sound, and so within the darkened kitchen, everything appeared calm. But after only two minutes of filming, suddenly balls of light pierced the darkness; orbs, seemingly dozens of them, swished through the kitchen in all directions.

They moved from the back of the kitchen to the front and from the left to the right and back again. Appearing out of nowhere and dissipating into thin air. They passed right through the tables and into the ovens, through the walk-in box, and through the rolling racks across the floor. One orb could be seen pulsing blue and red.

"Wow! What a show," Joe beamed. This went on for a full minute. Not like they were all out at the same time, but more like passing each other by, like cars on a freeway. A couple of seconds would pass and a few more would show up and zoom past the lens.

Oh, make way, we were putting on a stage production of a Broadway musical. Did you see my tap dancing? Geez, I told you it's like Grand Central Station here at times and you must've heard of the lost souls roaming the earth. Well, some of them are almost zombie-like, trying to drag us with them. There are hundreds if not thousands of them at a time combing the earth. They want our energy to keep going, they are so lost, constantly in search of something. The children and I hold tight and keep our distance when we hear them coming. It's a thunderous wave, almost like an earthquake. We crouch down in the hallway away from them.

I'm not giving in to that. If I'm here for a reason, then that reason must be to protect Annie and apparently without help it might be a long-drawn-out process. But how long do I have?

As we watched, we noticed a lot of activity was happening between the oven and the walk-in box.

"This area seems to be a hot spot," Joe observed.

"No wonder we all seem to drop things there." I was amazed.

"Maybe they're knocking the trays out of our hands?" Kate added.

"So, I have to ask, is this orb thing the dead guy in the back or something completely different?"

"Not sure, Gerard. It could be another spirit coming through, whereas the guy in the back looks to be a bit more stationary. A spirit can come and go while a ghost tends to stay put."

"Are we standing on a path of sorts for ghosts and spirits?"

Finally, Joe suggested, "I think Kerriann and I should come back later and do an investigation. We'll bring sound recorders for EVPs and magnetic detectors."

"What's an EVP?" I asked.

"It stands for electronic voice phenomenon," Joe explained. "We try to record spirit voices, or any sounds they make."

Ha. That stupid thing doesn't work. Franco tried it and asked us stupid questions. He got nothing from us. We hated him.

"Terrific," I deadpanned. "Say seven p.m. when we close."

Kate asked, "Are we were going to have a séance?"

"Not quite," Joe folded his arms across his chest. "An investigation is a little different and not so devilish or mystical. We don't want to wake the dead. We just want to see who is still hanging around."

"Oh, boy. What are we getting into?" I muttered.

But Kerriann and Joe assured us it would be fine.

"Wow, this was a refreshing change from the norm. What do you think, Steve?"

"I think you're all nuts," he shot back. "Come on, really? Ghosts and dead people in the back?"

"Uh, dead people are ghosts, Steve. Just saying," Kate smirked.

"Ha-ha-ha." I always laughed when I was nervous.

"Look, you girls go home and don't worry about it," I tried to sound brave. "No one will bother you."

"Otherwise, I'll be busting some dead zombie skulls," Steve interjected. "Okay?" Steve was one real reassuring guy. Wink-wink. He liked to get to the point without any issues and was a firm believer in *you mess with me and I'll mess with you.*

The chefs departed—no pun intended! Rick and Lucas finished cleaning up, and I set the cameras on continuous record again.

From that day on, I did this every evening. Sometimes the cameras would capture orbs, sometimes a lot of them and other times only a few. Some would appear as soon as the lights were turned off while others took a few minutes to appear.

Sometimes there were so many orbs it looked like they were having a wild party in my pastry shop.

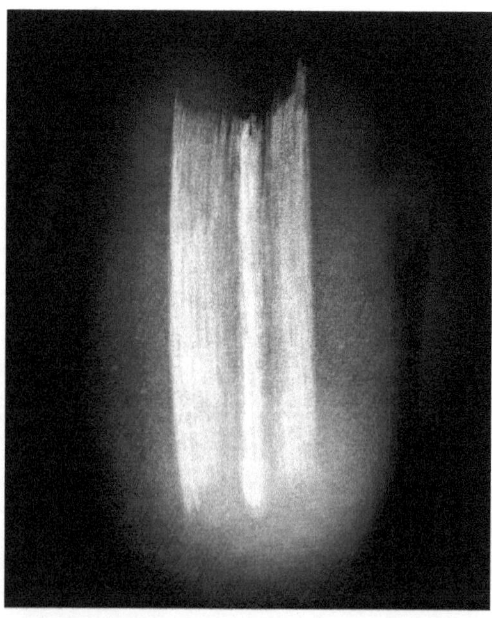

Pignolia Cookies

Preheat conventional oven to 350 degrees or convection oven to 325 degrees.

12 oz (3/4 lb.)	*Almond paste*
½ cup	*Granulated sugar*
1 cup	*Powdered sugar/Confectioner's sugar sifted.*
4 oz	*Egg whites*
1-pound	*Pignolia nuts*
#805	*Plain pastry tip*

Separate eggs until you have four ounces of egg whites in a measuring cup. Sizes of eggs may vary. Keep the egg whites on the counter and save the yolks in the refrigerator for another use.

Prepare and sift the powdered sugar into a bowl or on parchment paper and set aside.

In a four-quart stand-up mixer with a paddle attachment, break the almond paste into small pieces using your fingers or grate it into the mixing bowl. Add the granulated sugar. Turn on the mixer to the first speed on slow. Mix for five minutes and pour in one ounce of the egg whites. Mix for five minutes, always keeping the mixer on the first speed.

Start alternating the remaining egg whites and powdered sugar in three turns, ending with the powdered sugar.

When combined, stop the mixer and scrape all around the mixing bowl. Mix again for two more minutes at a slow speed. There should be no lumps of almond paste left. If so, break them apart and mix again for another five minutes at the first speed or a higher speed to beat the lumps out.

Remove the batter from the mixer.

Line a cookie tray with parchment paper and fill a pastry bag with some of the batter using a medium plain tip. Pipe quarter-size dollops of the mixture two inches apart. Apply a generous amount of pignolia nuts. Remove any loose ones on the tray, saving them for the next tray.

Bake in the preheated oven for about five minutes. Turn the tray around and bake for another five minutes or so depending on your oven, low fan if using a convection oven. The cookie should be lightly browned on the sides and opaque on top.

Cool the cookies on a baker's rack.

Remove the cookies from the parchment paper and store in an airtight container in the refrigerator for about two to three weeks.

Yields approximately five dozen cookies.

CHAPTER 22

LATER THAT EVENING, WE had an investigation. Naturally, of course, it rained. Not a thunderstorm rain that would scare the bejesus out of me, but a gloomy, foggy, spooky rain all the same.

The only one to join me was Hana. Everyone else bailed for whatever reason, so I asked my friend Phil to join us, and Steve hoped to come by later.

Kerriann and Joe started with a kind of introduction into the investigation, which they followed with a question-and-answer session. We gathered around the marble-top table, which held EVP recorders and a couple of heat-sensitive light indicators in the center of the kitchen.

The first spirit who came through was ... did I just say that so nonchalantly? Never mind, I'd never had a spiritual reading or visited a psychic, and I wasn't sure if I believed, but I tried to be open-minded about the whole thing.

Joe reasoned, "Some people who come through may or may not be connected to you directly but may just be passing through." Joe slipped into a trance-like mode and channeled the spirits of the afterlife.

The first spirit to come through Joe was Hana's grandfather. He had passed away when she was only ten years old.

Joe said, "I have a person here who passed about eighteen years ago, who says he is your grandfather, Hana. Is your grandfather here with us in this world or has he passed to the afterlife?"

"He's deceased. He passed about fifteen years ago."

"Okay, fifteen years ago, not eighteen. He's standing at your right side."

Hana turned to her right and whispered, "Hi, Grandpa."

Kerriann acknowledged her. "You don't have to whisper; they can still hear you."

Hana was moved. "I was so close to him as a child," she said wistfully.

At which point Joe acknowledged it was indeed her grandfather, and he was saying hello, adding, "He says he's always by your side, even here in the bakery."

Shortly afterward, a female spirit came through Joe, once again acting as a medium. She was looking for someone named Andy, saying Andy, whoever he was, was a "cutie." I couldn't place the name and had no idea who Andy was.

Uh, hey, Grandpa, nice to meet you but I need to talk to this guy. Now, if you'll excuse me, um, hello, Joe. Come back here so we can speak privately. My name is Eddie.

Joe kept picking up on a male who he believed had been murdered in the back of our building many years ago. "Again, he's telling me he's black or in the back, but he's so garbled I can't make out most of what he's saying. Sometimes a medium can't understand a spirit, whereas another medium can." Finally, Joe walked to the back of the kitchen to talk to him.

While he was gone, we spoke with Kerriann about life after death and what supposedly happened to our spirits, how it might be possible for them to live on. She told us, "After death, some people's spirits linger and wait for their loved ones before moving on, to join them, perhaps. Some stay just to see what's going on among those still alive, and some just are not ready to move on. In other words, we are all free to go to the light after we die but some choose to stay here, and this seems to have happened to the guy in the back."

Yeah, that's what you think sister. Now, Joe, you have to listen to me. I don't have enough energy to convey all the information I need to, but Annie is in trouble.

What's your name? How did you get here?

My name is Eddie. I parked my motorcycle in the bowling alley parking lot. It was my bike and these so-called friends thought I took money to buy drugs and…

Speak slowly I can't understand you; you sound garbled and there are too many spirits trying to push through to get my attention.

Good God, what does it take? Get the hell off me and out of my face. This is my time, get away, you don't even live here. This is my space, Dude, stop pushing me around. Who are you people? Where did all these spirits come from? Don't push me. Arghhhh!

"I'm trying to listen but you're fading away. Well, this is unfortunate." Joe returned and told us the dead fellow had been involved in some type of drug deal or money was stolen. "It had to do with money. It happened, from what he's saying, at the bowling alley across the street, where the supermarket now stands. He parked his bike there. He says, 'My bike, my bike.' It must've been a while ago, about thirty years ago." But Joe had a real tough time understanding him. He couldn't get his name.

We all listened with fascination.

"Wait a minute, he's back, he says, tell Phil"—meaning the friend I'd brought along for this wild ride— "to tell his friend Ben. He knows."

Phil was dumbfounded. "How does he know about Ben?"

"Who's Ben?" Joe inquired.

There's no use, I can hear Joe, but I'm stuck in the middle of all these dead skulls. So here goes, if he can hear me so be it. Ben is married to my friend, Christopher's little sister, Kelly. She has to know about me. This is the only connection I can find here. Chris was a good friend. I am so tired. I have to go rest, this was exhausting.

"Ben is my handyman. He was at my home today painting the bathroom. He's something of a local historian."

"Huh, maybe he knows something about this," I asked. "When did this guy die, Joe?"

"Sometime in the early eighties or late seventies. Going to say around 1982." Joe relayed what he was told as Phil started texting Ben with the information we had about the possible murder.

The rain had stopped, and Kerriann went outside to take some photos of the front of the store. When she returned, we shut the lights off in the kitchen. Hana stayed nervously right by my side, but Kerriann continued to take some photos even though it was dark. "Sometimes I catch orbs in the photos," she explained. Joe and Kerriann walked around the kitchen in search of spirits. It's one of the most bizarre things I'd ever witnessed.

Joe left his EVP recorder on the center table. Phil, Hana, and I kept our eyes on the monitor, thinking maybe we'd catch an orb floating by. Phil walked over to the middle table, and that's when Hana and I simultaneously felt a strange sensation. It passed between us, chilling our souls, and sung, "Hello" in such a whisper of a way that you might doubt your senses, except that it was so clear and so definitely in your ear that it was impossible to deny.

You, young lady in white, you know me. Please wait. What's your name? Please help me, I can barely move. Tell them who I am. I, I, am …

We both looked at each other at the same time. "Did you hear that? It was right in my ear." One of us said that—I cannot remember if it was Hana or me. Shivers went up my spine just like the first day we saw the space and in an uncomfortable way! Hana said she felt the exact same feeling.

She grabbed my arm and moved closer to me, "I don't like this."

I smiled to try and reassure her, but I'm not sure she was comforted. "It sounds like the same voice that called my name out a few times." We heard a strange sound that was unfamiliar, more like a grunt than anything else. We looked at each other with the same expression, "What the heck was that?" But the answer eluded us.

Later, when we turned the lights back on, Kerriann showed us the photos she'd just taken. And there they were, one orb here, one orb there, a few orbs outside, one that was tremendous in size to the others and whizzing above the store. "If you zoom in to enlarge the photos, you can see a face in them sometimes."

"Whaaat? Are you kidding me?" I was joking… at first.

"No, sometimes there are faces in them," Kerriann grinned. "I have one at home with a dog's face. I'll look at these later on the computer and blow them up on-screen for a clearer resolution."

At this point, Joe encouraged us to try asking the spirits a question. You can imagine the response. We started blurting out predictable questions like, "Why are you here? Who are you? Do we know you? What are your names? Do you like it here?" That is, until Hana quipped, "What, do you like French pastries or something?" that cracked us up.

Still, no audible answer was heard, but Joe said he would check his EVP recorder later the next day.

No one close to me came through, like someone from my family or someone I might have known in the past. Maybe this place was haunted, and maybe we had intruded into their space. I started to think maybe we're not supposed to be here, until Joe remarked, "My impression is they like having you here, and they feel extremely comfortable with your patisserie being in this space."

"But Joe, we don't want them to stay and cause havoc on a daily basis. We want them to leave. In fact, who is behind all the mischief around here?"

"I can't see anyone who is owning up to it. You must ask them to leave and mean it, but most of them have been here way before you."

"So, we have squatters with no names."

Everyone laughed at my joke.

And just at that moment, Steve finally arrived, and Joe turned to him and added, "They love your sense of humor, Steve."

"Great, I have a fan club from beyond the grave," Steve blurted. We all had another laugh.

There was one more thing to check out, and that was our creepy, windowless hallway. I escorted Joe and Kerriann to the back door. I reached for the push-bar handle, but then I paused, sheepishly admitting to them I'd never made it through all the way.

"Why?" asked Kerriann.

"This is why," and I opened the door. It opened with such a loud *CREAK!* no amount of grease would be able to fix. Slowly it opened, just like a horror movie in slow-mo. The creaking noise got louder and steadier until the door was fully opened. You couldn't make it stop by pushing slowly or quickly.

"Oh, my God," Kerriann exclaimed. "Are you kidding me? This is so creepy. Gerard, you saved the best for last."

Joe led the way, pointing to the single swaying-ever-so-gently light bulb—we willingly let him—and he immediately came up with the notion, "This's where the guy who was stabbed hangs out."

I sighed knowingly; it had to be the guy I'd felt pass by me.

As they walked through the hallway, Joe smelled something like burning sulfur, and both got bad vibes from all around. He spun around in a circle, "The air is heavy with a sense of sadness and neglect. Soul upon old soul clustered in the still air."

I stayed back, holding the door open wide with my left arm and peering from behind them as they moved through.

Then I saw it. *BAM!* It was right in my face. I screamed aloud, "Oh my God! Is this a joke?"

Joe and Kerriann turned back and yelled, "What happened? Did you see a ghost or something?" Utterly speechless, I silently, ominously pointed to the stone wall in front of me, for there, carved into the dark-green-painted concrete wall in a hideously tortured scrawl, was the name ANDY.

My heart dropped.

Never noticed Andy's handiwork before, and yet there it was in five-inch letters, clear as could be.

"You sure pick a fine night to discover it," Joe huffed as he held a hand over his beating heart after I explained this.

"But Joe, you said earlier today a woman asked about Andy, saying he was cute?"

"Don't know," was all Joe muttered running his fingers over the carved letters like an archaeologist finding unhidden treasure as the paint cracked and pieces fell. "We never did figure that one out, at least not yet."

"So, is Andy the name of the guy who was murdered or the name of the killer?" I released my grip on the door, hearing it crack a few times. "Maybe the dead guy scrawled the killer's name as he was trapped in this hallway, not able to open this bolted door, slowly dying from a stab wound, trying to leave a clue as to who murdered him." My heart skipped a few beats as I realized what I'd just said.

"Good detective work. Maybe so, but the dead guy isn't saying much." Joe smiled again. "He is fading out, running out of energy, and I still can't figure out if he is black or saying he's in the back. He's so garbled to me."

By this point, they had had enough of the creepy hallway, and I slowly let the creaky old door close while peering around it to catch a final glimpse.

We all returned to the living in the kitchen. The lights flicked over the table, and I could swear I felt a knock or bump under my feet as I stood in front of my marble table.

Kerriann let out a gasp. "You better see if you can fix the light," she exclaimed. "Because otherwise it may be someone is trying to tell you something. Orbs like electricity and energy. They can actually cause the lights to flicker."

"The lights are new, and after hearing all you had to say, I'm starting to believe an orb, spirit, or ghost is causing it to flicker."

Kerriann looked concerned, especially when she saw how apprehensive I was. "I think we have enough information from this investigation to call it quits for the evening. I'll call you if I see anything else in the photos. Thanks, Gerard, for having us over." Kerriann reached out to give me a hug. "Good night."

We all shook hands with Joe.

And that was it. "That's it? No big finale? No exorcist or casting of spells to keep the evil forces away?"

"Noooo." Kerriann laughed. "It's not like that, but we can have the bakery smoked with sage to help keep the spirits away. Let's see what Joe picks up on the EVPs before doing anything."

Steve, Hana, Phil, and I wondered what was next. I didn't have long to wait, because the next day Phil called me all frantic. "You aren't going to believe this."

"Uh, I'll believe in anything now," I replied.

"The guy who was murdered is real." Phil was ecstatic. "My friend Ben got back to me this morning. It seems Ben's wife remembers the story of someone being murdered outside across from the bowling alley a long time ago when she was a freshman in high school in the early eighties, but she can't remember the person's name. He died just the way Joe described it."

I was numb. I had a spirit of a dead man living in my pastry shop. I hoped he liked my baking. "That's crazy. So, we have a confirmation, and this is legit?"

"Yeah, I guess we do. Tell the ghost I said hello."

"Ha-ha, I don't think so."

Phil laughed as we said goodbye and I hung up the phone.

Hana and I were in fairly good spirits as we told Kate and the chefs all about the past evening's events. At least now we had some type of clue as to who the dead guy was, but part of me thought of Annie's story about JT stabbing Eddie to death around the same time. I wondered if they were connected.

Meanwhile, Steve was out front behind the counter, helping customers, and the chime on the front door kept going off. The door was not moving. *Beep-beep-beep* in rapid succession. A pause for a minute or two—then it would go off again.

Yo, Gerard my man, it's me, Eddie. You guys got it right. JT did it. He's after you if not all of you. Can you hear me? Open your mind, Gerard, I know you can do it. I'll beep the hell out of this door until you listen to me.

This went on for almost two hours. Finally, I yelled out, "Hey, er, Andy, we know you're here. Knock it off!"

And then it stopped.

Dude! My name is Eddie, not Andy. I feel like I get scolded around here more for trying to do the right thing!

Seriously. It stopped.

"You tell 'em who's boss, Rardy. Oh, yeah! You, ghost, got nothing on us. Ha-ha!" Steve laughed and fist-pumped the sky.

"So, you really think his name is Andy?" Annie was cracking eggs for brioche.

"I don't know but the chime stopped going off, so maybe it is." I was about to go back to work and turned back to Annie. "Was Eddie African American?"

"Eddie? No, Eddie was Irish. Why?"

"Just wondering if your story about Eddie is related to what we just found out about the dead guy in the back. He kept telling Joe he's black or in the back."

"Oh, yeah, no, Eddie was a white kid, and like I told you, I had left Harrington before Eddie was killed. Last night's story sounds like a random drug murder at the bowling alley. It was always full of shady people. I guess that's why they tore it down and put the supermarket up. No one went there anymore."

"Geez."

Geez is right. You people are twisting so much information into a misinformed tale. Stick to the facts.

Kerriann called later in the morning. "Hey, Gerard," she was quite excited, "I just emailed you the orb photos from last night. Blow up the photo of Joe walking to the back of the kitchen and look at the orb on the right; you'll see a face."

"Are you serious? Who is it?"

"Don't know but you can definitely see a face in it. Maybe it's Andy."

"Okay, I'll check it out. So now what do we do? Nothing?" I had to know what was next. I told her about the chime on the front door going off.

Kerriann laughed, "I guess they want to reach out to you and say hello. I'll try to look through some archive folders at the library when I can, to see if Andy was murdered in the alley. But don't hold your breath, with two kids, a dog, and a crazy schedule, it may be a few weeks before I can do anything further."

"Yeah, sure, no problem." I couldn't ask more of Kerriann. She had been super nice to help in the first place.

"But still I was so surprised no spirits came through for me. I was a little disappointed."

"It doesn't work like that all the time," she explained. "I'm going to write about the investigation in my column in the local blog. It comes out Monday, so you can read about our findings and maybe it'll draw some ghostly business." Kerriann laughed.

I thanked her again and said we would keep in touch. But as soon as I got off the phone, I couldn't wait. I wanted to see the face in the orb.

CHAPTER 23

I OPENED THE EMAIL and looked at the photos. The ones taken outside the store surprised me the most. They showed several orbs up in the sky above the store, one with multiple colors like an exploding nuclear atom of some type—and huge. It was the biggest of all the orbs that were visible.

Then I clicked on the one where Joe was walking to the back of the kitchen. I was on the left, across from the oven. The photo was taken in the dark, but I clearly saw Joe's back as he walked away. On the right was the oven, and a small orb hovered near the stain-less-steel hood.

I started to enlarge the photo, nervously. What would we see? I called Steve and the chefs over to check it out. Alex and Vincent were working that day, so they came over to look, too.

I started to make the frame bigger, and slowly an image started to appear, and it was a face.

Alex and Vincent exclaimed, "No way! That's crazy."

Kate let out a gasp.

Hana cried out and covered her mouth, "Oh, my God, that is insane."

Ever the nonbeliever, Steve waved it off, "That's photoshopped."

"No, Kerriann wouldn't do that." I cut him off. "Wow, this is nuts."

It was definitely a face. A little blurry but clear enough to make out the features of sunken eyes, puffy cheekbones, and a wide, leering grin.

Then it hit me. "Maybe it's Andy."

"Andy who?" Steve wondered.

"You know, the guy who wrote his name on the wall."

"Yeah, right." Steve was doubtful. "Andy died and he's living here in the bakery. Are you kidding me? Come on. I wouldn't live here, there are ghosts here."

We all chuckled.

Dude, you people are bugging out. That's not me, that's not me. And who the hell cares about Andy? I don't even know the guy. He doesn't live here. I do.

I tried to rationalize it, "Well, maybe he died and he's one of these orbs now."

"Call the media. 'Hello, media, how are you? Did you hear about a guy named Andy? 'Cause there's a ghost here that looks like him.'" Steve was laughing, but his voice was cracking. So, I knew that even he was a little shaken up by the face in the orb. But then, always the businessperson, he got back to being serious.

"Come on, let's get back to work," he ordered. "Hey, Vin and Alex, make sure you dust up here on the hood where Andy is hanging out. Hey, Andy, I hope you're not throwing those buckets at me, because we're going to dance if you are," Steve ranted.

The orb face made us all feel a little uncomfortable as it was disturbing and strange to say the least. The kind of thing that just made you wonder, was it real? Yet there were no faces in any of the other orbs in the photos, just that one.

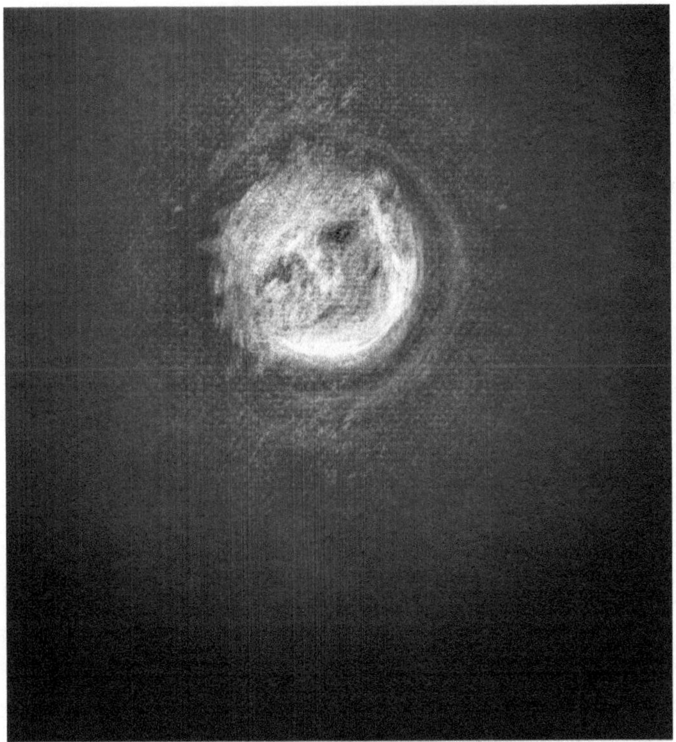

By midday, Joe called with information on the EVPs. Seemed like he had picked up a few sounds. "One sounds like a woman singing hello."

I stepped out of the noisy kitchen to take the call outside in front of the store and thought it was the sound Hana and I heard.

Some of the sounds we could only make out as grunts, but there was one that seemed to be dragged out, as if someone were talking in slow motion. It came right after Hana asked the question, "What, do you like French pastries or something?"

The answer was the word *French* delivered in a long, deep, dragged-out breath of air, sultry, as if someone said it while exhaling a lot of air.

It was a man's voice, and Joe seemed convinced that there was some connection with the dead guy.

I told him what Phil told me and thought maybe Andy was the face in the orb. But Joe did not pick up on Andy as we spoke, and in his view, the dead guy, being Andy or not, black, or not, was the only spirit who came through all the way, and we had no proof that he was the orb face in the photo.

The other spirits were just passing through, Joe conjectured. But I was more concerned with the face and woman's voice singing hello.

He gladly replied, "We'll do it again and see if other people will come out."

I closed my eyes and sighed. "Again? I thought this was it, we were done, and the hauntings would now be over. Tell me it will stop, Joe."

"See, for a medium, the spiritual world is never done. Your spirit will live on, and sometimes it may be here or there, but never everywhere. If the spirit isn't here at the time that I am open to them or they don't want to speak out, then we won't know who they are. It can take a few times for them to trust us and for them to come through. Not every spirit wants to say hello, and besides, communicating, making noises, banging on walls, and making spatulas move is extremely draining on them. That's why they like to be near electricity, they recharge themselves."

I listened intently, trying to understand all of what Joe was sharing. It was new to me and quite interesting if not scary.

I told Joe what had happened this morning. I was working at my table making tart shells. The mixer behind me was on high speed, loudly whisking genoise batter.

The radio tried to output more volume than the mixer, and everyone was at their stations working diligently. I'd just laid the dough on my table and reached out to put the rolling pin back on the sheeter when, abruptly and with no warning, it was as if a man was right next to me speaking in my ear. "Hey, Gerard," a voice yelled. I froze and stopped in mid-motion. The hairs on the back of my neck stood up.

It came out of nowhere literally.

I know what I heard. I stayed frozen in my tracks. I did not know what to do. Should I ignore it or answer it? Then I smiled and blurted, "Someone just called my name in my right ear."

Everyone stopped what they were doing and stared at me.

Steve questioned while grinning, "What did they say? Is it fresh?" Laughter erupted and I shook it off.

It was then that I remembered that I was standing right near the spot where Kerriann had picked up some electromagnetic charges during the investigation.

I listened for a while, but nothing seemed to be there. Softly, I whispered, "Hello?" hoping to elicit a response, but nothing. It was a weird feeling. I hoped I wasn't going crazy.

Joe laughed on the phone. "Yes, someone is trying to connect with you, and no, you are not crazy, but probably sensitive to being a medium of some sort."

Joe, I'm getting very tired of this. Tell him it's me, Eddie. I'm right here in front of him.

"As I am talking to you now on the phone, there is a guy standing in front of you wearing a leather jacket, jumping up and down, almost trying to get your attention. It looks like he has a motorcycle next to him."

I turned around so fast I almost bumped into a woman passing behind me. "There's no one here, Joe." No one near me or in the street or passing by on a motorcycle wearing a leather jacket in June.

"He's about five feet away by the curb."

"I don't see anyone fitting that description, Joe."

Silence.

"Joe? Joe?"

The conversation went dead, and that lovely sound of the phone being off the hook triumphantly played, *bahh-bahh-bahh*, right in my ear.

"Damn it!" It scared the crap out of me. I lost Joe on the phone, probably because I traveled too far away from the landline telephone base. I looked around again, but no one fit the description. I even stared at pedestrians passing by the café and got weird looks back. "What am I doing? This is ridiculous."

I went back inside the patisserie, deciding not to call Joe back. The whole experience was getting out of hand. Maybe Steve was right, and we were all going off the edge. Time to come back to reality. *Whatever that is.*

Kerriann published all these findings in an article that appeared in the local newspaper and in another feature article for her weekly blog.

I wasn't sure how my customers would react to this ghostly publicity, but I figured, what the heck, it might help business. I even posted all the links to Fiorello's website.

Later in the afternoon, Jon and Constantine had just finished sweeping the floor by the flour bins while I prepped some molasses cookies. We were listening to random songs playing on Indie Artist radio on a chill afternoon, until…

"Did you do that?" Jon asked me.

I looked up, and as he pointed toward the wall, the two of us witnessed three of the whisks swinging from left to right in unison. "Uh, no, not me," I answered. I was standing two yards away from where the whisks were hanging. "Look where I am," I argued. "I couldn't possibly reach that far."

"Then how the hell is it happening?"

Neither Jon, Constantine, nor I could explain it other than to say maybe the ghost was doing it.

I don't think that's a good idea, Grace and Charlotte. Constantine is a bit nervous around us. I don't think Gerard would appreciate your help right now either. If this boy leaves because of us, I think Gerard will get mad, and I need him on my side right now. So, please, no pranks.

"Are there really ghosts here, Gerard?" Constantine scanned the kitchen from side to side.

"I think so. I have no other explanations for the strange things that keep happening around here."

"Any idea who it is?" Jon asked.

"Haven't got a clue, but I think there's more than one ghost. Just have that feeling. It could be a guy named Andy, and there is a young woman's voice around here, too. She has called my name a few times."

"And you're not scared?"

"I am, but as long as nothing harmful happens to anyone, I'm trying to manage this ghostly phenomenon along with the business, my investment, staff, a pastry competition coming in two weeks, crazy guys showing up and now ghost-hunting mediums."

Jon laughed a bit nervously. "All right, so if you're not scared, then I'm not scared, but how are you keeping it together?"

"Speak for yourself, Jon." Constantine stopped sweeping and stared at both of us.

"Are you okay, Constantine?" I was concerned; these kids were seventeen and still youthful with a mature disposition.

"I don't know. I never had to deal with anything like this, and I'm not a fan of horror movies."

"I don't know, and neither am I, but I feel like this whole thing is an adventure and we are running with it. But I can feel the stress and gray hairs coming out."

Jon laughed a bit more sincerely. "Ah, you look good, G. you still have a few black hairs left."

I smiled as we watched the swaying whisks slow down, but what had started them moving in the first place, we had no idea. I was listening to the lyrics of the song playing and I almost laughed with terror.

Ain't no ghosts in the graveyard.
That's not where they dwell.
They are right behind you, clear as a bell.
Night stalkers sneak through when you least expect them.
Reaching out to say hello.
It is what it's not.
And always what will be.
Floating around for eternity.

CHAPTER 24

Well, hello, young lady, you're back.

I didn't think I'd see you when nothing was happening around here. What's your name, if you don't mind me asking? And no running away this time until we have a conversation. I'm lonely, too. By the way, you giggle a lot.

Okay, I'll stay for a little while but only because you need me and thank you, my name is Mattie.

Mattie, what a pretty name. My name is Eddie, nice to meet you finally.

Nice to meet you, too, Eddie, but I already knew who you were.

So, why do I need you?

You need to protect a few people around here, especially Gerard. I like him, his baking reminds me of my mother's and her peach pie. It was so yummy; I could almost taste it.

He's an amazing baker but I, I have to protect him?

Yes, and Annie, too. That guy, JT, is up to no good. They'll need your help.

How do you know this?

I can see the future, well, parts of it anyway.

Really? I can't see anything but what happens here and I'm kind of stuck here. I can't see past these four walls sometimes.

I was stuck here, too, for a while. My family owned this land around the time of the Revolutionary War. I tap Gerard's feet sometimes to remind him to get off my resting place. Franco did it all the time too and I warned him, but as you know, Franco didn't listen to us.

Wait, what are you talking about?

I'm sorry, are you upset with me? When I hear that tone of voice, I know people are upset with me. I upset so many people, nobody wants to listen to me.

No, no, no, don't be upset. I don't want to upset you, I'm happy to talk to you. I won't ask questions like that. I'm sorry.

I have to go…

No, no, please stay, you have to help me. You said I need to protect Gerard and Annie. How do I do that?

Hmm, okay, I'll help you, but you'll need energy, a lot of it. You'll need to fill yourself with a maximum amount of energy in a short period of time. You might think you'll explode, but you won't. Then you'll be able to move things with strength and precision.

You'll have to show me. I, I don't want to mess things up, especially at a critical time.

It's easy. I'll show you and you might even be able to show yourself to people every now and then, too.

Like you did?

Uh- huh, like I do.

Wait, come to the back of the kitchen, Gerard is coming in to work.

This morning went pretty smooth around here, no paranormal activity, no bumps, no sounds not much of anything. Until mid-morning.

There were four fluorescent light fixtures in the main kitchen area, each consisting of four bulbs, and the one fixture over my table that, on occasion, flickered on and off.

From time to time, I still felt a banging from the ground beneath my feet. These things seemed to happen randomly, at various times and unrelated to one another.

One of the four bulbs went out. But then an hour later, a second bulb blew out. *Great*, I thought. I needed reading glasses as it was and couldn't see what I was doing. But in the next hour, the first bulb turned back on again. "Yay." Much better. I looked at it with questionable curiosity, thinking maybe it was an energy source for the orbs.

I was making rugalach cookies and spreading raspberry jam over the dough. I laid the offset spatula down and went to grab the box of chocolate. As I turned around, I knocked the spatula off the table, it dropped to the floor right in front of my marble table. But before I could pick it up, Kate stepped back and accidentally kicked it under my table.

"Oops. I am sorry. I'll get it,"

"That's okay, I got it." I bent down on one knee and reached under my table to retrieve it. But as I withdrew it from underneath, the wooden handle happened to tap the floor several times.

Thud, thud, thud. It didn't sound right. Then I tapped around a bit, farther away from the table, and I heard a distinctly different sound. *Tap, tap, tap.* "This can't be."

Hana walked over. "What's wrong?"

"Listen." I tapped around again. Kate turned around and we listened. *Tap, tap, thud, thud, tap.* "The floor is hollow here."

Hana's glasses almost slipped off her nose, "Whaaat? No way!"

"Yeah way, this is messed up." I got up so fast. "I stand right here all the time. Right here! I'm standing on hollow ground! It's solid all around except for right here in front of my table. This is where I feel the banging under my feet. This is nuts." I dropped the spatula and took two steps back.

Jada, Annie, Antonio, and Laurent looked on and could clearly see my distress.

Kate was cautiously inching backward, away from the spot.

"Yeah, when we built this kitchen..." I trailed off, trying to recall the renovations we made. "Wait. These are the original tiles. These were here when we moved in." The area over the hollow ones hadn't been disturbed since we moved in. "Maybe it's a hollow grave," I blurted.

"What? That's crazy talk." Hana stepped back even farther.

"Think about it: I feel banging, knocking, whatever you want to call it, under my feet sometimes." I paused and thought about the clear connection. "And the lights above my table flicker all the time." I gazed up at the lights and now I stepped back from the table, too. "What did the previous owner do, build this place over a cemetery, like in that movie?

"Well, we do have ghosts, Gerard," Kate joked. "Are you going to break it open?"

"Hell no, are you kidding me? Leave the dead alone. The less we know, the better off we are. Right? Do you really want to see a skeleton or a bag of bones?" I was like, *this was surreal; this cannot be happening!*

"Maybe Jimmy Hoffa is in there," Steve chimed in. We all laughed and that broke the tension.

I washed off the spatula and walked back to my table. "Maybe I'm just starting to go crazy or maybe I'm really onto something." I had to finish making the rugalach. I felt like I was on some wacky game show, and I made sure to step over the hollow spot over and over.

"Step on a crack, break your mother's back," Steve joked. Laurent and the other chefs laughed too.

I did not. "Ha-ha-ha, I forgot to laugh. Don't you people have something to do other than make fun of me and this freaky situation? Huh?" I looked around the kitchen and no one answered me.

"Calm down, I was only joking with you." Steve was trying to be sincere.

"I know, but why am I the only one these things are happening to? What did I do that was so terrible?"

Kate rubbed my shoulder. "It's okay. We're all in this together."

"Thanks, but I think these ghost things are out for me. I keep stumbling, literally, upon more and more. There must be a reason for all this. Are we standing on hallowed ground, and they want us gone? Maybe, therefore, the old pizza guy went crazy and had a heart attack."

"Stop it. Now you're scaring me." Kate folded her arms across her chest. "There are spirits here. I get it. We all get it. Why they want to haunt a bakery I don't know. Maybe we should call a priest and hang crucifixes over our workstations, but I'll be damned if I throw in the towel for you and Steve. No way. You guys worked so hard to put this place together. And your immediate success? No little ghost is going to kick us out of here. Halloween is one day, not every day. You hear me, ghost? Although Halloween is my favorite holiday." Kate paused and then shouted out, "Leave us alone and go haunt somebody else!"

Everyone else kept their head down and worked. Steve rolled his eyes with a chuckle and went out front to help a customer.

I stared down at the floor, "Hey, I don't know if someone is in there, but I must work here. So, excuse me for living."

But I had to wonder if the flickering lights and the knocking from the floor were related.

Uh- oh, I think they're on to us. This is not good. A few more instances like this and I think some will start leaving. I can't have that happen, not now.

As midday rolled around and the chefs were finished and gone, Nora answered a phone call. "Hey, G, a lady on the phone wants to know if the bakery is haunted. She read an article about it this morning."

I thought, *Oh God, it is out there. Now the whole town will find out and I will be labeled as the crazy ghost baker.* "Just tell her you're not sure but that the carrot cake is to die for."

"Are you serious? I just got a chill." Nora questioned me.

"Yes. I'm sure the customer will laugh."

Oh, man, this is going to get played out real fast. "Next thing you'll hear is customers wanting to speak with Casper, the head chef."

"It's better than having a dead guy pick up the phone." Constantine snickered as he passed me to help a customer.

"Where do you want me to put the rugalach you guys made?" Julie was standing there with the tray in her hands, looking at me for a solution.

"Um, in the cookie case."

"Um, there's no room."

"Um, make room."

Constantine and Nora were helping customers and had just returned to the kitchen to refill some pastries.

"Pretty busy today." Constantine pulled out a tray of mini pastries from my marble table.

I'd just laid down the last cookie and went to wash my hands. But just as I got to the sink, I heard Julie scream, accompanied by the crashing sound of a round metal cookie cutter tin hitting the floor, spraying cookie cutters everywhere.

No, no Charlotte. What did you do?

Julie was holding her hands to her mouth, and a visibly trembling Nora was pointing to one of the shelves.

It seemed Constantine was walking past the table when suddenly the cookie cutters fell off the shelf over my table at his heels, smashing to the floor. Only, according to Nora, they didn't so much fall as leap off that shelf. Nora swore she saw them fly off the shelf. Julie and Constantine started to laugh nervously, but not Nora.

"That's it. I'm done," she ripped off her apron and tossed it into closet. "This place is haunted, and you people are crazy for staying here."

"Nora, wait a minute, maybe there's an explanation. Maybe it was—"

"I don't need an explanation. I'm out!" She practically ran through the door.

The three of us stood there, not knowing what to say, until Steve popped his head in the kitchen, "What the hell happened to her? Did she see a ghost or something?"

Nora quit and never came back.

Rugalach

4 oz	Cream cheese (soft, not whipped)
4 oz	Butter (soft)
1 Tbs	Sugar
1 cup	All-purpose flour, sifted.
	Raspberry jam for spreading.
	Almond flour
	Semisweet chocolate chips
	Milk for coating
	Granulated sugar for glazing

In a five-quart stand-up mixer with a paddle attachment, add softened cream cheese and butter and mix till smooth. Add the sugar and mix on a medium-low speed. Stop and scrape the bowl completely. Turn the mixer back on and combine everything again for about two minutes. Set the mixer on its first speed and slowly add all the flour. Stop and scrape the bowl, return the bowl back to the mixer, and mix till everything is combined.

Remove the dough from the mixer and place it on a tray lined with parchment paper, lightly floured. Dust the top of the dough lightly with some flour and use your hand to flatten down the dough. Form a square that is about one-quarter inch thick. Wrap the dough in plastic wrap and refrigerate for one hour or until it is cold and solid. This can remain in the refrigerator for another twenty-four hours if needed to work with it at another time.

Preheat conventional oven to 350 degrees or convection oven to 325 degrees.

Roll the dough out on a lightly floured work surface to one-eighth of an inch or thinner into a six-inch by twenty-inch rectangle. Divide the length into two pieces.

Spread the raspberry jam across the length of the dough. Generously spread the almond flour onto the raspberry jam and follow it with the chocolate chips.

Roll the dough up toward you lengthwise.

Brush the top of the rolled log with milk. Coat the top of the log with a sprinkling of granulated sugar evenly.

Cut the rugalach into one-inch logs and place them on a parchment-paper-lined tray. Space them out by an inch or two.

Bake them for seven minutes. Rotate the tray and bake again for another five to seven minutes or until the rugalach has a light golden-brown color.

Makes two dozen.

Enjoy!

CHAPTER 25

SEVERAL TIMES THAT WEEK I woke up at 2:19 in the morning. I don't understand why and had tried to go back to sleep, but I wound up thinking about the ghost and the patisserie till I knocked out again. But this time it was different. I was wide awake, could not fall back to sleep, and thought I should search the internet for some answers.

I got out of bed and shuffled my groggy way to my desk. The first thing I searched for was the meaning of the number 219. It happened to be an angel number, *symbolizing service to others through living, serving your life purpose and humanity. Angel number 219 tells you to focus upon your career and life purpose.*

"Huh!" And then I thought, *well, I know my career and life purpose are for me to be at the bakery in a few hours to work a full tiresome day, because something or someone keeps waking me up at 2:19 in the morning. So, please stop it and let me sleep.*

I searched through the Town of Harrington website, but all I came across were roadblocks saying *sites under construction* and felt I was getting nowhere. But I did find out some history of Harrington. It was founded in 1653, and Nathan Hale was one of its occupants during the American Revolutionary War for the Battle of Long Island.

I scrolled farther down and saw the heading "Colonel Gilbert Potter, Revolutionary War hero, lived on a farm on what is now Wall Street." I clicked on it and found he was buried in the old Harrington Cemetery by Town Hall. *Thank God he is not buried on Wall Street.* I clicked on a survey map and could not believe that the corner of Wall Street was where his home and farm were located. Which meant to me that the patisserie was on his land and not on the Indian burial ground where the post office was now located. *Thank you for that. I think I'll have to go to the Town Hall and ask for some more information.*

I continued searching the internet and typed in Harrington, New York, Main Street land survey 1980. It showed the store locations. There was a pizzeria in the same location as my store called Franco's Pizzeria. *I guess his business was quite successful to last all these years.*

Time was ticking. It was about the time I usually got up. I'd have to do more research later if I could stay awake. I jumped in the shower and drove to work, arriving at five a.m. to find Annie's car in her usual spot.

I looked over with a smile as I pulled in, only to find her car empty. *Where is she?*

I quickly looked left and to the right and saw no one at all walking around the parking lot. No text messages or missed calls from Annie, and I started to think of the craziest ideas of where she might be. Or even worse if JT was behind this and she was now missing.

I exited my car with my messenger bag in tow and looked in her car windows. She was not sleeping in the back seat and her doors were locked.

Car headlights startled me; Hana pulled in faster than anyone I'd ever seen. She parked on the other side of Annie's car with an inch to spare before hitting the curb. I cringed that she was going to hit it and she exited faster than she parked.

"Morning, Rard! What's up?"

"Hey, Hana, good morning."

"Annie's here?"

"Don't know. I just arrived myself. Her car is here but I think that's it."

"Well, that's weird."

"No sense in waiting around. She probably won't materialize out of thin air."

"Ha! Maybe she is a witch and if we say hocus pocus, she will show up."

"Uh, let's not and say we did. We have ghosts, spirits, and a dead guy living in the back of the kitchen. I'm good."

"I was joking."

"I know." We walked to the patisserie. "I couldn't sleep last night. I woke up at 2:19 again. I've been awake searching the internet for any information about the previous owner, land, town, and history of Harrington. Nothing much comes up worth noting."

"Oh, geez, Rard, you need to sleep."

"Yes, I do, I feel like I'm running on fumes lately." I reached inside my messenger bag for my keys.

"Uh, Rard? Hocus pocus." Hana pointed to the patisserie's front door.

"Oh, boy!"

Annie was sitting in the shadows of the morning light against the front door. She saw us approaching and stood up before we arrived. Wiping her chef pants off, she greeted us with a whispered "Good morning."

"And good morning to you, Annie. Are you okay?" I put my key in the lock.

"Yeah, I'm fine. I just had an all-nighter. Danny is with his father for two days, so I went out with my old girlfriends, Nettie, and Marie."

Don't worry, my friends, I kept an eye on her. He lurks in the dark but he's afraid to strike, too many wanderers on the streets tonight. She's only been here for about an hour, and he's been there for less. I would've slammed him into the street if he'd tried to step over here.

"Nice, you had a chance to tie one on, as they say." We headed into the patisserie, locking the door behind us. I glanced across the street, and there I saw the cigarette smoker was back hiding in the dark shadows. The glow of the cigarette was all I could see. Was it a coincidence that this person in the dark would always smoke a cigarette when we came to work or am I getting paranoid that someone is watching or stalking us. Chilling, to say the least, as I could feel the chills running up my back.

"Yeah, you can say that. I wound up crashing at Nettie's and came straight here."

I backed away from the door and followed Hana and Annie into the kitchen.

"You're not afraid of being alone with JT out there?" Hana turned the ovens on.

"No, not at this time of day. Everyone's sleeping if you know what I mean."

"Should be sleeping," I muttered.

"What?"

"Nothing. I was just talking to myself." I didn't want to alert anyone of my paranoia of the cigarette smoker across the street. They're all starting to think I'm nuts anyway.

I set my laptop on the marble table and began to stream some rock 'n' roll from the classic rock station. Ovens on, all systems go. After filling the proofer with croissants, we started scooping muffins.

Hana informed me. "We're running low on oatmeal muffins. We'll have to make more today."

"Okay, I'll put it on the production list. Would you like some morning brew?"

"Absolutely."

"Me, too," Annie replied. "In fact, just pour some milk in the whole pot and give me a straw."

Hana and I both chuckled.

I went to the front of the store, got a fresh pot of morning brew going, and headed back into the kitchen.

I may have to do something if he comes in here. Let's see if I can remove a knife. My God, the magnet strip is stronger than I thought. I may need to work on this. Oops!

But just as I passed through the swinging door and approached my table, a paring knife came flying off the magnetic strip and slid across the length of my marble table, falling to the floor on the other side.

"Whoa! Hana, did you see that?" I was so shocked that I almost tripped, pointing at the knife, "That knife just slid across the table!"

But Hana had also seen it, and before I got the words out, she yelled, "I saw it s-sl-sl-slide behind your laptop before it hit the floor!"

Annie turned around in a hangover daze. "What happened?"

I walked around the center table and stood next to Hana, kind of afraid to get too close to my table and laptop. Annie crept up behind me. We stood still, looking at the magnetic wall with the knives and spatulas all in a row with my wooden-handle paring knife missing.

Hana whispered, "I saw it! I… I saw it fall off the wall and slide across."

"I did, too." I took a deep breath and sighed. "Now what?"

"You're asking me?" Hana slowly scooped the batter out.

"I didn't see a thing." Annie whispered.

It made me angry, and I slowly walked over to the space between my marble table and the dough sheeter, picked up the knife off the floor, and said aloud, in my most commanding voice yet, "Hey! Spatulas are okay but no knives! You got it, ghosts? What the hell are you doing here? What do you want from us, or do you want to help us?"

Silence. No grunts, no banging noises from the back, no voices in my ear.

Damn it! That was sloppy. Sorry, everyone, my fault. I was only trying to be on guard in case JT tried to come in here.

The front door sounded, and Kate came in, startling us. "Morninnnng!"

I turned around, "Really? Watch yourself, they are throwing knives this morning."

Hana filled her in on what had just happened. We all gathered by my table. I took the paring knife and demonstrated its flight from the magnetic strip, across the marble table surface, and down to the floor. Hana supplied the color commentary.

Kate shuddered, "You two just gave me the chills." She hurried herself toward the sinks to wash her hands, when surprisingly a spoon flew out of the utensil caddy and crashed to the floor.

Kate screamed out, "Ahhhh! Oh, my God! That spoon just jumped out and flew at me."

No, no, no, Grace, leave the utensils alone. They don't need our help at the moment. I already freaked them out with the knife.

But I want to protect them, too. If we all grab something and throw it at the monster, then maybe he'll leave and won't come back.

Clever idea but I think we have to practice when the chefs aren't around. Oh boy, we really scared them this time.

I looked at Annie as we jumped and turned around at the same time. "Oh, no, what was that?" I hurried over to the sink next to Kate and noticed along with her that the metal utensil caddy was swinging wildly from side to side.

"What in the world? Look at this!"

Hana came running over, and the four of us stood there, dumbfounded, and silent, just watching the caddy swinging back and forth. There were a few utensils still in the caddy, a mini-spatula, and a plastic scraper.

Kate shook her head, "I'm ready to go home. This is creeping me out."

I looked down at the spoon on the floor.

"This is too much for me. I just got here." Kate continued, "I need a cup of coffee and then maybe I'll go home," and with that, she headed off to the front of the store to pour a cup of morning brew.

"Wow. Do you think this ghost really wants to help out?" Hana was trying to find a reason for what had just happened.

"Maybe it is that dead guy, Andy, or maybe it's someone else. Maybe your grandfather or maybe the ghost wants to chop us up and throw us in the ovens."

Kate interjected, "Stop it, Gerard, and you, too, ghost! But whoever it is, they're scaring the crap out of me." She was trying to hold her cup steady enough with both hands to take a sip.

The thought was in my mind that this incident seemed a bit more serious. "Kerriann said they can't hurt us, but I'm not too sure about that anymore." *Perhaps I should not have said that.*

If a ghost was able to pull a knife off a magnetic wall, then they are just short of dragging us around the kitchen. Why did they do that? And where did they go? Why not stay? Is Andy or Hana's grandfather behind this? "I need a cup of coffee too."

I went out front to pour a cup and almost lost it. *Why is this happening to us?* My hand was shaking as I poured in some half-and-half. "There has to be some sort of answer for all this."

"You okay out there? Who you talking to?" I could see Kate standing in the doorway.

"I'm okay, just a bit shaken up."

"I see that."

I whispered, "Where's Annie?"

"She just went to the bathroom."

"Hear me out. This ghost person thing or things, I feel, is trying to communicate with us or trying to help us. Does that sound about right?"

"Yeah." Kate didn't sound convinced, and I could see Hana's twisted face maybe thinking, *Gerard is nuts trying to rationalize this.*

"But if we start adding all the things up that have happened in the past two weeks, it's as if they're playing with the utensils just like we do, wanting to help in the kitchen."

The children do want to have fun in the kitchen, that's for sure, Gracie just wants to help, and Charlotte can get underfoot. Sorry, but they can be persistent. They wish Hana would make peanut butter chocolate chip cookies, they smell incredible while baking and are quite delicious from what I remember.

"And you think this is, okay?"

"No, Kate, it's not okay. None of this is okay. It is just something I've been noticing, and I'm sure you all have, too. Besides, I'm trying to get past my idea that Annie is involved in it somehow."

"Why would Annie be involved with ghosts?" Hana asked, shaping the Cantucci biscotti dough into logs.

"Shh, keep your voice down. I don't know. It doesn't make sense, but my sixth sense is telling me she is."

I walked back to my station while Kate went in the walk-in, Annie exited the bathroom and Hana was putting trays full of cinnamon Cantucci biscotti in the oven. This recipe was handed down from my grandmother. It was sturdy, dense, and full of flavor.

For whatever reason—I guess I thought Hana had finished putting the biscotti into the oven—I glanced over at her station to ask her a question.

Immediately I was horrified to see a shadowy black figure leaning on her table, facing toward the oven. It looked like one of those depictions of the Grim Reaper, only the figure had no scythe. I did a frightened double take, but in the space of a split second, the black figure was gone. I, however, was frightened out of my wits.

"What the hell was that?" I blurted.

Jeepers creepers, Shadow man is back. No, no, not here, please not here. The last time I saw him was the day before Franco died. I need your help, Mattie. Mattie, help me, we have to push him away. Grace and Charlotte stay back. Arrghhh!

Hana glared at me, "What the hell is what?"

I think Hana was beginning to question my sanity at this point. I tried to explain.

"It looked like an outline in black of a distorted person leaning sideways on one arm on your table, facing the ovens." Now it was my turn to have the shakes; I could not believe how rattled I was. I was trembling. I was seeing things. "It was a weird black figure of a person of some kind. Like a shadow-looking person, a hunchback maybe."

"Uh-oh, that's no good. Shadow people, no, please say no," Kate had a tray of eggs in her hands. "Make it go away, Gerard."

"I wish I could," I sighed. "But I did see what I saw. Why did I see that? What is happening with me?"

Kate narrowed her eyes to me. "Shadow people are evil. Don't even think of it. This is one crazy morning."

"You know, it just seems lately like more and more things are happening to me, or I should say, us. But I, I know what I just saw and I'm not imagining it."

They stared at me, no doubt thinking I was crazy or on the verge of losing my mind. Kerriann must've been right—I was sensitive to the spirits. They knew who I was. Did I have a connection… or was I somehow the connection between their spirit world and the real world? I wasn't quite sure where this whole experience would take me, but it seemed to be getting way out of control.

Even though music was playing, the four of us were quiet. I hated a quiet kitchen, and Hana asked if there had been any orb activity last night, so I played back some of the videotape. But as I viewed the tape, I saw this strange stick light thing materialize out of the wall, fly across the kitchen, and disappear out of the camera's sight.

"Whoa! Check this out."

We all gathered around. I played it back and a few gasps were heard. "What the hell is this now?"

As the video played, the stick light materialized again, coming right out of the center table in a swirling motion before dashing off toward the back of the bakery.

"Ah, hello. Who are you?"

"Really, Rard?" Kate looked on. "Okay, I think we need to breathe for a minute."

"Yeah, I don't like the look of that either." Hana was slowly shaking her head. "Don't look at it. Shut it off!"

The stick light orb thing zoomed all over the kitchen, appearing out of nowhere and then disappearing back into nowhere, just as the one on the first video had done.

It passed through the tables, refrigerators, and ovens, and it passed directly in front of the camera time after time. For over an hour, it zipped around the kitchen. I had the distinct feeling, whoever this was, he or she knew the camera was filming and decided to put on a show.

I felt like a true ghost hunter. Whatever it was, it clearly wanted us to see it.

Of course, we want you to see it! We're trying to get your attention and it seems like Mattie's bright soul has finally done it. She loves ballet and she loves to dance. You need to listen to us. Kerriann is right, we're trying to talk to you, and I am so tired of repeating myself like a broken record, but I'm running out of freaking ideas.

By the way, you can thank your lucky stars we were here when Shadow man showed up, otherwise, we would've had another death around here and we'd never forgive ourselves. Someone is on the short list, and you can thank me later for saving your life. It's not often I get to do that, but I'm happy to do so. And in my opinion, dude, you owe me one.

Mattie teased and tricked him into following her and sent him off with the lost souls as they came combing the earth. She is quite powerful as she flew between the souls like a ballet dancer in a war zone, while Shadow man became entangled. I stayed low and watched as he was tackled and absorbed into a massive orb. His cries were muffled by the wind. Even the dead die again.

No rest for the weary as I'm learning a powerful ghost is better than a resting one. So, I guess we won't be seeing him around here anymore and everyone gets to live another day.

Now, if you'll all excuse me, I do need to rest.

CHAPTER 26

I CALLED KERRIANN LATER that day to tell her about my new findings. She'd never heard of such a thing, but then she and Joe had never seen a massive orb before either.

"This is something new and noteworthy. I feel like this place is turning into a vortex and the gates of the netherworld are opening up," I stammered.

"Gerard," she spoke calmly, "Talk to it and see what it wants."

"No way, I can't do that. That is your job, I'm not a medium."

"True, but it appears that it's you they want to talk to. They know you're sensitive to seeing and feeling their presence as spirits. They're connecting with you, or they're trying to. I'd try to talk to them. Maybe they'll answer back. It's worth a try."

Kerriann's gentle expression changed, her voice hardening. "Did you tell them to go away? Tell them they're not welcome here?"

"I did, yes."

"Keep doing so. Maybe they'll get the hint and leave."

"Should I threaten them with a rolling pin?"

Kerriann laughed.

I laughed a bit as well, visualizing myself performing a magic wand act with a rolling pin in hand.

"Well, you'll be happy to know I did some homework and found out that from the late 1800s to the 1950s, there were row houses where your bakery now stands. I'm not sure what went on in those homes, but maybe if you go to Town Hall, they can give you an idea of who lived there. Maybe Andy or the woman who calls your name owned the land or was murdered there."

"Row houses?" I shook it off. "I don't have time for this investigative work. It's a process."

"Maybe in a few weeks I'll have more time and we can go to Town Hall together and go through the archives."

"Okay, sounds good. The pastry competition will be over, too."

"Perfect, but really, Gerard, when you feel them near you or when an incident occurs, try envisioning everything in white. White light is angelic and heavenly. It protects us. Try wrapping the spirit or ghost in white for protection, pink for love, green for hope, and send them to the light."

This whole ghost thing was about to go to the next level. "Can't I just come to work and bake?"

"You don't sound convinced. Try it, it might help."

I told Kerriann we would give it another try. But the fact was, there had been a dead guy chilling in the back of the building since the 1980s. If there were other spirits hanging around, perhaps they'd lived in the row houses she mentioned. And who knows? Maybe there was a shallow grave under my feet. At this point, I held out little hope any of her advice would work.

I hung up the phone and called Phil for Ben, the handyman's phone number. Maybe he was my lead in finding out what and who had been here before us. Phil warned me that Ben probably wouldn't pick up the phone and it might take him a while to return my call. He's set in his ways so to speak. So, I left a message in hopes of setting up a date for a chat about the history of the land. Perhaps his wife could shed some light on the murder of the guy in the back from the 1980s.

CHAPTER 27

THERE SEEMED TO BE a pattern emerging with these ghostly disturbances. I noted they mainly happened in the wee hours of the morning when we first arrived and stopped sometime during the day. Maybe they needed to rest after scaring us. I know I needed rest after they scared me. Besides trying to manage my kitchen, I was now on the watch for any paranormal activity.

I had to make a test run baking the gavajunes. Laurent rolled out the brisée dough and cut five-inch circles from the one-eighth-of-an-inch sheet of dough. Annie prepped my mother's gavajune recipe with a warning to follow the recipe exactly.

She gave me the eye. "Seriously?"

I smiled back. "Now you know how anal I can be."

Annie laughed at my stress-induced micromanaging.

"Hey, Hana, would you like to work with me next Monday at the Prestigious Honoré Award competition?"

"I'd love to, but I can't, it's the only day I can get my car in for an inspection, sorry, but I'll still be there in spirit for the award ceremony." Hana smiled from ear to ear.

"No problem." I smiled back. "It's okay."

"I'll help you!" Annie spoke up. "That's if you'll want me to?"

"Of course, that would be great."

"Thank you. I'd love to work at the event and meet some of the other top chefs. And besides, I could use the extra money." Annie gave me the eye again. "I'll get paid for this, won't I?"

I laughed. "Of course, you will. I'll pay you in gavajunes, all you can eat."

Annie and Hana laughed.

I left the kitchen to make myself an espresso.

"What are those pink and white swirly things in the cookie case?" I heard a customer ask.

Raquel was busy making the customer a cappuccino, and the noise level was a little high with the frother. So, her question was projected a bit loudly.

I pointed to them, "Those are peppermint meringues."

"Oh, I love," she cheered, so I offered her one.

"Wow, these are so good and not too sweet, incredibly good. Can I have a pound? I'm going to a party tonight and they'll be perfect."

"Sure, we can do that. That's a lot of meringue, you realize. They're noticeably light in weight."

"The more the happier. There'll be a lot of kids there. Are you the owner?"

"Yes, I'm Gerard."

"The owner of the haunted bakery! I saw the article in a local blog. Is this place really haunted?"

"At times, yes. Other times it's just a delicious pastry shop."

"That's funny." She smiled. "I'm Diana. Nice to meet you."

"Nice to meet you as well."

Raquel started to fill a box with the meringues. "It's nice to finally know your name," Raquel joined in. "We refer to you as the pretty cappuccino lady who sits at the table by the window working at her computer."

"Oh, that's so cute. It's a great spot." Diana gave me a bright smile. "So nice and calming. No one to bother me and I get a lot of work done."

I thought to myself, *she should've been here when the guy stabbed his own hand with a fork.*

Raquel handed me the meringues. "I'm happy we made it work for you. Here are your meringues." I realized the box was big enough to fit an eight-inch cake for ten people.

"Oh, my gosh, you're not kidding. That's really a lot of meringue." She laughed, as if a little embarrassed at the size.

Then unexpectedly, she asked, "Have you ever thought about consulting a medium? For the ghosts or spirits, I mean. Or whatever you want to call them."

I was intrigued, with tilted head and raised eyebrows (or so I imagine), I replied, "We had one spiritual investigation, but it didn't convince me on what's going on around here and I'd have no idea who to call. Why, do you think it'll help?" I needed help.

"I don't know about helping," she leaned on the counter as if to whisper me a secret, "but it might give you some answers. There's a medium in the next town over who is supposed to be particularly good. Her name is Ciara."

"Really? I'm not too sure..."

"I'm going to see her in a few days. I'll let you know how it goes."

"Why? Do you have ghosts, too?"

"Not that I know of, but I thought I'd check it out and see who is on the other side. You never know. Maybe an old uncle left me some money and it's buried in my yard under the birdbath." Diana gave a laugh.

"Ha, which would be great, a buried treasure. Maybe he hid a map under a floorboard," I joked. "Here's my card, I'm always here, so please do let me know how it goes. Have fun tonight and it was a pleasure meeting you."

"Yes, it was nice to finally meet you, too, and that flourless chocolate cake is to die for. I had it last week at a party."

"Thank you, but don't say die. There seem to be a few dead people around here already."

Diana laughed. "Oh, dear!"

Peppermint Meringues

4oz.	Egg whites
250 grams	Sugar
	Pink or Red food coloring a drop
	at a time for a bright pink color.
1 Tbs	Organic peppermint extract

Preheat conventional oven to 200 degrees, high fan, or convection oven to 200 degrees.

Set up a heat-proof mixing bowl for a five-quart stand-up mixer over a double boiler with the egg whites and sugar. Whisk the meringue mixture slowly and constantly over the double boiler until it reaches a temperature of 160 degrees. This may take ten minutes or so.

Once the temperature is reached, carefully remove the bowl with oven mitts. Set the bowl into the mixing unit and use the whisk attachment on high speed.

Let it whip for about ten minutes or until the bowl has cooled down. The whites should look glossy and hold a stiff peak. Add the peppermint extract and whisk again for two minutes.

Remove the meringue from the mixer and place half of the mixture in another bowl. Add the pink food coloring a drop at a time and whisk gently to reach your desired color. Light pink is best so as not to make the meringue too watery from the added food coloring.

I like to use an 846-star tip for the best results. Insert the tip into your pastry bag. Scoop a little bit of plain meringue and place it to the side of the opened bag. While holding it open, scoop some pink meringue and place it on the other side of the bag. Close the bag, pushing the meringue toward the tip.

Start piping rosettes onto a parchment-sheet-lined tray. After the second rosette, you should see the pink and white swirls piping with ease. Refill the bag the same way and continue.

Place the trays in the oven for at least one hour.

The meringues should be hard on the outside and slightly soft on the inside.

Makes approximately four dozen. Store in an airtight container for four weeks.

Enjoy!

CHAPTER 28

I WENT BACK INTO the kitchen with an espresso in hand, eager to share the discussion I had with Diana. "The customer who was just here told me about a medium who might be able to help us."

"Well, what are you waiting for? Let's go." Kate chuckled.

"Soon, I hope."

Hana was in the midst of battling with a spatula constantly flying off the pot's handle at the stove. It was her third try.

"I think my grandpa is playing with the spatula."

We stepped back from the pot again looking at the handle. It stayed balanced as it usually did, or the way normal spatulas did, and it didn't move.

"Thank you, Grandpa!"

Thump! Thump!

Hana shrieked as Kate grabbed my arm, just shy of digging her nails in. We glanced toward the back of the kitchen where the noise came from.

I whispered, "They heard us. I don't think they're happy with us for yelling at them."

I'm not happy either and it bothers me to no end that you'll listen to Hana's grandfather, Kaito, playing with a spoon but not to me when it comes to life and death situations. There seems to be no way I can get through to you people. Wait. What? Oh no, not you guys again.

We all looked a bit wild-eyed and crazy. Maybe we were, but we didn't like what was happening.

"I'm not happy with them scaring me, either." Kate waved as she walked into the refrigerator.

I walked back to my worktable to help Laurent when Kate came running out of the walk-in refrigerator with a tray of eggs in her hands, screaming out, "Someone just whistled at me when I was getting the eggs."

She practically threw the eggs on the table. One rolled off and Hana reached over the table to stop it.

"What are you talking about?"

"You know the catcall whistle construction guys use on girls as they pass?"

"Yes?"

"That's the one." Kate huffed.

"Maybe it's the fan and it needs some of that instant grease stuff," Annie suggested.

"No, no, no, I know what I heard." Panic set in as her face turned red. "I have to go back for some butter. Wish me luck."

"Do you want me to go with you?" I offered my assistance but was hoping she would say no.

"No, I'm okay, I got this." Kate returned to the walk-in, "Hey, don't you whistle at me, damn it."

The door closed behind her.

Hey, you guys, leave the lady chefs alone. We don't want any trouble around here.

A second later, she busted through the door. "Okay, I'm not going back in there. I'm too scared."

"Sounds like someone likes you," Laurent joked.

"You're hilarious Laurent. Now, you can go back in there for the milk and for whatever else I need today. Okay?"

"Sure. I'm not scared."

"Well, I am!" Kate's face turned an angry red.

"Okay, okay, no worries." Laurent smiled reassuringly at Kate.

Those damn rum runners, the two of them, always showing up to taunt me, too. I have to show them who's boss every now and then, otherwise, they'll wreak havoc around here. Dude, I've seen them in action when Franco was here, it was the first time I met them. He nearly shot his sandwich maker, Javier, with the gun he kept in the kitchen drawer. Javier nearly lost his lunch when he saw the rack move by itself and the oven doors open. He claimed the place was haunted but Franco reassured him it was defective, but on this day, Franco was in quite the mood; he drank too much the night before and came to work with a terrible hangover. The rum runners, Giuseppe, and Richard showed up and antagonized the hell out of him.

I was a bit frightened myself, so I went to the back of the kitchen and watched. I couldn't believe my eyes. They were relentless, provoking Franco to no end. I'm not sure of their history with him, but they pushed him, smacked him, and pulled his cap off and flung it across the room. They even tossed flour in his face. Javier stayed perfectly still in place with eyes and mouth wide open with mozzarella cheese in hand, watching the hat hit the oven doors.

Franco screamed, "Leave me alone, you two. I'm in no mood for your antics."

But they didn't. Giuseppe flung the pizza peel, nearly hitting Javier in the head as it slammed Franco in the gut. Javier had quick reflexes and ducked out of the way, screaming profanities for all to hear. He stood up in time to hear Franco cry out in pain.

"That's it, I've had it with you two." He reached into the kitchen drawer and pulled out his gun.

That was when I realized he could see us. He could actually see ghosts.

He waved the gun around and spotted Richard hiding behind Javier. Javier ducked down below the prep table as soon as he saw Franco point the gun at him.

"I see you, Richard, now it's time for you to die again." He fired two shots.

One bullet ricochet off the mixing machine to the stove and right back at Franco with one hitting him in the thigh. He screamed plenty of obscenities along with Javier. Franco dropped the gun, collapsing to the floor, while Javier ran for the door. "You're a crazy son of a bitch!"

Giuseppe and Richard disappeared faster than the bullet.

So yeah, they're relentless in their hauntings, a cat whistle is nothing, Kate. Good move for speaking back.

Way too much had happened in this one day for me to understand. But there was more.

Vincent pushed open the swinging door. "Hey, G?"

"Hey, Vin, what's the matter?"

"You remember that crazy guy who was in here last week?"

"Yeah?" I looked over at Annie, who stared back and forth between Vincent and me.

"He was just here."

Annie rushed to my side.

Oh, no. "Yeah and…?"

"Nothing. He bought a croissant and left. No questions or problems. His hand was all bandaged up though."

Annie and I both felt relieved "Okay. Make sure you call me next time he shows up. I don't want him hanging around here. Make sure everyone knows it."

"All right, sounds good." Vin let the door close and went back to work.

Annie had that nervous look on her face again as I tried to comfort her with words. "No one will hurt you. He is apparently insane and not welcome here. I'll make sure of it. I promise."

"Thank you. I'm sorry to trouble you with my drama."

"No trouble. It's this ghost thing that is bothering me."

As midafternoon approached without any further incidents, I thought, *I really need to stay focused on the competition.* I didn't want to say it out loud, but with all the paranormal activity in the café, I was quite surprised no more staff members had picked up and walked out.

Given all the latest press coverage about fine pastries and ghosts, we were remarkably busy. With Nora and Julie gone, I needed more help, so I had brought on a new hire. "Hey, everyone, this is Aly."

Aly was greeted with hellos and smiles all around.

"Steve will show you what to do. The chefs are leaving, so you'll have plenty of space to fill the orders he is setting up for you."

"And we are out." Kate patted my shoulder goodbye as all the chefs made their way out of the kitchen.

Hey Gracie, I'm going to walk Annie to her car. You're in charge, so keep an eye out for trouble, yell for me right away if anything happens. I'll be right back.

Hana wished her well. "Good luck, Aly. See you tomorrow!"

"Thank you. See you tomorrow!" Aly swiveled around to meet Steve with boxes in hand.

"Okay, Aly, first things first, go wash your hands and put some service gloves on."

"Yes, sir."

"Then when you come back, Gerard will have you pack this order of tarts for tomorrow morning. Super easy. Put the tart in the paper cup and then into the big box. Simple."

"Got it. Sounds easy enough."

"Perfect. I must help some customers." Steve gave me the nod, sort of the opposite of giving someone the eye.

Aly returned from the hand sink with a smile. "Okay, let's do this." She looked around the empty kitchen. "Am I the only one working?"

"Uh, yes, for now. Jase and Jon are running late with their summer-school sports, which means you'll have to put the garbage out by four."

"Oh, yay. Fun first day."

I laughed as well. As glamorous as pastries were, there was always an ugly and mundane side such as taking out the garbage. I had no intention of telling her about the hallway yet.

I sat on a stool by my marble table with my back to Aly, finishing some paperwork. She was quite the chatterer, telling me stories and asking if I knew so-and-so and such and such. I tried to concentrate on reading my electric bill…until…

"So, is this place really haunted?"

I cringed. The realization was a bit frightening. I spent fourteen hours a day trying to establish this business, and all I was starting to hear from customers was this.

"Yes, I believe something ghostly is going on."

"The whole town is talking about it!" Aly exclaimed.

"So why did you come here for a job?"

"Oh, I'm not scared or anything. I'm a bit nervous, but as long as nothing happens to me, I'm okay."

Aly wiped her hands, palm upon palm, and walked to the other table for her water bottle. As she turned with the water bottle in hand, she saw it happen right in front of her own eyes and froze.

"Did…did, did you just see that?"

I turned around on the stool. "See what?"

"That! That paper cup went from here to the edge of the table and curved around it without falling off. Oh, my God!"

"Wait, what happened?"

Panic set in as she raised a shaking hand to her mouth. "I just saw that paper cup move, and it was like, it, it followed me. Is this a joke or are you playing with me?"

"I'm over here. I'm not playing with you. Maybe you're playing with me, or the so-called ghost is."

"I-I-I don't think I can do this."

"I'm sorry, but you're freaking out over a paper cup that may have moved. Maybe the wind from you walking away did it, or are you playing with me and making this up?"

"I'm not playing." Aly stammered. "The cup moved about two feet this way and another foot that way."

I stood there with my arms folded and thought, *Here goes all the media hoopla around town talking about everyone seeing ghosts now.* I wasn't sure if Aly was looking for attention, lying, or, it really did happen, but it scared the crap out of her.

"This place is really haunted. I, I can't!" Aly was shaking a bit and never took her eyes off the cup, blindly grabbing her hoodie out of the closet. "I can't do this! I'm scared. I have to go."

And go she did. Right out the door.

I did not say a word.

Steve came through the swinging door. "What happened?"

"I'm not quite sure but I think the ghost was playing with her."

"The ghost?"

"Yep."

"This has got to stop."

"Eeeee-yep!"

CHAPTER 29

"YES, MAY I HELP you?" Steve's voice rose over all the conversations that were happening at once in the café.

"Yes," said the man in the suit. "I'm looking for a birthday cake for my daughter's birthday today, but I see you don't have any."

"I beg your pardon, sir, but these are all our cakes. We write happy birthday on a plaque of dried fondant and put it on the cake."

"Oh, but they look so fancy, not birthday-ish at all."

"Well, we tried to put candles in the cakes and keep them lit for questioning customers like you, but they keep going out in the refrigerator case here for some reason."

"Oh, I see. Wait, what?"

Steve laughed. "I'm sorry, question time is over. I have a cake in the oven. This young lady would love to help you. Thank you. Raquel, he's all yours."

"Yes, sir, which cake would you like?" Raquel stepped up to the counter, and I stepped back from the doorframe.

"You are too funny, Steve."

"I know. I love to leave the customer speechless."

We both had a good laugh.

"Where are those boys? Garbage has to be put out."

"They said they would be here by four, but it's four fifteen now."

"C'mon, let's take the garbage out ourselves." Steve was egging me on. "It's not too busy right now. Raquel and Deanna have the front covered."

"I'm not going through that hallway." I stood my ground.

"We'll go together. It'll take five minutes. I've been in there quite a few times, and nothing has happened to me or our employees."

I bit my lip with hesitation. "Only if you stay by me."

"Yeah, sure."

I let out a huge sigh and took a deep breath, trying to shake off my nerves. "Okay, let's go," I committed. I wasn't scared in my kitchen. I felt safe and I needed to get over my own fear. It was just a hallway. Speaking in public was my biggest fear and I had overcome that. *Damn, why did I agree to this? There go those nervous butterflies again. Ugh!*

"Hello? Are you listening to me?"

"Sorry, I zoned out."

"Stop being afraid. It's just a hallway and I'm right here with you."

"My protector." I batted my eyelashes and laughed.

"And your dishwasher and floor mopper if those damn kids don't show up soon."

Steve pushed the metal door open. The rusty spring-loaded hinges cried out. *CREEEAK!*

Steve put the rock in place to hold the door open. Where the eight-pound rock of a boulder came from, I'll never know. Smooth all around, it probably came from someone's front yard as a marker for a driveway. It's been in the hallway since we first saw the vacant space. It does its job of holding the door open, that's for sure.

"Ready?"

"As I'll ever be."

"Bags first, then the boxes."

We picked up two bags each and entered the hallway. Steve led the way, passing under the slightly swaying light bulb. I wondered if it swayed all the time. The gentle movement was so hypnotic. As I entered, I had a good look at the name *Andy* scrawled on the wall. It looked like it'd been etched with a box cutter or a nail. *I hope no one died where I am standing.*

To the right was the alcove entrance to Mr. Clayton's art studio. The wooden door was a solid brown with multiple splashes of paint around the doorknob. Streaks of yellow, green, and red ran down the door as if someone needed to rid their hands of paint. Empty paint containers and brushes stacked themselves on the floor, waiting for their turn to come back to life on a new canvas. Two blank pieces of paper were tacked to the door at almost knee height, with an open can of what looked to be red paint to the side of the door with small paintbrushes on top of the can.

"You with me?"

"Uh, yeah, I'm with you. Just enjoying the sights." I had a double take at the paint cans. *Wait a minute. The red paint is used on the paintings by the children. What are they doing in the hallway?* I passed under the single bulb and looked up at the dim light.

"Not so bad, right?"

"Not yet."

I could see the curved wall ahead of Steve as he entered the darker part of the hallway.

"We're almost there… a few more feet."

As far as I was concerned, I felt like we had traveled five feet too far. I looked over my shoulder to see the lit kitchen behind me, the stone propping the door open. *Okay, good,* I thought.

Rounding the curved wall, we were plunged into darkness, the dim swinging bulb, along with the kitchen light fading away. I gulped. In the darkness, I wasn't able to see anything, not even Steve, who was six feet away.

"Why doesn't the landlord fix the lighting in here?" I asked Steve.

"I don't know, maybe he doesn't know about it."

"So, we walk in darkness with garbage bags in our hands. I'll call him tomorrow. This is ridiculous."

"He's not here. He went on vacation, remember?"

"Oh, yeah, that's right. He's kind of odd in a way."

"Yeah, I totally agree. Something is off."

Steve pushed on the security door ahead of me, letting a slit of light through, which made all the difference. I immediately felt better as he pushed the heavy door open, flooding the hallway with afternoon light. I breathed a sigh of relief as I stepped out into the light of a scorching summer day.

The alley ahead of us looked shorter than the hallway, but the debris scattered about was interesting. There was an old wooden ladder on its side, at least ten feet long, a few clay flowerpots, empty, but one overflowing with cigarette butts from the neighboring restaurant. The kitchen door was held open by a rope tied around the doorknob, stretched to a rusted nail on the wall. Latin music poured out at a higher volume than a normal kitchen would allow. Two corroded rolling racks and a mop bucket guarded the gate to the street.

Steve put his bags down to push open the locked gate. "You, okay?"

"Yeah, I think so, much better than I thought I would be. No anxiety attacks yet if that's what you're wondering."

"Good. See? It's not so bad. I'm not sure what you're so afraid of, other than spiders, snakes, and now ghosts." He poked me in my side, making me jump and laugh.

"Did you notice the red paint and blank canvases on the small easels by Mr. Clayton's door?"

"No. Was I supposed to?"

"Well, yes, they are at knee height, with brushes and open paint cans. You know the paintings by *the children*."

"No, I didn't notice. Show me when we pass it again."

"Okay." We plopped the garbage bags down on the curb.

"Are you okay with this competition event on Monday?"

"Yeah, I think so. I'm just looking to get our name out there. Winning, would be the icing on the cake."

"You're going to blow them away with the carrot cake and those gava-junes. No one makes anything like that. No one."

I smiled. "I hope not."

I glanced at the alley we had just come from and the neighboring building. Something made me look up at the building, which is a local bar, the narrow building squeezed onto a postage-stamp-sized lot. I could see a staircase through the French doors leading to the second floor, carpeted with a red rug that looked like it had seen better days. Never really knew there was an upstairs, the place was so small. Something about it gave me an eerie chill.

"Come on, break is over." Steve put his hand on my shoulder to push me along.

Back through the alleyway we walked. Through the maze of debris, I peeked into the restaurant's open door. "Hola!" I waved to the pot washer, and he nodded back.

Steve pulled open the large heavy metal door, allowing us back in. I watched the sunlight disappear as he closed it, smothering us in complete darkness.

WHAM! The door closed tight.

"Why did you close the door? We have to head back out."

"I don't know, just a force of habit of closing doors. All right, let's go get the boxes."

Steve led the way as I followed close around the curved wall, catching a glimmer of light coming from the kitchen. I sighed some relief as the kitchen door stayed open with the rock holding the door firmly in place.

Raquel popped her head into the doorway as we were halfway through. "I've been looking for you guys. I need some help out front."

"Okay, I'm coming," Steve replied.

Raquel was looking around the hallway as we approached. "This hallway really is creepy looking. Yikes."

"Shhh, you'll scare Gerard." Steve winked at her.

"I'm fine. Go help the customers. I'll be here waiting for you to come back to do the boxes."

"You sure?"

"Yeah, I'm fine. I want to check out all these paint supplies. You think Mr. Ernie Clayton would mind?"

"Why would he mind? He is such a nice guy. Maybe he put them there because he doesn't have the heart to throw them away."

"See the easel and red paint?"

"Yeah. That is weird, I don't think it was here yesterday. Why would he leave them set up like that?"

"I don't know."

"Just leave them. I'll be right back. Come on, Raquel, let us go and serve the multitudes."

As they walked away, I pulled out a few palettes tucked between the cans and the shelves. The first one I pulled out was small, made for a child. I couldn't get a finger in the thumbhole. Then again, my sausage fingers were too big for many things. "How adorable is this." I ran my fingers over the beautiful red, blue, green, yellow, and white merging into a pool of abstract art. Sort of like when we start to make carrot cake with white flour as the base and we add the spices in heaps, separate from each other, cinnamon, nutmeg, clove, salt, ginger, and sugar. All separated in the bowl as an artist's palette is ready to become a piece of art or a delicious cake.

CREEEAK!

That sound! I knew that sound. I looked toward the door, which was about fifteen feet away, with the rock in place. Crouched down like a catcher waiting for the pitch, I was about to put the palette back when I heard it again.

Now, Gracie and Charlotte push the rock away. Hurry, before he sees it.

CRRRREEEEAK!

"Huh?" Scared, I froze in place. I felt if I moved, I'd be caught sneaking around. Artist's palette clutched in my hand; I watched the Rock of Gibraltar stone move as the door let out its warning cry... *CRAAACK.* It scraped along the concrete floor an inch and I gasped. The rock was wobbling against the concrete floor, scraping the ground, and moving my way. Mesmerized, I watched it move. Gripping the palette in my left hand and a painter's brush in my right hand, I cried out as if the painter's model had moved to the left and destroyed my profile view. *How could this be happening?*

"Nooooo!"

The rock moved away from the door, freeing it from the doorstopper that it was.

Now, slam the door closed. I have my hand on his shoulder.

The door started to close faster than normal.

It was too late to do anything. Away it went, slamming into the door-frame with a deafening crash that shook me within and without.

"Oh, my God! Oh, my God! Noooooo!" I broke free, dropping the palette and the brush. Reality set in as I ran to the door to try and catch it. No luck, a little too late, as I banged on the door, groping for the handle.

"Where's the handle?" Right side, left side, in the middle, nothing.

"Hey!" I screamed out. "Steve, open this damn door!" I took a deep breath. "Nice joke, now open this damn door!" I kicked it a few times with my leather clogs. I stopped, stood still, my own harsh breathing the only sound as I listened for someone on the other side. I kicked the door repeatedly as I banged it with my right fist, screaming out for someone to open the damn door.

My heart was racing as the fear was setting in, trembling as I turned around. "Oh, my God, this can't be happening to me. Damn it!"

I yelled one more time at the top of my lungs. "HEELLP! OPEN THIS DAMN DOOR!"

Silence.

I felt my pockets for my cell phone and knew it was on the charger in the kitchen.

The single swaying bulb in front of Mr. Ernie Clayton's art store was my only light, pitch-darkness lying ahead.

Slowly I raised my head to look up at the bulb as the hallway suddenly began to fill up with light. A sigh of relief escaped me as I saw the curved wall ahead. It became too bright, and I could hear a humming sound getting louder and louder, like a mixer starting low and pushing the lever higher and higher. It was almost deafening. I looked up again and saw the brightest bulb ever.

"Oh, God, this is not good!"

Blinding white light filled the hallway. I covered my eyes with my left arm just in time as the bulb exploded, shattering glass everywhere. I felt something hit me as I stood still in silence.

A piece of glass hit the floor as I lowered my arm.

"STEVE, OPEN THIS DAMN DOOR!"

Darkness settled all around me.

No answer. I kicked it again and again. "Damn it!"

Tap, tap, on my shoulder. I felt something and I swung my arm around so fast into thin air. No one was there, I was breathing heavily, blinded by the light, feeling terrified. *This cannot be happening.*

Stay calm, I thought. I put my hands out and found the art studio alcove. Kicking a few cans aside, I banged on the door. "Ernie! Hello? Anybody here?" No answer. I knew there would be no one there but I had to try.

Gerrraaaaarrrrd!

A voice called my name. Tingling sensation up and down my spine. A man's voice this time, right in my left ear. It was so close I nervously shifted to my right, knocking empty paint cans off the shelves in a thunderous crash. I fell halfway to the floor, crying out, "Damn it!"

As I regained my balance, I heard a piece of wood snap below my feet. Probably one of the painter's palettes or easels. *I have to get out of here.* The musty hallway was becoming quite pungent with dampness and the smell of mold—not good for my asthma, or anxiety.

My right leg felt wet along my thigh and shin, like I had dipped one leg in a swimming pool. I patted my leg and what seemed to be water turned out to be paint. God only knew what colors they were. Probably red.

With my heart in my throat, I took baby steps into the hallway, away from the alcove, kicking a few cans out of the way. Right hand along the wall, left hand out front, I closed my eyes. I couldn't see anything anyway, but with my eyes closed, I could envision the hallway better… and I'd rather have them closed just in case I came across something I didn't want to see.

Ring around the Rosie, a pocket full of posies, ashes, ashes…

I heard the old nursery rhyme and a few giggles from what sounded like young schoolchildren. The singing ended abruptly as I heard something like a whisper that was not clear. I continued my shuffle. Someone or something was there with me, a ghost or spirit. Then I felt it, the cold wave of pressure passing through me. I walked right into it. "Oh, God, oh, God, please make it go away. Please, leave me alone. Please, I'll never come in this hallway again."

Aaaaaannnnnnnn.

Something was whispered inaudibly in my ear by what I believe is the ghost. I shook as something pushed me from behind. I swung, flailing out with my left arm as I was pushed again into the wall.

"Get away from me!" I screamed, frightened out of my mind. I opened my eyes, and there was nothing, nothing to see and nothing to feel.

Help!

"Go away," I swung my left arm around while feeling the wall with my right hand. *I am almost there. I am almost there. I have to be.*

Annie!

"Oh, God, make it stop. Please stop it. Let me out of here!" Then I thought of something Kerriann had said, and I yelled, "I don't know who you are or what you want from me. I want you to leave us alone. Go to the light! Go to the light!" All I wanted was to see daylight again.

Help. Listen to meeeeeeee.

I heard whomever this ghost was, pleading with me. "I can't help you. How can I help you? Go to the light!"

Nnnnnnooooooooooo!

He heard me. What the hell? I had to be close to the exit.

You are in danger.

"Leave me alone!

I took a deep breath trying to ignore what I'd just heard and then, bang, I hit the door, walked right into it, almost smashing my face. I pushed on the lever aggressively. The crack of sunlight coming through was so calming as I opened the door all the way. "Thank you! Thank you!"

I held the door open and turned around to look in the hallway. Nobody was there to be seen. You can't see the unseen. Slowly I let the door close with a huge sigh. I tried to calm down as I leaned my back on the door. My hands and pants were doused in red paint. Looking through the alleyway, I could hear people talking, car horns blowing, and birds chirping. One bird landed on the old wooden ladder and began chirping. It looked like a wren or sparrow of some kind, flapping its little wings, crying out for something. I locked in on it and it hopped right toward me.

I scared myself into thinking the bird was crying out to me like the ghost had. Was that even possible?"

The restaurant side door flung open, and the bird took off.

I followed his takeoff. "Got scared, little guy? I know how you feel!"

"Hey, *mi amigo?*"

Startled, I waved to the pot washer guy from the restaurant, who was dragging on a cigarette as if he were sucking on a straw.

"*Que pasa?* You have a problem painting the walls, or painting your clothes?"

I smiled and laughed. "*Si, muchas problemas!*"

I had my chance. How frustrating is this? I save up my energy and for what? This guy won't open up to me at all. Stubborn as hell, too. I don't know what else to do, I'm done.

CHAPTER 30

THE NEXT MORNING, I wanted to sleep in, so I messaged my staff that I would not be able to open up. I really needed the rest, even if it was for another fifteen minutes. I was still shaken up and disturbed from trying to escape the hallway. Something was happening in a more freakish way than I could ever explain and someone from the other side had tried to communicate with me.

Steve thought I was crazy and told me to ignore it, but I could not. I couldn't even sleep. This ghost, invisible man, spirit, Andy…whatever you want to call it, was reaching through for help. I needed to find out who this guy was, but not by being locked in a hallway. Maybe Ernie Clayton knew who he was. I should've asked him when we spoke, but he was so concerned about *the children* I didn't want to sidetrack him.

I found it weird how he called the kids coming into the class *students* and the ones that painted the drawings, *children*. He had said, "They are called children." And the paint setup in the hallway, paper at knee height on easels, open paint cans, and brushes… Were the ghosts' children?

I sat at my kitchen table with my laptop and wrote everything down that could be a clue as to what or why we were being haunted. I searched for any information I could think of. I typed in murder, ghost, Harrington, 1980s, bowling alley, the neighboring addresses, fire, children, painters, and Andy.

Nothing came up worth looking at. *I need to go to the Town Hall.* One thing I did note from searching was that Harrington and neighboring town Cold Springs used to be whaling towns. Walt Whitman, the famous poet, was also from Harrington. Indian burial grounds were here, too. There were quite a few tribes before the first European settlers.

Wow, this town goes way back, I thought. When we moved here from the city, we had no idea of the history of Harrington or Long Island, for that matter. The town offered the small, quaint village appeal, plenty of restaurants, shops, and New York City is only thirty minutes away.

Nothing about ghosts, and any murders that came up were random. Nothing that I could pinpoint to my problems.

The ghost said, *Help me Andy, please, no,* and *Gerard. If I knew who Andy was, maybe I could help. Or maybe I can search for the right answers.*

I gave up and headed for the shower.

CHAPTER 31

I SHOWED UP TO work at six-thirty a.m., only to have Kate and Hana tell me about how Kate had been whistled at in the walk-in refrigerator again.

"It was loud and clear, right in my right ear. I said to Hana, 'You go in there.'" Kate pointed at Hana, and she said, 'No, I'm scared.' So, I went back in and spoke firmly, 'Don't you whistle at me, you ghost!' And of course, the door slammed behind me, freaking me out." Kate took a breather, as if she were reliving the event again.

"Are you okay? You're turning beet red."

"No, I'm not okay. Damn thing grunted at me! I'm not going back there again. That scared the hell out of me. I'm still shaking."

I bowed slightly, "Well, you do look awfully pretty this morning, Miss Kate."

"Oh, stop it." She was in my face. "No makeup and my hair tied up under my hat. Yeah, I look real pretty, just play back the video. Maybe something is on there."

I thought to myself, *Maybe the ghost is trying to get Kate's attention now, since I ignored him or them?*

I played back the video recording. Although of course the kitchen was dark, the audio quality was usually rather good. Initially, we could hear the faint sounds of Kate and Hana opening the front door. First, the distinctly metallic sound of the front door key sliding into the lock, followed immediately by the sound of the lock turning and the door opening, then the alarm being turned off. Normal.

Hana and Kate could be heard chatting, even if their exact words were hard to make out.

And then there was a loud sigh, perfectly audible.

Kate grabbed my shoulder and froze. We all looked at each other. "What was that? Was that you?" I asked them.

"How could it be us?" Kate shot right back. "We were in the front of the store. That sounds like it came from right here in this kitchen."

And it did. It was a loud sigh—like the person or spirit or whatever was standing directly in front of the camera. Sort of like it was saying, "Great, here they come. Got to go. Playtime is over." It was creepy to say the least, and it was the first time we caught an actual voice or sound recording.

Kate was right. On the one hand, there simply hadn't been enough time for either of them to get into the kitchen to have made such a sound so close to the camera. And besides, we reasoned, we would hear the kitchen door opening before we heard the sighing sound.

The video continued to run as they entered the kitchen and put the lights on, and then I fast-forwarded to the part where Kate came running out of the fridge, but we couldn't hear any whistles or grunts. Of course, that might easily be due to the thick, insulated walls of the fridge, the ovens, and the exhaust fan whirling—and the door slamming shut.

"I guess whoever whistled was disturbed by the two of you coming in to work today. Lucky me getting to sleep in an extra hour," I spoke sarcastically with a big, evil grin across my face.

Hold on chefs, where's Annie? How come she didn't show up yet? I was just waiting for her in the parking lot. Oh no, it's Giuseppe and Richard, what are you two doing here?

My two chefs were not grinning. In fact, nobody was grinning after I told my tale of getting locked in the hallway.

"Uh, so, how long are we going to keep doing this?" Kate finished rotating the croissants in the oven, folded her arms across her chest, and faced me.

"Doing what?"

"Getting scared out of our minds every day is what I mean. These things are happening more often and disturbingly."

BOOM, BOOM!

What did I tell you two? Stay out of here, beat it. This is my place.

Oh, tough guy, Eddie, shooting off his mouth again.

Go haunt someone else Richard.

We were just having fun with the ladies.

Yeah, what's it to you, little Eddie?

We stopped what we were doing and looked to the back of the kitchen as a thunderous banging noise came from the back-door area—well, at least it sounded like it did.

"See?"

"Sounds like you woke the beast, Kate."

No time for fun, Giuseppe, just leave the chefs alone.

Sounds like Eddie, here is looking for a rum runner's rumble, Richard.

He's nothing but a piss ant. There's two of us to one of you. Let's get him and knock his head off, it'll take him a while to find it. I'll show him who's boss around here.

You two idiots need to back off and take a chill pill. I'm stronger now and they have power, too.

Them? The living ones? Not a chance. They're weak like you, Eddie, pushovers, and unfocused.

Sounds like we need to reclaim our turf, Richard. You know, Eddie, we were here, some fifty years before you, trapped and weak too.

Awe, what's a matter Eddie, you look like you're going to cry. Why are you backing away big boy Eddie? It's time to rumble.

Get him!

BOOM, BOOM!

Again, the banging noises in the wall, but this time they were closer by the sink area.

"Do something, Gerard." Kate threw her hands in the air as she stepped away from the oven.

"What do you want me to do, for God's sake?" I had reached for a whisk to mix the lemon curd that was on the double boiler. I could feel the tension mounting.

"Do what Kerriann said to do," Hana egged me on.

They both looked scared and nervous, putting all their hope into me.

The banging was right in front of us, coming from the oven area in the overhead hood, so loud and in direct range.

I extended my right arm with the whisk as my magic wand, twirling it as if I were going to pull a rabbit out of a hat, and shouted out amongst the noises in the kitchen, "I wrap you in white for protection, red for love."

"Pink! Pink!" Kate yelled out to correct me.

"Uh, yeah, white for protection, pink for love, green for hope, and send you to the light!"

And at that moment, whatever was in the kitchen with us took off and flew up the exhaust fan in the overhead hood with such a whirlwind it sounded like a bushel of leaves from an autumn harvest being pushed through a fan, where the fan struggled for a moment and then whirled up on a faster speed, spewing whatever went through it to the other side.

"Oh, my God!" Kate cried out. "You did it!"

"That was crazy." Hana rushed over.

I stood in the same spot for what felt like an eternity, staring at the whisk in my hand. *Did I really just do that? Make the ghost or whatever leave?*

"You're a freaking magician, Gerard."

"Ha! I really don't know what just happened here."

"You got rid of the ghost." Kate came over and hugged me. Hana joined in as we felt overwhelmed from a whirlwind morning.

"Are you two, okay?" I looked from Hana to Kate and back to Hana.

"Yes!

"Yes, we're fine." Kate wiped away a tear.

"Oh, don't cry." I put my arm around her shoulder.

"I cry at everything."

"Stop, Kate, or I'll cry, too." Hana took her glasses off to dab her eyes with a paper towel.

Just then, the kitchen door flew open as Jada and Annie came in to work.

"What's going on?" Jada gave a weird look as she hung up her hoodie.

Kate could not wait and blurted out, "Gerard got rid of the ghost."

"Good, maybe now we can work in peace." Jada clapped her hands. "I'm getting tired of this ghost stuff anyway."

"Amen to that!" Annie smiled.

We all let out a small chuckle.

"I made an appointment with Kerriann and Ben the historian for next Thursday at the library, and I'm going to go to Town Hall today to see if I could find out any information on this property."

"Like what?" Hana asked.

"I don't know, maybe see what buildings were here before us or who lived here. Anything at this point would be good."

"Oh, cool. Doing some detective work on the side." Hana nudged me. "Can I join you? I love historical stuff."

"Sure. We can take a ride over later."

I really wanted to go alone for the purpose of looking into Mr. Clayton from next door and to see if there were any records of children who died here. I didn't want my chefs to think I'd become morbid thinking dead ghost children were involved in this, too.

"I just want to say one more thing. I have a lot invested in this place, and it's proving to be one of, if not, the best pastry shop around. I have an incredible partner to help me make it happen, and most importantly, I have an incredibly talented group of chefs right here in front of me who can create the most delicious cakes and pastries Long Islanders have ever seen and tasted."

I paused as my staff caught me becoming emotional.

"We had a medium here who claims someone died back there in the hallway, and for whatever reason, this ghostly person is reaching out to us for help. I don't know why, and I'm sorry, Mr. Andy the ghost, if that's your name, but we can't help you." I spoke loudly enough for people on the street to hear me. "So please go to the light, rest in peace, and leave us alone!"

Kate fisted the air. "Give me another amen to that."

Jada chuckled and the tension in the room broke.

The telephone rang behind me, startling me as I looked at the time. It was 7:01 a.m., and the morning staff was not here yet. "Good morning, Fiorello Patisserie, may I help you?"

"Yes, may I speak with Gerard? It's Diana."

"Hi, Diana."

"Oh, hi. I'm rushing to get the kids up and ready for school, but I wanted to tell you I made an appointment for you with Ciara for Sunday evening. I hope you don't mind, but it's all she has available, and I told her how desperate you are to find out who is haunting the bakery."

"Oh, wow, okay then. That sounds doable. Thank you. I'll look forward to it."

She hung up before I could say goodbye. My staff was looking at me for some news I could share.

"That was Diana. She made an appointment for me to see the medium, Ciara, Sunday night."

Hana stopped what she was doing and peered at me over her glasses. "This is crazy. I hope she has some answers."

"I hope so, too, because it's Sunday night and Monday is the pastry competition."

Kate cut me off and blurted out, "Maybe she could come here instead?"

"She doesn't even know me."

"She's a medium, maybe she does."

"Well, if she's a medium, then she knows how I'm feeling right now and how disturbing I find this whole thing. Maybe she can just call me and tell me to turn the oven up to five hundred degrees, put the exhaust fan on high with the oven door cracked open, and play the song 'Spirits Busting Through the Night' and hopefully the ghosts will get sucked into the oven as we run around the kitchen sprinkling holy water."

We all had a good chuckle.

Rick, Lucas, and Jase interrupted us by coming through the kitchen door.

"What, did you guys' all carpool or something?"

Lucas smiled and looked around the kitchen. "Why was everyone laughing?"

"Oh, just another day at Fiorello, Lucas, just another day."

"Oh, cool, I thought maybe it was a good joke."

"No jokes, only customers coming through the front door. Let's go, guys."

"We got it, G," Rick reassured me as they went behind the counter to help the first few customers of the day.

I had a few minutes before setting up for a normal workday. Well, whatever was normal lately was not normal. Or maybe it was the new normal? And sticking with that, I played back some of the notification videos from last night. The usual orbs passing through after closing time, which was the norm these days, but what caught my eye was this stick light-looking thing again.

But this one came right out of the center table in a swirly tornado fashion and danced around the kitchen. It was zigging and zagging, as if it were putting on a show for us.

"It knows we can see it."

"What are you talking about?" Annie looked over my shoulder.

"This stick light orb thing. It's putting on a show for us."

The chefs gathered around as I played the video clip over again, watching it rise in a circular motion right out of the center table.

"Amazing, simply amazing." Kate looked in awe and then jabbed me in my side. "Is this the thing that whistled at me? Is that what you think?"

"I do not know what to think. I really don't."

"That looks like a piece of paper flying around," Jase butted in as he passed with a basket of almond croissants for the display cases.

"How is that a piece of paper spiraling right out of the table?"

"I don't know." Jase spoke with a tremble; I could hear it in his voice as it cracked.

"Jase, I wish it were as simple as a piece of paper but think about it and I'll try to be rational about it. Paper does not materialize out of a table and fly around a room for twenty-four minutes, swaying, zigging, and zagging around a closed-door kitchen with no air blowing around from different vents of forced air keeping it afloat."

"Yeah, well, it looks like paper, and I don't believe in ghosts, so it's a piece of paper, period."

"Okay then." I looked at Jase as he took the tray of almond croissants to the front. Jase turned away to finish his task at hand as I looked to Hana and Kate.

They both shrugged their shoulders.

"I guess it's easier to not believe in ghosts than try to rationalize it for whatever it's worth or to believe in something you're frightened of." Annie excused herself as she weighed in on the topic.

"Do you believe in ghosts, Annie?"

"No, not really. I find all of this interesting, but it doesn't affect me."

"Really? I thought you did."

"Nothing can hurt you if you don't believe in it."

"Huh? I never thought of it that way."

"Yes, well, you believe in God, fulfilling life's goals, creating a successful business, fi nding the right someone, acing a test, jumping over hurdles, and all things good. Say it, manifest it, and believe in it. I choose to stay positive, but life ever after and ghosts, eh, not too sure about it and not for me."

Kate shook it off . "Well, I believe and I'm not giving in to this nonsense. I'll bet you Ciara will tell you what it's all about on Sunday."

I watched the video one more time and thought to myself, *I hope so, too.*

See, I told you two fools they have power. Woo hoo! That was slam-ming! Now who's bugging out? Stay away from here or I'll have them kick your ass again! Damn, I almost lost all hope but I think we are start-ing to make some ground. My faith is starting to build back up again.

CHAPTER 32

HANA AND I TOOK a quick ride to the Town Hall that, to me, felt like chasing a dead end with nothing worth finding. Just a gut feeling.

"May I help you?" said the grizzly security officer who looked like he had lived a long life.

"Yes, we're looking for the office of records."

"What kind of records? Albums? Forty-fives?"

He caught me off guard and started laughing, the harsh, ragged laugh of someone who smoked too many cigarettes for far too many years.

"Quite funny, sir, but we left the turntable at home."

"Oh, that's a good one, too." The guard laughed again with a bit of a jiggle.

Hana whispered, "Everyone's a comedian."

"Yep. Everyone wants to do stand-up for whatever reason."

"I beg your pardon?"

"Oh, I'm sorry. Don't worry, we're in a bit of a hurry."

"Yes, yes, indeed. Everyone who comes here is in a hurry. The office is down the right corridor. It is the third room on the right. Just ask for Gail."

"Thank you, sir."

"Have a good day and don't forget about the B-side. Always something good to listen to."

"Ha," I laughed to humor the gentleman. "Will do."

I escorted Hana down the corridor.

"Well, here it is, Hall of Records." As soon as we entered the room, which resembled a small library, we were at once greeted by the clerk in charge, a studious and knowledgeable-looking middle-aged woman. Her head was down in an index file with a pile of folders on the left and a pile of ledgers on the right, and without lifting her head, "How may I help you two?"

"Hi, are you Gail?"

"Yes, I am." Gail looked up and pointed to her name tag. "What are you looking for? Information on some land, taxes, real estate, public information, or someone you may know? You name it, I'll help you find it."

Gail finally looked at us with a wide, friendly smile.

"We're looking for some information on what was once located on Main Street before my pastry shop was built."

"Pastry shop? There's a pastry shop on Main Street?"

"Yes, where Franco's Pizzeria used to be."

"Oh, I know where you are. Haven't been there yet. Is it good?"

Hana chimed in, "Not only good, but probably the best pastries on Long Island."

"Wow, that sounds promising. What are you, the taste tester?"

"I'm Hana, Gerard's chef. I should know." Hana nodded towards me and extended her hand for a handshake as Gail walked around her counter.

"Nice to meet you, Hana, and you must be Gerard, then?"

"Yes, nice to meet you, Gail." I shook her hand.

"What's the name of your bakery?"

"Fiorello Patisserie."

"And you didn't even bring me a cookie?" Gail folded her arms across her chest and pouted for a moment before smiling. "I'm only joking. I could spare a day or two without a cookie." Now tapping her belly. "So how can I help?"

"Well, I'd like to know some background information on what businesses occupied my space and if anyone with the name Andy was involved."

"Hmm, ok, uh." Gail took off for the far wall, where all the ledgers involving Main Street were located. "Andy who? Or is it, Andrew? Or was Andrew his last name?"

Hana and I both looked at each other at a loss. "I haven't a clue."

"I need some more information if I'm going to help you."

"I think this guy, Andy, was murdered inside or outside of where the patisserie is now located. He's haunting the bakery."

Gail froze in her tracks and stared at me with wide eyes. No one said a word. It was one of those epic moments when someone drops a bomb.

Gail busted out laughing, loud and clear. "That's the funniest thing I've heard all day. Oh, my gosh."

We, on the other hand, did not laugh, and when Gail settled down, I flat out spoke, "Yes, the patisserie is haunted."

"Oh, dear, you aren't joking, are you? So, you want me to help you find a ghost?"

"Yes, something like that, or help us figure this mystery out."

Gail shook her head. "I'm not a ghost hunter, but you can look through these ledgers and try to find the information you need. Don't think you'll have enough time to do so today, but you can come back Monday with some chocolate chip cookies, and I'll help you." Gail smiled cheerfully.

"Why, thank you, but I can't come back Monday. Perhaps Tuesday?"

"I can hold my appetite for cookies till then."

Hana and I both laughed. "Okay, we have a date. In the meantime, may we look through some of these?"

"Absolutely. I must finish up a few things. If you need anything, I'll be right over there."

"Wait one moment. Don't you have all this on a computer? It would be quicker."

"Yes and no. We did not convert all the town records, so many files and only me to do so. I can search a person and most tax info if it is after 1990. Anything before that would have to be manually searched through the ledgers starting from here. This section is when Harrington first settled in April of 1653. Follow the wall to the 1700s and so on."

"Ugh."

Hana looked around the room. "We'll be here all day, maybe three, and we only have twenty minutes until closing."

"I had the feeling this would be useless. What about the 1980s?"

"They are over here."

I whispered to Hana, "Joe said something about the dead guy having been murdered in the early 1980s."

"You're right," Hana agreed. "We should at least look up something while we're here."

"Right over here in this section," Gail pointed. "Nineteen eighty is here on the left top shelf and has five ledgers flowing right into 1981 and so on."

"May we have a look?"

"Yes, of course."

Gail reached up and pulled down the first of many. "You had said something about what was on Main Street in your space? Correct?"

"Yes."

"That should be toward the middle of the ledger." Gail looked at her watch. "I really have to start closing."

"Please, go do what has to be done. We're sorry to bother you."

"No bother, I'll be over there if you need me."

I quickly opened the ledger, and I did find Mr. Clayton's art studio but nothing about the space next door, where my shop is located, or what had once been Franco's Pizzeria.

"Maybe the space was vacant at the time," Hana suggested.

"Maybe we better go and come back next week. I feel stressed just knowing we have fifteen minutes to find a needle in a haystack."

"Yeah, we're not going to find anything right now."

I put the ledger back and we thanked Gail for her time.

"Come back Tuesday, okay?" Gail escorted us to the door.

"Yes, it's a date, have a nice weekend, Gail, and thank you again."

"You two do the same."

We walked down the corridor and passed the security desk, where the guard was entertaining himself laughing with another citizen looking for help.

And of course, I'm fashionably late to the party, but better late than never is what I always say. Let's see, hmm, here it is.

Gail slung her purse over her shoulder and grabbed her keys, ready to close up for the day when she heard the noise behind her. *FA-WUMP* She knew what the sound was because she had heard it several times before but only when someone dropped a ledger. It startled her nonetheless, because nobody else was in the room and she most definitely did not drop a ledger on the carpeted floor, making that *fa-wump* sound that she was so familiar with.

She slowly turned around and surveyed the ledgers. She spotted the empty space on the shelf almost at once.

"Dear God, how did that happen?"

After laying her keys and purse back on her desk, she walked over to the bookshelf with the missing ledger.

Gail gasped to not only find the ledger on the floor but also to find the ledger opened to the police reports from September 1982.

"Oh, dear, this is odd." She wondered if this was what the bakers were looking for, but how did the ledger fall to the floor?

Gail surveyed the room again. "Hello, is someone here?" She looked at file after file, ledger after ledger, and book after book, but there was not a sound, and there was no reply. She quickly turned around. *Where did that chill come from?*

It came from me, Gail. I'm right next to you. Show them this next Tuesday so they can find their answer here.

After searching unsuccessfully for a possible straggler, she closed the ledger and put it back on the shelf. Giving the Hall of Records one more glance around, she gathered her things, shut the lights, and locked the door behind her.

CHAPTER 33

I WAS THE FIRST one to arrive at the patisserie before five a.m. I loaded the proofer with all the breakfast items for the day. I went back into the walk-in to get the muffin batters. Two by two, I brought them out and placed them on my table. I happened to glance at the monitor that showed the front of the store, and much to my surprise, I saw that stick orb moving toward the front door.

This was live, not from a recording. It was happening as I stared at the monitor. The only thing separating this stick light orb and I was the wall separating the kitchen from the café area.

I reached over gingerly and lowered the volume on the radio, "Hey, good morning. Where're you going?"

It heard me!

The orb stopped short of going through the glass door and made a U-turn instead, heading back toward the kitchen.

"Oh God!"

I don't know what compelled me, but for some reason, despite this new phenomenon, I backed away from the monitor briefly, as if it was just too surreal, looked to the kitchen door as if it were going to open, and went back to the walk-in to get two more muffin buckets. As I stood in the walk-in alone with the fan blowing frigid air around me, I felt my heart in my throat as my nerves kicked in.

I took two more muffin buckets, pushed open the door, surveyed the kitchen, and placed them on the table next to the others. I stared at the monitor screen: the stick orb was gone. I glanced toward the front of the store, and there was nothing to be seen. I calmed down a bit, thinking it was gone. I really didn't want a close encounter of the third kind, or any other kind, for that matter. I have had enough *encounters* lately.

Then I felt that pressure of something in front of me. It screamed at me!

Hi Gerard, it's me, Mattie.

It was like a whale's cry, so loud the sound was ear piercing. It literally blew me back, like a full-body flinch. It was horrific in every sense, and I simply cringed with fear. Somehow it was a roar and a scream at the same time. It was a sound unlike anything I had ever heard before. I backed away from the table right into the proof box. It was more like a backward stagger, and I instinctively raised my hands as if to push back. I felt like it was right on top of me and right in front of me, hovering close. It was… there, but where? I could not see it. What the heck was it?

"Whoa!" I exclaimed as I stepped back again, regaining my balance. Was it trying to talk to me? It's one thing to watch a video of an orb but to have an encounter with one was frightening to say the least.

Trying to make sense of this—and compose myself at the same time—I uttered, "Hey! Uh, good morning." I kept my hands out in front of me. "Who, who are you? Andy? What are you?" I never trembled like this before.

There was no answer. Not another sound. I backed away again from where I stood to the other side of the center table, toward my marble table, picking up a rolling pin on the way.

I held it like a baseball bat, ready to have a dueling match with the stick light orb, if that was what it was. The silence seemed to last forever. I had attempted to communicate directly with a spirit or foreign being, and it had tried to talk back to me. Or so it appeared.

Now, I spoke with a nervous tremble in my voice, "I have to get back to work, okay?" I motioned outward with the rolling pin, as if trying gently to bunt it away, backing up a little more as I did so into the corner of my dough-sheeter. I felt as though it was right there in front of my face. And it probably was.

Oh no, I scared you. I'm so sorry. I just wanted to say hello. Eddie went to walk Annie from her car. I better go, I'm so sorry. Please forgive me.

My heartbeat was pulsing, and my mind was racing, or was it the other way around? I was too delirious to tell. I stepped to the side and started for the walk-in refrigerator to get the last of the muffin batters. But then I looked over my shoulder at the monitor and saw that darned stick orb pass over the counters and beeline for the front door once again. Only this time it left. I could finally exhale, and I dropped the rolling pin on the center table.

"What the hell was that?" I asked the empty kitchen, and when it didn't answer, I answered my own question. "I just had a spirit encounter with a ghost or whatever."

I hung my head low and sighed. *Dear God, please make that thing stay away from here.* I returned to the walk-in and gathered the rest of the batters, trembling with every footstep but kind of laughing nervously at the same time. *Was that real? What just happened? Am I crossing over that veil and reaching the spirit side? Or am I just so sensitive that they really are trying to communicate with me?*

I took the last bucket of banana muffin with me and courageously looked at the monitor. Nothing was there. As I was putting muffin cups in the baking trays, I heard the front door lock click open. It was 5:24 a.m. My gaze shot up to the monitor. Not again!

But luckily it was Kate and Hana arriving for work. I watched intently to see if the stick orb might be following them, but thankfully just human beings entered the store.

They greeted me with a bright and cheery, "Good morning!" in unison as they entered the kitchen.

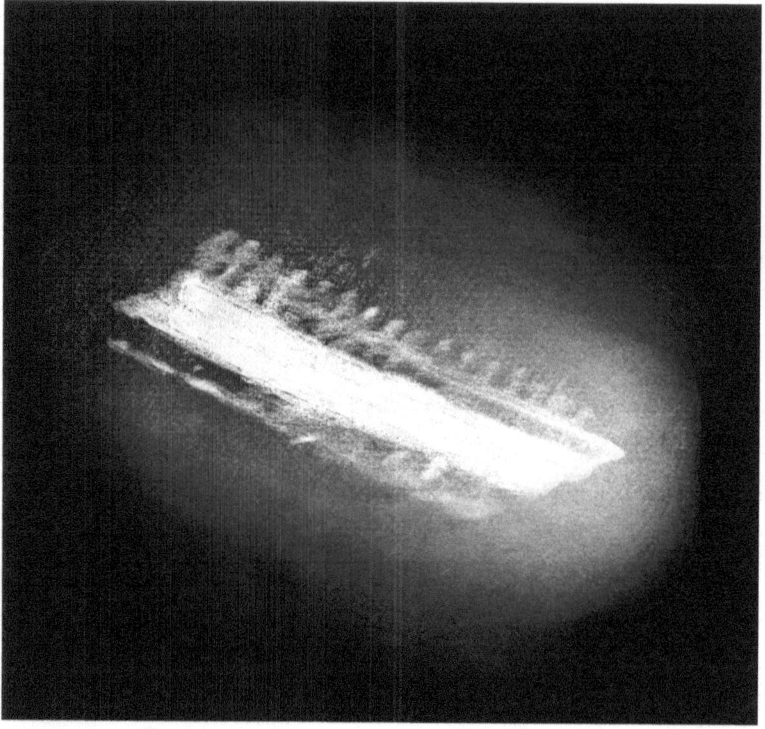

"Good morning, my ass!" I was so tense.

"You have no idea what just happened to me."

As I explained, they took turns glancing nervously at the monitor, either hoping to see the stick orb themselves—or maybe hoping *not* to see the stick orb themselves!

Hana was curious, "Who do you think it was?"

"I haven't a clue, but my money is on this ghost of ours, Andy, but I didn't see a name tag on it." I was still trembling.

Kate laughed. "A name tag. Ha! My name is Casper, what's yours?" Hana laughed, too.

I wasn't quite ready to give in to the humor. If they'd been here during my encounter, they would not be laughing.

Kate headed to the front to make coffee—some strong morning brew, I hoped. I kept one eye on the monitor just in case.

"Are you all set for Monday?" Hana asked, scooping the blueberry muffins.

"I'm good, but I'm not sure about Annie. She always seems preoccupied, like she is waiting for something to happen. This JT guy is really messing her up. I think she's afraid he might hurt her or her son."

"I feel the same way. It's like she's always in deep thought."

Kate pushed through the swinging doors with three fresh cups of morning brew. "Here we go. I heard you. I think something is up with Annie, too, and I know it's about that creepy JT guy. She told Jada she's afraid to leave her house. She comes to work and goes home, locks the door, and does not go anywhere. Her mom does all the grocery shopping."

"That's not good." I took a sip of coffee. There's way too much in my head to handle.

The front door opened, and I glanced at the monitor as Annie and Jada walked in. We all raised our eyebrows and changed the subject.

"Good morning." Jada walked in first.

"Morning, Jada. Hey, Annie."

Morning, Gerard. How is everyone?"

Good morning, everyone. Hello G-man!

"Just dandy, another day, another haunting."

"Oh?" Jada hung up her sweater.

Oh? Who was here my man?

"Yeah, Casper came by to say hello and Gerard lost his cool." Kate waved hocus-pocus fingers at me.

"Why don't you go in the walk-in for a while and wait for your whistler?" That wiped the smile off her face.

Those rum runners are back?

"You got me on that one. Touché. Now I'm not going in there." Kate grabbed a muffin scooper to help Hana instead. "I'm staying out here all day." She pointed to Hana, Jada, and Annie. "You three can deal with the walk-in thanks to boss man freaking me out."

"Ha! Nice, smooth move." I folded my arms on my chest and leaned onto Kate's shoulder. "I'd be happy to assist, Miss Kate. Not fun feeling this way, is it?"

"No, it's not. You better get some answers from the medium tomorrow night."

"I hope I do because Town Hall was useless. We only had like five minutes to do any research, so we may go back on Tuesday."

The medium reading is tomorrow? I better go with you. This may be my last chance to warn you. And by the way, I found the journal you were looking for. Gail knows, she will show you on Tuesday.

Annie pushed through the swinging doors for some coffee. We all looked at each other. Kate gestured for me to talk to her.

"Why me?"

"You're the boss."

"Yeah, and…? I have four female chefs here. Maybe it's a sensitive woman's issue."

"Oh, my God, are you kidding me?"

"No, I'm serious."

Just then, Annie returned with an apron, and we all focused on the deer caught in the headlights or should I say the elephant in the room.

"What's the matter?" Annie made eye contact with all of us and jumped to a conclusion. "Did I do something wrong? Did I screw up a recipe? Are you firing me? Oh, my God." Annie began to shake and cry at the same time. She had kept her troubles to herself lately, but sad and moody had become her norm. Something was bothering her, and now she was breaking down.

"No, no, no one is firing you." I looked at Kate. "See what you did?"

Kate smirked. "Annie, I'm sorry, but what's going on with you? You're so distant lately and it's showing." Kate turned to me. "Happy now?"

I shook my head, smirked back, and gave Annie a quick hug. "No one is firing you or wanting any drama."

"I really don't want to bother everyone with my personal issues." Annie sniffled back the quick tears and runny nose.

Kate blurted, "Hey, look, we all have issues, and at this time in the morning, we can share our lives with one another. Talk about the good and the bad. It's called coffee talk and we hash it out. Nothing wrong with it. It helps the soul. We can help each other, so spill it. It's better than crying behind a mask."

Silence fell but for the convection ovens behind us.

Annie opened up. "I'm embarrassed, as much as I don't want to be. I have a fantastic job, a great boss, and I love you guys for all you teach me. But... but..." The tears started again. "I can't keep living like this."

We all had the same questioning look on our faces.

Hana pushed forward. "Living like what?"

Annie had our full attention, and I was waiting for her to say she was going quit. Waiting for those two words that every executive chef hated to hear when business was going well. Those two words stressed me out because then I had to find someone else to fit in with the team.

"I live in fear every day. I wake up in the morning and check on Danny, I check on my mom, I check the doors, and then I get ready for work. I dress in the dark, afraid of putting any lights on. Afraid he might see me. I enter the garage with a baseball bat, just in case, as I get in my car and gun it out into the driveway. I'll mow him down and kill him, I don't care."

Trembling, Annie took a sip of coffee as Kate and I made eye contact. I watched her roll her eyes. I knew what Kate was thinking and knew Kate would've had this guy knocked out already.

"JT?" I asked.

"Yes, JT."

"Can't you get a restraining order?" Hana closed the muffin buckets.

"No, he hasn't done anything to me to issue one. The police called my encounter with him a 'mild threat.'" Annie made air quotes.

"Geez, a threat is a threat. What does one have to do to be protected these days?"

"I know, Hana, believe me. I'm living in fear from a crazy guy who just got out of jail for murder instead of feeling safe, like a normal citizen. He's in my head, and I'm freaked out that he's coming for me. Coming through that door when we least expect it."

"Don't think like that." Jada was rubbing her arms. "You're freaking me out, and I'm getting goose bumps all over my arms."

The front door opened. The chime went off like clockwork

We all jumped as Laurent and Antonio walked in the kitchen.

"Oh, my God, you guys scared the crap out of me,"

Hana joked, but I could tell she was scared regardless

Laurent now took rein of the jokes, "Why, is it Halloween already?"

We all laughed.

"Annie, the other day you said something to me about only being afraid of what scares you. Please don't let this JT guy scare you. You're not a believer in ghosts, but I am, and they try to scare me, but I won't let them know I'm afraid anymore. Although an hour ago it was another story. Don't ask. I don't want you to be afraid of this guy. He won't hurt you, nor will he try to scare you, knowing he can go to jail again."

"You don't know JT. He'll do what he wants. He has no morals, no fear. He thrives on terrorizing people, and he likes it when you are afraid of him. It gives him power and control."

"I wouldn't give in to such an asshole. I have the right to my own life. He has nothing on you or me. Fear no more, promise?"

Annie hesitated at first, "Okay, I promise I'll try. Now what happened this morning?"

"You don't want to know." I smiled and so did she. I had lit the firecracker chef up again, giving her some more hope.

And I will protect you as best as I can. I'm stronger here than I am outside of these four walls, building energy from the ground up, thanks to Mattie. If he comes in here one more time, I'll bash him into the wall and then out the door. He'll never come back, he'll run in fear because I'll terrorize him forever. You're safe here, I promise you that.

The rest of the day went well for a busy Saturday until Steve called me, midday.

"I can't come in. This cold came on like gangbusters, and I don't see an end to this misery."

"Oh great, you'll have to stay home, and I'll close the shop. Not a big deal."

"Sorry, Rard. I don't want to get anyone sick.

"Yeah, sure, not a problem. Make some tea and rest up."

"Already on it. Keep an eye on those kids up front. Make sure there are enough boxes and doilies separated."

"All right. I'll talk to you later."

"Bye."

I hung up the phone with a deep sigh of more to do. The kitchen was busy, and the front of the house was as well. I told Lucas and Raquel to stay on top of things up front while I continued working in the kitchen.

I overheard a customer asking Robert what had been made today and what was fresh. Robert replied politely, "Everything is made fresh on a daily basis."

"Yes, but what was made today?" the woman asked.

I heard her plea that left Robert confused on how to answer, so I stepped in. "Yes madam, as the young man said, everything is made fresh on a daily basis."

"But what was made today? Like a few minutes ago?" She was adamant about the pastries being made fresh. "In fact, can I try your cannoli cream? I want to see if it's worthy."

I could feel my blood pressure rising. *How dare she.* I tensed up at once. Robert backed away as he saw the expression on my face tighten. I was trying to think of something to say in a polite but sarcastic way, but the customer decided to add fuel to the fire.

"One more thing, sir, if I have a dinner party at seven, would you be able to make a tiramisu cake at six and I can pick it up at six forty? Can you do that or is that too much to ask?"

I was ready to boil over. My stress level had risen lately due to the ghost stuff and the competition on the horizon, but I took a few deep breaths before answering with a smile. "Madam, if you need to have everything made that fresh, then I suggest you go home and make it yourself."

I smiled from ear to ear as I watched her jaw fall to the floor. "Well, I never!" was all she could muster.

"Well, I never either, madam. Now, may this young man help you with our fresh selections of pastries?"

She did not say another word as she purchased a box of mini pastries, including cannoli. When she left, I was met with a roar of applause from the customers waiting in line.

I chuckled, relieved that the whole encounter had ended on a positive note.

CHAPTER 34

THE FOLLOWING MORNING, HANA and I unlocked the front door and walked in as usual, the alarm beginning its countdown beeps, also as usual. But we also heard the beginning strains of "Sunday Blues" by Old Chaos blasting at a shouting level. If you know the beginning of the song, it is kind of haunting. A synthesizer beat at its best. To our dismay, the music was coming from somewhere inside the shop, and it was deafening.

I shut off the alarm as we slowly, cautiously, approached the POS digital cash register sitting on the customer service counter. It was turned on and playing music on the loudest volume setting. But how? By the look of the on-screen display, it appeared as though someone had been trying to put in a pass code. All I could see were covered-up characters. Had someone tried to hack into the POS?

Now "Sunday Blues" was going into full swing. I didn't know what to do. I looked at Hana and she took a step back. "Oh, my God! Oh, my God!" was all she was able to say.

Cymbals clashed in crescendo. The vocalists were starting to sing, "*Ahhh ahhh ahhh.*"

I stared at the screen in the still-darkened room, "That song is in my private music library. How is it playing? Why is it playing?"

For a fleeting second, I thought maybe an intruder was hiding in the kitchen and trying to hack in. JT? Maybe he was lying in wait, ready to slaughter us one by one, but why? There was no money in the register. We never left money in it overnight anyway. The alarm had been set but obviously hadn't gone off during the night. The cameras were on. There was no sign of a break-in, at least not through the front door.

We stepped back from the register and started for the kitchen door. I went straight for it, but Hana arced in a wide turn as if to say, *I am getting as far away from that thing as the room will allow.*

I flipped on the lights and surveyed the kitchen. No one was there, and nothing appeared out of order. We walked through the kitchen to the swinging door and to the back of the register counter.

Old Chaos sang away: *"How come you treat me like you do? It's Sunday morning blues."*

I felt like I was back in a night club in 1986. Was this another clue? I had no clue what to do. I tried to swipe the screen to unlock it, but it did not work. I tried to clear the password out.

Delete, delete, delete.

Finally, to my great relief, that worked.

I fumbled for my phone to try and record the wackiness when I realized we had the cameras, although, this certainly gives you an idea of my confounded state of mind at that point. I tapped on the music icon, and I could see the song "Sunday Blues" in play mode.

I hit the pause button and it stopped. Hana did not leave my side. "What is happening? This is so crazy. How did it turn on?"

"I have no idea," I scratched my head. "I think I better play back the camera recording to see what happened." I supposed that I could have forgotten to turn off the POS, but that would have been highly unusual; turning it off at night was part of my routine. I tried to compose myself. I logged into the POS as usual and set up the cash drawer. I was disturbed, shaky, and on edge. I would've lit a cigarette, but I quit almost twenty years ago. So, I made a pot of coffee to calm my nerves. Yes, really.

We were still freaking out as I turned my laptop on. Hana began loading up the breakfast items in the proofer as I logged in to my security camera account.

"What do we do? Keep working?" Hana looked around the kitchen in hopes nothing else was going to scare us.

"I don't know what to say or do. I'm literally shaking."

"Me, too. I don't like this anymore."

"I don't either."

Rage took over. I was angry and anxious and frustrated, so I yelled at the top of my lungs, "Leave us alone already! What do you want from us, damn it?" I paused and listened. Nothing.

No answer, no stick light orb or banging in the walls. Nothing but the anxiety in my throat. "Get out of here!" I yelled with my scary voice.

BANG, BANG resounded from the back of the kitchen. Hana jumped and grabbed my arm.

"Leave us alone, damn it! Go haunt someone else!"

The light blinked over my table. Was that an acknowledgment?

It's no use, Mattie. We tried everything to get their attention, and nothing worked. I mean, we get their attention, but they don't want to listen. I don't know what else to do.

You're right, Eddie, don't get upset. I don't like you when you're mad; it's scary, even for me. I'll admit, they're good bakers but bad listeners. My mother would've scolded me for not listening to her. Maybe it was the song the children selected and if Mr. Clayton was here, we wouldn't have this problem. He would've listened to us and warned Gerard about JT and his no-good doings.

I know, I know. We have one last chance tonight. Will you be there?

Yes, we will all be there.

We better rest up; it's going to be a long night.

Calm came over me and I felt it was gone. Had yelling at it worked? We viewed the monitor and saw the stick light orb leaving through the front door.

"Oh, my God, there it goes." Hana pointed to the monitor. "What is that thing?"

"I don't know," I replied as I watched it float away.

"Is it an alien? Why is it bothering us?"

"Exactly! What does it want?"

"I don't know, but I'm really freaking out here."

"Me, too, Hana, me, too."

"I don't think I can do this anymore. I was speaking to the other chefs yesterday, and we agreed that if this doesn't stop, we're leaving."

My heart sank. "Hana, please hold tight. Maybe the medium will give me the answers we need."

"Gerard, it's been weeks, and it seems like they're closing in on us. How long before one of us gets physically hurt by this thing?"

"I don't want to believe they'll hurt anyone."

"I don't want to either, but it scares the crap out of you and me every day."

I was at a loss for words as I sighed.

I scrolled the video back to the point when Hana and I had entered the shop. Then I moved the cursor back another thirty seconds. That was it. All was quiet in the store. Hana and I watched with anticipation. And sure enough, the POS started up all by itself and then the music. It began playing a classical song, I couldn't put my finger on. But then, clearly visible in the video, the keypad display popped up on the screen. Hana and I both gasped.

Was I being hacked? The music changed abruptly, like someone flip-ping past stations on the radio. First a one-note blast too short to recognize the song, followed by the beginning of a disco song from the late seventies." Hana and I laughed for a brief second.

Then it quickly switched to "Sunday Blues." Our mood changed, as we next heard ourselves coming through the front door and saw our own reactions to the welcoming tune.

I leaned in closer to the laptop when, in a moment of sheer mind-bending shock, we clearly saw the cursor moving across the screen as if someone or something was trying to log into the POS.

Not only that, but in the video, as I reached across the counter for the display screen, the keyboard instantly dropped down out of sight.

"Wow, Hana!" I exclaimed. "Did you see that? It's as if they saw me reaching, 'Uh-oh, he's here. Better run.' And they dropped the screen down." We couldn't believe our eyes, so we reran the video.

"You're right," Hana leaned in. "It looks like someone is actually trying to log in for you." She took a step back. "This is too scary for me."

We watched this sequence about five times.

"I wonder if the code they were typing or the songs that were selected mean something?"

"Maybe a clue of who the ghost is?" Hana suggested.

Maybe it was a message for us. But I couldn't make it out, it was typed in so fast. So, I joked, "Yeah, the ghost is a disco queen from the late seventies who loves punk rock and classical music at night."

Hana let out a nervous laugh. "Thank God it's Sunday and it's just the two of us right now."

"After yesterday, I don't know if I can explain this."

We said nothing to each other for the rest of that morning as we tried to concentrate on baking breakfast. Occasionally, one or the other of us muttered, almost involuntarily, "I just can't believe it."

Vincent and Lucas came in at seven. We told them about our adventure earlier that morning and showed them the video. They couldn't believe it either.

All Lucas had to say was, "Damnn! This place is haunted!"

About fifteen minutes later, Vincent came running into the kitchen, shouting, "Freaking geez, the music is playing again!" Hana and I made eye contact, dropped what we were doing, and rushed to the front of the store.

It was the B-side to Sunday Blues, 'Monday is Not Far Away.'"

Children, that's enough. They aren't in tune with us. We scared them more than we thought, but I do like this song, Gracie. Nice choice.

Thank you, Eddie.

Come on, let's go, we have to rest up for tonight.

Okay.

"Geez, G! What the hell is going on?" Vincent threw his hands out.

"I'm starting to freak out."

Lucas examined the POS closely, saying finally, "This is weird, your music library isn't open, and this song is not even in rotation." Lucas sighed. "I'm with Vin, I'm starting to freak out too. You better call an exorcist or something."

Fortunately, there were no customers in the store at the time. I logged in to the music player and pressed Stop. "Maybe someone is trying to hack the system."

Hana whispered audibly, "Why is this happening again? Is this another clue?"

"Well tomorrow is Monday, but I just don't know anymore; I just don't know."

CHAPTER 35

FOR THE REST OF the day, I felt emotionally torn, pulled apart, especially with the hauntings. Although I tried to ignore it, it always stayed on the back burner, waiting to pop the lid off the kettle. My chefs were about to bail and all I wanted to do was reset and start over.

My main focus was the Prestigious Honoré Awards the following day and prepping the recipes that are needed. I made the GF dough, enough for six dozen cookies, and set the waffle iron next to the closet so I wouldn't forget the main attraction. There were no more distractions from ghosts, staff, or customers for the rest of the day, and I was able to work at my own pace, prepping the gavajune recipe and brisée dough.

I used the dough sheeter to my advantage and rolled it out thin enough so as not to tear when Annie and I filled them up in the morning at the event. They had to be made fresh; I didn't want the mixture oozing out before I put them in the oven by filling them now and having them sit overnight in the refrigerator.

Hana made the carrot cake and the six individuals beautifully, one for each judge and some extras just in case one broke.

As we finished up that afternoon, Hana gave me a hug for support. "Call me tomorrow and fill me in on the details."

"Okay, I definitely will."

"And good luck tonight."

"Thanks. I'm so nervous. I feel like I'm going to trial and this medium, Ciara, is the judge and jury."

"Don't feel like that. She's there to hopefully help you."

"Yeah, we shall see."

In an *hour and a half*, I would be sitting with a medium, talking about God knows what, maybe ghosts and dead people. I wasn't so into the plan, but I needed to find out what the hell was going on in the shop before any more of my staff quit, I had a heart attack, or someone got dragged down the hallway.

How I held it all together, I will never know. Steve had no idea how I remained calm through so many high-drama situations. Too bad he couldn't come with me. The summer cold he came down with had him coughing every five minutes.

I had to thank my dad for the calm genes, and personality, but I worried like my mother. I wasn't perfect, hence the reason for another gray hair.

All was quiet. The day was done.

Pushing through the kitchen doors, I checked that the cases were closed, counters cleaned, table and chairs in order. The cappuccino machine was still on. Those kids always forgot something. I made an espresso for myself, as if I needed more caffeine to calm my nerves. I never had an espresso in a ceramic cup; usually it was a paper cup and, in the kitchen, no glassware in the kitchen. God, forbid it broke, sending glass everywhere.

I ran the reports for the day and set the empty cup and saucer on my marble table. I walked to the back hallway door to make sure it was locked, not afraid anymore for whatever reason. I think I'd been scared enough to know someone was trying to communicate with me, not to scare me, and I was about to find out why.

A little apprehensive about this medium appointment, like I was about to go into a meeting, and I was about to give a speech, (public speaking is not my gig), I grabbed my messenger bag and put on my hoodie. Exiting the quiet kitchen to the front of the store, I heard a loud noise behind me.

CRASSSHHHH! CLINK, CLINK, CLINK!

I stopped dead in my tracks, a chill racing up my spine. Two people walked by the front door, which was maybe six feet away, laughing. One smacked the other on the back, having a hilarious time, while I stood frozen in time, afraid to turn around. The ghost scared me again. I took a deep breath and slowly exhaled, closing my eyes, trying to find the Zen I used to know.

I turned around and faced the kitchen door. I had to go back in there and see what had happened. I just had to. In my peripheral vision, I could see the swinging door was moving back and forth, back, and forth. Just like the day I had seen a figure in it and when the weird guy JT was here.

I swallowed hard, opened the kitchen door, and flipped the lights on. I looked immediately over to where I had set my espresso cup and then down to the floor. Shards of the broken ceramic cup were scattered about.

I shouted. "Leave me alone already, damn it!"

I reached into the closet for the broom and dustpan. I cleaned it up quickly, cursing away with every swing of the broom.

"You freaking dropped it! You should clean it! Stay out of my kitchen and out of my store! You hear me?" Nothing. I heard absolutely nothing. I threw everything in the trash, shut the lights, and bolted for the front door as rain started to fall.

CHAPTER 36

APPROPRIATELY, IT HAD RAINED all afternoon, and there was a chilly mist in the air, quite dreary for the month of June, so once again, I felt like I was in a scary horror movie, just shy of blinding flashes of lightning and ear-splitting cracks of thunder. Ciara's studio was above a small clothing store on Main Street in Cold Springs.

I drove up to the address Diana had given me, put the car in park, and released a big, heavy sigh, because for me, that released a lot of anxiety, of which I had plenty at that moment.

I thought about just leaving, but by that point I felt so compelled, as if drawn by some unseen force, there simply was no turning back. I had to know about the unknown and who or what was haunting my pastry shop.

The old building in front of me dated from the early 1700s, as most of the structures along Main Street in Cold Springs did. I took a deep breath and entered the foyer. A clothing store to the left had a Closed sign hanging on the glass door, and directly in front of me, a staircase with a sign pointed up. It read "Readings by Ciara."

I felt my heart leap up a notch as I started up the slanted staircase, which was lasting proof of how old the building was.

Ten steps up to a small landing, then a slight turn to the left and a few more steps up to the second floor. Cream-colored walls surrounded me, and in a dark corner of the landing, a small table with a vase of dried flowers sat on a yellowed doily that could've been knitted by a widow in the 1700s, forlornly waiting for her seafaring husband to come home from a whaling expedition but never did.

There was a hallway ahead and I had an eerie feeling come over me. I called out, "Hello?" but no one answered. There seemed to be no one around. I began to wonder if I had the wrong address. There was yet another flight of stairs to a third floor, but just as I started to venture up, a woman violently opened a door up there and leaned over the railing. She glared down at me, the intruder. I gasped, "Hello. Are you Ciara?"

She had a look as if I had rudely awakened her from some deep, ageless sleep. Or maybe she was the widow who knitted that doily three centuries ago.

Her eyes narrowed as she gave me a stern look, with a crooked smile, said tersely, "Second floor."

"Thank you," My heart was pounding like a jackhammer.

As if for good measure, she added, "This floor is a private residence." She then buttoned her lip and picked her chin up and gave me that chilling *so there!* Look.

I smiled back. "Sorry about that. It's my first time here and I didn't see a sign."

"There's a sign on the table. It's down the hall." She almost had to stop herself from leaning too far over the banister and pointing.

"Okay, thank you. I'll take another look."

I turned around quickly and vaulted down the two steps in one bound, peering down the hallway, trying to imagine where to go now. All was silent except for the *click* as the old woman up above closed her door.

My nerves pulsating nearly out of my skin, I started down the dim hallway anyway.

The door on my right was closed and locked.

There were more doors on my left and one straight ahead.

I stammered, in some desperation now, "Hello? Hello, Ciara?"

Again, there was no answer. Then I realized that the second door was slightly ajar. Boldly but fearfully, I pushed it open a bit more with my foot and echoed out, "Helloo?" Okay, now I was freaking myself out. Soft lights were on, and a trestle table sat squarely in the middle of the room. Drawings and paintings hung on garish pink-and-lavender-painted walls, but they all seemed a blur; I couldn't make out what the images in them were, but it seemed peaceful and calming. And still no answer, and apparently no one here.

I turned to leave and started back down the dim hallway when, like a shot, I heard a deadbolt unlock, and almost simultaneously a doorknob jangled open behind me. I whipped around so fast that I think it took my teeth two extra seconds to catch up with my jaw! I watched the door creak open, and a young woman floated toward me. She was talking on a cell phone, and music came wafting out from the studio behind her. "Hello. Are you Gerard? No, not you, Dad," she spoke into the phone.

I only nodded.

"My appointment is here, Dad. I have to go. Yes, I'll call you tomorrow. Okay, bye." She hung up her cell phone. "I'm sorry I'm late. I got caught up."

She offered me her hand with a sweet smile. She was a lot younger than I imagined, pretty, with a gentle, strangely ethereal presence.

I shook her hand in the hallway and she welcomed me into her studio.

I was still nervous. I sat at the trestle table, taking note of the two fist-size crystals and four votive candles. She lit the candles and sat across from me, all the while smiling and calmly explaining what might or might not happen during the reading. Why sometimes people might come through for varied reasons and why not all of them might be appearing specifically for me. And she pointed out that not all mediums are the same.

"Is this your first spiritual reading?"

"Yes, yes, it is."

"I want you to relax and clear your mind. You may ask questions, but usually the spirit will come through first and reveal who they are."

"Okay."

"Any questions? Oh, by the way I love your pastry shop, those coconut macaroons are to die for."

I shook my head smiling and sighed.

"Okay then, let's begin."

I adjusted my chair, swallowed hard and sat forward. "Yes, ready."

She began doodling in her notebook, making circles next to circles, and drawing bars between them, connecting the shapes as we went along.

I recorded the whole reading.

Coconut Macaroons

Preheat conventional oven to 350 degrees or convection oven to 325 degrees.

2 1/2 cups	Desiccated coconut.
1 cup	Granulated sugar
1 Tbs	Corn starch
6 ounces	Egg whites
1/4 tsp	Pure vanilla extract

Double boiler

Thermometer

One-ounce ice cream scooper or larger

Use a metal mixing bowl that can fit over the double boiler. Fill the pot with water so it does not touch the bowl. Turn the stove on to boil the water.

Place the mixing bowl on your work surface. Place the coconut and sugar in the bowl and mix together with a rubber spatula. Add the cornstarch and mix. Add the egg whites and vanilla extract and mix until it is completely incorporated.

Place the mixture over the double boiler. Lower to a low boil. Stir the mix occasionally every five to ten minutes to cook evenly. It should take close to forty-five minutes to an hour to reach a temperature of 150 degrees.

At this point, remove the mix from the boiler and let cool down for at least thirty minutes so the mix is workable and cooler to scoop.

Using a one-ounce ice cream scooper or larger (in which case baking times can take longer), scoop haystack mounds on a parchment-lined baking tray about two inches apart. Place the tray in the preheated oven for five minutes. Turn the tray and bake again for another five minutes or until the macaroons take on a light golden-brown color.

Remove from the oven onto a cooling rack.

**Baker's note: For a variation, dip the bottoms of the macaroons in melted dark chocolate.*
When completely cool, place in an airtight container in the refrigerator or freezer for up to three weeks.

Yields about three dozen.

CHAPTER 37

I WASN'T SURE WHAT to expect if some apparitions were supposed to appear. I told Ciara there seemed to be a lot of orbs and ghostly spirits in the bakery, and I'd like to know who they were.

I also told her about the earlier investigation with Kerriann and Joe. But I didn't tell her everything. She didn't want to know. She said the spirits would tell her. Whatever I told her was public knowledge already. Yes, I was a little skeptical, and I wasn't sure how much she knew about me. But I figured, *she is a medium, right? Shouldn't she be able to find all the other stuff on her own?* So, for example, I did not tell her about any of the hauntings that had been happening, nor did I give her any information about my family.

It was not like I had to wait for the reading to begin, it just did.

"Do you know a Dani?" Ciara blurted out.

"Is she living or passed?" I asked nervously.

"Living."

"Yes."

"Doesn't seem like a connection. There is a woman here" (I wasn't sure exactly where "here" was), "telling me and showing me the number five. Hmmm, I am not sure if she is connected to you or is someone you know. I'll pass on her for now."

She drew the letter V on a piece of paper and asked if I knew a woman whose name started with that letter.

I couldn't place the letter V with anyone I knew, past or present.

Then Ciara spoke, "There's a woman at your shop who works for you. She helps with the making of cakes. She's there a lot with you and her grandfather says he helps her."

"Whoa!" *Second time Hana's grandfather came through. I guess he is there a lot!* I confirmed it with Ciara.

"He likes to play with spoons and he's always by her side, as if he's assisting her with her tasks."

I think my eyes bulged out like a cartoon character. How could she know this? Her expression was like a big question mark. I told her about the time the spoon kept falling off the pot handle, and how Hana felt his presence around her occasionally. I told her about the shadow figure and how, for reasons I couldn't explain, I thought it might be Hana's grandfather.

"Shadow figure? You can see shadow figures?" Ciara questioned.

"Well, I saw a black shadow figure. I've never seen one before, but I know what I saw." I was getting a little nervous again. "I've never seen anything like it."

"Yeah, that's not good." Ciara paused, shaking her head. "White spirits are good. Shadow people are not good." Ciara was not smiling. "Send it to the light."

"Oh, boy," I muttered.

"Hmmm, let's see who else is there," Ciara smiled coyly. "This woman I passed on earlier, she's pushing through again. She's still showing me the number five, and she's all over the place, running from this house to that house. She feels everything has to be done quickly. She knows you, and I think the five means she passed away sometime over the past five years."

She drew the letter R on the paper, and I gulped. I started to put two and two together and realized that this was Steve's mom, Rose, coming through. "Dani is her granddaughter." I told Ciara that I validated her presence.

I did not know what to say, so I simply said, "Hi, Rosie.

Ciara giggled out a laugh. "There you go. Hello, hi there."

"She's showing me that she stays with Dani's daughter, Liv. She is not directly related to you but to someone you know with the letter S." Ciara scribbled on the paper as she connected a few more circles with bars. "Is there a Steve? Do you have a partner named Steve?"

"Yes, Steve is my partner and alive."

"Yes, he is among us."

There seemed to be no particular rhythm to the circles or bars, but she kept furiously doodling and connecting things up.

I told Ciara, "Rose was Steve's mom, who passed away a few years back, and she had five children."

Ciara seemed to confirm this, saying, "Oh, now the five makes sense. She loves helping at the bakery. She says that one time she stopped a fire in the ovens."

"Hmm, really? I'm not sure about that, we have never had a fire." We were this deep into the reading before I realized that I was apparently communicating with someone who had died.

"She's showing me that she likes to play with the timers on the oven."

I let out a big laugh. "Oh, my God! That's why the all the timers keep breaking. There was one day when I burned five trays of triple chocolate cookies because the timer didn't go off." I was starting to enjoy this. I missed Rose; she was a great lady and a wonderful mom to Steve.

"Well, there you go; mystery solved about the broken timers," Ciara, laughed happily.

The connection to Rose was strong, Ciara indicated, and she related to me things that only Steve or I would know.

"There is a man behind Rose… his name begins with the letter J— James or Jimmy. Sound familiar?"

I asked if James was living or deceased.

She said he had passed, and the name James was right.

Steve's dad was called Jimmy, although his real name was Vincent. Don't ask. My dad, who was still indeed alive at the time, was named Gabriel, but everyone called him Bobby. Believe me, I don't get it either.

Ciara muttered, "There are a lot of people here. There are two women off to the side trying to get through, but Rose is holding firm."

I glanced at the clock on the wall and realized we were well past the thirty-minute session. *Wow, time flies when you are hanging out with the dead!*

Next Ciara asked me if I knew a woman with the letter J and another with the letter M.

At the time, I had to pass on these two, because I did not have clue. I realized later that these women were Steve's grandmothers from both sides of the family. Josephine and Mamie.

Ciara pointed at me, "J knows how you and Steve met. She helped push you together. You were in an open field; you and Steve were the only two people there. Is this right? Can you confirm this?"

"It's true," I engaged. "We met on a beach at six thirty in the morning. And we were alone."

Ciara smiled. "Well, there you go. The spirits are right."

A gust of wind passed through the room from a window that was slightly cracked open, and all four candles blew out just like in all those scary movies. Ciara looked at me with a cheery face, "Oh, that always happens."

I peered at the open window. I was not smiling. "Uh-huh."

Ciara relit the candles, composing herself and said Rose was stepping aside to let another woman come through, and with that, she drew the letter A on her pad. I told her I knew someone with the letter A.

"But this spirit is showing me that she has two names."

I did not say anything at first, but all I could think about was my aunt Angie. I waited for more information.

"This woman stands in front of another woman with a letter A name as well. The first woman is younger than the second, and I think this must be a mother-daughter relationship." Ciara was moving her hand from front to back.

I smiled broadly. "Ciara, this is my aunt Angie and Grandmother Anna."

"They're related to your father?" Ciara looked up to me from her doodling.

"Yes," I replied eagerly.

"She, your aunt Angie, is showing me that she is sending healing to your sister. She spends a lot of time with your sister. Is your sister sick or is something wrong with your sister?"

"Was," I spoke clearly. "She just beat ovarian cancer."

"Well, she is praying over your sister and showing me healing and calming motions of a patting over the chest." Ciara demonstrated the motion with her own hand.

I felt tears well up in my eyes. I missed my aunt. She died too young at sixty-eight years old. Grandmother Anna was the only grandparent that I ever had the opportunity to know. She passed away when she was ninety-seven when an aneurism burst in her stomach.

"They're showing me that they're sending your father healing as well. They are rubbing his knees and pushing him to get up and move around. Pushing him right up and out of his chair."

I burst out laughing. How could she know this? I was enthralled, "This is surprising. My dad has water on his knees and always complains that they bother him at the youthful age of ninety-two when he goes bowling."

One of the interesting things I found out after all of this was that my parents had had their own experiences with spirits. Since the day my grandmother passed away, they reported occasionally seeing white shadowy light figures pass through rooms and hearing strange thumps they could not account for. They also claimed that things in their home were sometimes inexplicably moved…or feeling like the chairs they were sitting in were suddenly bumped by some invisible thing. So now, I don't know which place was haunted more—the pastry shop or my parents' home. But one thing seemed clear from the session with Ciara: it sounded like my aunt Angie and my grandmother Anna were keeping in touch.

I asked Ciara if she would like to see some of the photos and videos of the orbs that we caught flying around the bakery. I was thinking maybe she could identify these orbs with names; was this even possible?

She was in awe as I showed her the still photos that were on my phone. It really was an impressive album of photos captured by the security camera video recorder.

"What is that?" Ciara was engaged.

"That's what I'd like to know. Or better yet, who is that? Any ideas?"

She was looking at the video of the stick light orb that had danced around the kitchen for over an hour.

The stick light orb glowed bright white. "I'm not sure who it is, but I feel like it's more angelic and less of a nuisance. I've never seen anything like it."

"So, I've had two mediums and a ghost hunter look at this, and nobody has a clue to what it is," I lamented. "Is it an entity? Did it come out of a vortex?" I was really starting to believe there might be a real danger.

She was blown away by all the activity.

"Wow, your shop is highly active." She handed my phone back to me.

"Whoever this is, they want your attention. I don't think it is dangerous at all. They want you to know that they're in your shop. They are trying to reach out to you. They know you are sensitive, and they also know you can see them as well as feel their presence. I think they're trying to contact you, but I believe they're scaring you and your staff more than anything else."

"Yes, they are, and the other medium said almost the same thing."

"Well, there you go. Your family is trying to help and assist in the bakery."

"Could you please ask them to stop? I love and miss them but it's way too much for us to handle these scary moments."

"Yes, I already did. You can do this yourself; you know."

"I've tried," At that point I was willing to try whatever she might suggest. "Is there something else I could do?"

"You pray. Just as you pray to God for help, love, and protection. You pray to them to send them on their way toward the light. Imagine colors to help you. Paint them and their spirit in pink for love, green for health, and white for protection. Then send them on their way. When you send the rent check, electric bill, or whatever every month, do the same thing. Wrap it in colored papers, too, keep the energy flowing from the bakery to wherever it has to go."

"I've done this before, and it doesn't work. Well, it did work once. But they keep coming back! I'll try it again," I thought back to what Kerriann had said when she told me almost the same thing. *It did not work then, but would it work now?*

Ciara kept doodling. "See, it did work. Keep saying it."

"What are the ramifications from doing so? What might happen? These ghosts aren't going to get mad if I keep trying and do anything malicious, will they?"

"No, no, they won't hurt you. They won't stay if you don't want them there."

"Okay, I've heard this before, but paranormal activity happens all the time lately, and I've been pushed and shoved, even a knife has fallen from a magnetic rack and slid across my worktable. I'm willing to try something, even if it's again."

"You have that much paranormal activity?"

"Yes."

By this point, the reading had been going on for more than forty-five minutes, and I still hadn't heard anything about Andy. My nerves were quickly becoming short.

Ciara grabbed my hand. "Trust me, I know what I'm doing. There is a spirit that is hanging out"—she drew the letter E on her pad—"he's showing me a hallway kind of alley behind your store. He is telling me that he was murdered there in the early '80s. Oh, and by the way, he loves the French desserts."

Here it was, the moment of truth.

"You mean the letter A, not E, right?"

"Uh, no, it's the letter E."

"Is he Andy?"

"No, no Andy." Ciara smiled. "Okay, who else is there?"

"Wait! Who is this guy with the letter E?"

"I'm sorry, he moved on and let the woman who is still hanging around from before with the letter V come through. She is showing me that she's connected to your mother. Maybe she was a sister, a friend and cousin perhaps? She's showing me that she is paralyzed on her left side."

"Oh, my God," I stuttered, "that's Vivie, my mom's cousin. She had a stroke years ago and was paralyzed on her left side. She died a few years later."

"Well, she hangs out with you and feels there is a connection between her son and you. She loves the way you make blueberry pie."

I let out a soft laugh. "I make a blueberry cobbler."

Ciara looked up at me, "Regardless, she loves the way the pie comes out. It looks so homemade."

"Her son Anthony passed away years ago when I was a teenager. He used to pass by our house on a Saturday, and my mom would make him a peanut butter and banana sandwich. I remember that was the first time I ever tried one."

Sadly, Anthony died in his early twenties. "Hi, Vivie!" I called out. I really liked Vivie, always happy and never had a terrible thing to say about anyone. "But Anthony is not any of the letter A's you've been talking about, is he?"

"No, no, he's not."

I hoped Ciara would circle back to the guy with the letter E, but instead she continued, "You have another chef who works for you, a young woman. I am getting the letter A from her great-grandmother on her mother's side. She is showing me that she also passed a few years ago and that she's proud of her great-granddaughter, is it Christine or Kristy?"

I added, "It's Kate, with a K."

"Okay, yes, she is acknowledging this. She says her name is Ann and she stays with Kate a lot. She is quite proud of her."

Wow. "I will tell her."

"Did you own a dog, uh, a white dog? Not like a tiny dog but a little bigger, so if it sat in your lap, you would know it. He's sitting right here now. I feel his weight on my lap."

"Yes." I smiled widely. "His name is Figaro. He was a West Highland terrier, and he was a medium dog, maybe twenty pounds or so. He had cancer and passed away when he was almost thirteen years old." I gave a whistle to him.

"Oh! He perked up. He feels the love," Ciara moved her hands around her lap. "He stays with Rose when he isn't with you. I wouldn't be surprised if you tripped over him because he is always around your feet. He's extremely comfortable with you, by your side all the time. Did you put a carpet by the garage steps?"

"Yes, I did."

"He doesn't like it there. He thinks you'll trip on it."

"Okay, thanks, Figs," I smiled. I missed him but I hoped he wouldn't come back to life like that demonized cat from the pet cemetery movie.

CHAPTER 38

CIARA SCRIBBLED THE LETTER M on the notepad and then started making a new section of circles, connecting them with bars.

"There is another presence there that isn't connected to you or the store but to the land. I am getting the letter M. This spirit is young and a female. She's all of about nine years old."

I could not place any relative that had died that young. *Where is Ciara going with this?*

"She's young in age but her spirit is old. She's been gone for an exceedingly long time. I'm getting the late 1700s somewhere." Ciara spoke as if in a trance. "Honest, I'm not making this stuff up."

"Are you identifying all the orbs that float through my patisserie?"

"Yes, I believe so."

"How many people are there?"

"I'm not sure but there seems to be quite a few who want to say hello."

"Unbelievable."

"So, this young girl was killed accidently by her mother. She was out playing, and her mom was screaming, 'No! No!' from somewhere in the house. She ran into the house to see what was happening."

Ciara gasped for air and stopped.

"Oh, my God. What happened?" I asked. My left foot was nervously tapping away as if I were trying to keep the beat to a great song from the 1980s.

Ciara paused and looked at me. Her face had gone pale. Her eyes looked gaunt and deep-set as if she had just seen a ghost.

"I think this young girl is buried in your shop."

"*What?*" I gasped. "Are you serious?"

She nodded.

I looked from side to side and caught a breeze from the open window as the curtains billowed out toward me. My eyes opened wider, and I'm sure my mouth opened wider, too. Not sure if it was in horror or nervousness or both.

The truth was that I'd had a feeling something like this would happen. *Here we go with dead people buried in the bakery. Please don't call the health department!* At that moment, my heart rate jumped. All I could do was stare at Ciara as she doodled, apparently thinking, and occasionally tapping with her pen.

I waited for her to continue, extremely anxious about what would happen next. My mind raced around the kitchen at the bakery. *Where? Where? Is she below the roofline on the grade-level side of the building, or maybe somewhere under the back alley where Andy hangs out? Is Andy her protector? Did he somehow know her, even though their lives were so far apart? Maybe someone in my family knew her. But that is impossible, of course.*

What the hell is going on? I have to ask a question I'm sure of. "Is there an Andy in the hallway?"

"Andy? No there is no Andy. No Andy before and no Andy now. Who's Andy?"

"I… I do not know. I thought he was the ghost who is bothering us."

"Really?"

"Well, his name is scrawled on the hallway wall, and a ghost woman asked Joe, the other medium, where is Andy. So, we all think the ghost is named Andy."

Ciara flat out said, "No Andy here at all."

"I'm so confused."

"Hmm. I'm trying to listen to this young girl's story. I'm getting the letter M for Mary, Marty, Mattie, Matilda. She is acknowledging Mattie. Matilda is her real name and she's so young. She is crying softly and I'm trying to make her stop so I can understand her."

"Oh, my God. Is this a joke?" I laughed a nervous laugh like I was prone to do in situations like this.

"I don't joke. Not with this anyway." Ciara was serious.

"Okay, sorry about that. I'm simply confused by this information, I guess."

"No problem. Things happen all the time that may or may not concern the person who is getting the reading. But she lived there in the late 1700s. Potter, Potter was her last name. Matilda Potter. Mattie. She likes to be called Mattie."

"Oh, dear God. I came across some information indicating that. Revolutionary War hero Gilbert Potter had a farm on the land where my store is located. Uh, hi, Mattie." I tapped my nervous left foot.

"She is acknowledging you; she likes you, the pastries, the chefs, and she loves Steve. Oh, wait, she is claiming to be the white light stick-orb you have seen zipping around the kitchen. She said she tried to speak to you recently."

My jaw dropped. I think I was more frightened now knowing that the stick-orb is a nine-year-old girl who screamed at me. "This is absolutely insane."

Ciara ignored me. "She is incredibly happy your pastry shop is there compared to what it used to be before. She says it was dark and forgotten, and it was not a happy place. The man who owned the pizzeria was mean. She says she's happy he's dead."

"Did she kill the man?"

"She says no, but she is laughing. She liked to scare him."

"Geez, Louise! It used to be a pizzeria. The space was empty and abandoned when I first saw it. There was mold on the walls, and it was dreadfully cold. We gutted most of the place from floor to ceil…ing," I trailed off. Suddenly, all I could think about was the hollow floor in front of my marble table. No, it could not be! I froze and looked up at Ciara.

"Mattie is telling me the story. She was playing outside on a swing her father had hung from a tree branch. He was not home that day. He was a patriot, helping to secure the bay from the British during the Revolutionary War if they were to land. Mr. Cleary, who owned the general store, also went to the bay, leaving his son William behind to help Mrs. Potter move furniture into her new sewing room. Something happened. Mattie heard her mother scream out, 'No, let go of me!'

"Mattie ran into the house, yelling for her mother.

"'Momma? Are you okay? Momma, where are you?'

"She let the screen door slam behind her as she entered the kitchen.

"There was shuffling and banging against the wall upstairs. It sounded like it was coming from her bedroom.

"She heard her mother cry out again. 'Stop it! What are you doing? Let go of me!'

"Then she heard a smack sound. Not like the smack she would get on her bottom from being a bad girl, but a loud smack, and her mother let out a cry. 'No, please, please stop it!'

"Mattie ran up the back staircase to find her mother.

"As she reached the top of the stairs, she saw William trying to rip her mother's blouse off. She saw the floral fabric tear and the pearl buttons hit the floor. One by one, they bounced on the wooden floor until they started to roll.

"'Momma, Momma!' she called, and her mother turned around to see her standing there. So did William.

"With a wide swoop of his hand, he struck her mother with such a force across her face. Mattie cried out, 'No, don't you hit my momma!'

"Her mother staggered backward and lost her footing, blood gushing from her bottom lip as she crashed into Mattie. She reached desperately but was unable to catch the young girl as her body twisted and went falling head over heels backward down the flight of stairs.

"There was an awful thud when her head hit the floor at the bottom of the stairs.

"'Mattie!' her mother screamed from the top of the stairs, looking down in horror to where her little girl lay still. A large pool of blood started to form under Mattie's head.

"Seeing what had happened, William ran down the main staircase and out the front door. The door stayed wide open as the midday sun poured through and warmed the floorboards. He was never seen or heard from again. Mattie was laid to rest at the bottom of a green, grassy hill on the family farm."

When Ciara finished recounting this horrible tale, she looked exhausted, like she had been possessed. We sat in silence for a long time.

I shook with disbelief and kept thinking of the hollow floor.

"Ciara, there's a section of the floor in my kitchen that's hollow. When I stand there, I swear I feel tapping under my feet. Could that be her resting place?"

"It could be. Yes. She's acknowledging that it is."

I was beside myself. "Holy crap! You have got to be kidding me! My patisserie is haunted by more people than any scary movie I have ever seen. *Murdered* people. What the hell? Excuse me! Pardon my French, but what the heck?" (I did not actually say *heck* in this instance.)

I was ready to stand up and get the hell out of there!

"It's okay, Gerard. I am a little shaken myself. Mattie says she is happy to finally be acknowledged. She doesn't mean to frighten or cause harm to anyone. In fact, she really enjoys your baking and loves it when you make a peach pie. But it's not a regular pie, she says, because it's open with no top and the dough is flaky."

"Wow, she really watches my baking. That is actually a peach paysanne. Fresh peaches and blueberries on puff pastry."

"Yes! That's the one she means. It reminds her of her mother's baking."

"Is she really buried in the bakery?"

"Well," Ciara sighed. "The farm was located across the street from where the big supermarket is on Wall Street. In fact, there is a Harrington Historical Landmark sign on the corner claiming Gilbert Potter lived there. I doubt any of her remains are still intact. It's been over two hundred years, but her spirit is still alive."

"Apparently," I huffed.

"Mattie has one strong spirit. We need to send her to the light along with the other spirits. If you like, I'll come to the bakery in a week or so to smoke it out with some sage."

"Will my family members stay, or will they be smoked out, too?"

"No, they'll stay because they're part of you and those who work with you. But the others will have to go."

I got up to stretch my legs and looked at my phone. I had been there way too long, over an hour. Boy did time fly when you were communicating with the dead. But more questions remained. "Others?"

"Yes, there are others."

"I'm sorry if I've overstayed my welcome. But are you saying there are even *more* other ghosts there?"

"Yes, would you like to hear more? And don't worry about the time. I'm finding all of this quite fascinating."

I hesitated at first, then decided I needed to know more. I did not believe that all of the banging and voices we heard were coming from a young girl, Rose, Hana's grandfather, Kate's great-grandmother, my grandparents, my aunt, and Figaro.

"Yes," I replied, "tell me more." I sat back down.

CHAPTER 39

CIARA IMMEDIATELY PICKED UP on some young men from the late 1920s or early '30s.

"They're showing me there was a speakeasy of some kind, either right in the building where the bakery is or near there. Whichever it was, these spirits liked it there. Your pastry shop is comforting to them. Who doesn't like the smell of fresh-baked croissants and cookies?"

I laughed at Ciara's sweet humor.

"I'm getting the letter J, like Joseph. Are you Joseph?" Ciara spoke aloud and kept doodling. She appeared to be listening intently, as if in a classroom taking notes and trying to comprehend what the teacher was saying.

"I don't think his name is Joseph. I am getting more of an Italian name for Joseph. Is your name Giuseppe?"

That is all it took! Ciara breathed a sigh of relief. "That was a tough one. Do you know of a Giuseppe, maybe in your family history?"

"No. I have a brother Joe, but he is alive." I tried to think quickly, but it wasn't quick enough as Ciara continued.

"Hello, Giuseppe. Why are you here?" Ciara looked across the table but not directly at me. "I think someone else is here with Giuseppe. Is there someone else here? Are you friends with Giuseppe? I am getting the letter R, like Richard. Is your name Richard?"

Ciara paused again, staring at the space to my right. *She can see these people.* I wondered what they looked like.

"What are you looking at? Is he standing next to me?"

"Yes, he is a young, handsome man. Wait, he's stroking his mustache and combing his hair for me." Ciara laughed and I chuckled with her.

"He's acknowledging his name is Richard. So, now I have a Giuseppe and a Richard here. Wait! Giuseppe is trying to tell me something." Ciara sat upright. "He says the distillery was where the pastry shop is among row houses of some kind? Do you know any history of the years gone by on the land? Huh. It seems like they were killed there. Young guys, early twenties, I believe."

I muttered, "Great, more dead bodies."

Ciara shot me a stern look, dismissing my humor.

"A speakeasy, huh?"

"Yes. Back in the Prohibition era."

"I'm not from Harrington, but according to the landlord and some town folk, there were row houses on the property back in the 1950s. So, I'm guessing maybe the houses were there longer than that. How did these guys die?"

"They were ambushed."

"They were what?"

"Like a hit. A Mafia hit," Ciara continued. "They were working."

She paused, then shared Giuseppe's story.

"It was the early 1930s, during Prohibition. Their boss was not satisfied with the going on at the speakeasy, and they pulled a hit on Giuseppe and Richard. It seems they were skimming some alcohol off the top and selling extra bottles for their own profit. There were four or five men who shot up the place. Giuseppe and Richard were both shot in the back trying to run away." Ciara sighed. "They didn't make it."

"Geez. Do they know who murdered them?"

Ciara stopped doodling. Maybe it was a moment of silence, but I sat perched on the edge of my chair.

"They're shaking their heads. They don't know who shot them."

"But why are they still here, Ciara?"

"They're stuck," she replied, referring to Giuseppe and Richard. "They're having a hard time moving on. They don't want to go to the light."

"What do you mean?"

"I think they prefer to stay there," Ciara answered. "They like the pastry shop and they like being ghosts… doing a little haunting, creating a little mischief."

Great, I thought.

Ciara paused, took a sip of water, and asked, "Giuseppe, are you the one who whistled at Kate in the walk-in refrigerator?"

How does she know about that?

Then she asked, "Do you like Kate? He said yes, he is the one who whistled at Kate. He didn't mean to scare her but wanted to say she's pretty."

"Well, she is."

"They are quite sorrowful, but they like you, your staff, and all the pastries you make."

"Thank you, guys."

"They are acknowledging you."

"But please don't whistle at Kate anymore."

Ciara laughed. "He says okay, he won't, but he'll whistle at you instead."

I laughed out loud. These two guys had a sense of humor.

"They also say they're sorry if they hurt anyone. They did not mean to. They were having a bit of fun, letting you know that they were there."

"Well, they could've called first or knocked on the door." Then I had an aha moment. "Wait. Are they the ones who bang on the walls and call my name?"

Ciara quietly doodled. "Hmm. They say no, it's not them. They're saying it defensively, no, not me, no, it's the other guy."

"What other guy?" I did not hesitate with my response. I didn't think these were the guys banging on the wall either, but they knew who was. "The guy in the back of the patisserie?"

Ciara appeared to be struggling to understand them. "They're talking at the same time in broken English. It's hard to understand their Italian accent." She showed me the *calm down* motion, her hands waving downward, and then she smiled. "Okay, there's another guy who hangs out in the back of your shop and they say it's him. He bangs a lot out of frustration when he gets mad, or when he wants to start a fight with us."

"Fight? Ghosts fight? What's his name? Is it Andy?" I leaned in on her desk in hopes of an answer. I felt my heart in my throat, thinking I was finally going to meet the ghost.

"They left." Ciara stopped doodling and leaned back. She held on to her pen, tapping the paper. Slowly she raised her gaze to me and repeated, "They left. It was like someone pulled them away."

"They left? What do you mean they *left?*" I looked around the room, toward the door, and back to Ciara. "How's that possible?" I banged on the desk in a bit of frustration.

"They said what they had to say and left. They're no longer here, but they made room for two little girls to come in."

"I don't understand this. What is this medium afterworld like? What are they doing? Taking turns in a phone booth where only one person can talk to you at a time and then walking away to let someone else speak?"

"Good analogy. I like that, and yes, it's sort of like that. I can see through a small portal, and I'm channeling through you and all your connections who have passed to the next realm."

I was speechless.

"There's a little girl here," Ciara pursed her lips. "But it's not Mattie. She is showing me the letter G. Actually, there are a few girls here, all young, maybe eight or nine years old."

I sat back and almost felt like admitting defeat. I had no idea what was going on anymore. The whole thing was completely crazy. But I wanted to know about the guy who been banging on the wall.

"I'm seeing the name Gracie. Is your name Gracie?"

"Oh, no, please, no more dead children." That's all I could think about.

"I don't like it when children are involved either," Ciara grimaced and suddenly got serious. "Hello, Gracie, was there a school? There are a bunch of little ones there. They're all right here next to us." Ciara was looking toward the edge of the table. "Gracie was there a school where the bakery is?" she asked a second time.

I just listened, and for a few moments, there was an eerie silence.

"There are three more young girls with you." Ciara paused. "She is showing me the letter C for Charlotte." She started to speak but paused, as if questioning herself. "Were you girls in a hospital?"

My heart sank. There might be a young girl buried under my worktable and now three more young girls were hanging around the bakery. It broke my heart when I heard of a parent losing their young child or that a child was abused.

"Was there an orphanage there?" Ciara spoke gently, trying to establish some trust. "They said yes, there was an orphanage there or somewhere nearby. Oh, dear," Ciara shouted, "Oh, my God! I didn't see that coming." Clearly agitated and terribly upset, she was trying to shake it off. I wasn't sure what was wrong.

"You, okay?" I reached across the table and held her hand.

"No! I hate it when young children are involved. It's so sad. It upsets me."

"I'm sorry. I didn't come here to upset you."

"I do this all the time, and I get so incredibly sad when young children never had a chance at life, or their lives were cut short for whatever reason."

"I feel the same way. Now, we have a bunch of dead children there. Bad enough, I thought it was only one spirit. What happened here?" I released her hand and settled back.

Ciara finally raised her head slowly, like someone coming out of a deep sleep. She was trying to stay connected to the children. "They were sick," she began to explain. "No one murdered them. There was an orphanage there or awfully close by. They were children who had been displaced during the Civil War."

"The Civil War?" I nearly jumped out of the chair. "How can that be?"

"There were a lot of orphanages all over Long Island. Adults were caught up in the war, and most of them never made it home."

Ciara composed herself. "I keep hearing that children's song 'Ring around the rosie, a pocket full of posies.'" She glanced at the edge of the table for confirmation from the girls. Then she asked Gracie, "Did everyone get sick? Were the people nice to you?"

Channeling Gracie's answer, Ciara spoke softly, "They got sick with some type of flu and pneumonia, like a plague of some kind. That's where the nursery rhyme comes in. They all died. No one hurt them; they just died of a sickness."

Then Ciara tried to lighten the mood, asking, "Gracie, do you like to play in the kitchen at the pastry shop?"

This caught my attention.

"They're trying to help out." Ciara's hands hovered over the table, almost pretending to roll some dough with a rolling pin. "They especially like it when you make cookies, Gerard. Gracie, do you like to play tricks on Hana with the oven doors?"

Ciara smiled and giggled lightheartedly, trying to let the children see it was okay to have fun.

"Oh, my God, we just found the culprit. See? I'm not crazy. There are little dead kids helping me out. That's all. Nothing wrong with that, right?"

Ciara laughed. "You have to show them how to turn the trays in the oven now."

I forced a short laugh, shaking my head as I tried to fathom this whole bizarre scene unfolding right before my own eyes in my own pastry shop kitchen. I hoped Ciara was feeling okay. I felt a bit traumatized, although I kept thinking, *everyone gets to go home at the end of their shift, and I have to spend more time there than anyone else! I am always there.*

And yet, was it really so bad that the spirits were always there with me, too? It now seemed clear they were not going to leave, not all of them at least, and the ones who were family either to me or Steve or my chefs, well, I didn't want them to leave—as long as they behaved, of course. One thing was certain: I would never have to feel alone again when I happened to be by myself working in the kitchen in the wee hours of the morning.

Ciara interrupted my ruminations.

"Don't worry," Ciara extended her hand over the table. "Rose keeps them in line. She will not let them get out of hand. She doesn't let them out front. She lets them play in the kitchen. She's in charge and they know it."

"You go, Rose. Thank you. I miss you." I made a cheering gesture with my bottle of water.

"Rose said she misses you and Steve, too. She said she's enormously proud of you both and all your accomplishments."

"Thank you, Rose."

Ciara continued, "The girls like to paint. Do you have painting materials in the bakery?"

"Oh, my God, the… the children. Jeepers creepers, the children who painted the pictures next door." My mind was about to explode. Ernie Clayton's children.

Ciara looked like she was trying to listen to me and to the children at the same time. "Yes, they like to paint next door and red is their favorite color. They said Mr. Clayton is so nice to them, and he always has the materials ready for them to use. Mrs. Clayton looks over them now and she wishes she were still alive to taste your pastries, they are picture perfect." Ciara chuckled. "She said pun intended."

I smiled back. "Thank you." My voice cracked. "Your husband is a gentleman."

"Are you okay, Gerard?"

"I think so. That really shook me up."

"Me, too. I'm going to send them to the light now. I want to send them all to the light. You can go to the light and rest. You're safe, and your stories have been told. You can all go now." Ciara made hand gestures as if to wave them away to the heavens.

"This was crazy even for me." I took a sip of water. "I never expected the orphanage connection."

Ciara nodded. "Neither did I. Neither did I."

Yet I was left wondering where this Andy guy was. Maybe he, and perhaps Mattie, too, went to the light, now that Mattie knew we were aware of her and that we knew the sad story of her life cut short.

"I think we did enough for one night," Ciara sounded rather exhausted. "The only other presences were the patriots at the time of the revolution, although it also appears that there were Indian burial grounds on the other side of the parking lot. Over behind the movie theater, across from the post office. I don't see any other spirits hanging around there. Right now, that is!" She started to laugh. "Tomorrow may be another story."

I laughed, too.

"I think we're good."

I closed my eyes, took a deep breath, and exhaled slowly, trying to find a peaceful place. So many things to think about.

"Uh, wait a moment." Ciara held one finger up, stopping me in my tracks. "There's one more person here. The guy with the letter E is back. He said he was waiting for everyone else to finish. Now he wants your attention to talk with you."

"Me?" *So much for that Zen moment.*

"Yes, his name is Eddie, and he wants to tell his story."

"Who is Eddie?" I was almost afraid to ask. "Is he the guy who bangs on the walls?" My palms were sweaty, and I was getting a bit anxious again.

"He says yes, it's him. He's sorry to be scaring you but he needs your attention."

"Why?" I crossed my arms over my chest and sat back. "Why is he bothering me all the time?"

Ciara nodded her head. "He says his name is Eddie, not Andy."

"Wait! What? How is this possible? Who's Eddie? Annie's old friend? What the hell is he doing here, and where's this Andy guy?"

Ciara showed me the calming motion now with her hands and waited for me to calm down before continuing.

"He's Eddie, not Black or African American but Irish, Black Irish." Ciara looked to me for confirmation.

I spoke in almost a shout and was quickly reminded of what Joe Giaquinto had said—that there was a black dead guy who had been stabbed in the back of my store. "Wait, what?" Way too much information for me to absorb, but the light bulb just went off in my head.

"And he wants you to know Annie is in danger."

"Annie, my chef? How is she related to this?"

Ciara looked confused for a moment. "He says it has to do with Jackson or a Thomas, and he wants to tell his story."

"I'm lost. I don't know these people, Jackson, or Thomas. I don't get it. Hey, wait a minute, is Eddie the guy who was murdered by JT?"

Ciara furrowed her brow. "He says after he tells his story you'll understand."

I took another sip of water before settling back. I looked at the clock. "Ciara, I've been here for an hour and a half. Are you sure you're okay with this?"

"Yes, quite sure. This sounds important. Let's see what he has to say."

I have to get up in six hours for that pastry event.

Ciara looked at me and confirmed, "You'll be fine."

Stunned, I just looked back at her and thought, *did she just read my mind?*

"Shall we begin?"

"Yes, please continue."

Ciara relayed the conversation between her and Eddie as he told his story.

"It was September of 1982. He says he had graduated from high school and taken a job at the Italian restaurant on the corner of Wall Street and Central Avenue. He's showing me a narrow building. Do you know this building?"

"Yes, the alley rides alongside it." I remembered looking up at it the day I had been locked in the hallway. "Was he trying to talk to me in the hallway?"

"He says yes." Ciara nodded. "How did you get locked in the hallway?"

"Well, that's another story. He scared the crap out of me, you know."

"He says he's sorry, but he needed your attention."

"Well, he has it now."

"He said good, finally." Ciara smiled as if she was on his side.

I shook my head. "Whatever."

"He says he was working at the restaurant for two months when it happened."

"When what happened?"

"When he was murdered," Ciara said this nonchalantly as if it happened all the time.

I remembered the story Annie told us, that JT murdered Eddie. I guess I was about to find out the true story.

CHAPTER 40
Eddie

"EDWARD, CAN'T YOU STAY home at least one night, for goodness sakes?"

"Mom, they need me at work."

"But every day?" She crossed her arms as she stood in the kitchen doorway glancing at the kitchen clock. It was two forty-five in the afternoon.

"It's not every day. I was home yesterday."

"Yesterday was Sunday, and you didn't even come to church with me."

"I was tired, Mom. I needed to rest."

"Rest? I don't rest around here. Why should you? What do they have you doing every night? It doesn't make sense to me."

"Nothing makes sense to you since Dad died. I skipped college to get a full-time job to support us, and you still complain." Eddie put on his leather jacket against the cool September day. "Do you really want to have this conversation again?"

"Edward, please, I don't like those guys you work for, and I know your father wouldn't approve either. You're not even twenty years old yet."

"I will be come November. They treat me well. I'm like a nephew to them."

"More like a flunky or a gopher."

"Yeah, okay. Just because I was left back in grade school, I'm a flunky and an idiot, but I bring home enough money to pay the mortgage and the electric bill every month."

"I want you to go back to school and stop working for those men. They are nothing but trouble, and you know it! Mrs. Boccabella told me so."

"It's all talk, Mom. Mrs. Boccabella thinks her cat is still alive and should mind her own business."

"She says they're mobsters, and they gamble upstairs in the restaurant. Is that true?"

"I have no idea what you're talking about."

"Who bought you the motorcycle?"

"Never mind."

Edward resembled her husband in so many ways—the high cheekbones, blue eyes, straight black hair, and dark complexion. Black Irish rather than the lighter-skinned ginger Irish from her side of the family.

Gripping his arms, she spoke softly, hoping he would listen. "Edward, please listen to that inner voice in your head and do what's right. Don't get caught up with these guys. Return the motorcycle and accept no gifts. Work for the paycheck with no favors. They're nothing but trouble, and once they rope you in, they'll own you and not let go."

Her tears started to fall as she rested her head against his cold leather jacket, hugging him tight.

"I don't want to lose my son."

"Mom, you're not going to lose me, ever. I'll always be here taking care of you." Eddie kissed the top of his mom's head. "We're going to be okay, promise. Now, I have to go to work."

Releasing her hold on her son reluctantly, she wiped away the tears and forced a smile. "Please be safe on that thing."

"I will, Mom, promise."

Eddie gently closed the door behind him, hopped on his motorcycle, and drove slowly down Willow Avenue. After turning on Soundview Road and a quick right onto Hollywood, Eddie opened the throttle and felt the engine roar as he held on tight, tasting the exhilarating freedom most bikers felt when they rode.

Slowing down for the red light at the corner of High Street and New York Avenue, Eddie spotted his friend Brenden coming out of the Stop Light convenience store. Eddie pulled into the parking lot, catching Brenden in his tracks like a deer in his headlights.

"You son of a bitch, you nearly ran me over. Where in the hell did you get that thing, Eddie?"

"My boss, Mr. Carlucci, bought it for me." Eddie was beaming as he shut the engine and lit a cigarette.

"Wow, nice gift. What did you have to do to earn this? Have sex with his ugly daughter?" Brenden laughed at his own joke.

Eddie chuckled. "No dude, nothing like that. He saw my beat-up bicycle and wanted to buy me a new bicycle. I guess he had this in mind instead."

"Nice, real nice."

"Thanks. What are you up to?"

"Ah, not much. I start classes Thursday at Hofstra, so I bought one last six-pack to hang out with boys." Brenden nodded his head in the direction of the convenience store as Johnny, Kenny, Christopher, and JT exited with brown paper bags of snacks and another six-pack of beer.

"You still walking around with your brother's fake ID?" Eddie asked Brenden as he smirked at the guys approaching.

"Of course," Brenden laughed.

"Is that Eddie on that hog?" Christopher led the group. "Wooo eeeee!"

"Hey, what's the lowdown, Chris?" Eddie smiled.

"Damn, look at Eddie on the big wheels," Johnny teased.

"Yeah," Kenny reached for the cigarettes. "He looks like James Dean on that thing. Gimme one of those cigs, Eddie."

Eddie handed a cigarette over and locked eyes with JT. "What up, JT?" It had been a while since they last spoke.

JT nodded back without a word.

Kenny kicked the front tire. "Who did you steal this from?"

"My boss, Mr. Carlucci, bought it for me." Eddie beamed, feeling proud.

"Say what? No way." Christopher stepped back to take the bike all in.

"Your boss bought you a motorcycle?" Johnny looked angry, like he could not believe it. Could not believe someone would do that for Eddie. It was the same look as when one of his friends took the last can of beer and didn't ask him if he wanted it first. The same look as when a girl was interested in all the other guys but him.

"Yeah, he felt bad I was riding a beat-up bicycle and…" Eddie was cut off.

Johnny laughed. "Yeah, right. You have been up there gambling every night and taking home the cash. Nobody buys a nineteen-year-old kid a motorcycle after his bicycle loses its training wheels."

JT laughed at the sarcastic joke.

"Well, it's true. The guy likes me. He wants to help me out since I lost my dad."

"He's probably sucking off Mr. Carlucci at the end of the night for money. Ha-ha-ha!"

"All right, I've had enough. I have to go." Eddie put on his helmet.

"Hold up, we've been giving you our graduation money all summer to gamble and get some weed for us, and you show up on a brand-new motorcycle?" Johnny pointed his finger in Eddie's face. "This doesn't sound right to me. Sounds like you've been skimming off the top, taking a few bucks for your own pocket, huh? Making that summer cash really grow."

"I ain't been stealing from you guys. I played the numbers for you like you told me to. Some win, some lose." Eddie started his engine.

"Sounds like we've been losing more than we're winning. My boss at the bowling alley never bought me a thing, not even a free game." Kenny was annoyed as he stood next to Johnny, waiting for that moment when a fight would start, and you needed two more fists to break some heads. "I have to pay for sodas, too."

Eddie shot back, "Sounds like there's not much money in cleaning balls. Maybe you should ask Johnny for a raise the next time he asks you to clean his balls."

Brenden and Christopher burst out laughing.

Eddie drove off as Johnny and Kenny finally got the joke and gave him the finger. JT stepped between them, grabbing them by the shoulders. "Don't worry, boys."

CHAPTER 41

EDDIE DROVE HIS MOTORCYCLE to the far side of the bowling alley parking lot, away from all the other cars. He flipped the kickstand down, grabbed the helmet, and jogged to the corner.

Crossing Wall Street, he waved to Mr. Carlucci and his friends, Carmine, and Mario. All in their late sixties, dressed nicely in button down dress shirts that were a little too tight around their big bellies. The three of them were inseparable, always together, either talking on the bench in front of Mr. Carlucci's restaurant, Basta Pasta, smoking cigars, drinking wine, or having a good laugh.

Mr. Carlucci shook his head as Eddie crossed the street. "But where did you park the motorcycle, I gave you?"

"In the bowling alley parking lot."

Mr. Carlucci stood up slowly, grabbed his cane, and walked with Eddie to the alley. "Why did you park it over there? Go get the motorcycle and park it here against the wall. This way I can keep an eye on the gift I gave you. *Capisce?*"

"Gabishi?"

"Ca-ca, no ga-ga, no gabishi, its *capisce*. It means *do you understand* in Italian."

"Oh, I'm sorry, Mr. Carlucci. I didn't understand what you were saying. No *capisce*."

Mr. Carlucci laughed. "No *capisce!* That's funny." Carmine and Mario joined in the humor. He lightly smacked Eddie's cheek. "You're a good kid, Eddie. Now go get your motorcycle. My boys will be here in a little while to play cards, and you'll have to set up the table upstairs."

"Yes, sir. I *capsici.*"

More laughter erupted from Carmine and Mario.

"One more thing. What did your mother say when she saw the motorcycle?"

"Well, she's not happy, Mr. Carlucci. She wants me to give it back."

"It's a gift, Eddie. No one gives me back a gift."

"Okay, Mr. Carlucci, I understand. I'll tell my mother it was a nonreturnable gift."

"All right, let's go then." Mr. Carlucci gestured to the lot across the street and watched Eddie cross. "Hey, Carmine, send his mother some flowers on my behalf. Have the note say, *you raised a good son. I will keep an eye on him. Sincerely, Mr. Carlucci.*"

"Yeah, sure, boss."

Eddie was back with his motorcycle in no time. Mr. Carlucci escorted him to the alley and showed him where to park it against the building, leaving enough room for the neighboring restaurant's trash.

The metal door at the end of the alley banged open as a man with two bags of garbage struggled out of the doorway and entered the alley. "Hello, Mr. Carlucci."

"Good evening, Mr. Clayton. How are you today?"

"I'm fine. Just another day at the art studio. Well, what do we have here? A new set of wheels?"

Mr. Carlucci laughed. "This cane I carry is to help me walk, not to swat flies. I doubt I can even reach over the seat without falling, let alone sit on it."

Mr. Clayton laughed. "Oh, the angst of getting old. I'm feeling the aches and pains now, and I'm younger than you."

"Yes, wait, arthritis will come fast and furious. But not to this young man. Eddie, this is Mr. Clayton. He owns the art studio around the corner."

"Nice to meet you, Mr. Clayton. May I help you with the trash?"

"Why, er, yes, that would be great. Thank you, young man."

"Sure, no problem." Eddie took the bags to the curb.

"He just started working for me at the restaurant, and he's going to be parking his motorcycle here. I think there's still plenty of room to pass."

"Absolutely. Is he handy? Maybe he can fix that door for me. The damn thing doesn't want to open at times, and it doesn't want to close either, leaving it wide open. I think the damn door has a mind of its own."

"I'll call my guy, Jonas, in the morning and see if he can come by and fix it for you. He's a great handyman."

"That would be great. Thank you, Mr. Carlucci."

"You're welcome, enjoy the evening and say hello to your lovely wife for me."

"I will and you do the same. Nice to meet you, Eddie."

"Nice to meet you, too, Mr. Clayton."

They watched Mr. Clayton enter the hallway at the end of the alleyway. The door, as mentioned, did not want to close. Mr. Clayton threw his hands up in the air and left it ajar.

They entered Basta Pasta, and Eddie ran up the steep staircase, leaving Mr. Carlucci on the main floor to have an early dinner with his friends in the back of the restaurant.

Once upstairs, Eddie set up like he always did, turning the lights on and opening the corner window for some fresh air. He peered out the window gazing over Wall Street up to Main Street as the evening was turning to night, then down onto the alley, where his shiny new bike was parked. Eddie smiled proudly and felt good about life. *I should be able to save enough money by year end to go back to school part-time, and with Mr. Carlucci's help, Mom and I should be okay.*

He pulled the tarp off the card table and folded it neatly, put on a new plastic tablecloth, and checked all the chairs for any debris. Cocktail napkins for drinks and glasses for water were set for six people. The side table was prepped for the deck of cards, and Eddie counted out the five-hundred-dollar cash draw for poker chips. The cassette player was turned on with a stack of old crooners waiting to be played.

Wineglasses were set on the bar with two bottles of Chianti from Italy. Mr. Carlucci's cousin Marco owned a winery. Eddie filled the ice bucket and put two bottles of scotch and anisette on the counter.

Lastly, Eddie pulled the tarp off the crap table and turned on the overhead lights. He ran his fingers along the green felt and picked up the dice. "Come on, baby, let's roll a seven." Shaking them in his hand and blowing on them for good luck, he tossed them across the table. "Come on, baby, come on, baby!" Eddie watched the dice bounce to the far wall and stop. He shook his head in disbelief. He had rolled craps, a one and a two. "So much for that."

"So much for what?"

"Good evening, Mr. Carbone." Eddie was startled as the guys came up the stairs, catching him at the crap table.

"What happened, kid? Did you crap out again?" Mr. Carbone laughed.

"Sal, leave Eddie alone." Carmine took a seat at the card table.

"Why? Maybe the kid wants to win back all the money he lost this summer." Sal smiled and put his hands on his hips. "Maybe the kid wants to try to win the money back and stake his new bike."

Sal and Carmine turned to Eddie, waiting for a response.

"I… I don't think that's a good idea." Eddie's heart was beating a mile a minute.

"What's not a good idea?" Mr. Carlucci made it to the top of the stairs with Mario, Gino, and Frankie.

Sal folded his arms across his chest. "The kid wants to play craps. If he loses, I get his new motorcycle."

"I didn't say that!" Eddie stammered gripping the crap table's chip holders.

Mr. Carlucci held up his hand. "Hey, Sal, why would Eddie want to risk his new motorcycle? Hmm? Is this just another way to get something from me? Or another way to try and break this good young man over here?"

"Oh, no, I would never take anything from you, boss, never." Sal pleaded. "I was only playing around with the kid."

"Good." Mr. Carlucci patted Sal on the cheek. "So, the next time you want to play around with Eddie, you talk to me first. *Capisce?*"

"Yes, boss."

"All right then, let's play some poker, boys. Eddie, get the boys a round of drinks and bring the cards over along with the poker chips."

"Yes, Mr. Carlucci." Eddie did his task and locked eyes with Sal, who snarled as he was setting down the chips. *This is not good*, he thought. *This guy has killed people before. I know it.* Eddie broke his stare. "Uh, what can I get you, gentlemen, to drink?"

The drink orders were placed and delivered. Eddie cleaned up the bar and put the empty bottles in a box to be brought out to the alley for recycling day. "I'll be right back, Mr. Carlucci. I want to take the bottles down."

"Okay, Eddie, bring up some gelato for the boys on your way back."

"That sounds good." Carmine smiled and rubbed his belly. "Summer's over, so I can gain all the weight I want now."

Sal was quick to respond, "Looks like you already started."

Eddie heard them laughing as he raced down the steep stairs only to stop at the bottom of the landing, looking through the French doors to see Brenden's car parked right out front with the trunk open. Brenden was in the driver's seat, looking toward the alley, when he saw Eddie. They stared at each other, a look of guilt racing over Brenden's face before he turned away.

Eddie walked out the front door, past Brenden's car. He tried to get Brenden's attention, but he would not look his way. Eddie turned to the alley and stopped dead in his tracks.

"What the hell are you guys doing to my motorcycle?"

"Taking back our money you lost." Johnny laughed as he downed his beer.

"What's the matter, Eddie, you don't like to share?" Kenny slurred, holding Eddie's motorcycle helmet as JT tried to pick up the bike.

"Hey, that's my bike! Leave it alone!"

"Sorry, Eddie, they brought me here. I had no choice." Christopher spoke apologetically as he looked on from a position by the wall.

Eddie turned to see if his friend Brenden was watching any of this. No such luck. He had a white-knuckle grip on the steering wheel, staring straight ahead with blinders on. Eddie turned back in time to hear Christopher shout, "Look out!"

It was too late. With brute force, Kenny swung the helmet against Eddie's head, making him stumble and lose his balance. Eddie slammed into his motorcycle sideways and dropped the box of bottles.

"What the hell was that?" Carmine was startled as they all turned around.

Sal was closest to the window and jumped up first to look. Shocked at first at what he saw, but he then smiled with contention. Fists were flying, and Eddie was getting the crap beat out of him. "Ah, it's all good. The kid dropped the box of bottles. He's okay." Sal cranked the window closed. "Getting chilly in here."

"You gonna play cards or tell us about the weather?" Carmine laughed at his own joke.

JT lifted Eddie off the collapsed bike and swung a fist solidly into Eddie's gut, knocking the wind out of him. He dragged Eddie by the collar with his boots dragging deeper into the alley and dropped him on the ground.

Johnny and Kenny laughed as they looked on with glee.

"Aw, Eddie fell down!" Johnny kicked him in the side. "What's that nursery rhyme, Kenny? Ring around the rosie?"

Eddie rolled over, coughing up blood.

"Yeah!" Kenny laughed it out, "Ashes, ashes, Eddie falls down."

Johnny and JT guffawed as they continued to kick Eddie while he was down.

"Hey, leave him alone, guys!" Christopher nervously called out.

JT rushed over to Chris and got up in his face. "Oh, Chrissy, why don't you go sit in the car with Brenden like a good little girl and leave us men to finish our job, okay?" JT jabbed Christopher in the chest.

Christopher did not hesitate, and without a word, he looked back at Eddie and ran to the car.

"Where's our money, you prick?" JT pulled Eddie up with his hair. Eddie screamed out only to be silenced by Johnny throwing more punches to his stomach. JT let him go as he doubled over to the ground.

The hallway door suddenly banged open from a gust of wind through the alley.

"Come on, boys." JT grabbed one arm, Kenny the other, and Johnny took aim. He kicked Eddie right in the balls. "Why don't you tell Mr. Carlucci to clean your balls."

Eddie cried out, and Kenny laughed. "Stop being such a baby and take your whupping like a man."

"Johnny, hold the door open," JT demanded. "Throw him in here."

Kenny kicked Eddie a few more times in the side, and Johnny punched him in the face. JT propped him up against the wall. "Don't ever steal from my friends again, you understand, dickhead?" He turned to Johnny and Kenny. "Okay, boys?"

Before they could answer, JT reached into his back pocket and pulled out his hunting knife. It glimmered in the alleyway light.

"Do it!" Johnny yelled out. "Stab him once for me!"

JT did not hesitate. He stabbed Eddie in the stomach.

Eddie let out a gut-wrenching breath, reaching for JT's arm. Blood spilled from his lips as he gasped for air. JT stabbed him again as Eddie moaned out for help.

Johnny looked over his shoulder to make sure no one else was around.

JT leaned into Eddie and stabbed him one more time in the heart. "This one is for keeping Annie away from me."

Eddie reached for JT's hand again, gurgling something incoherent, and fell still.

JT pulled the knife out, slowly wiping it across Eddie's shirt. "Let's go, boys."

Johnny was in shock, frozen and sober. "Is… is he dead?"

"We'll soon find out, won't we?" JT exited the hallway into the alley nodding for them to follow.

Kenny followed suit, pulling Johnny by his sweatshirt. "No, did this just happen?"

JT slammed the door shut, putting the knife in its sheath and back in his pocket. They exited the alley to find Brenden and Christopher had driven off. They were gone.

Ciara sighed and took a deep breath. "Wow!"

"Holy cow. JT murdered Eddie. Oh, my God. I have to tell Annie."

"Wait a minute, calm down, Gerard."

"No, no, no, wait. So, the guy in the back is Black Irish, not Black. Joe, the other medium, said the guy in the back was Black and named Andy. But he's a white guy named Eddie, and JT murdered him."

"Yes, yes, he did. Eddie wants you to warn Annie to be careful. He says JT is coming for her and you if you get in his way."

"He already has. He's been to the patisserie twice, as far as I know. Annie is freaking out over it. Now what? So, who the hell is Andy?"

"I don't know. There is no Andy here that came through."

"So much to take in. I need to listen to this reading over again to try and understand it all."

"Yes, I agree. So much has been said, I don't even remember half of it!" Ciara chuckled.

"What about the other spirits that are roaming around?"

"The others are fine, and they won't bother you. I mean, they've been there for so long; they are comfortable with staying put, and probably will never leave. Family will always stay, too, because they are connected to you."

"I am sorry for staying so long." I was trembling inside and felt like a nuisance.

"Not a problem, Gerard. It was an incredibly enjoyable reading. I had fun, and I hope you did, too. I hope you got some answers to your mysteries at the bakery."

"I did, but I wouldn't exactly call it fun. I would say it was remarkably interesting, and it kind of opens my view on life after death. Thank you for taking the time to do this reading." I stood, a little wobbly on my feet after the emotional roller coaster. I had to get in touch with Annie immediately.

"It was my pleasure. I'll call you in a few days. Maybe I'll come by the bakery this week and smoke it with some sage."

"Yeah, sure, that sounds good." She escorted me to the door, and I looked around the room for a final time. Just thought maybe I would see a ghost fly by, but the room was calm and silent.

"Remember what I told you," Ciara instructed, "when you feel their presence, or if they're bothering you, mentally wrap them up in pink, green, and white and send them on their way to the light."

"Okay, I will. I'll give it a try again." I shook Ciara's hand, and she pulled me in for a hug.

"Have a good night; you'll need to rest up for tomorrow's event."

"I know; now I'm nervous about everything else."

"Don't worry, you'll be fine and happy with tomorrow's results. Just take care and watch your back." Ciara smiled her contagious smile.

I shot Ciara a look before she gently closed the door after me. I walked back through the hallway to the twisted staircase. I looked up to see if the old widow was going to give me a wink good night, but she must've been involved watching a rerun of *Murder or Nothing*.

I headed down the stairs, relieved that the reading was over. I have to process what I have just learned. Thank God, I had recorded it all.

CHAPTER 42

STEVE WAS SKEPTICAL ABOUT the whole reading after I played it back for him.

All he said over and over was, "Is she for real?"

I could not blame him, but some of the things she told me were true, things she said that only I'd know. Too much had happened in such a brief period. Steve listened intently when his mom, his dad, and Figaro came through.

Steve sniffled and coughed a few times. "She could've looked it up."

I handed him the box of tissues. "How could she do that? She doesn't even know you."

"I don't believe in all this voodoo stuff. Something isn't right."

"Well, I believe in what she said. So much of it was true." I headed to bed; it was getting later than I wanted.

"Tell me again in the morning. I can't think straight with this cold."

"Fine. I have to get some sleep anyway. Big day tomorrow."

"I know, don't worry. You got this."

"Thanks, Steve, everybody says the same thing, don't worry but as usual I worry."

I could not wait to play the recording for my chefs. Maybe Annie could now get the restraining order she needed to protect herself from JT. That's if the police believe in ghosts.

CHAPTER 43

I WAS ON FOUR hours' sleep, feeling hungover, tired, and drained from Ciara's reading. It was four a.m., and I sat in my car thinking about the day. I couldn't wait for today's competition to be over, and it hadn't even started yet.

I texted Annie. *-Are you on your way?*

-Running late.

-Should I wait for you? I have so much to tell you.

-No, go ahead. I'm sorry, I need another twenty minutes.

-Okay.

-Sorry, Danny is sick. Waking my mom now, and then I'm leaving.

-Okay, no problem.

I hesitated to type *no problem*, but I gave everyone the benefit of the doubt.

When I arrived at the shop, I inserted my key as I normally did and heard someone cough behind me in the distance. I turned quickly only to find no one there. I scanned my surroundings. Someone had definitely coughed. It was then I spotted the lit cigarette in the vestibule of the bar across the street. Someone was hiding in the dark, again. Maybe, it was someone who lived above the bar stepping out to have a smoke. I just wasn't sure.

I stepped inside and turned off the alarm. Looking out the glass door, I could still see the cigarette being puffed on, as the amber glow grew brighter in the darkness. I ignored it as I needed to start working.

I walked through the café to open the kitchen door, then paused to wonder if I would come face-to-face with paranormal activity.

Slowly, I opened the door and flipped the lights surveying the kitchen; it looked in order, nothing flew around to grab my attention. I set my messenger bag down on the table and set up my laptop to stream some music. "I know you're all here."

Yes, we are dude; we're all exhausted from last night's reading with Ciara. She is spot on, very calm, clear, and easy to speak to. You should see her again. She has more to tell you, but she won't interfere with life. She will not change the course of what is about to happen. She cannot alter the outcome. It's not her place to do so, but she did warn you, so be ready, my friend.

No reply.

"I guess that's a good start." Heeding Ciara's advice, I spoke firmly. "Thank you for all your help around here, and I'm sorry most of you passed so tragically." I paused, still no noises or voices to be heard. "I have an important day today and a lot of work to do. So please leave me alone. Okay?"

No reply.

"That goes for you, too, Eddie, now that I know your name. I'll tell Annie what you said when I see her. So, I wrap you all in pink for love, green for hope, and white for protection and send you on your way to heaven. Go to the light and leave the bakery alone."

G-man, I thought we straightened this all-out last night. They are lovely colors, but nobody is going anywhere. We are just getting started.

Again, there was no reply.

I sighed a sigh of relief. "Okay, then and let's do this."

I marched to the front of the store to make a pot of morning brew. While it brewed, I peered out the front window to see if Annie was there or if the smoking person was still across the street. No one was there. I blew a sigh of relief. It was time to start my day.

At four thirty, Annie still had not shown up for work. Now I was getting angry. I could have asked Kate or Jada to help me, so I sent Annie another text.

-Are you okay? Where are you?

I put my phone in my pocket and continued cooking. The GF dough was made, and I put it in the walk-in refrigerator. I crossed it off my list and put some pan spray and powdered sugar in a bag alongside the waffle iron in the closet. Done. "Here we go, Grandma, wish me luck."

I checked my phone for Annie's reply. No reply but an error message saying, *failed to send text.* So, I sent another text and immediately received the same response.

"What the hell is with her phone?" I muttered. "I can't do it all but sometimes you have no choice."

I turned the music up a little louder with some classic rock and roll and finished sautéing chickpeas in butter, added the walnuts, honey, and jam. I always think of my mom when I make the recipe, and how I covered myself in chocolate. I laughed at the memory.

I added the melted chocolate to the mixture when I heard the front door sensor sound off. I moved the big bowl of gavajune mix to the middle table and gazed at the monitor. No one was there. I thought maybe Annie had come in.

I was stirring the mixture when I heard the front door sensor beep again. I looked up and saw someone at the front door. It looked like Annie. Then I did a double take. There were two people at the door. The door was swinging open and closed, sending the sensor off along with the bell chiming in. Something was wrong. It looked like the two people were struggling when I heard Annie scream out, "Get away from me."

I froze; everything moved in slow motion. "Oh, my God, it's happening." *JT.*

Annie came rushing into the café, JT a few feet behind her.

As I turned to open the kitchen door, Annie came barreling through, sending me into the closet. She stumbled forward, tripping over me to the kitchen floor and slid on her stomach. JT stood in the open kitchen doorway, surveying the room. Not seeing me in the closet, he let the door close behind him and took a few menacing steps until he stood over Annie, squirming on the floor.

"How nice of you to get down and ready for me, but I'm not sure if the music is to my taste so early in the morning. Perhaps a little Beethoven would be good for some kitchen carving."

Annie screamed as JT grabbed her foot and held it up, making her almost do a handstand.

Still out of JT's sight in the closet, I slowly inched up to standing upright.

"Where's that faggot baker boss of yours?" JT demanded. "In the bathroom hiding. Hmm? I don't want him to miss the show."

"I'm right here, you asshole!"

JT dropped Annie's leg, snickered his devilish grin, and pulled out a large hunting knife from his waistband.

Annie screamed scrambling away as JT turned to face me.

I was ready and caught him off guard. I saw the surprise in his face two seconds before I swung my grandmother's waffle iron with all my might right in his gut, knocking the wind out of him.

I slammed him right into the wall and heard something crack, maybe one of his ribs or his body impacting the wall. I stepped back out of his reach and watched as he stood hunched over, crying out in pain. I looked around the kitchen for something, anything, to help me defeat this guy knowing the waffle was too heavy to swing around like a sword.

I reached for a rolling pin, the closet thing I could grab as the lights above my worktable started blinking. Then the other kitchen lights overhead did the same thing until the kitchen was filled with a strobe light effect.

"What is going on?" I shouted out, keeping my eyes on JT.

Screaming, Annie stood up and rushed to my side as we backed away from JT toward the swinging kitchen door, knowing the main door was too close to where JT was.

Propped up against the wall, JT was holding his stomach as he tried to stand. "Where the hell are you?" he shouted.

We did not dare move. I heard the scraping of the chef's knife against the magnetic board and slowly turned my head in its direction as it detached. It looked as if someone was having a challenging time removing it because the magnetic hold was stronger than they thought. The knife fell to my worktable. Annie and I gasped out loud as the knife flew across the kitchen, stabbing JT in the stomach.

JT let out a wretched cry as another chef's knife flew across the kitchen, stabbing him for a second time in the stomach.

Annie tucked her head into my chest, unable to watch. I put my arm around her and held her tight.

JT screamed in pain. "You bastard! I'm going to kill you both."

He could not move as the knives had pinned him to the wall, piercing right through him as blood sprayed out. The lights in the back of the kitchen by the sink started to grow brighter and exploded in a burst of shattering glass. The oven doors blew open, and the walk-in compressors stopped humming, but the rock and roll music continued playing a bit louder drowning out JT's screams. The lights above us kept the strobe light effect going as JT's hunting knife levitated before us and floated its way to JT.

Annie seized the moment, darting away from me and toward JT.

"Annie, wait!"

She reached for the hunting knife, locking eyes with JT, and screamed, "You bastard, die already!"

JT cried out. "No, no, no!" as he tried to deflect the knife.

I watched in horror as Annie pushed the knife forward. "No, Annie! Oh, my God!" I reached for Annie's shoulder as she shrugged me away.

Panicked, JT gripped the sharp serrated blade coming for his chest. Blood dripped from his hands as he tried to stop the movement of the knife. But Annie was stronger, his grip around the blade useless, as the knife pierced his chest and entered his heart.

I turned away.

Blood spewed everywhere as JT fell still.

Annie cried out, "Die, you evil bastard!"

The lights above my worktable grew brighter, almost to a blinding light, and then fell dark.

The music continued with guitar riffs and drums drumming as Annie backed away from JT, covered with blood. "Oh, my God. What just happened? What did I do? I felt like my body was taken over."

Annie sobbed hysterically as I tried to calm her, but then suddenly we witnessed an apparition. I had no other words for it as the shape of a person materialized before our eyes. It looked to be a young man, Eddie, I believed, as he smiled at Annie and me.

"Yoouuuuu arrrreeee saaaffffffe noooooooowww."

He smiled and blew a kiss to Annie.

Annie smiled amid the shock and tears. "Ed, uh, Eddie?"

He nodded ever so slowly. She reached for his hand as he reached for hers, touching, glowing fingertips with a gentle touch as blood dripped.

"Oh, my God!" Annie sobbed as tears rolled down her cheeks.

Eddie turned and faced JT; whose body now lay limp as his ghostly image materialized before us. Eddie reached forward, grabbing JT's image by the throat, and both vanished into the wall.

The lights above us slowly grew dim as the knives fell, crashing to the floor. The compressors started humming again, and the ovens turned back on. JT's legs gave way, slumping his body, leaving a smudgy trail of blood on the white wall.

"Oh, my God!" Annie backed up against the side table as the lights came back on in the kitchen.

"What just happened?" I think my eyes bulged as I gasped.

"He's dead, right?" Annie approached his still body.

"Yes, Annie, I believe he is. I cannot believe what just happened, but I have no choice. This just happened, didn't it?"

"Yes." Annie continued to cry. "Oh, my God!"

Blood splattered on the center table and on the outside of the mixing bowl with my gavajune mix in it. Although I couldn't see any blood on the surface, it did look like raspberry jam to some extent. *Damn it!* I thought.

Annie put her hands on her hips and immediately snapped out of her horrified trance. "We have to get rid of the body."

"Annie." I walked around the center table. "Seriously, we have to call the police."

"And who's going to believe that a ghost did this?" Annie threw her bloody hands out toward me.

"You have a point, but there's a dead body here." I felt nauseous, so many thoughts went streaming through my head and not good ones.

Annie took the knives to the sink and washed her hands. Crunching over the shattered fluorescent glass, she put some food handler gloves on and repeated, "We have to get rid of the body."

"No, no, no." I watched her in motion. "What are you doing?"

"I don't know. Panicking, I guess."

"The hallway." The idea came quickly to me. "We can put him in the hallway for now until we figure this out." I can't believe I just said that.

"Yes, exactly. I bet nobody knows he's here. We can put him out with the trash." Annie came back with a few garbage bags. "Think you better call Kate and ask her to go with you to the competition. I'll stay here and clean up."

"Whoa, wait! What? You want to stay here with dead JT?"

"Yes, here, open the bags up."

"Annie, you are freaking out. We must call the police."

"No! If you call the police, I am gone." Annie narrowed her eyes to me. "I'll disappear Gerard. I won't stay around for this. You have the competition to get to, or you'll have to face the police on your own."

"Forget the competition." I folded my arms across my chest.

"Forget nothing. Go! I'll take care of this, and you take care of you. I'm done with him terrorizing me. I need to move on." Annie tore off her bloody chef's coat and threw it in the garbage bag.

I gave Annie that questionable and unsatisfying look, trying to think of my own options. I looked at the time and gave in.

"Please, help me drag him." Annie stood there in a bright white T-shirt and extended her hand with some latex gloves for me.

"I think I'm going to be sick." I dry retched at the task in hand. "We should be calling the police!"

"Can't tell anyone. Dispose of the body, and no one will know."

"Sounds like you've done this before."

Annie took a second before replying. My eyes lit up again. "Uh, no, just watched too many scary movies."

"Uh huh." I felt my nerves jump, thinking JT may not be the only killer in this room. "How do we explain the gashes in the wall?"

"We plaster them with buttercream."

"Say what?" I found her comment almost comical, knowing toothpaste was always a quick fix for a home remedy.

"Pull!"

Annie was stronger than I realized as we dragged JT through the kitchen, leaving a trail of blood into the hallway. I gulped at the thought of getting locked in there again, especially with a dead body. But the rock held the door open, and we pushed his body against all the other garbage bags from Sunday night.

We stepped back into the kitchen and slammed the creaky door closed.

"Now, call Kate."

"It's almost six a.m. I have to leave soon. There's not enough time for all this. Damn it!" I complained again. "Why the hell do they have to have the baker competition so freaking early?"

"Go, Gerard. Please, go, I will take care of this mess. It's all my fault anyway." Annie let the tears flow again.

"This is insane. I cannot believe we are doing this. Come with me. We can come back later and clean up."

"No." Annie folded her arms across her chest and stood her ground.

I tried to plead with her. "We can tell the police we found him outside in front of the store, and we dragged him into the kitchen, or he slipped and fell onto some knives."

"Ha. Good luck with that." Annie grabbed a bucket for my gavajune mix and started pouring it in. I wanted to stop her and have another look at it, just in case I saw some trails of blood, but she was quick.

"This is your time to shine, to win this thing—for you, for your future, and for Fiorello. Don't worry about me, I'll be fine. Life goes on." Annie set the bowl down and wrapped her arms around me for a supporting hug.

"Please, call Kate and go. Just wash up and change your chef coat first. You got a little blood on your sleeve."

I stood in silence, thinking how incredible the last month had been. I didn't want to miss out on this opportunity to showcase Fiorello Patisserie. "Damn it!" I ripped my chef coat off and took a clean one out of the closet.

"You got this, Gerard!" Annie smiled for the first time.

I called Kate and woke her up. "I need you to come with me to the Prestigious Honoré Awards."

Gavajune

CHAPTER 44

I PICKED KATE UP and filled her in on what happened. I think she said *oh, my God* at least fifteen times.

"And you left her there?"

"What am I to do?"

"I don't know what I would've done, but at a minimum, I probably would've run out into Main Street screaming at the top of my lungs."

"Yeah, I thought about that, too."

"Come on, we're here."

I called the patisserie, and there was no answer. I called Annie's cell phone and received a recorded message. *Sorry, the number you dialed is no longer in service.*

"Did you dial it right?"

"Yeah, she's in my contacts. I'll try a text message again, but it keeps coming up failed to send."

"Maybe she's too busy chopping JT into tiny pieces to hear the phone ring." Kate gave me that wide-eye staring look.

"You're as crazy as this whole morning has been," I joked.

"Nah, you're crazier."

"Agreed."

We both laughed.

"Maybe she shut her phone down?"

"Don't know, maybe, but I did text her at four in the morning, and she replied. It's weird."

"The whole thing is weird, let's go."

We entered the convention hall and Mary Cartelli ran right up to us.

"Good morning, Gerard. So happy you made it. It's so exciting to have you and chef Kate here. I hope you brought the carrot cake?"

"Of course, I did."

"Oh, good." Mary smiled from ear to ear. "I've been hyping you up, and I'm sure the judges will die over it."

"Oh, God, please, I hope not," Kate whispered as we stepped behind the table in our show booth.

I gave her the stink eye this time. "Thank you, Mary. I'm sure the judges will love it."

"Good luck to you both and to Fiorello Patisserie." Mary stepped aside and left us to set up our booth and prepare the gavajunes to bake off.

Kate cringed at the thought of blood being in the batter. There was no proof of it, and I was quite sure it hadn't been tainted with blood. I could almost swear on it. Almost. I checked my phone again. Still no reply from Annie, just the same error message.

I was starting to feel frustrated and anxious. "I should've called the police."

"And tell them what? A ghost knifed a guy to death in the patisserie's kitchen. Gerard, we are all in on it now. Maybe Annie is right. Put him out with the trash and pray this ghost thing is over and done with."

"I don't know. I can't think straight for anything right now."

An announcer's voice spoke over us. "Good morning, and welcome to the Prestigious Honoré Awards 2006. We would like all pastry chefs entering the best dessert category to bring their dessert forward to the judge's table. Please no labels or any information on your dessert or where the dessert is from. This is a blind taste challenge, and we want everyone to have a fair shot at this. Thank you, and good luck to you all."

We brought the carrot cake over on the provided platters and hurried back to our station.

"I hope no one dies from the carrot cake."

"Oh, Kate, knock it off."

"It was just a joke." Kate rolled her eyes and nudged me.

I looked up and saw the judges starting to make their rounds. I heated up the waffle iron, and by nine a.m., we were ready for our first tasting.

The GF cookies came out flawless. I did not burn one. My grandmother and aunt Angie would be proud of me. I'm sure they're looking over my shoulder as I flipped the heavy iron.

A few of the judges nodded with delight and took some notes. They then tried the freshly baked gavajunes, and with hope in my heart of success, they delivered.

"Wow. This is incredible. I've never had anything like this before. It's quite delicious. Never knew chickpeas could taste so good."

"Why, thank you, for the kind words."

The second judge agreed. "The flavors explode. What are the ingredients again?"

I explained—butter, sugar, chickpeas, chocolate, honey, orange zest, cinnamon, nutmeg, walnuts, almonds, and raspberry jam. I waited for a reply after the judge took another bite.

"There must be a secret ingredient in here. I cannot put my finger on it, but I taste something else. Is there an herb or another spice that you forgot to mention?"

"Uh, no other spices or herbs."

Kate elbowed me and whispered. "Oh, my God."

I smiled back to the judge. "I assure you, there are no secret ingredients other than a labor of love."

"Whew, that was a good answer," Kate whispered.

"Thank you very much Chef and Team Fiorello."

We both nodded as the judges moved on, and Kate felt relieved. The judges made their rounds from booth to booth, eating their way around the event.

"Still no answer from Annie." I stared at my phone in hopes of a message magically appearing. I called the bakery, and there was no answer. I started to feel uneasy and thought maybe she did call the police, and they would burst through the competition doors and arrest me in public for murder.

Kate sent her a text and called her. She, too, received the same response as me, nothing. "Something is wrong here. You should call Steve or the police."

"I can't call the police now. I left the scene of the crime and could be implicated in the death of JT., and I sent Steve a text. No answer yet. He must still be sleeping."

"Attention, please!" The announcer was quite pleasant. "The judges have tallied up their votes and scored in each category. We will announce the winner in the best childhood dessert and cookie category first. Followed by best pastry chef, best pastry shop, and finally, the best dessert of the year!"

Everyone applauded as the announcer held the envelope with the results up in her hand.

"Good luck to us."

"You did an amazing job, Gerard. Win or lose, you already won."

"Thanks, Kate. Although we have a dead body at the patisserie for a consolation prize."

Kate rolled her eyes.

The time came to announce the winner for best childhood dessert and cookie. Kate and I held each other's sweaty palms as the judges announced the third-place team.

"I wonder how Annie is doing at the patisserie. Maybe she's in trouble."

"I'll call Steve again and ask him to meet us there when we're done."

The judges announced the second-place team.

"Damn, I think we lost," I whispered to Kate. "I can't believe it."

"Shh, don't think like that. We have to stay positive."

"I don't have much more in me to think positive. I'm terrified thinking about Annie being alone in the patisserie."

"Wait, they're going to announce the winner."

"We are proud to announce the winner of the Prestigious Honoré Award for best childhood dessert and cookie. This year's winning dessert is totally different than anything we have ever tasted. It is full of unique flavors that explode on your palate. I hope there is more of this incredible dessert for everyone to try. Without further ado, the winner of the best childhood dessert and cookie is…."

CHAPTER 45

KATE CALLED HANA ON the way home from the award ceremony and asked her if she had heard anything from Annie. *Not at all* was her reply. "It's too strange to piece together. Hana said she'll meet us there in five minutes. She just finished with her car inspection."

I pulled up in front of the patisserie and at once peered through the window. The lights were still off, and the front door was still locked.

"Hey, Rard? Are you going to help me with these awards or what?"

I opened the back of my SUV and helped Kate unload everything onto the wheeler. The golden whisk for best pastry chef, the etched golden plaque with Best Pastry Shop on Long Island, the platinum cookie tray for best cookie, a bronze rolling pin for best childhood dessert, and a crystal cake stand for best dessert. My carrot cake blew them away.

I opened the front door and lifted the wheeler into the café. "The alarm's not set. Maybe Annie is still here. Hey, Annie!" I yelled out as my heart filled my trembling throat.

"What are you two doing in here?" Steve bellowed from behind us in his scary voice.

We both screamed out in unison.

"What the hell is wrong with you?"

"Oh, my God, Steve, you scared the crap out of me." I punched Steve in the arm. "Damn you. We're freaking out enough today."

"Well, it *is* a haunted bakery!" Steve started laughing a rough, dry, raspy cough and coughed some more.

"Are you okay?" I put my hand on his shoulder.

"Sick as a dog. I should be at home in bed. Instead, you drag me out at this ungodly hour."

"It's ten thirty."

"Whatever. Congratulations! I knew you would win." Steve gave Kate and me a hug. "Now what happened around here?"

"Well, now the patisserie is even more haunted." Kate gritted teeth with a nervous laugh.

"What do you mean?"

"JT is dead, and Annie is missing." Kate blurted it out.

"Kate!" I shot her a glance.

"Well, he asked!"

"I wanted to tell him about this morning."

The front door behind us blew open and Hana entered. "Hi, everybody. So, did we win?"

"Every category," Kate cheered.

"Yes!" Hana threw her fist in the air. "Woo-hoo! Congratulations."

I gave her a hug. God, I really needed a hug. "But we have other problems in the kitchen now, I'll bet."

"What do you mean?" Hana looked from Kate to me. "Where's Annie?"

Before I could answer, Steve opened the kitchen door with a sneeze and put the lights on. "Are you scaredy-cats coming in?"

I looked past Steve into the kitchen. "Annie?" The floor was cleaned, and the blood gone. Not a trace of it anywhere. The wall was clean other than the three knife marks. I ran my finger over the cuts in the wall.

"What's going on?"

I looked from the magnetic bar wall in front of my marble table to the wall where JT had been stabbed. All my chef knives were back and in size order.

"Annie?" Steve called out. "Why are the lights out over the sink?"

We all fell silent.

"They exploded when Eddie was here," I answered quickly as I surveyed the kitchen for blood stains.

"What are you talking about?" Steve demanded.

"It's a long story." I tried to smile. "Where the hell did Annie go?"

Steve pulled on the walk-in refrigerator door handle and freezer door handle. Both doors were locked. He unlocked them and found nothing unusual inside.

I walked to the sink area myself and discovered no broken glass on the floor at all. All the bowls I'd used were clean above the sink drying.

"The hallway. I'll bet you Annie is trapped in the hallway like I was."

The four of us proceeded to the hallway door and I yelled out, "Annie, are you okay?"

No answer as Steve pushed the heavy door open. The creaking door hinge sounded the same as it had on the first day, we looked at the space. Scary in every way, although right then I felt terrified. The four of us peered into the vacant hallway. There was nothing but the rock. Not a piece of trash or garbage bag to be found.

"Where's the body?"

"The body?" Hana poked her head through. "What happened this morning?"

"This can't be happening, but it did happen. No question. The lights are busted and there are knife gouges in the wall." I looked to Kate for confirmation. "The video!" I ran back into the kitchen, turned on my laptop, and opened the security app.

"Gerard, what the hell happened this morning? And where the hell is Annie?" Steve folded his arms across his chest, sounding more nasally than ever.

"The cameras are offline. No way. Are you freaking kidding me?" I scanned the complete system. "Not a single recording from this morning. Eddie must have drained all the electricity. There's nothing here. Nothing since last night."

"You're a freak, Gerard! Doesn't anything work around here?" Kate blurted out.

"But it happened! I saw it all happen." My heart raced as I questioned my mental state. Had it all been a dream of some kind? Then, out of the corner of my eye, I spotted a red envelope we use for gift certificates hanging on the clipboard of the daily list. "Hana, there's a red envelope on the clipboard. I didn't put that there. What is it?"

It took Hana a second to realize what I was talking about, but she grabbed it and handed it to me. "It says Gerard, Steve and my Fiorello friends."

I didn't want to read what was inside, so I handed it back to Hana. "Please, you open it."

Hana tore it open. "It's a recipe card for Annie's ricotta tart." Hana flipped it over. "There's a note on the back." And read it aloud:

Dear Gerard, Steve and my Fiorello friends,

As you can see, I cleaned up. I shut my phone down earlier this morning, as you probably know by now from trying to call me. I'm sorry to leave this way without saying goodbye, but I must go. I've been living in fear for far too long. Danny and I have an opportunity for a fresh start to live with my cousin in New Jersey.

Please do not try to find me. I've caused enough trouble and grief in your world to last a lifetime. Thank you for all you have done, and today was totally unreal, beyond anything I've ever witnessed. I can't explain it, nor do I want to relive it.

I've left you this recipe to remember me by.
Till we meet again in life after death.

Annie

"Wow. She left us." Hana handed me the note.

"Can I see it?" Kate snagged it from my hands.

"Ahh-choo!" Steve sneezed.

"Bless you. Are you okay?"

"Yeah, this damn cold won't let up." Steve sniffled.

"Did she say anything to the two of you or Jada?" I asked Hana and Kate.

"No, not a word about leaving," Hana answered.

"She must've been planning this for a while to shut her phone off and plan a move. But why would she do it today, the day of the competition?" Kate placed the note on the center table.

The front door chimed open. We all looked to the monitor and saw a woman enter the café.

"Hello? Are you open?"

Steve headed for the door. "I'll go see who it is. Maybe she is a real person. Excuse me please."

"I am so confused." Hana sighed.

"It's okay, Hana. I'll tell you later." Kate leaned on the table rereading the note.

Steve popped his head back into the kitchen. We all gave him our attention. "Uh, Ciara is here."

"What? I just saw Ciara last night, why would she come here today?" I followed Steve to the front counter.

"Hi, Gerard, I was in the neighborhood and thought I'd stop by."

"Yeah, sure, hi, er…we're closed today, but can I get you anything?"

"No, I actually came by to sage this place out."

"Oh! Sure, come on in."

"What is she talking about?" Steve whispered in my ear. "Is she really going to do it now?"

"Just go along with it, please," I quickly whispered back. "She said she'd come by in a week, so this is a surprise. I didn't think today. Uh, Ciara, I'd like you to meet my partner, Steve, and my chefs Kate and Hana."

"Nice to meet you all. You were all in Gerard's reading last night."

"Oh? How so? What happened?" Hana questioned me.

"A lot. We need to catch you and Jada up on a lot of details, but if I remember correctly, your grandfather likes to play with spoons and hang out with you."

"Spoons?"

Ciara started to walk around the kitchen as if she could not be bothered by the small talk.

"Yeah, remember how the hard spoon kept falling off the handle?"

"Oh, yeah. Hi, Grandpa." Hana giggled.

"Why the unexpected visit, Ciara?" I wondered if she knew what had happened to me that morning.

"Well, I did say I'd drop by, and I was in town. I also wanted to make sure you were okay." She frowned. "A lot went on this morning around here. I can feel it. I can sense it. The spirits are telling me everything will be okay from now on. The, how should I say it, *the drama*, for lack of a better explanation, is over." Ciara smiled and circled her arms around, bringing her hands together, ready for a prayer in meditation mode.

"Yes, a lot of drama this morning, but was it real? I'm still in shock."

"Why are you in shock, Gerard? What happened?" Steve elbowed me.

I spoke softly. "Eddie killed JT this morning." There, I said it, loud enough for Steve and Hana to hear.

"Who's Eddie?" Hana scrunched her face.

Steve tapped my shoulder for my attention. "Wait, are you saying Eddie, the ghost, killed JT?"

"Yes. It was real. It happened. Those awards I see in the box are real. It all happened." I sighed with a heavy deep breath.

"I have no idea what's going on." Hana looked to us for answers.

"Neither do I, Hana," Steve rolled his eyes.

"I'll tell you the whole story. JT followed Annie into the patisserie this morning, I whacked him into the wall with the waffle iron, and Eddie threw the chef knives across the room right into JT's gut, pinning him against the wall. Annie finished him off with his own hunting knife in the heart. Eddie materialized as an apparition and grabbed JT's ghostly image and vanished into the wall."

"What the hell!" Hana stepped back from the table and was side-stepped by Kate.

"You're losing it, Gerard. This ghost crap has got you fantasizing stories," Steve chimed in.

Kate for once kept her comments to herself and blankly stared at everyone's reaction.

"It happened! I swear."

Ciara reached into her large bag and pulled out a crystal rock. "Yes, it happened." Ciara placed it on the middle table. We watched in silence as she reached in again, this time pulling out a large clamshell, a lighter, and a white box marked Dried Sage.

Were we about to witness a magic trick of some kind?

"There's a lot of good energy in this room. Most of it comes from you, Gerard, and your staff. Were you and Kate married?"

"*What?*"

"I feel there's an extremely strong connection between the two of you."

"I'm his work wife, if that means anything."

"It means a lot," Ciara teased.

"And then what am I? The mistress?" Steve put a hand on his hip.

We all chuckled.

She told Kate and I that we might've been married in a previous life. She told Steve his parents had nothing but love for him, and that they were immensely proud of him.

She put a few pieces of sage in the shell and tried to light it. It took a few tries to stay lit and then it kept going out. Were the spirits doing this on purpose to prevent the smoking? I was somewhat torn by this. There were some spirits I wished would leave—but hoped some would eventually continue to stay with us—despite their shenanigans. I feel the patisserie is a place of comfort for them.

I asked Ciara if Eddie, JT, or Mattie were present.

Ciara turned my way as if suddenly struck without an answer to the question. "You know, I don't feel their presence at all. There's nothing but family and love here."

"Whose Mattie?" Hana asked.

"Just a young dead girl buried somewhere in the bakery." Kate was back in form.

"What?" Hana shouted.

Steve rolled his eyes this time. "Maybe our grandparents chased them away."

Kate cheered. "Yeah, you get 'em, Grandpa."

Hana and I laughed nervously.

I showed Ciara where the hollow floor was.

She asked, "Do you want to break it open?"

"Whhaaat? No way! I'm not waking up the dead."

Sheer horror came over Hana and Kate. They slid their way to the far side of the table, inching toward the kitchen door.

Steve spoke sternly, "If you break that open, I'm never coming back into this shop again." Then he, too, got up, joining Hana and Kate near the door, like they were all about to make a run for it.

"Look at the scaredy-cats," I laughed, but then quickly agreed with them. The floor would stay intact. I did not want a mutiny on my hands.

"Who knows what's under there," I gulped. "Let Mattie's bones lie, and all will be well. We know she is here… somewhere. No exhumations!" That seemed to reassure them. Me, too!

As Ciara moved farther into the kitchen, she picked up on a group of old spirits in the corner area of my table, and a few stuck in the walk-in refrigerator. She smoked them away with love, hope, and white light for protection.

Next, she moved into the back hallway where she voiced. "Hello." She felt no threat at all, yet throughout the shop, she felt the heaviness of old spirits who were stuck, who had not moved on. That hallway was scary enough. Never mind having it full of spirits from the 1700s.

She braved the walk down the hallway, following it around and outside to the front of the building. Not a sign of JT's body or Annie anywhere. When she came back, she said she felt a sense of energy flowing. We opened all the doors, allowing a refreshing wind to sweep through.

The unknown haunted the patisserie, any number of the spirits of people from the past that seemed to be coming and going at will. Perhaps we were the gatekeepers to some sort of otherworldly vortex.

Looking at the early still photos of the stick-like orb, which at that point I hadn't seen in a few days, I asked, "Ciara, do you think this is Eddie?"

"It could be, but it also could be anybody. I don't feel Eddie's presence here at all. Maybe he did leave. If you ignore them, they'll go away. Eventually. Hopefully."

"How about JT?"

Ciara closed her eyes for a second. "No, no JT. I believe Eddie took him to the other side, probably dropped him in hell." Ciara smirked and continued. "Hmm, I think Eddie left with that girl, Annie. He is now a free spirit, no longer chained to this place as a ghost. He settled the score in getting his revenge or should I say sweet revenge." Ciara chuckled. "He is free to roam."

I breathed a sigh of relief but wished she had sounded more definite, but I was afraid to ask about this morning's events but happy knowing the patisserie is basically ghost free.

I took a deep breath for courage and glanced at Kate, and as if on cue, she told Ciara about my magic power of sending the spirit up the exhaust fan.

Ciara gave us a good laugh and addressed Kate. "When you feel scared, I want you to wrap yourself in white for protection. In fact, all of you, imagine the whole kitchen in white. Wrap it in pink for love, green for hope, and white for protection, and send the spirits to the light."

"Easier said than done, but I guess it works. I mean, we actually saw it work." Kate nodded in agreement.

"Yes, it does work," Ciara smiled.

"Thank you so much for coming here and for smoking out the bakery."

"You're welcome. Nice to meet you all." Ciara smiled and shook everyone's hand goodbye.

I escorted her out to the front door, where she grabbed my forearm, "I know what happened this morning, but I didn't want to sound an alarm to the others. Everything will be okay now."

I gave her a hug. "Thank you."

Annie's Ricotta Tart

Preheat conventional oven to 350 degrees or convection oven to 325 degrees. If using a convection oven, select the low fan.

¾ lb. (12 oz)	Ricotta cheese
1 Yolk	
3 ¼ oz	Granulated sugar
½ tsp	Sweet dark rum
¼ tsp	Vanilla extract
1	Lemon: zest half of it
2.5 oz	Semi-sweet chocolate (grated)

18-inch tart/pie shell lined with sweet sucrée dough*
Cheese cloth or strong absorbent paper towels

Make a sweet pie dough recipe using our pâte sucrée recipe first. This way the dough can rest for at least an hour in the refrigerator before use.

We like to use fresh ricotta when available. Place a strainer lined with cheesecloth or paper towels over a bowl, leaving an inch between the strainer and the bowl. Place the ricotta in the strainer and pat down with another paper towel or two to help absorb the excess liquid. Place the ricotta, strainer, and bowl in the refrigerator while prepping out the other ingredients.

In a mixing bowl, separate the egg, saving the egg white for another use. Add the sugar to the yolk and whisk together until combined. Add the rum, vanilla extract, and lemon zest and whisk.

Remove the ricotta from the refrigerator and gently squeeze out some of the remaining liquid. Add the ricotta to the yolk mixture, discarding the liquid and paper towels and cheesecloth. Whisk together, breaking up the ricotta.

Remove the whisk and switch to a rubber spatula to fold in the shaved chocolate.

Pour the batter into the prepared tart or pie shell.

At this point, the tart can be baked as is or the remaining dough can be rolled to create a decorative or lattice top. Egg wash the lattice or dough cutouts with an egg yolk for a nice golden color before the pie goes in the oven.

Bake for twenty minutes, turn the tart around, and finish baking for another twenty minutes or until the lattice is has a light golden color and the filling has a light amber color. The center of the tart should be a solid jiggle, not a loose jiggle.

Remove from the oven and cool on a baker's rack.

Refrigerate after it cools down and serve.

** Baker's note: you may use your own pie dough
recipe or purchase sweet pie dough from your local supermarket.*

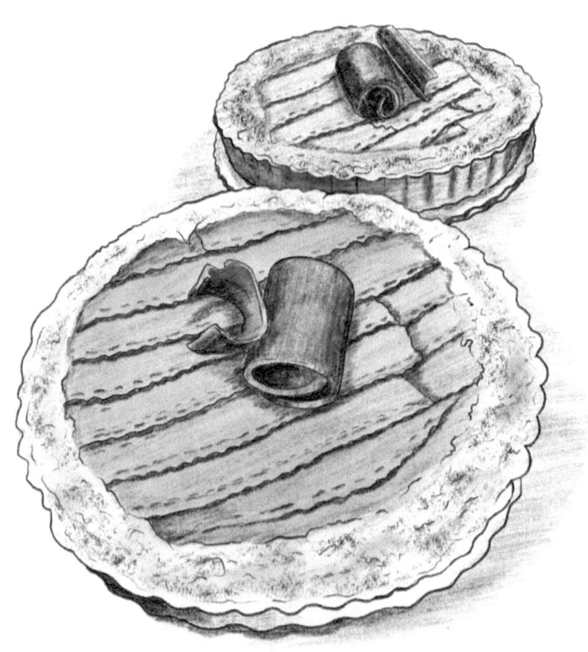

Pâte Sucrée

½ pound	Unsalted butter, soften at room temperature
250 grams	Granulated sugar
3	Extra-large eggs at room temperature
500 grams	All-purpose flour
½ tsp	Baking powder
1/8 tsp	Salt

In a five-quart stand-up mixer with a paddle attachment, cream the butter to soft pomade consistency. Add the sugar and mix until it is incorporated. Stop the mixer and scrape down the sides with a rubber spatula. Add the eggs one at a time until incorporated before adding the next one and mix again on a slow to medium speed. Stop the mixer and scrape down the sides again.

Sift the flour with the baking powder and salt. Set the mixer on the slowest speed and add the flour mix. Mix until it is incorporated. Stop the mixer and scrape down the sides again. Mix again for another minute or two to make sure the dough is fully incorporated.

Remove from the mixer onto plastic wrap. Form a disc about a quarter-inch high. Wrap fully and refrigerate for at least an hour or until the dough is firm.

Remove the dough from the refrigerator, remove the plastic wrap, and roll the dough out on a lightly floured surface. Add flour as needed to roll the dough to an eighth of an inch thick to fit an eight-inch tart or pie shell. Remove the excess dough from the borders and reroll the dough to make a decorative cutout top or a beautiful lattice. If the dough is too soft to use, refrigerate it to chill and reroll it.

Save the remaining dough wrapped in plastic wrap in the refrigerator for one week. Another beneficial use of the dough is to make cutout cookies.

CHAPTER 46

TWO WEEKS LATER IT was business as usual. No stick light orbs, no voices in my ears, no paranormal activity either. Although now we were selling gavajunes like crazy. Silvia came in and bought four for her bridge club. I was featured in local papers, including a full spread in the *Long Island Post* by food critic Mary Cartelli.

The word was out; everybody wanted a gavajune, a GF cookie, and a carrot cake. I was so proud of my staff and my accomplishments.

Not a single word had been spoken about Annie or JT. We never heard from Annie, nor did we know what she did with JT's body. I was sure she would come around again one day, when she was up to it.

"We're all cleaned up, G." Lucas lightly smacked my shoulder with a roll of paper towels.

"All right, cool, let's go home."

"Wait, G. I have a question for you."

"Yeah, sure, what is it?"

"Do you think, uh, maybe you can teach me or train me on how to become a pastry chef? I can work full-time this summer and learn how to bake like you."

"Serious?"

"Serious. With Annie gone, I figure you can use a new chef, and when school starts up again, I can work after school and weekends."

"You must be here at five in the morning. Are you aware of that? No partying the night before, and you must be ready for some demanding work."

"I'm ready to do this."

"All right, then. Tomorrow morning be here at five a.m."

"Wait, what? Tomorrow?"

"Yes. You said you were ready."

"Okay, okay. I'll be here. No more mopping for me."

"Ha! No more mopping, we'll get the other guys to do it."

Lucas left the roll of towels standing upright on the middle table, and we exited the kitchen.

"Thank you for staying late to help clean up."

"Not a problem, G. I'll see you tomorrow morning."

Lucas was such a great kid, and for him to follow in my footsteps was a total honor. Maybe I could pass the torch one day.

The next morning, I was the first to arrive at the shop, mostly because I hadn't slept well. Maybe, I was keyed up, but I kept waking up, like every hour. It seemed like I always woke up precisely at 2:19. I still don't know why. Nor did I know why I looked through the patisserie's windows with ghostly thoughts again, half expecting to see lights flashing inside the kitchen, or some other weird, unexplainable phenomena. But the shop looked quiet, and all appeared to be as normal as normal could be.

I turned the lock and opened the door, which set the alarm warning off. I input the code for the alarm, closing the door behind me with the spring-loaded bell ringing above. It was four fifty in the morning, the chefs, and now Lucas would no doubt be in soon. *Maybe I should wait for them.* Something about the morning had me on edge.

I looked across the street at the bar's vestibule and didn't see the cigarette smoker. I guessed JT was the smoker, stalking us the whole time, watching our every move. Just thinking that sent a chill up my spine. I turned around and headed toward the kitchen door; might as well get started. I had a lot of work to do.

As I grabbed the kitchen door handle, I caught a glimpse of a car pulling up on the street. I turned back and looked at the front door. Had I left it open? *Yeah, I think so,* I thought. They had the key if it was locked.

I flipped the kitchen lights on as I entered and froze in my tracks. "What the…!"

The roll of paper towels Lucas had left on the table had unraveled at least three times around while still standing upright.

I set my messenger bag down on the side table and just stood there speechless for a moment. I didn't want to touch it. On the one hand, I was a little bit afraid. Maybe it would reach out and bite me, or the towels would wrap around my hand and then up my arm and around my neck to strangle me to death like a possessed roll of paper towels. Tomorrow's headline: "Baker dies by roll of paper towels wiping him to death." On the other hand, I wanted another witness to corroborate what I was seeing.

I heard the front doorbell chime as Hana, Jada, Kate, and Lucas came in, followed by Antonio and Laurent.

They immediately sensed something was wrong. I kept shifting my eyes over to the roll of paper towels on the table, trying to send a silent message.

"Are you okay? What's wrong?" Kate asked. "What happened? Did the ghosts do something? I thought they'd been all wrapped up and sent into the light."

Hana approached the center table and was about to instinctively grab the roll of paper towels.

"Don't touch them!" I yelled out.

Hana jumped back.

"When I left last night, Lucas cleaned up and left the paper towels on the table."

"Yeah… and…?" Kate questioned me; her anticipation that I was about to tell them something creepy made her voice about an octave higher than normal.

"Look at it. It's unraveled. By the look of it, at least three times around."

The shock on Lucas's face was priceless! "Damn G, how's that possible?"

"You're right. It does look like it unraveled at least twice." Kate walked around the table.

"Someone is playing tricks on us again." Hana did not love these new shenanigans either.

"So, what do we do?" Kate implored.

I reached for the cleaning supplies in the closet. "We leave the spray cleaner on the table tonight, too, and see if they clean the kitchen."

Everyone cracked up. That's all it took to break the tension.

"I'll make the morning brew," Kate sped off to the coffeemaker.

I grabbed the roll of magic paper towels, rolled it up, and set it on the side. We continued to set up for the morning. It was getting late.

A little later, I played the video back from the previous night's events. We could not see any orbs or ghosts flying around the kitchen, but then I played back the clip that showed the roll of paper towels unraveling by itself.

It started to open. Then nothing. Then more. Exposing at least one full sheet. Then it paused. Then it continued to unravel. It looked like some invisible hand was tugging on the end of the towel as if trying to take a sheet off. All I kept thinking of was the little girls singing, *Ring around the rosie, a pocket full of posies, ashes, ashes…*

I showed this mesmerizing sequence to my chefs, and we must've watched it a dozen times. We speculated that maybe it was the air conditioner. We tried to prove the ghosts wrong, experimenting to recreate it ourselves. AC on and nothing happened. Move the roll, turn the roll, rotate the roll a little bit, tease the first sheet out a little bit to give it a running start. No matter what we did, we couldn't get it to happen a second time. Was it one final trick?

Not a final trick, but more like the children wanted to hang streamers and welcome me back from the 'Road to Hell, but the paper towels were a bit heavier than they thought. The children and Mattie are incredibly happy I'm back. I must say I'm happy, too. I kind of missed this place and realized I've been trapped here for a purpose. Now, I am a free spirit to fly and happy to call Fiorello Patisserie my home.

And one final note if I may, dude, the road to hell is exactly what you think it is, terrifying to say the least. Thank God, I was only transporting a devilish psycho and not staying to meet the devil himself. Besides, JT's inaudible screams will haunt me forever. So, tell me, what are we baking today?

THE END?

EPILOGUE
Summer 2023

AT A LITTLE PASTRY shop in Huntington, New York, where the hauntings continue, I wrote this story. Sometimes it's knocking on the wall, timers going off, door chimes ring, a voice is heard, a shadow is seen, or a utensil twangs. An orb or perhaps a legion of them is sometimes detected with security cameras. And the stick light orb appears now and then, zooming across the kitchen in the middle of the night.

Can it truly be said that the spirits of our loved ones, our parents and grandparents, close relatives, and friends, and even our beloved pets (and possibly a couple of strangers) may somehow remain among us after they have passed? Certainly, I don't know the answer to that question. And while it could quite conceivably be a comforting thought to us, that is, the living who miss them, I wonder about it from their perspective. Because when we say goodbye to our loved ones who depart from the strife of this life, we always wish for them nothing less than eternal and everlasting peace and happiness. So, all I can say is, if all of you dear folks are still hanging around amid the craziness and chaos of my pastry shop, I hope you are all having a wonderful time!

In the meantime, it is business as usual at Fiorello Dolce Patisserie.

In loving memory of my friend and spiritual medium
Diana Cinquemani - Fritze

In memory of
Eddie
Matilda
Grace and Charlotte
Giuseppe and Richard
Andy (whoever you may be)

Ann Orsini - Fioravanti ~ Gabriel Fioravanti
Anna D'Adamo - Fioravanti ~ Giacinto Fioravanti
Antoinette Torelli - Orsini ~ Raphael Orsini
Rose Marinello ~ Vincent Marinello ~ Connie Marinello
Mary Orsini - Cartelli ~ Joseph Cartelli ~ Alberto Orsini
Frank and Adele Orsini ~ Angelina and Leo Denaro
Phyllis Orsini - Moccia ~ Al Moccia
Vivie, Dolly, Lucie, Lydia and George Torelli
Norma and Dominick Trombetta
Grandmother Mamie ~ Grandmother Josephine

Figaro Fiorello (forever in my heart)

To our dear customer friends who are no longer with us,

Ernie, Clayton, Barbara, Kathy, Morris, Ruth,
Joe and Jonas, rest in peace.
We miss you.

JT and his friends (Fictious Characters)

ACKNOWLEDGMENTS

PRIMARILY, I'D LIKE TO thank my lifelong partner, Steve, for his ongoing love and support through all the ups and downs during the process of writing The Baker's Ghost, may the adventures continue. Thank you, Figs, for forever being by my side.

A very special thank you to my editor Caroline Tolley for her advice, dedication, patience and for believing in me and this project. Yes, I'll send you a pound cake. Thank you, Amy, Art and Heather, for the copy-edits.

Thank you to my book designer, Glen Edelstein, for putting this novel together. It's amazing. A big (braciole) thank you to the very talented graphic designer Domenic Rizzotti, for the incredible illustrations. IG@ Domenic.Design.

To my amazing family at Fiorello dolce patisserie, the names go on and on. My ex-Kristy, my brother Miguel, sis Meg, Brian(BVas), my son Blake, Jackie, Angel, Macrina, Derrick, David, my No.1 Jess, Isabella, Eric, Nick, Andy, John, Jake too, Samantha, Heidi, Ginny, Chris A., Luke, Dave, Ben, Lorraine, Mark, Alexie, Domenic, Rachel, Elvis, Anthony, Michael(-Mikey), Zack, Matt M., Derek, Caitlin, Alex, Matt C., Joey, Ralph, Christina, George, Adam, Cameron, Kimi, Nikki, Chris M., Kelly, Ava, Big Mike, Ryan, Camille, Elyssa-xo, Katie, Kat, Sam, Myka, Jose, Will, Dillon, Luca, Christian, Jordana, Elizabeth, Zeke, Sadia, Cole, Joe, Jak, Vanessa, Andrew, hunting knife hand models Marcus and Greyson, stop eating everything, and through the echoes Jack and Jon. A special shout out to Thea and Ralph, Lucy and Karl, Kathy and Gene, Alessandra and Virgilio, Barbara Jo, Tricia and John, Maryann, Angela (Big Ang) and Glenn.

To my book club members Marianne from the old neighborhood, Marianne from the new neighborhood, Linda from the Bronx and Theresa from the south, who read every draft, Barbara from the north, and Ellen from the west, thank you for your feedback. And to Jzach, Bobby, Pat, and Mark, cheers.

A Big Thank you to my dear friend and fellow author Jeannine Henvey for keeping the hopper full, fire burning, the sweet morning laughs about everything and the incentive to keep writing. We got this!

To my dear friend, mentor, and amazing author Alyson Richman, you are as beautiful as your words on paper, thank you for all your sweet advice and the cappuccino chats.

To author Kerriann Flannagan – Brosky, thank you for your incredible insight into the ghostly realm and your sweet love for the flourless chocolate cake.

To the poet laureate Richard Bronson and his wife Susan, thank you for your support. Poetry rocks!

To dear Diana Cinquemani - Fritze, Richard Schoeller and Joe Giaquinto, your spiritual readings are true, consoling, blessed and hysterical at times. You are gifted, and beautiful.

To the ghost hunters, Angela, and Bill Artuso. See, I knew something was happening here.

Brenden and Gail, Joe and Liz, the wine glasses are full, and the grill is fired up. Rob and Phil, always in our hearts. Jarrett, thanks for keeping my muscles loose. To my NYC radio friends Jim, Shelli, and Maria, thank you for keeping me rocking through it all and of course a shout out to Big E, grumpy Joe, and Trevor from Q104.3, for having Fiorello up at the studio all these years. To my old pastry family, Laurent, and Herve, you are always in my heart. Nino, Tina, and Charlie, thank you for letting Fiorello nest here. To Mark and Inge, we still have dinner plans. Tom and Judy, you are the happiest couple alive. Nancy, my oldest friend, cheers xo! Mark thanks for connecting the dots with Dave, keep on writing, riding, grilling, and drinking. To my west coast friends from PDX, Sheila, Dave and Shelly, cheers to black and white cookie and good old rock and roll.

Thank you, Rachel, for the weekly chats, fresh vegetables, miche bread, family stories, you are truly a beautiful soul. To Maryann, large latte, single shot, almost ready. To Gil, you brighten up anybody's day, you are a golden ray of light. To Madeline, the artist will live on with one brushstroke at a time. To Denise, I finally did it. To Risa, cheers to carrot cake and brownies. Dana and Joe, I know you want a black and white cookie, and Joanne, yes, we can write a book about it all. Yes Jen, the salted caramel tart will be back soon, xo. Karen and Joe, long live the lemon bar in a different time and a different life. Caren, we always have strawberry shortcake or red velvet. To sweet Joan, may everyone learn to be as sweet as you. Omid, Yoko, Dave, Liz, Remi, Rob, Cathrine, Dawn, Margy, Bonni, Zoom and Dilbert, always a pleasure chatting. Bobby and Amy, cheers. To my accountants Artie and Amanda, thank you. And to my dearest Kate, you always make me smile and inspire me to keep writing from the sacrum up, love you.

To our families, where would we be without our moms and dads? Barbara and Rich, Joe and Linda, Michael and Cecilia, Christine, and Junior, Geral, Joanne, Donna, and Mike. Rest in peace Anthony. To all our nephews and nieces Christina, Rich, Michael, Danielle, Kim, Jamie, Matthew, Kristen, Ryan, Gabriella, Michael, Lauren, and Michelle, followed by the great ones too. Love you.

Thank you, Newsday, for including Fiorello dolce Patisserie in your amazing feed me stories over the years. Peter, Erica, Joan, Scott, Corin, Marjorie and talented behind the scenes team. Cheers! And to News12, thank you.

To the wonderful people of Huntington, Cold spring Harbor, North-port, Huntington Station, Melville, Centerport and to the rest of the amazing Long Islanders, thank you for your love and support over the years at Fiorello dolce Patisserie.

To Phyllis and Al Moccia, Adele Orsini, John and Bill Lucas-Takacs, love you.

Sending hugs to my fantastic cousins, Nancy, Richard and Barbara, Janet, Joanne and Peter, Ralph and Iris, Donna and Jack, Joe and Rose, Lisa and Keith and Domenic and Kerri, Annette and Deb. Cheers to Clason Point!

PHOTO CREDITS

Orb face photo – Author and ghost hunter Kerriann Flannigan Brosky

Orphans in hallway - Angela and Bill Artuso, from Gotham Paranormal Research Society.

Back cover illustration – John Evangelista. Thank you, Angie Evangelista, Tommy, and Maria Vilardi for the beautiful drawing.

Documentary video – The Ghosts of Fiorello by Christopher Mavrogian.

Interior Illustrations – Domenic Rizzotti IG@Domenic.Design

Thank you, Pastry Chef Kristy Chiarelli, for your research and development assistance with the recipes. You are an incredible chef with a sophisticated palate. I bow to the queen.

Recipes:

American Cheesecake	pg. 112
Annie's Ricotta Tart*	pg. 299
Blueberry Muffin	pg. 31
Coconut Macaroons	pg. 237
GF Cookies	pg. 24
Mexican Wedding Cookies	pg. 52
Pâte Sucrée	pg. 301
Peppermint Meringues	pg. 181
Pignolia Cookies	pg. 139
Rugalach	pg. 164

The story you just read started off as a work of non-fiction based on the ghostly hauntings at Fiorello Dolce Patisserie in Huntington NY, which are real and true. However, when I found out about Eddie and how he died, I felt compelled to add more to the story. So, I gathered the information that was given to me by spiritual mediums along with my own intuition and combined it with fictional characters and storytelling of tell how Eddie died.

Names have been changed to protect the innocent.

Peace, love, and life ever after.
Wrap them in white for protection,
pink for love, green for hope and
send them to the light.

Enjoy life. Eat chocolate!

ABOUT THE AUTHOR

PASTRY CHEF GERARD FIORAVANTI had been baking for twenty years and writing for five, when he discovered his patisserie was haunted. Originally from the Bronx, he now lives in Huntington NY creating amazing desserts at his Patisserie, Fiorello Dolce. Home of the Frenagel™ and classic French pastries with some of the best croissants on Long Island.

He is the winner of the *Foodnetwork* show, *Bake you Rich,* a former NYC radio morning show sidekick and featured on award winning shows, NBC NY Live, *Restaurant Hunter, News12, The Ghosts of Fiorello,* and in *Newsday / Feed Me* publications. The Baker's Ghost is his first novel.

* 9 7 9 8 2 1 8 2 5 8 2 5 2 *